THE CRIMINALIST

EUGENE IZZI

AVON BOOKS ◆ NEW YORK

AVON BOOKS, INC.
1350 Avenue of the Americas
New York, New York 10019

Copyright © 1998 by Theresa Izzi
Interior design by Kellan Peck
Visit our website at **http://www.AvonBooks.com**
ISBN: 0-380-97540-8

Library of Congress Cataloging in Publication Data:

Izzi, Eugene.
The criminalist / Eugene Izzi.—1st ed.
p.   cm.
I. Title
PS3559.Z9C7   1998   98-18658
813'.54—dc21   CIP

First Avon Books Printing: October 1998

AVON TRADEMARK REG. U.S. PAT. OFF. AND IN OTHER COUNTRIES,
MARCA REGISTRADA, HECHO EN U.S.A.

Printed in the U.S.A.

FIRST EDITION

QPM   10 9 8 7 6 5 4 3 2 1

THE
CRIMINALIST

Novels by Eugene Izzi

The Take
Bad Guys
The Eighth Victim
The Booster
King of the Hustlers
The Prime Roll
Invasions
Prowlers
Tony's Justice
Tribal Secrets
Bulletin From the Streets
Safe Harbor
Players
A Matter of Honor
The Criminalist

As Nick Gaitano

Special Victims
Mr. X
Jaded

THE CRIMINALIST

CHAPTER 1

"**D**ADDY *DON'T!*"

Her husband's scream terrified Ellen, and she popped up in their bed like a marionette on a string. "Tom!" She shouted the name in panic. Her immediate, disoriented terror receded incrementally as her mind made the connection that she was in her own bed, in her own home, on the second floor of their house on Chicago's Near South Side. Tom was having another nightmare. She could feel him thrashing around beside her.

Breathing heavily, one hand clutched to her breast, the other grasping her stomach protectively, Ellen lowered her head and took deep breaths to try to calm herself. She realized that she'd somehow twisted her back when she'd popped up in bed. Tom's night terrors had finally caused her more than fear and disturbed sleep. A snake of strong resentment reared its ugly head before she forced its fangs closed and sent it back where it belonged.

A certain amount of anger, however, seemed appropriate, under the circumstances. Ellen allowed herself that, gave in to it at the same instant that she realized it was up to her to awaken her squirming husband before he harmed himself in his sleep.

Awareness came slowly; Ellen blinked her eyes rapidly to try to hasten it along. She turned on Tom indignantly, then stopped at the sight of him, and gasped.

This was the worst one yet.

Tom had stopped moving. His eyes were open wide now, and he was reaching toward the ceiling, as if he were grasping for salvation, as if something that could save him was directly above him, just out of reach. His entire body was stiff, the veins in his neck were distended; every muscle was taut, long fingers stiffly groping.

"Tom!" Ellen jerked back to her side of the bed, then fearfully leaped out of it. Her husband's head was toward her now as he subconsciously sought the source of his name, needy, vacant eyes, widely glaring.

Ellen stepped back and reached out a tentative hand, then pulled it back, suddenly frightened.

What was she afraid of? Ellen scolded herself. This was *Tom*, her husband for more than seventeen years.

But the look on his face, the hunger in his eyes, conspired to almost convince her he was someone other than her husband, someone less, more primitive; someone far more frightening.

"TOM!" Ellen shouted his name now, no longer worried about frightening him. She was worried for Tom, but she was even more worried for herself.

"DADDYYYY!!!!!!!!!!!" Tom's prolonged scream first made Ellen jump, then galvanized her into movement. She hurried to the other side of the bed, struck out with a trembling hand, and slapped Tom across the face as she loudly hollered his name.

Empty eyes blinked, then fluttered.

"Tom, wake *up!*" Ellen had his left arm now, was shaking it hard, calling his name. His eyelids continued to flutter, as if he were fighting his way toward consciousness. He slowly lowered his arms. He turned an uncomprehending gaze toward her as he began to hyperventilate.

He was back, shaken and staggered, nearly unrecognizable, but still, this was Tom.

Ellen leaned into him, sat down on the edge of the bed and pulled him into her arms, holding him, shushing him, rubbing him, whispering as she comforted.

"Tom, it's all right, it's okay, it was a nightmare, that's all;

2

just a bad dream." Tom's body stiffened again for an instant, then relaxed, as if a snatch of the dream had come back to him for just a second.

"Ellen?" The relief in his voice, the gratification in his awareness of his safety with her, was almost enough to calm her. To cover her anger at him, Ellen squeezed him even harder. "Ellen? Oh, Jesus, oh, dear God . . ."

"It's over, Tom." Was there derision in her tone? Ellen hoped there wasn't. Tom clutched at her, mumbling apologies even as he fought for breath. He sat up and Ellen moved a bit, giving Tom room without relinquishing her grip. She felt a spasm of pain in her lower back and bit her lip, but did not comment. He'd feel bad enough as it was without knowing that his delirium had caused her physical harm.

"Oh, Ellen, did I do it again?"

"I don't mind; it's all right." She could feel his entire body shaking as he fought to retain the emotional control that had always been so important to him. Tom was no longer sobbing, but still apologizing, worried about her, cursing himself, as if he had control over his dreams, could somehow make them sweet and pleasant, rather than ugly and bitter. Ellen held him close.

She didn't ask him what he'd dreamed about. She suspected that she knew, although she remembered him shouting something about his father, rather than about his first marriage; he hadn't shouted Nancy's name. Ellen continued to hold on to him tightly, until his shaking stopped. Tom, now embarrassed, gently disengaged himself from her and sat up straight, put his feet on the floor, then leaned over and held his head in his hands.

"My *God*."

Ellen rubbed his back. She could feel the weight of the world between her hand and his shoulders. She repeated the only thing she could think of to say, trivial, perhaps, but appropriate.

"It's over, Tom."

He looked at the clock. It was just after eleven. In less than an hour, it would officially be twenty years since he'd been arrested for the murder of his first wife, Nancy. Ellen suspected that she knew what he was thinking. They'd been through this before, to a certain, lesser degree. She repeated herself once more, wanting to say more, but unable to think of any words that could bring comfort to her husband.

"It's over."

"*Over?*" Tom echoed, a single, simple word, infused with disbelief.

Later, Ellen would reflect upon this moment and wonder if Tom had somehow known that it was only just the beginning.

A few minutes after midnight a wino came staggering out of an alley on East Chicago Avenue. He was white-faced, screaming, pointing back toward the alley in accusation with one hand, the other clutching the lifeline that was his bottle of port wine. Some passersby ignored him, others walked around him; some stopped and stared at him with amusement, making fun of him, looking down on him. Some of them were half drunk themselves, but were blissfully, frightfully ignorant of the fact that they were in a different stage of the same disease that had consumed the man they were mocking.

"It—it—*back there*—" The man's terror was real and alive, a bright sun immolating him, penetrating even his dark alcoholic cloud. Wide eyes glared at all the strangers as he pointed, his head jumped from side to side as he sought to communicate with his fellow man, shouting unintelligible words that no one would have paid any attention to even had he spoken them in cultured, measured, articulate tones. He was just a wino, freaking out. Unexpected entertainment for the urban late-night pub crawlers, the shift workers heading home, the Blockbuster Video crew next door who were just getting off work, the street predators, other beggars, and those who were just out for a late-night stroll on a beautiful evening in May.

Frank Moran stood back, alone and apart from the crowd.

They were to be begged from, not to be merged with; never to be joined. There would be no hand-holding from Frank Moran; he existed without partners or friends. But there would not be any ridicule from him, either; he himself had been made fun of too often, and, having felt mockery's sting, he rarely belittled his fellow human beings by exhibiting such behavior toward them. He had his own way of dealing with his many resentments

4

toward the human race, other than pretending he was better than they were at any given moment in their lives.

Frank quickly took in the man's image, deciphered it in ways that could only be learned through long, tough years of experience gleaned by living on the street.

The man had probably gone into the alley so he wouldn't have to share his wine with his confederates, who were sitting just across the street in the Water Tower Park. He had stumbled onto something in there that had scared the living shit out of him.

Frank watched the man, gave him a long, studied look.

There were old and new urine stains covering the front of his shiny pants. He wore a long coat in mid May. His beard was full gray; it had been several months since he'd shaved. He more than likely hadn't shaved since he'd had his last shower, which would have been at a homeless shelter, back when it had still been frigidly cold, and he'd been forced by his survival instinct to come in off the street. Most of the homeless people Frank had known—and he'd known many—preferred the streets to shelters, where you had to pray before you could eat, where your few possessions were taken from you right along with your dignity. The man appeared to be in his midfifties; say, ten years older than Frank. He'd been out here for a while. Probably for years.

Not the sort of man who would easily be frightened. Frank squinted at him. He decided that this seemed to be exactly the sort of man who should unveil grim secrets. A demented messiah, ranting to the disbelieving.

Frank had seen all that he needed to. The man had now drawn a large and boisterous crowd. This was the very heart of downtown, the jewel of the city, and Frank knew that the police would be arriving at any time. He knew that he had to get out of there, fast.

He briefly wondered how much trouble it would be to grab the man's bottle, as sort of an ironic twist, then shook his head in self-disgust. He wasn't that bad yet. Or anymore. At least not today. Besides, he didn't need to draw any attention to himself; he was now only an observer, and could not allow himself to be distinguished as a participant.

There were thirty-two begged-for dollars in Frank's pants

pocket, and plenty of change that he hadn't counted. He'd get by for tonight. He already had a rented room that had been paid for a week in advance, and more than enough money for a hot dog, fries and a Coke, the staples of his diet. He had enough for cigarettes. And enough for the all-important bottle of cheap whiskey that would get him through another night, a bottle which, throughout his entire adult life, had taken an absolute and complete precedence over food, clothing, cigarettes, and shelter.

Frank took a last look at the crowd that had formed around the wino. The man was now shouting as he fell to his knees, pulling at the long, gray, stringy hair of his head with the hand that wasn't holding the bottle. The man was now keening. Young males laughed; their female companions made compassionate sounds. Now that Frank wouldn't be begging from them, he let his derision for them show.

Some of them, Frank knew, would wind up right here, like the man down on his knees. Others would wind up like Frank: alcoholic but ambulatory, able to think, beg and hustle, somehow existing through the worst of times, and through times that got slightly better. They would be in and out of detox centers, thinking after each release that they'd finally beaten their addictions. Frank could scan the crowd and see which ones were in danger; he'd always had the eye. Not that any of them would believe it was coming if he went up to them and told them, warned them of what lay ahead. They were young, carefree, out drinking on a beautiful Thursday night in May without a single care in the world.

Frank hid his contempt for the sort of people who would think that the wino had been born that way. It was easy for him to do, as he'd been hiding his hatred for as long as he could remember, only letting it out when he was certain that no one was watching.

Frank heard the single, short, bloated blast of a police siren. A squad car was making its way toward the crowd. He turned and walked away, not too slowly, not too quickly, not doing anything that would draw attention to himself.

Frank Moran was a survivor, a wily, haunted veteran of late-night, big-city streets. There were times when his appearance and demeanor degenerated to the point where he was almost indistinguishable from the screaming man before him. But unlike some of his brethren, Frank, due to necessity, force of will, and a judicially ordered twenty-eight-day stay in an alcohol rehabilitation program in Portland, Oregon, the previous February, had rehabilitated himself to a point where he was now able to maintain himself. He looked like a middle-aged, recently unemployed factory worker. He had learned that it was easier to beg money from people if they could, in some small manner, identify with you. So Frank dressed decently, took showers, brushed his teeth, and shaved as regularly as he could. And he never asked a woman for a dime, he begged from men only. Which didn't mean that women never gave him any money.

Frank had discovered that if you looked down when women passed, if you acted passive and submissive toward them, they would sometimes open their purses and offer something to you. If you approached them, though, they became intimidated, and either ignored you, walked more quickly, or, confronting their fear, faced you head-on and told you what they thought of you. Frank had learned many years ago that he couldn't take much of that sort of treatment without striking back, especially when he'd been drinking.

Which was the reason why he just drank enough through the hours that he spent begging to enable him to maintain a slight but constant, mind-numbing buzz.

It was after the day's survival money had been earned that Frank allowed the creature within him full reign.

Frank wondered how long it would be before he once again ended up like the wino. He wondered how many of the sneering tough guys in the crowd would be at his present level by the time he reached the wino's. He wondered about his two brothers, men he didn't see but once every three or four hard, brutal years. Frank passed through Chicago more often than that, but he only rarely attempted to contact his brothers.

The last time Frank had seen him, Tommy had finally finished his residency and had started his career as a staff member in the psychiatric department of one of the local hospitals, Frank couldn't remember which one. Frank had told him that their other brother, Terry, was still a cop. Terry hadn't bothered to come over and see Frank at their mother's house; the two of them had never gotten along very well, even when they were just kids. Frank now wondered if their mother was still living. He did not wonder about their father.

He wondered if he should stick around until the cops showed up and found whatever wretched treasure awaited them in the alley. He wondered if anyone would pay attention to him; a skinny, middle-aged vagrant on the periphery of the crowd.

As he started to move away from the alley he wondered how long it would take, alone in his rented room just down the street—but an entire world away—with the door latched and the light out, to drink himself into oblivion. An indecisive man, Frank made an immediate decision. The demon was calling impatiently, and Frank had to put him to sleep. He picked up his step a little, until he felt the pain in his stomach.

At the corner, Frank stopped, eyes wide, and put a hand to his chest. The pain had spread, up into his chest. Was he having a heart attack? Was he dying? His heart began to pound loudly, it seemed, in his ears. His heartbeat overwhelmed any street sound, his panic any sense of his physical surroundings. Frank's world dwindled down to the sound of his heart, and his pain.

Frank stumbled against the wall of a building, and leaned against it, trying to catch his breath. He muttered a sound, then bit his tongue; he couldn't allow himself humiliation, he might attack someone tonight if they tried to mock him as they had the wino. Fortunately, no one was paying him any particular attention, everyone seemed in a hurry to get up the street, to see what the crowd was doing in front of the video store

Frank took fast, shallow breaths, afraid to breathe too deeply, thinking something inside him might rip apart if he did. He was overcome with his fear. If he died here, if he even fell unconscious here, they would blame him for what had happened back *there*.

He felt a sudden, overpowering sense of guilt, of shame. He lowered his head, bit his lower lip, and tried not to cry. He shook his head back and forth, slowly at first, then more rapidly, as the pain stayed with him, rising, cresting, then, blessedly, beginning to subside. When he was able to, Frank pushed away from the building, and began to stumble slowly down the street.

CHAPTER
2

The plainclothes patrol officer's name was Terry Moran, and he was in his usual state of mind—one of barely controlled rage—as he stomped up North State Street, alone, heading back toward the main downtown area. He was as used to the grip of his anger as he was to the sight of his face, so he was unaware that there was anything unusual in his manner as he headed toward the heart of the city. He turned his back on the wind and lit a cigarette, walking backward, too angry to stop.

Tall, trim, in his early forties with a full head of hair that he combed straight back, in gray dress pants and leather shoes, wearing a dark sports coat over a yellow shirt, Terry looked more like a midlevel gangster than a cop. And he behaved in the manner of gangsters and cops; he walked tall, with confidence, and his eyes were vacuum cleaners that never stopped shifting, seeing all, but lingering only on the things they registered to be a threat to either himself or the public at large.

From the train station on South Michigan Avenue and Randolph Street, then north all the way up to Elm Street, was Terry's private district. He walked Michigan Avenue only, but he was on call to walk the few blocks west down to Wells if he were needed. He had a counterpart he rarely spoke to, a woman detective who walked the other side of the street, who also was responsible for handling disturbances in Streeterville, what they called the "New East Side," and all points east, right up to the lake.

Terry didn't care for the woman; he didn't acknowledge her existence, even when she radioed for help and he was near enough to offer it. Terry thought that women police officers should never have been allowed on the street. It was one of the many things about the department that Terry passionately hated.

Terry had been a mile and a half from the southern edge of his working zone, almost back to his station house, when the radio on his belt had crackled. It was his own fault, and he knew it. If he had called for a squad car to take him back to headquarters, he'd have been on his way home by now. Well, not exactly home, that wasn't where he planned to go tonight . . . but off duty, at least.

But he wouldn't have called for a squad, not for personal services. He suspected that no one would have come for him, they'd all claim to be busy. Terry knew that he was a better cop on his worst night than any of them were on their best, and still he had to take it when they looked down their noses at him, when they acted as if they were better than he was; it was a constant source of anger, the main source of Terry's loathing. Trapped in a system that treated him as a pariah, having to work every day with all those coppers who smiled at Terry to his face but whispered about him in ugly tones just as soon as his back was turned.

Terry was supposed to have gotten off duty at midnight. He'd made plans for after work. And then they'd radioed him the news that he had to work four hours past the end of his shift. Comp time, which, theoretically, he could take back when he wanted it, as long as there were other officers available to cover his beat. Terry knew that plenty of other officers would have ignored the radio call and gone off duty anyway, claiming the next day not to have gotten the call: You radioed me, boss? Jesus, are you sure? He knew of other, more secure veterans—men with Terry's number of years in the department—who would have simply told the watch commander to go to hell.

But Terry couldn't do that.

They had Terry Moran over a barrel, and everybody, including

Terry, knew it. He had no more chance of being able to pull seniority than he had of making sergeant; options open to twelve thousand other police officers had been shut off to Terry, twenty years ago this very night. He smiled grimly as he thought that this night was an anniversary; the anniversary of a rupture that the police department had never allowed to heal.

Terry had just spent eight hours working, on his feet for most of them. Well, actually, he'd worked seven. He'd taken an unscheduled hour of personal time that nobody had to know about, to do something that he had finally come to realize had to be done. Something he wanted to do. Something he *needed* to do.

But he didn't have to tell his sergeant about that when the man had called to inform him that Terry had to work over. Requested, was the term the sergeant had used. But he had made the request in much the same manner that a flight instructor would use to request a novice to pull the pin on his parachute after jumping out of the plane. Terry was single, and twice divorced. His superiors were aware of this, and often used it to his disadvantage. Still, Terry had given the man a halfhearted argument from a pay phone on Wabash after the so-called request had been relayed over the radio.

Terry's thirty-two-year-old black superior had chastised him for calling in from the street; he had something to say? He should say it over the radio. Terry hadn't done so because all radio transmissions were recorded. The sergeant then told Terry that he didn't have any right to complain: he was in plainclothes, wasn't he? He was working a cherry assignment. The unspoken statement was that Terry was still a patrolman after twenty years in the department, and would retire as such—if they didn't find a way to take even *that* away from him. When Terry would bring it up, and his reasons why he believed he was still in patrol, his sergeant would say he was paranoid, that a lot of guys retired out of patrol. And now that the weather was good, the sergeant pointed out, there were a lot of coppers with far more clout than Terry had who would covet a cozy, safe, downtown assignment.

The sad thing was, if any other officer wanted it, even one with less seniority, they'd get it, and Terry would be back in uniform, back working a patrol car, by himself. The sergeant's threat had served its intended purpose. Even if they kept him walking, if they decided to keep him in the Community Policing program, they could shove his ass into Englewood or one of the other undesirable neighborhoods, and there wouldn't be a thing he could do about it, because Terry had no clout. More than once, the union itself had pointed out to Terry that he was lucky to still have a job.

Walking on State Street, Terry, as he did throughout most of his waking hours, seethed.

His radio was clipped to his belt, on the left, his weapon was on the right. At least they hadn't shoved a partner onto him; that was one of the few bright spots in Terry's life. Although no officer had ever come right out and said it to his face, Terry suspected that no other officer *wanted* to work with him. All these years later, he thought that the stigma of that long-ago night still tainted him, and it didn't matter to his fraternal brothers that the union had gotten him reinstated in his job, it didn't matter that he'd been cleared of any wrongdoing following a large and long departmental hearing, it didn't matter that the state's attorney's office had dropped their investigation of him not long after he'd taken his first and only polygraph exam. They still held it against him. The self-righteous bastards that they were.

Terry believed—without doubt and with all his heart—that he was a marked cop because of what had happened twenty years before, and that he would be so marked for the short time that was left in his career. Too many questions had never been answered, too many threads left dangling.

In the cynical police world, innocence had to be proven by the accused, and *everyone* was guilty of something. The suspicions about Terry's involvement in the brutal slaying of his sister-in-law had been set in place before he'd ever been suspended, before any questions had ever been asked by any investigative agencies.

The state's attorney's halfhearted announcement that there was no "evidence" directly linking Terry to the slaying was as much an indictment as that which would have been handed down by a grand jury, if the case against him had ever gotten that far. The man could have cleared him, without losing face, without having to apologize, but he hadn't. Instead, he'd cast aspersions, and they'd stuck to Terry like scarred skin through the twenty years that had passed.

There was more than one officer in the department who had killed; some in the line of duty, others under less-sanctioned circumstances. It wasn't unusual for an officer accused of murder to be supported rather than shunned by his fellow officers. Sometimes, even under the most suspicious circumstances, the officers in question were sainted, as their motives had been judged to be pure, and who knew the trials of police officers, the stress, the risk, the fear they lived with, better than another officer? Fundraisers were always being set up for coppers who had been implicated in dirty shootings; there was at least one commander Terry knew of who'd had three such fundraisers held to help him out, and the commander had been a torturer, would use the old, electrical black-box technique on murder suspects, shooting electricity into their groins in the station house basement. If a guy like that could be granted forgiveness, why couldn't it be granted to Terry?

What had caused Terry's banishment had been the nature of the crime: There were too many coppers who had seen, heard, or read about what had happened to Tom's wife. Too many officers who believed without doubt that Tom, or Terry, or the two of them working together, had killed Nancy Moran in the most horrific manner. Terry believed in his heart that there were still a great many officers who believed that he was a psychopathic killer.

It wasn't the sort of thing a man ever got used to, no matter how much time has passed. Particularly in an unsolved, cultlike murder which had already been dredged up by the media once— ten years ago with sidebars concerning everyone involved: WHAT-EVER HAPPENED TO . . . ? (Terrence Moran, brother of the accused medical student and himself once a prime suspect in the murder, was reinstated into the Chicago Police Department after a three-month investigation. He still works for the police department today . . .) Written with foreboding.

In such matters there was only one rule of thumb: The department never forgets or forgives.

Terry had no doubt that rookie officers were warned about him up front, as soon as they were assigned to his district, told to stay away from him, and told the reason why. Veterans, although polite to his face, shunned Terry socially. He was a member of nothing except his union; not even the Emerald Society would have him. He could not remember the last time he'd had a drink after work with another police officer, male or female, black or white. It would have to have been when he was a rookie, before Nancy had been murdered. He'd been a popular guy until the murder, had been pegged at the Police Academy as a real up and comer, as someone to keep an eye on.

But all that had changed after Nancy had been killed.

Some officers had actually approached him, especially in recent years, trying to establish relationships, but Terry had suspected they were doing it more out of pity than anything else, and he had snubbed them, sometimes brutally. He had gotten this far without any of them, he could hang on for another three months, until his retirement.

This far was a plainclothes, single-man assignment, walking the downtown area and making sure no citizens—particularly the rich ones—came to any harm.

It was Terry's job to know all the winos, all the junkies, all the beggars, all the gold-chain salesmen, all the *StreetWise* newspaper vendors. He had to keep his eyes open for the hustlers, the scammers, the muggers, and the crazies. There wasn't a night that passed where he didn't radio for a squad, sometimes a dozen times over the course of an eight-hour shift. The squads responded swiftly, as it wasn't a personal request. It is legal to beg, but it is illegal to block egress; to stand in someone's way, to bump them, to grab their arm, to threaten them. There were plenty of people who worked downtown who were willing to file police complaints over such minor assaults to their vanity.

Terry's job was to keep the peace in the high-rent, mostly commercial district, to make sure that nobody came to any harm in downtown Chicago between 4:00 P.M. and midnight. There were a number of apartment buildings on Terry's beat, too—particularly on the Near North Side—but for the most part, on Michigan Avenue at least, it was office buildings, late workers, the streets, and the scum that worked them.

Terry's resentment bubbled over as he thought about his own "work." He'd arrest an overly aggressive panhandler, call for a squad, and they'd take him in, run the paperwork, and the offenders would be cited, receive a *ticket* for Christ's sake, and would then be detained in lockup for a couple of hours as punishment, and be back at their work before Terry took his lunch break.

This fucking city.

Terry tossed his cigarette into the gutter, then shoved his hands into his pockets, shaking his head as he walked. He made sure that the hem of his sports coat on both sides covered his radio, his weapon, and his belt badge.

Terry didn't know it, but his lips were twisted into an expression of disgust. Terry didn't know it, but his eyes were blazing with anger. Terry didn't know it, but other pedestrians passed him with apprehension; he was a source of fear for them, rather than one of solace.

He didn't have to do any paperwork, wasn't chained to a desk all night, bored to death as he typed the reports; that was another one of the few bright spots in an otherwise dark, mind-numbing job. On the other hand, the city had just suffered through one of the most brutal winters in its history, and Terry had been out there, walking like a crazy man down deserted downtown streets, with taxicabs trailing behind him, their drivers hoping he'd come to his senses.

Cold weather made for desperate men, and desperate men were dangerous. Terry was desperate during summer's peak; winter brought him to critical mass.

On some nights, though, he even enjoyed it, when his isolation made Terry feel like the king of Michigan Avenue. On other nights he'd sunk into depressions so deep and brutal that he'd been physically shaken at the thought of what he might do if he were called upon to perform his duty. His fantasies, at those times, were frightening even to him.

On top of all his other problems, the sergeant's warning was in the front of his mind, giving Terry yet another cause for concern. Now that the weather had broken, he'd bet, some bastard with connections would take his job away from him.

Terry noticed someone approaching him specifically, walking at an angle so that they'd meet in a few more yards. He stopped daydreaming and was immediately alert; his hands came out of his pockets. Downtown or not, the city was dangerous after midnight. Terry felt a calmness wash over him, warned himself to stay in control. Most days, it worked. Other days it didn't.

The man was tall, young, muscular, and black, wearing a uniform of some kind that had patches on the upper sleeves. As he came closer, Terry stopped and stared at him, awaiting the man, who, surprised at Terry's reaction, paused for an instant, hesitated, as if wanting to turn and walk away before overcoming his trepidation and moving the few feet that put him into Terry's space.

" 'Scuse me, sir, don't be afraid . . .'' the con man's usual aproach, spoken halfheartedly, as if he knew that Terry was different, that someone was wrong this time.

Terry wasn't afraid, and there was nothing in his demeanor to prove otherwise. He just stared at the man with a deadpan expression. The man's expression, on the other hand, was pained, as if he were embarrassed, or shamed. He cast off his initial caution and dived into his spiel.

"Excuse me, sir, don't be afraid; I don't mean you no harm. I'm with security, see my badge?" There was indeed a shiny badge pinned to the chest of the dark blue uniform. As he'd stepped in close, Terry had noticed the dark blue stripe down the middle of the man's pants legs. "I lost my wallet, or somebody stole it from work. I only need five dollars for the train ride home. I'll pay you back—can you help me out?"

"Where do *you* work security?" The man was stunned by Terry's question, as surprised as he'd been when Terry had stopped to watch his approach. He'd obviously been used to working his scam while walking hurriedly beside the pigeon, using his size, his uniform, and the cheap tin badge—subliminal symbols of authority—as intimidators to get what he wanted. The man looked at Terry now, eyes widening as his initial suspicions were confirmed. He began to turn, but Terry smoothly grabbed his upper arm and spun him around. "Don't do anything stupid," Terry said, then added with a smile, "Not yet."

He had his right hand on his weapon now, a lightweight Glock fifteen-shot that was in the man's plain view as he turned back to face Terry. The man's eyes were glued to the weapon, he didn't even seem to have noticed the badge clipped right beside it.

"Fuck this, I'm through with it." The man was openly belligerent now. Terry wouldn't let him be for long.

The man tried to pull away; Terry squeezed his arm and softly said, "You're through with this when *I* say you're through with it." The man looked around, panicking, wondering what to do. Terry knew that if it was daylight, with crowds around, the man would have made a move, tried for sympathy while he played the race card, hollering at the State Street shoppers.

That wouldn't work at this time of night; even on such a lovely night as this one, there weren't ten people in sight.

Which left the man only two other options; acquiescence or violence. Terry, sizing up the situation, welcomed, hoped for, the latter.

"I asked you, where do you work security?"

"The McCormick Convention Center." The man's heart wasn't in it, he was just lying due to habit, it was what you did with the Man. He didn't seem to understand that Terry might now be able to add impersonating a federal officer to the other charges against him.

Terry kept his hand on his weapon, but let go of the man's arm, blatantly tempting him to run. Terry wouldn't shoot him, would rather chase him down and beat the shit out of him if he tried to escape on foot. He enjoyed testing himself against younger men who were bigger and more solidly built than himself, although the occasion to do so was rarely presented. This man, at this time, on this night, seemed to have been sent to Terry by a kind and benevolent god.

The way the man was dressed, in this getup, led Terry to believe that he could get away with it, too. This wasn't some one-legged homeless beggar, someone the public would feel sorry for. This was what they most feared encountering while they busily commuted back and forth to their safe, white suburbs: an aggressive, urban, black, street hustler.

Terry smiled up at the man, then nodded his head, as if in self-doubt.

"We'll see about that. You just stand right there for a minute." The guy seemed to be dense. He didn't move. Terry shook his head and unclipped his radio from his belt, took his eyes away from the man, then said, "Do me a favor, would you, pal?

Take off. Go ahead, run." He spoke into the radio, gave his situation and his position, and received confirmation, all the time waiting to hear the scuffle of the man's feet, Terry looking across State Street at the entrance to a subway station, rather than at the man.

He was disappointed in the man's reaction. In this part of town, at this time of night, he would have only three or four minutes at most before a squad car rolled to the curb.

The man was now openly frightened. "Oh, don't do this to me, come on, man, I ain't did nothing. I ain't out robbing old ladies, I ain't snatching chains or cutting wallets out of pants, shit."

"Those your only options?" Terry clipped the radio back to his belt. He still wasn't looking at the man. "You could run, if you want to. Big guy like you, young, tough buck, with those long, fresh legs, hell, how's an old man like me ever gonna catch you?"

The man's reaction was immediate. His face fell, and he stood stone-still. "Don't shoot me, man, I didn't do nothing violent."

"Shoot you?" Terry looked at the man now, amused. "I wouldn't shoot you. Not unless you draw down on me first."

"I ain't got no gun, I swear to God!" The man was sweating now, terrified. Terry couldn't stop smiling at him.

"I give you my word, I won't shoot you."

"Won't plant no drop piece on me?"

Terry pursed his lips and shook his head, then watched as the man weighed his options. For a moment there was a sly look in his eyes, as if he were about to make his move, but then his shoulders slumped, and he shook his head, dropped his gaze to the sidewalk.

"Where'm I gonna *go?*"

"Dressed like that, not too far." Terry didn't allow his disappointment to show. He stepped back, out of range, and told the man to assume the position against the Woolworth's window. As he roughly frisked him, he spoke to him, still softly, still without malice.

"There's two women working Michigan Avenue, north of the bridge? Wear patches on their faces, clean clothes, tell you they need money to get to a battered women's shelter. There's a guy in a van drives the homeless people around, from place to place, dropping them off on busy sidewalks during different times of the day. He's a pimp for the homeless, you kow who I mean? A nigger, like you. Medium height, with a beard? The star of his stable's that ugly, little old white bitch in a wheelchair, holds her hand out all day begging for pennies. He's going down, too, man, I can't wait to get him alone."

Terry searched the man's crotch area, digging deep with his fingers. The man jerked upright, shivered, and made a high-pitched squeal of pain, but didn't otherwise resist. Terry had to fight the urge to squash his scrotal sac.

Of all the many things that Terry Moran hated, cowards were at the top of the list.

He finished searching, finding nothing, spun the man around and didn't even give the respect of cuffing him as he said, "I got junkie *StreetWise* vendors on every fucking corner; I got niggers strolling my beat trying to sell lead chains sprayed with gold paint to conventioneers; I got shoeshine scammers everywhere I look, telling tourists it's only two bucks for a shine, then demanding five after they do the job. I got fat old ladies taking dives in McDonald's and Burger King, hoping to make their fortune with an injury claim."

Terry saw the squad car turn onto State off Adams. He swallowed his disappointment; he'd have another opportunity, with another player who wasn't quite as perceptive as this one, who couldn't see past Terry's badge and into what was inside him. Maybe he could still get this guy to swing at him, entice him into a fight. The sight of the squad car might give him false courage, now that he understood that he was no longer alone with a man who wanted to hurt him.

"I want to tell you something, broham, I spend every goddamn day of my life listening to bullshitting assholes like you. What you want to do, the only thing that's healthy for you, is stick to the 'double-l' theory from now on. Know what 'double l' stands for? Lawsuit or lottery. You stay the *fuck* out of downtown from now on, you understand me?" The man, shivering with terror, nodded his head rapidly as the squad car pulled to the curb. Terry made a face, shook his head, and grabbed the man's arm. He shoved him toward the uniformed officer who got out of the passenger side of the car.

"Con artist, pretending he's a security guard lost his wallet."

The officer spoke to the con man, rather than to Terry. "Another one? What are you, stupid? When are you guys gonna get creative?" The man held his arms out to the officer, ready, anxious to be handcuffed. The officer made a whirling motion with his finger.

"Turn around. You know the drill."

"Man, get me *away* from this guy." The officer smiled at Terry, then slowly shook his head.

"What's the matter, *Officer*, Patrolman Moran put a scare into you?"

"Get me *away* from this crazy motherfucker!" He had turned, was now being cuffed. He looked up quickly, met Terry's gaze, then lowered both his eyes and his tone of voice. When he spoke now, he was begging. "Please, man, get me out of here."

The driver, still behind the wheel, laughed loudly enough for Terry to hear. The other uniformed officer finished cuffing the man, turned him around, put his hand on his head and shoved him into the back of the squad. He looked down at his hand, then wiped it rapidly on the side of his pants, as if the man's head had somehow caused it to become contaminated. "What's the matter, our Officer Moran remind you of a vampire?" Terry, stoic, heard the driver laugh again.

It was their pet name for him, the Vampire, most often used behind Terry's back. Nancy's body had been drained of blood when the priest had found it, just before early mass.

Just before the squad door was closed on him, the con man in the back seat said, "He remind me of *Satan*, what he remind me of."

Terry heard the two cops' laughter as the car pulled slowly away. He nodded his head, decided there were better things for him to be doing tonight besides being made fun of by a couple of coppers who'd been in nursery school when Terry had graduated from the academy.

Terry closed his eyes and cleared his mind of thought, stood stock-still in the middle of the concrete State Street sidewalk, his face contorted, concentrating. After a moment he opened his eyes, and then he smiled.

He could get away with it tonight.

He could keep to his original plans, and he wouldn't get caught. He'd always been able to tell such things, though he wasn't sure how he could do so. He had closed his eyes and thought about it, and now knew in his heart that no patrol sergeant would be looking for him tonight.

There was a certainty to his step as he headed north this time, Terry no longer angry, no longer filled with hate. For the first time in months, Terry Moran felt just the slightest twinge of happiness, along with a frail spark of hope gently tugging at his heart, a heart that had been beating without either emotion for almost as long as he could remember.

CHAPTER
3

Area One Violent Crimes Homicide Specialist Dominick DiGrazia stopped at the red light, then did a double take when he noticed the large, boisterous crowd gathered just ahead on Chicago Avenue, between Wabash and State. He saw a single squad car angled out into the street, lights flashing, its back end blocking the farthest eastbound lane of traffic. DiGrazia immediately turned on the flasher in his unmarked squad, hit the siren and blew the light, then raced the half block to the crowd.

He knew the crime scene was going to be bad when he saw the cop throwing up in the gutter.

The uniformed patrol officer was leaning against the squad car, holding himself up with one hand on the trunk. He was holding his other hand over his belly, as if doing so would keep his intestines inside. DiGrazia pulled the new Impala next to the squad, shut it down, and got out.

The sick officer's female partner was hard at work several yards away, looking pale herself, but not giving in to her fear—or to anything else. DiGrazia recognized her from the 28th District, right down the street—he worked out of the same building himself, upstairs in the Violent Crimes squad room. The sick young patrolman didn't look familiar to DiGrazia. He was undoubtedly one of the new officers, and one with a lot of clout if he'd pulled an assignment at the Chicago Avenue station house straight out of the academy.

Officer Janice Constantine had somehow single-handedly managed to cordon off the mouth of the dead-end alley with yellow crime-scene tape, and she was now standing in front of it, arms out wide, trying to hold off the crowd of citizens who were trying to peer into the alley. Several tourists were lifting their cameras over her shoulder, shooting pictures into the alley. The bright, sudden flashes got on DiGrazia's nerves, though he was unconcerned about their lack of respect for the dead. During sixteen years of police work, having worked twelve of them as a detective, he'd grown used to the base, gross ignorance often displayed by the taxpaying public.

"Goddamnit, I said get *back!*" Constantine shouted. It was more than a one-person job, and her credibility with the public wasn't being helped by the fact that her partner was throwing up less than ten feet away. DiGrazia wondered about the character and intelligence of people who would want a personal, close-up look at the sort of thing that would make a Chicago police officer sick.

"Well, praise sweet Jay-zuss," Constantine said, as DiGrazia approached her. DiGrazia nodded at her noncommittally as he pushed his way through the crowd. When he got to her he reached for the radio attached to her leather belt, but she pulled away. "I've got a call in for crowd-control officers; they're bringing barriers with them." DiGrazia nodded again. Constantine didn't seem to notice. "You want to help me with the crowd? We got to get them back before the media shows up."

"How long you been here?"

"Two or three minutes, I guess; seems like two or three hours." She grabbed at a camera as the bulb flashed; the man shooting the picture pulled it out of reach just in time. "Goddamn you, *give* me that!"

DiGrazia was as surprised as he was impressed. In under three minutes they had seen whatever was in there, and the male officer had used the remaining time to evacuate his stomach, while Constantine had spent it putting up crime-scene tape, calling for assistance, and fighting off the vultures. He was glad that he'd stopped. There weren't many veteran cops like Constantine left, and the few who were still on the department—who hadn't become lazy, cynical, and apathetic over the years—deserved all the support they could get.

"HEY!" DiGrazia screamed it at the top of his lungs, and the party atmosphere immediately changed to one of foreboding. "Step back!" He waded into them with his arms out, forcing them back, first to his right, then to his left. The crowd stopped where he left them, didn't try to advance. "Everyone. That means you too, mister." DiGrazia twisted a video camera out of a man's hand, leaned down so he could speak directly into the owner's face. DiGrazia towered over him, and the man wasn't small.

"This is impounded evidence; the camera's *mine,* you got it?" Other cameras disappeared into pockets and purses; were hidden behind frightened backs. DiGrazia in his shirtsleeves was impressive enough. He was made even more so by the weapon that was clipped to his belt on the right side, next to his star, and by his convincing air of authority.

He turned away from the man as several other squad cars and a police department equipment van pulled up to the scene. "Well it's about time," Constantine said. DiGrazia joined her at the tape.

"I think they'll stay back, now. You want to go see about your partner?"

"Fuck him," Constantine said. "He let the guy who found the body get away, Nick."

"There's a witness? That makes things easier."

"Like hell. It was just a wino. He couldn't have witnessed anything; he probably just contaminated the scene." Constantine lowered her arms as the crowd was pushed even farther back by the other officers. She took a handkerchief out of her back pocket and wiped the sweat off her brow, taking her hat off to do so, then setting it far back on her head. DiGrazia saw the circular sweat stain under her armpit, and looked away. Whatever she had seen back there in the alley had badly shaken her, but she hadn't let it stop her from performing her duty.

DiGrazia thought that her partner, on the other hand, had no business in police work. If you couldn't back up your partner, no matter *what* the situation, then you were better off working night security in Bloomingdale's, because once the word got out about you, it was all over for you in the department. DiGrazia looked back at Constantine, and she gave him a weary smile.

Constantine appeared to be at least fifteen years older than DiGrazia, which would put her somewhere in her early to mid-fifties. He smiled back at her, two veterans standing shoulder to shoulder as uniformed officers pushed the greedy citizenry back.

"How did you get that tape up, what with the crowd pushing all around you?"

"Same way you would; I intimidated the shit out of them. But they started to outnumber me." DiGrazia grunted a small laugh at her choice of words. "There were plenty of them out here when I first rolled up, but when they saw the squad, they *swarmed*. I was worried that one of them might get back there, sell his story and pictures to one of the tabloid TV shows. Thank God we got the barriers up before the talking heads showed up." Constantine was referring to the television reporters.

The bags under her eyes seemed deeper in the brightness of the flashing squad-car lights. He remembered she'd had a reputation for being a heavy drinker at one time, but he'd heard that she'd given up drinking some years back. Yet the puffiness that more often seemed to plague female alcoholics was still evident in her cheeks and around her eyes, made more noticeable by the pastiness of her skin. Constantine had a reputation, too, for being quick on her feet, for being smart, funny, and tough. She was also twenty pounds overweight, with short, straight, stringy, dyed blonde hair. The two of them relaxed as the crime scene became completely secure. Constantine was out of breath, her chest heaving from her exertions.

DiGrazia knew scores of police officers who lifted weights every day, massive specimens of bodybuilding bulk, who neither smoked nor drank, who wouldn't eat red meat. But if he was walking into a pitch-black apartment where an armed and barricaded suspect was hiding, he'd prefer a cop like Constantine at his side over any of them, any time.

Constantine at last caught her breath, then took her hat off again, took her cigarettes out of its inner band, and lit one up as the uniformed officers placed the wooden barriers twenty feet from them, on either side from the alley's mouth, forming a fence that extended a few feet out into the street, until at last the area was completely sealed off.

"Young wimp-ass punk, look at him," Constantine said. "Thank God we didn't walk in on the killer. I'd probably have gotten my throat slit while Goldilocks over there overdosed on his own sensitivity. You watch, he'll tell me that his inner child made him run away."

"You all right?" DiGrazia asked, and she looked up at him. Her expression was serious, her usually hard eyes pleading.

"Nick, it's the worst thing I've ever seen." DiGrazia looked at her in surprise, but made no comment. He suddenly knew that he would have to enter that alley. "How'd you beat everybody else over here?" she asked.

"I didn't. I didn't even have my radio on. I saw it from the street, I was just going home."

"Off duty?" Constantine was looking at him strangely. Di-Grazia was six feet, three inches tall, and weighed 212 pounds. He carried very little fat on his frame. He had a reputation for dogged intelligence that was overshadowed by his reputation for being mean, surly, and short-tempered with subordinates. He knew about it and didn't mind, used both to his advantage whenever he could. But now DiGrazia looked away, slightly embarrassed, and shrugged.

Constantine said, "Take a little advice from an old street copper, Nick. Get back in your car, right now, and continue whatever off-duty activities you had planned for the evening. You do *not* want to see what's back there. Let whoever's on call handle it, there're other dicks who can handle the call. This ain't yours, Nick; take it from me, you don't *want* it."

DiGrazia didn't know if Constantine knew enough about him to have done it on purpose, but she'd just effectively put him in the position where he had no other choice but to go into the alley and at least take a look. He looked over his shoulder without turning around, squinted into the darkness.

"I remember it being lighted back there."

"There's pieces of glass all over the ground."

"Check any for fingerprints, did you?"

Constantine laughed without humor. "Don't you wish you could be so lucky."

"Notice anything else unusual?"

"Unusual?" Constantine grunted sarcastically. "Yeah, I guess there's a few things back there you could consider to be *unusual*."

"I meant about the scene."

Another new Chevy Impala was pulling to the curb. Two heavyset, middle-aged men were getting out, leaving their bright red flasher spinning in the rear window. Both men had their suit jackets on. One was carrying a shotgun. They looked around at the crowd with a "We're-in-control-here," attitude, both of them appearing to be bored and cynical men.

Watching them, Constantine said to DiGrazia, "The lights were taken out earlier, probably during the daytime, where the sudden lack of light wouldn't be noticed by anyone walking by. Might be pellets we can match up later in their somewhere, so watch where you walk. The girl was killed somewhere else, then brought here. The witness, the wino, he couldn't have seen the killer, or he'd be dead now himself. All's I wanted him for was to hold him for you, or whatever detective got this. So he could tell you what he'd touched, or if he took anything from the victim's purse. It's still—" Constantine paused, then said, softly "—on her person. It hasn't been opened, I don't think. If it was, it was opened by someone with a really strong stomach."

"That, or by somebody desperate. You say you think she was killed somewhere else?"

Constantine grunted. "No doubt in my mind."

"How you figure?" The two Homicide cops were standing a short distance away on the curb, conferring with the male officer, who had by now composed himself enough to be able to speak to them. One of the detectives was looking down at the puddle of vomit with distaste; the other stepped back as the young man spoke to him, offended by the smell of his breath. Still, neither man yet approached them, preferring to speak to a smelly, rookie male officer than to a female with more time on the job than anyone else at the scene, and who had more street savvy than the two of them combined.

Constantine was a hardened veteran with nerves of stone, a heart that had steel grates built around it, and emotions that had been cauterized by more than twenty years in the department. She ignored the same snubs that younger female officers would file sexism complaints over, but that didn't mean that she didn't feel them, that she wasn't hurt by those snubs.

DiGrazia, for his part, simply felt disgusted.

Looking coldly at the Homicide detectives, Constantine said to DiGrazia, "There's not a lot of blood in there, there's hardly any at all."

"Well," DiGrazia dragged the word out, then stopped. He didn't want to point out the obvious to her, she'd been around long enough, she deserved more respect than that from him. Even if he'd never heard of her, her conduct tonight had proved that much. He said, "Would there be? The victim might have died right away."

"You'll see what I mean when you go back there."

The two Homicide detectives were walking toward them now. A uniformed patrol officer pushed a barrier aside so they could pass on to the scene, then immediately replaced the barrier behind them and turned back to the crowd. A phalanx of officers guarded the barriers, ignoring the catcalls and shouts and whistles, the drunken insults, exactly as they'd been trained to. DiGrazia was no longer needed, but curiosity made him stay.

"Thanks for stopping, anyway, Nicky, I appreciate it." Constantine said, as the detectives came up to her. DiGrazia recognized one of them, the man with the shotgun, though he couldn't remember his name. They worked out of the new West Side building, he remembered that much. Shotgun pointed at the tape with his weapon, made a gesture with it as if he expected Constantine to lift it for them.

"What am I, your trainer? Are you Mike Tyson?" She turned to DiGrazia. "This nitwit look like Mike Tyson to you?" DiGrazia didn't try to hide his smile as Constantine paid them back for their silent insult. The detective with the shotgun looked quizzically over at him.

"This yours, DiGrazia? We got the call." There was a note of hope in his tone. He waved the shotgun over his shoulder. "Kid says it's ugly back there."

"I think he might have been too busy throwing up to have picked up any lasting impressions," DiGrazia said.

"Guts everywhere," Constantine said. "Laid out all over the place, boys." The detectives ignored her.

The one without the shotgun said, "Mitchell told us you're DiGrazia."

"*Dr.* DiGrazia. Got shot by the guinea last year. Made the headlines," his partner added, as if DiGrazia needed no more of an introduction than that. DiGrazia felt the scar on his belly begin to itch, and he had to stop himself from reaching up to scratch it. He ignored the ethnic slur; it hadn't been aimed at him. What he would not forget, however, was Shotgun's making fun of Di-Grazia's doctorate degree in forensic science. He made a mental note to find out both men's names.

"I heard you're a hot dog." DiGrazia's face went blank as Shotgun quickly shot a look at his partner.

Constantine said, "Why don't you put some mustard on him and bite him then, you moron?" DiGrazia still said nothing. The detective looked at her sternly while Shotgun laughed, relieved that the tension had been broken. If he knew about what had happened with Tonce Alberti, then he was aware of the sort of violence that DiGrazia was capable of. He shook his head and turned back to DiGrazia.

Shotgun was the obvious spokesman for the two. His partner was strong, dumb, and tough. DiGrazia had seen enough of the type through the years to be able to recognize one on sight. Shotgun asked, "You from Twenty-eight?" DiGrazia nodded. Shotgun looked away, surveying the crowd, then looked back at DiGrazia. "We got called away while we was wrapping up a messy one down on Elm."

"*Elm?*" Constantine was shocked. Elm was the high-rent district.

"Seven-hundred West."

"Oh."

They meant the Cabrini-Green area, rather than the Gold Coast. What he was no doubt saying was that they had a slam-dunk ghetto murder: the corpse, the killer, and the weapon; more than likely a confession. They'd been called off it, so someone else would get credit for the pinch, if they didn't hurry back in time to process the suspect, and take his statement.

DiGrazia thought about his situation, pondered his options. He could take the case without a problem, he was a veteran Violent Crimes detective who'd been first on the scene, with the time and the clout to get the case, should he want it. The hot dog remark rankled him, and for a moment he was tempted to make these two earn their wages.

Then he thought about how they might do that, how badly they might screw it up. Constantine had said it was a female victim, that she'd never seen anything like it. He came to his decision as stark, false lights fell upon their faces.

The media had arrived; the Minicams were shooting.

The two Homicide detectives actually winced, as if they'd been subjected to enemy fire. Real life wasn't like the movies: A high-profile media case could sometimes be a career maker, but it was more often a career breaker, if the investigating detectives didn't solve the crime. Even if the detective didn't take any heat from the media and the politicians, even if it wasn't a solvable case, he could sometimes blame himself; the case could drive him to any number of self-destructive distractions. Any detective who didn't believe that only had to look at the once-shining departmental stars whose careers were now as lifeless as the corpse in the alley to see the sort of damage that a case like this could do. The department—and the ranks of departmental pensioners—was littered with bitter, drunken detectives who'd left a single, high-profile case dangling open.

DiGrazia knew one of them himself, quite well.

Which was another reason why he knew that he had to go into the alley.

"What do you think?" Shotgun said. "We need to get back if we're going."

"Go ahead back to Elm. I'll take it."

"I'll call it in; it's all yours," Shotgun said, relieved.

DiGrazia handed Shotgun the video camera. "Here. This is for you."

"Me?" Shotgun raised his eyebrows, smiled, and hefted the camera. "Hey. Damn." Shotgun inspected the camera with growing appreciation. "Thanks a lot, DiGrazia . . ."

His partner muttered to Constantine, "Thank God for affirmative action, huh?" and she responded by telling what he could do with his affirmative action, as the two of them bowed their heads, in the manner of criminals hiding from the TV lights, then hurried out of camera range. DiGrazia kept his face impassive as he heard a voice in the crowd shouting that he wanted his fuck-ing camera back, that cop with the shotgun was stealing his video camera!

Constantine, squinting at the lights, muttered spitefully at their backs.

"What's that, Janice?" DiGrazia kept his tone light, and the smile off his face.

Constantine looked up at him. He read her expression and raised his eyebrows, and she shook her head, as if her thoughts were unimportant. Both of them, however, knew better. She was worried about the sensitivity of the microphones that were now aimed in their direction. She hadn't survived in the department for as long as she had by speaking her mind openly in front of television cameras.

"Come on," Constantine said, "I'll give you the guided tour before the crime-scene techs get here." She lifted the tape, beck-oned DiGrazia forward, and he crouched down and stepped into the alley.

"Do I look like Mike Tyson?"

"You look crazy, you ask me. You should have left it alone. I hope it's been a long time since lunch."

DiGrazia, on a distant level, picked up the tight quiver of discomfort in her voice, but it didn't register in his conscious mind. Constantine's words didn't matter; he was thinking about her courage, her willingness to step back into a scene of unspeak-able brutality. He was glad now that he'd stayed, glad that he'd taken the case. He wondered how long he'd feel that way as he took slow steps into the alley, squinting at what was back there, propped up against the far wall, beyond the Dumpster. He felt a small, tight knot of fear in his groin as he noticed that the corpse was grinning at him.

Thankfully, the lights from the Minicams didn't extend this far back into the alley. The sodium-vapor lights in the narrow enclosure had, indeed, been smashed. Without taking his gaze from the victim, DiGrazia unclipped his mini–Mag-light and popped it on. He took small, slow steps forward, keeping as close as he could get to the alley wall without actually touching it. The scene had been contaminated by at least three people that he was aware of—the two police officers and the wino—but still,

DiGrazia was cautious, it was better—fresher—than he was used to. Step by step, he moved forward.

DiGrazia stopped three feet away from the first displaced organ. He looked down at it, moving the light away from the body for the first time in order to illuminate it. It appeared to be the liver. He put the light on each of the organs in turn, organs which were laid out around the body in an obviously symbolic manner; a madman's road map. At last he turned the beam back onto what was left of the woman's body and just stood there, taking shallow breaths through his mouth. He did not want to close his eyes, did not even want to blink. The dead woman's purse was in her lap, her hands carefully placed atop it, as if holding it closed from muggers.

Everything above the purse was pure atrocity.

Constantine spoke his name and he jumped. She squeezed his bicep with strong fingers. "Relax, Nicky."

"Dear Jesus God in heaven." His voice sounded strange to his own ears, as if he were speaking through a tin tunnel, from a long way off.

"I know, Nick, I know." Constantine kept her hand on his arm, as if doing so confirmed their humanity. The two of them stood there for what seemed like a very long time, DiGrazia considering the sort of human that could do this, Constantine beside him, silently waiting.

In a soft, gentle voice, DiGrazia finally said, "He glued her eyelids open, and he sewed up both sides of her mouth with fishing wire; that's why she seems to be grinning."

"That's what scared me the most. When I first came back here. That big, wide-open—cave—in the middle of her chest like that, and that smile." DiGrazia nodded. They continued to inspect the body. "You think there's a message in the purse?"

"I know what's in the purse."

Constantine removed her hand, puzzled. Pushing a step further, she said, "Don't tell me you've seen a case like this before, Nick," and DiGrazia turned to her, his face grim and pale, his jawbone tight.

"Yes," DiGrazia said, "Yes, I have." He reached into his pocket, pulled out his keys, and handed them to her. "I'll keep them out of here. You go to my car trunk, bring me the leather

satchel from inside. The camera equipment and the tape recorder's in it." DiGrazia had to think for a second. "Get a legal pad
off the back seat; the notebook's on the front seat, or under it.
It's got a leather cover, with my initials on it. Then get back in
here as fast as you can."

"You're doing the crime scene your*self?*"

"I'm trained and qualified. I'll do as much as I can. I don't
want any more than one criminalist back here with me. You tell
them that out there, out on the line. Tell them anyone else tries
to get past those barricades—and that includes the superintendent
and the mayor—they pinch them, and I mean *any*one. I'll cover
it for them later." Despite the urgency of his orders, DiGrazia
grasped Constantine's arm, keeping her from obeying them.

"You and I are the only ones who need to see this, and we're
keeping our mouths shut. I'm throwing up a wall of silence on
this one; no media, no bosses, no curious detectives, no uniforms
at all. *Nobody* gets back here besides the senior criminalist on call,
you see to that, Janice."

His voice seemed distant, distracted. Constantine looked at
him, and he let go of her arm. She walked away as DiGrazia
slowly turned and stood staring at the body propped up against
the alley wall.

CHAPTER
4

There is an informal meeting of inpatients at the Veterans Administration Hospital on West Chestnut Street. They meet every evening at midnight, a group of psychiatric patients who for whatever reason cannot sleep. They gather in a large, softly lighted room and drink decaffeinated coffee or pop, suck down as many cigarettes as they want to in the normally nonsmoking building, and take turns talking to each other into the wee, small hours without any authority figures breaking in on them with psychobabble.

The administration is aware of these meetings, and gives them its tacit encouragement. Men who cannot fit in on the outside are learning to socialize here.

There are Vietnam veterans who, more than twenty years after the end of that war, still cannot find a way to adjust to the regular world. There are alcohol- and drug-dependent men, some of whom have been through treatment here many times before. There are men who suffer from depression, and those who suffer from varying forms of schizophrenia.

The psychotics are kept in a separate ward, isolated from the rest of the hospital.

Most people in the outside world are not aware that this hospital has such a ward, or that the men of the ward have such meetings. In this area, on the Gold Coast, such knowledge would not be a good thing for these men. The neighbors would not stand for it if they found out that the mentally ill were being treated just down the block from their own expensive dwellings.

But they are here, and they have been for a very long time.

Of the dozen or so men of widely varying ages who were now in the room, six of them had killed, and the seventh was a murderer. Six had done their killing during wartime. The seventh man, Neal, was a twenty-four-year-old veteran of the Persian Gulf War who had performed his murder after he'd been discharged from the service and had returned back home, in a drug-crazed assault under cover of the nighttime. He had never discussed it with anyone, and he didn't plan to ever discuss it with anyone, not ever, not in this life.

Neal had checked himself into the hospital because he kept seeing the woman he'd killed coming at him in a recurring nightmare. He did not tell the doctors about this dream. He told the doctors he was depressed, that he thought he was losing his mind, that voices came to him in his nightmares, in every dream, and those voices encouraged him to kill himself.

The truth was that the woman had been visiting him on more nights than she didn't, her arms reaching, her decaying face smiling at him, her long hair flowing, the woman beckoning him into a lover's embrace. Neal would awaken, shrieking. Each time she visited, his more grossly decaying murder victim would get closer. Neal now dreaded sleeping, lived in terror of what would happen on the night when she finally, inevitably reached him.

Whatever the little brown pills were that Dr. Warren had prescribed for him had worked; Neal hadn't had the dream in more than three weeks. He didn't tell the doctors this, though, as he dreaded having to leave, he was afraid that the dream would come back once he was returned to the outside world.

There was a light rap on the door, then it opened a foot, and an orderly stuck his head inside. "Sarge?" the orderly said, and a tall old man with a huge belly that was stretching out the elastic of his pajama bottoms looked up and raised his eyebrows. The orderlies never bothered this group, unless it was an especially lively night with an inordinate amount of shouting. The orderly was getting a number of resentful looks from the residents in the room. The orderly didn't care. He had a knowing look in his eye; a shrewd smile creased his face. "Got a guy out here just wandered in off the street, wants to join your bitch session."

Puzzled, Sarge rose, pulled down on the T-shirt that had risen halfway up his stomach, and walked over to the door. The orderly lowered his voice to a whisper.

"Dr. Warren's on his way in, he wants you to keep the man cool until he gets here." Sarge looked warily out into the hall, saw who it was, then smiled, relieved.

"Come on in, Sailor," Sarge said to the man with the orderly.

Sarge waited until the door was closed again and the orderly's footsteps had retreated before saying, "Everyone? This is—"

"Eddie." Sarge looked at the man strangely, but Eddie did not respond. Sarge shrugged.

" *'Eddie'* used to—stop by—here regularly." Sarge tapped Eddie's shoulder lightly. "Haven't seen you in the neighborhood in a long time."

Now Eddie shrugged. Clearly nervous, he said, "I been away awhile. I figured you might still be having these meetings, or at least you'd be visiting. I wanted to see a familiar face, someone . . . " Eddie's voice trailed off.

Sarge covered for him by smiling, then quickly saying, "Well, I'm still here." He said it with a touch of pride, a psychiatric inpatient bragging on his seniority.

The men milled around; some of them squirmed in their seats a bit uncomfortably. Outsiders forced into close quarters with their own don't often adapt well to the company of intruders. Only their loneliness kept them from leaving.

"I—I've got problems," Eddie said. "I've been drinking too much, taking drugs, and I've been—really fucking up."

Several of the men laughed softly in understanding. Neither Eddie nor Sarge was offended.

Still smiling, Sarge said, "Pull up a chair and sit down, Eddie." He emphasized the name slightly, and would not do it again this night. "You wandered into an entire *room* full of drunken, drug-crazed fuck-ups."

*   *   *

A few minutes later, after coffee cups had been refilled and empty pop cans replaced, the discussion was once again joined. The lights had been turned off and candles had been lit. Eddie, having been softly requested to do so by Sarge, began to speak.

"Do you know what it's like? Any of you?" Eddie challenged the group. They were all very quiet now, listening to him, the intensity in his voice warning them of the import of the words he hadn't yet spoken. He leaned forward in his chair, eyes ablaze.

"I can't eat, I can't sleep! When I do sleep, I have nightmares! The guilt's eating me a*live!*" He looked around, saw that one of the men in the group had sat forward in his chair. The man had his elbows on his knees, and was staring at Eddie, as if Eddie had just put tin foil on the fillings of his teeth.

Eddie said, "The only thing I can compare it to, it's like a young Catholic kid jerking off, for Christ's sake! He's been trained all his life to *believe* it's wrong, he *knows* it's a sin, and still, he can't stop himself." Eddie took a deep drink of his pop, shook the can, then put it down at his feet. He hung his head, ran his fingers through his hair, and left them there. Head down, he continued.

"You tell yourself you'll stop. Every time is gonna be the last. You don't want to do it, you know you can't do it again, but sooner or later, the *urge* builds up, the fucking *NEED!*"

"It's all right, Eddie," Sarge, who was on Eddie's right, said very softly. He patted Eddie's shoulder, but Eddie pulled away roughly, accidentally knocking over the pop can. Brown fluid spilled out from the can, spread around the front of Eddie's chair.

"It's *not* all right, it's *not!* Do you have any idea what I'm talking about here? Do any of you?"

"Sure," one of the men in the back said, "you're talking about jerking off." Several other men chuckled.

"That's just an an*a*logy, goddamnit!"

"Eddie, keep it down, or the orderly'll come around. You ain't even supposed to *be* here unless you're an inpatient, unless a doctor checked you in, and you *know* they don't want you in here when you're drinking." Sarge paused, considering his chastisement. "And lighten up on the boys. We're all the same here, we all got the same two problems. We're crazy, and broke."

Eddie spun on him, eyes pleading.

"You understand, don't you, Sarge? Do you get what I'm saying?"

"Sure I do; you're describing a compulsion."

"That's ex*act*ly right!" Eddie turned to the crowd, sought out the man he thought had insulted him. "Com*pul*sion, man. That's what it is. Just like jerking off. A devout Catholic boy, he jerks off, and what happens? He's immediately filled with guilt, over-come by it, overwhelmed. He prays to God for help, begs God to forgive him, vows he'll never do it again, that he'll cut his dick off before he touches himself again."

Neal was watching Eddie with a look of profound understand-ing and concentration. Eddie's gaze gravitated to him as easily as if they'd heard the same, silent mating call.

When he spoke now, he spoke directly to Neal.

"And he sticks to the vow for a while, fighting against the urge, the need. And when he wants to do it again, he might even fall down on his knees at first, and pray until it goes away! He rationalizes; tells himself that if God didn't want him to do it, He wouldn't have given him such a powerful, uncontrollable urge." Eddie pondered this momentarily, and when he spoke again, his voice was soft and low.

"Then he forgets about God altogether as the urge comes back, getting stronger and stronger, and at last, no matter what he thinks he *wants* to do, he has to do it again, he doesn't have any choice."

Sarge said, "They teach us in here that there's always a choice, Eddie."

"They don't know shit." The man Eddie had been looking at, Neal, spoke quietly, backing up his newfound friend. "All of them, with their fancy degrees, their money, don't none of them know shit!"

If Eddie had been able to, he would have smiled. Instead he just nodded at the man, empathy leaping between them as lightning leaps between metal rods. Eddie blew his breath out, wiped at his tears with the back of his sleeve.

"Go on, man, what were you saying, before Sarge barged in?" Neal asked.

"I was saying, I was saying . . ."

Sarge shot a glare at Neal. "You were saying you had no choice," he said to Eddie.

Neal wasn't backing off. "Not that, Sarge, not *Eddie*, he wasn't talking about him*self*, goddamnit!" Neal said. "He was talking about the masturbating Catholic kid—how *he* doesn't have any choice."

"No, he doesn't," Eddie almost whispered. He leaned forward in his chair again, and looked directly at his soulmate.

"It's in his nature, part of what he is."

"Part of what makes him human?" Neal asked.

"God no, it's—less—than that; it's what takes *away* his humanity. It's part of—it's *inside* him—the need, the drive. And it overwhelms him, until he does it again, no matter what his intentions were."

"Does it ever get easier for him?"

Eddie thought about this for a moment. "No. It just gets worse. And worse."

Sarge said, "What if he stops being a Catholic?" Both men were glaring at him now. The rest of the men in the room were silent, watching, some concerned, others bored. None of them tried to join in. It had become a three-way conversation, three men speaking in analogies about a hypothetical subject whom they all knew was really Eddie.

"I'm serious," Sarge said. "What if he just decides to stop being a Catholic? Gives it up? Joins a religion that tells him it's okay to play with himself?"

Eddie thought about this a second, then shook his head. It was time to drop the intellectual facade. In a surrendering, desperate voice, Eddie said, "There's no religion in the world that would tell me it's okay for me to do the things that I've done."

That stopped them. Now all eyes were on Eddie, not just Sarge's and Neal's. Eddie stopped, aware that he'd overstepped his bounds, that these men now completely understood what he was really talking about. The thought frightened Eddie as much as it relieved him of part of his burden.

Sarge worded his statement carefully. "This ain't just about drinking, is it, Eddie?" He paused, but Eddie did not answer. "The—analogy—Eddie, what's it really an analogy for?"

"I can't tell you."

"But it's why you came back here, right? To try and control it?"

Eddie nodded, vigorously.

"And now, whatever it is, you're doing it again? Is that what you're saying?"

Once more, Eddie nodded, though this time slowly and cautiously.

"Do you want to talk about it? You can trust us, Eddie. I told you, we're all in the same boat here."

Eddie immediately shook his head. He bit his quivering lower lip. He squeezed his eyes shut.

Sarge gently placed his hand on Eddie's shoulder. *"Talk to us* about it, Eddie!"

"I can't!" The words were sobbed.

Sarge tightened his grip on Eddie's shoulder. "Will you talk to the doctor about it, Eddie, to Dr. Warren? He'll help you, man, you know him." Sarge looked around quickly, knowing that he might have just made a big mistake, that he might have said more than he should have, but nobody seemed to have picked up on it, no one was looking at him oddly, or in a way that made Sarge think that he might have betrayed a confidence. He turned back to Eddie.

"We can help you, Eddie, if you let us. We can help you out of your hell."

Eddie didn't understand what was happening to him. Something inside seemed to twist, turn, torturing him deep down in his stomach, the worst cramp he'd ever felt. He clutched his stomach, held it tightly, leaning forward in his chair as a high-pitched moan escaped him. Several men came to his assistance, holding him up, expressing concern. Sarge held him in once-powerful arms, patted his back.

"It's all right, Eddie, you go ahead and let it all out."

Was he crying? Eddie, doubled over, being held by Sarge, was stunned. He, the man who never expressed public emotion, was crying.

"Talk to us, Eddie, we'll take it all away, we can do that. We can help you. You wouldn't do it last time, but you've still got a shot at a life for yourself. You can do it, Eddie, you can get help."

Eddie pulled away and hugged himself.

"*I CAAAAAANNNNNNN'TTTTTT!*"

"Sure you can, Eddie. Sure you can." Sarge's voice was very gentle, reassuring in his ear. He had moved close in on Eddie now, put his arm around his shoulder again. Eddie tried to stop crying, wiped at the snot under his nose with the back of his hand.

"You don't believe you can talk to us?" Sarge gave Eddie's shoulder a manly shake. "Come on. You think you're gonna tell anyone in this room something he ain't heard before?" Eddie once more shook Sarge's arm off his shoulder.

Undeterred, Sarge said, "Then at least talk to Dr. Warren! He's helped more vets than any ten motherfuckers in Congress. You can tell him anything, he won't rat you out."

"I *did!*" It was a petulant whine. "And he didn't help me! He gave me some pills that didn't work, I don't think he even believed me!"

"Then fuck him. *We'll* believe you, Eddie. Tell us, man, we'll help you out. Every single swinging dick in this room is a veteran, just like you. We all know what it's like, what you're going through. We'll help you, we're on your side."

"What if you tell on me?" Eddie swiped at the tears with the back of his hand. He knew it was important to get himself back under control, but he wasn't sure he wanted to. Sarge's kind words, the compassion of the other men, it made him feel so safe, almost made him feel loved.

Sarge laughed off his concerns. "Hell, we couldn't tell, even if we wanted to. We can't tell no one shit." Sarge laughed. "Who'd believe us if we did? We're mental patients locked up on a psycho ward, for Christ's sake!"

"Oh, Sarge . . ." Eddie drew in a deep, shuddering breath. "I can't trust anyone." He looked up at Sarge, then around at the other men. His eyes were as hungry as his heart, and his words were now spoken with such an emotional anguish that they broke the hearts of more than one of the men in the room.

"Don't you understand how much I *want* to trust someone? Don't you know how I wish I *could* trust you?"

"You can!" Sarge looked at Eddie, calculating his next words. The room was silent as he thought. Eddie, suddenly realizing that he was the center of attention in a room filled with strangers, fought to control himself, then felt embarrassed. Sensing this, Sarge hurriedly, feebly said, "You can trust *us,* man. We're all on your side."

The other man, Eddie's ally Neal, said, "We didn't have that, nobody would ever get cured, would they? We had to trust each other. We're all the real help each other has in this world, man, don't nobody else give a shit. The doctors, they're just doing their job. They know if they say anything, you'd have a malpractice suit against them that'd set you up for the rest of your life. So what? Big deal. Money wouldn't make you better, money wouldn't heal you."

"But in here, Eddie," another man said, "what's in this room, it's like a miracle." Eddie looked over at him. He was a mousy little guy, old, older than Sarge, with wispy, greasy hair. Eddie had never seen him before in his life, and he wouldn't have given him a second thought had the two of them passed on the street, but the man was crying as he spoke. Eddie noticed that several of the other men were misty-eyed, too.

Eddie had wandered into a number of AA and NA meetings and had found nothing more than self-serving whiners who were there to seek sex as much as they were to seek help with their drinking. He could not count the many different church services he'd attended, seeking a spiritual avenue out of his pain, and finding nothing there but self-righteous, moral hypocrites. He had sought professional psychiatric help at this very Veterans Administration hospital, and all he'd ever gotten for his efforts was indecipherable nods, portentous hums, and medications that didn't work. Nothing had ever helped him. He had spent his life seeking approval, but he had still never felt as if he would ever belong, as if he would ever fit in, anywhere.

Until just this very minute.

He turned to Sarge quickly as the older man said, "Guys stay inside this shithouse just so they can come in here at midnight, Eddie, and be with their own kind. With other guys who understand what they're going through. Guys who'd do just fine on the outside, guys who won't even tell the docs anything, guys who could check themselves out of here any time, and go about their business, but who stay here, Eddie, just because of these midnight meetings."

Were they serious? Was that the way it was? It wasn't the way he remembered it, he could not recall feeling this sense of safety, the belonging before. But he felt it now. He was too confused at the moment to remember much of anything. Eddie wasn't sure yet, he was still too dazed to think straight, but he felt so relieved, so safe and loved at the moment, that he reached out and grabbed for the frail branch that was thrust into his own personal, churning river.

Sarge squeezed his shoulders. Eddie's body shook with his long pent-up grief. Eddie allowed a lifetime of suffering, terror, frustration, and self-loathing to bubble straight to the surface.

But he would still have to be careful.

There were too many men in the room, too many who would talk, too many who might turn him in. He would only trust one of them. Maybe two. The guy in the chair over there, staring at him, Neal, his name was. Eddie knew he could tell him. And Sarge. Maybe Sarge. Eddie wasn't certain about Sarge. Time would tell. It always did. His problem was that he didn't know how much time he had left; a heart attack seemed imminent, arrest would be worse than death. He had to get help this time, had to find someone he could talk to, and he thought that he might find his relief in the stranger, Neal.

He looked up, caught Neal's eyes, saw that they were shining. For the group's benefit, Eddie nodded.

Sarge said, "You mentioned Catholics, earlier. Were you raised Catholic? Well, no matter, God loves you no matter what religion you are, or were. And God's in this room, whether you want to believe it or not."

There was neediness in his tone as Eddie managed to say, "Can God forgive me? If I tell?"

"God forgives everything, Eddie."

Eddie pulled away, wiped at his eyes, but couldn't stop the flow of tears that continued to stream down his face. He heard Neal say, "And I forgive you, Eddie."

Sarge added, "We *all* forgive you. And we love you, Eddie, don't you ever forget that."

Someone else said, "Now you've got to learn to love and forgive yourself . . ."

They loved him? Would they still love him if they knew? If he told them what he *was*, what he'd done?

No!

He couldn't tell them, he couldn't say a word. He'd been through this before, the remorse, the pain. The false sense of hope that there could be some cure for him. It had been a mistake for him to call Dr. Warren, he didn't know why he'd done it, except that he was so afraid, so scared after what he'd done to the girl.

He shouldn't have called, he knew that now. And he had to get out of here before the doctor came and found him. The doctor would check him in, would keep him there against his will if Eddie wanted to leave. Eddie knew the drill: forty-eight hours locked up on a doctor's word alone, all the doctor had to say was that he thought Eddie was a threat to society or himself. Eddie had been there before. Why had he trusted a doctor? How could he trust these men?

Eddie felt his conditional humanity drifting away from him, felt himself shed it, the way a snake sheds useless skin. He felt his coldness coming back, uncomfortable but safer for him. He was always sheltered when he was inside the ice, nobody could crack through it and get at him. Eddie looked at his watch, then started, as if in surprise at the hour.

"Oh, man," he whispered, then looked up at the room in general, wide-eyed. "It's late. I've got to go."

"What? Don't do that, Eddie, you have to stay," Sarge pleaded. "Warren's coming in to see you, you probably got him out of bed. Stay, talk to us, talk to him. You'll be all right if you do, I swear to God you will be."

Eddie stood, shaking his head. "I've got to go."

"What's so important? You married now? Got a job? How long will either one of *those* last if you don't get a grip on these problems, man?"

Eddie seemed to ignore this, began to walk to the door. "Maybe I'll come back tomorrow."

Sarge was on his feet now too, following Eddie to the door. He grabbed Eddie's arm, and would never know how close he came to dying at that moment. Sarge watched as Eddie closed his eyes, opened his mouth, saw Eddie take in a long, slow, hissing breath. Something made Sarge let go of him. Still, he said, "Give me your word."

"Please come back." Eddie opened his eyes and saw that Neal now stood next to Sarge. Their eyes met, a decision was made, and Eddie nodded solemnly.

"If Dr. Warren'll have me, I'll come back tomorrow." He looked at Sarge. "I give you my word."

"Then why won't you *stay*—"

"Tomorrow," Eddie said firmly, then was gone.

CHAPTER
5

"**Y**ou took this on, on your own time; you actually *want* this fucking case?" Lt. Daniel Matthews of Homicide said, in a soft, near-incredulous tone. Matthews did not like the midnight shift, but it was all that was open for him if he wanted to stay in Homicide, and every detective in the department wanted to be in Homicide. Matthews had been doing some of his paperwork when DiGrazia had entered his office. Now he sat looking at DiGrazia oddly, his smile close to one of scorn.

"What's the matter, they don't work you hard enough on afternoons? You ain't got enough on your plate without digging into *my* watch?" DiGrazia wished that Lieutenant Bailey—his afternoon shift commander—was still on duty; both men were ladder-climbing politicians, but Bailey had known DiGrazia long enough—and had enough faith in him—to allow him to follow his instincts. As long as DiGrazia didn't blow a case, Bailey would give him his freedom.

DiGrazia never had, and didn't intend, to blow a case.

If Capt. John Parker had been in the building, DiGrazia would have been able to avoid this meeting entirely.

But neither Bailey nor Parker were here, and DiGrazia wasn't about to call either man at home and wake him up; he could handle this. The problem was that DiGrazia would now have to explain himself to Matthews, and that would be a waste of precious time.

"I wrapped up the Syrek shooting before I left for the night, got a signed confession from the killer. Got it on tape, too, sir. He can't correspond very well, so I did him a favor and helped him write it out." DiGrazia said, "I dropped a few mistakes in it, had him initial the corrections to help it stand up in court." He nodded at the mound of reports on the lieutenant's desk. "The paperwork's right there, somewhere in the pile. Lieutenant Bailey was already gone by the time I wrapped it up."

DiGrazia spoke to his superior officer in the lieutenant's office while Janice Constantine sat at DiGrazia's desk out in the detective squad room. She was visible through the lieutenant's dirty window. It was obviously DiGrazia's desk; it was the only one that wasn't abutted by a second desk, nose to nose. Constantine was now ignoring several cardboard warnings pinned to the walls, signs printed in large, red letters: NO SMOKING. There were several other detectives in the room who, following her lead, were now also smoking. The atmosphere on the midnight shift was more casual than it was when the brass were in their offices. Constantine dumped her ashes in DiGrazia's wastepaper basket.

The lieutenant said, "I don't know about you. I've got detectives who can't wait to get their asses out of here, and you can't wait to get back in. Come in on your own time . . ." as if this were unheard of, as if DiGrazia had to have an ulterior motive. DiGrazia did not think that a man like Matthews belonged in Command.

But he did not speak his mind, DiGrazia merely sat back and watched the dance the lieutenant often performed, a gambit that bought the man time to think, while it also kept most of the detectives he might be speaking with just slightly off guard. DiGrazia had figured out the diversional tactic the first time he'd witnessed it, so now he said nothing, giving the lieutenant all the time he wanted.

DiGrazia did not need to work very hard to be able to out-think such men.

"You know how many calls I've taken already this morning, from sergeants, other lieutenants, commanders, deputy *chiefs*, bitching about how you wouldn't let them inside the crime scene? I heard you took the pictures yourself. I heard you shut the scene *down*. What the hell was *that* all about, DiGrazia?"

"It's an outdoor murder, and I got there right after the victim was discovered. Who needs all those guys stumbling around, smoking, dropping gum wrappers, touching things, stepping on evidence? It was a nearly textbook example, Lieutenant, the scene barely contaminated, I got it almost fresh."

"Crime lab techs are livid, DiGrazia, textbook or not. They're threatening to file a joint complaint, saying you wouldn't let them do their jobs. I can't have a wildman shutting professionals out of their work."

"I'm a qualified technician, sir." DiGrazia spoke softly, not wanting to rub the lieutenant's nose in the fact that he was far better educated than the lieutenant was himself. DiGrazia wasn't being humble, he needed the man's approval on a couple of requests.

"I know all about your degrees, De*tec*tive. I know what you're overqualified for."

DiGrazia sat patiently and still, looking calmly at the lieutenant. Nothing in his manner exposed the dislike he felt for the man.

"It upset you that *I'm* in the lieutenant's chair, and *you're* still a detective?"

DiGrazia didn't bother to inform him that he had turned down many offers—for far more money—to work at various crime labs throughout the country, labs whose directors admired and wanted DiGrazia's professional expertise. He liked being a detective. He had never taken—nor ever intended to take—the sergeant's exam, as he would then be an administrator, rather than a working street cop. Matthews rocked in his chair, and DiGrazia gave him a small smile.

He said, "Listen, Lieutenant, why don't we just pull out our pricks, lay them on the table, and get someone in here with a measuring tape?" Matthews angled his head and gave DiGrazia a look of warning. "All right, I concede: Yours is bigger than mine. Can we stop all this bullshitting around now and get down to business? Sir?"

Matthews seemed mollified. He didn't know that, with the

exception of their captain, John Parker, DiGrazia absolutely refused to call any superior officer by his or her first name, even
when they were off duty and in a bar, or in a gym working
out together. Matthews took DiGrazia's liberal use of the formal
pronoun "sir" as a sign of DiGrazia's respect. DiGrazia spoke the
word with the direct opposite intent.

"So you wanted the case; all right, you can have it. Now,
what else do you want from me?"

DiGrazia said, "I want Constantine working with me."

The lieutenant dropped his smile.

"No uh-uh, fuck that, DiGrazia, this is Area One Homicide,
not some Boy Scout Troop." The lieutenant paused, but DiGrazia
did not respond.

Matthews said, "I got fourteen detectives out there you *won't*
work with, and you want me to drag an officer out of patrol?"

"Can you swing it for me, sir?"

"I can swing anything in this department, if I want to. But it
would be nice—before I pull strings and make more enemies
than I already have—if you'd tell me what's so special about
her that this case won't get solved if you don't have her by
your side."

DiGrazia took a second to glance at Constantine through the
window. She was stepping on the cigarette butt, crushing it out
on the hardwood floor. Her broad back stretched the uniform
blouse tight; he could see every seam of her bulletproof vest. He
could also see, from this point of view, the black roots at the
base of Constantine's hair. Constantine picked up the dead butt
and dropped it into the trash. DiGrazia felt the lieutenant watching her. He understood the lieutenant's point, but he was unwilling to concede it.

"Constantine's not connected to anyone, but she's one hell
of a copper. Everybody knows it, sir, it's a given. Even the state's
attorney's lawyers know if Constantine made the pinch and
wrote the report, it'll stand up in court. If she were a man, Lieutenant, she'd have been out of patrol fifteen years ago."

The lieutenant put a pained expression on his face. "Oh, don't
you start handing me any of that politically correct bullshit
now—"

"Let me tell you something, sir. Before I came up here, I

checked out her partner, Winston. I know whose nephew he is, I know you've had discussions about him with the sergeants downstairs. He's been in the department less than a year, and he's already being groomed for plainclothes, for TAC, just as soon as he's off probation."

The lieutenant showed a hint of anger. "Who the hell are *you* to come in here talking, with all the help you've had in your career? You want me to believe there's nobody behind the scenes calling the shots for you? As quickly as you got into Homicide? Not to mention detectives. Working alone, pulling strings when you have to; I know more about you than you might think, DiGrazia. Somebody powerful's on your side."

Matthews paused expectantly, but DiGrazia only stared back at him, impassively. When DiGrazia didn't answer for a full thirty seconds, the lieutenant said, "Where the hell do you *get* this information?"

DiGrazia continued as if the lieutenant had never made his outburst.

He said, "And none of you would have put an up-and-comer like Winston with a slacker, with someone who'd teach him how to hide out, or to sleep on duty. You made sure this kid got a field training officer that was the best you could find. I'm right, sir, and we both know it. The point I'm making is that Everett Winston is nothing more than a pretty, muscular, recruiting poster, just the kind we want in TAC, to go on television and schmooze for the cameras."

"Boy, are you reaching."

"I checked the time of Constantine's call, too, while I was downstairs. Let me run it down for you, tell you how this all happened. Nine-one-one never got a call on this, the two of them just saw a crowd formed around a wino on Chicago Avenue, and Constantine decided to investigate."

"How do you know Winston didn't make the decision?"

"She called it in."

"That doesn't mean anything."

"They get out of the car, immediately determine the wino's problem, walk into the alley, and into a scene of such brutality that even a twenty-year veteran like Constantine has never seen anything like it."

"Have you? Seen anything like it?"

DiGrazia immediately said, "No, sir, never."

The lieutenant was leaning back in his chair, slowly rocking, paying attention. He didn't show any reaction to DiGrazia's lie. "White girl, killed in the middle of the Gold Coast. Jesus Christ, let's hope that the killer's not a recent parolee."

DiGrazia said, "Winston's contribution to the maintenance of the crime scene's purity was to hold his hand over his mouth and keep the puke in until he got out of the alley and into the street. Before he even starts emptying his sensitive little stomach, Constantine radios for help, *then* gets the tape up, *then* fights off the crowd, does all this by herself, with no help from her partner, who's too busy entertaining the crowd by vomiting into the gutter. She called in from the alley, sir, at twelve-oh-nine. I got there no later than twelve-eleven. She did it all, by herself, in a little more than two minutes."

"Great recommendation for her. But do you know they got a manpower shortage in patrol? Winter's over, they can't get away with hiding out in their cars to collect a paycheck anymore. Cold winter, it was bad on their kidneys, their backs. Everybody's taking their vacations right now."

DiGrazia could see that he'd have to use more than Constantine's policing ability to convince the lieutenant that he needed her. Still, he didn't like to do that. He, too, already had enough enemies. He would give it another try.

"Let me tell you something else, Lieutenant. I helped with crowd control until the barriers arrived. I got to talking with her. She described a scene she'd looked at for maybe ten seconds with the minute detail of a photograph. Winston *still* isn't sure what he saw back there."

The lieutenant's eyes narrowed; a nasty grin creased his face. "Let me ask you a question, Dom—"

"Don't say it, Lieutenant . . ."

"—you fucking her?"

DiGrazia closed his eyes and lifted his head to the ceiling. He was far more relieved than he was angry; he knew from the question that the lieutenant would grant his request.

Matthews said, "What about Winston?"

"Lieutenant, I don't give a shit about Winston."

"You've got more friends in the press than I have. *And* in the department, *and* in the city council, too. If I give you Constantine—temporarily, for this case only, mind you—will you give the kid a break?"

The lieutenant was not stupid. This was indeed the ace card that DiGrazia would have used, had the lieutenant forced him to do so.

Trying to downplay his connections, DiGrazia said, "What the hell could I do to him?"

"His uncle's an alderman. They don't want him in uniform long."

"I won't have to work with him. He's fine with me, as long as he keeps his mouth shut to the press—and his uncle—and everyone else—about what he saw tonight."

"You won't tell any of your political buddies about this? Say, one of the alderman's rivals in the city council? Won't drop the whole mess into a friendly reporter's ear?"

"Where the hell do you *get* this information?"

The two men smiled humorlessly at each other.

"Do we have an understanding, Dom?"

DiGrazia decided to throw him a bone in appreciation, while at the same time thickening his curtain of silence around the case.

"Lieutenant, you don't have to worry about me. But if it was me sitting in your chair, I'd grab the phone just as soon as my insubordinate underling unassed my office, and I'd call whatever friends I allegedly have in the press. I'd tell them I'd owe them a huge one, each of them exclusivity on demand, on whatever case they wanted, if they held back on this one."

"Why would you want me—why would *you* do that?"

"Because your man Winston had puke all down his shirtfront, and they got him on videotape. Not to mention he was whiter than the Vampire."

The lieutenant began to reach for his phone, then stopped himself.

DiGrazia said, "And the captain thinks *I'm* the source of the leaks in this squad . . ."

"Was there anything else, DiGrazia?"

"Well . . . Two things. I'd appreciate it if you'd call downstairs and get Constantine assigned to me tonight, right away, before you call Channel Seven. She worked the scene with me, she ran the video, she drew the field sketches, she took notes—I need her right away."

"That's what I was getting ready to do. I wasn't calling Channel Seven."

"And just out of curiosity, with that Winston kid?"

The lieutenant waited.

"You fucking him?"

"Get out of my office."

"You just seem so . . . protective."

"DiGrazia, I won't tell you again."

DiGrazia rose, wanting to tell Constantine the good news. He heard Lieutenant Matthews punching telephone keys as he walked out the door.

CHAPTER
6

Dr. Cary Warren stuck his head in the door at approximately 1:15 that morning, and the talking immediately stopped. Every man in the room stared at him, as if he, one of the full-time doctors on staff, were an intruder. He put an apologetic look on his face, nodded at the group in general, his eyes searching the room, not finding the man he was looking for. He glared angrily at Sarge, who rose and sauntered toward him. Warren inwardly winced.

Sarge had read all the psychiatric manuals and all the self-help books, and he'd been inside this facility for something like seven years. Long enough that he considered himself Warren's colleague, rather than his patient. A psychiatrist rather than an alcoholic, paranoid schizophrenic, bipolar manic-depressive. Thorazine and lithium kept him even most of the time, and the staff had decided that it was best to allow Sarge his momentary delusions of grandeur; he was the sort of patient who hurt himself when such dreams were too obviously dashed. The myriad of long, thin scars that crisscrossed Sarge's body were manifestations of Sarge's propensity to cause himself harm when he was feeling even the slightest bit guilty. He'd been committed after his daughter had found him sitting naked in a Barcalounger, absently slicing into himself with a boning knife, watching *Wheel of Fortune* as a pool of blood formed around his shoes.

Sarge walked out into the hall with Warren, his manner confident and professional.

"Where is he?" Warren fought not to let his anger show.

"He's calling himself Eddie this time."

"He left?"

"He's in denial about his pathologies." Warren had to close his eyes for a moment. He opened them quickly, hoping Sarge hadn't noticed. "There's an overriding compulsion, but I don't think it's obsessive-compulsive, it seems more sophisticated than that, more within his grasp than, say, alcoholism or drug addiction, if you know what I mean." Sarge was not only playing shrink again, but now he was talking down to Warren. Warren nodded for Sarge to continue.

Sarge said, "He's become highly manipulative, emotionally as well as physically. It's very subtle, almost sociopathic."

"I see," Warren said.

"I'm not sure you do. The thing of it is, Cary, in spite of all that, I think he's on the verge of a breakthrough. He *almost* told us what was bothering him, I'm sure of it."

This startled Warren, but he didn't let Sarge know it.

"He did?"

"Yeah. He was right *there*, but he withdrew, extracted himself from the realities of his situation, and retreated emotionally. You could see it physically occur, the transformation was palpable."

"Where is he now?"

Sarge showed passivity for the first time since he'd stepped into the hallway. "I think we might have pushed him a little too far, too fast. We were telling him how much we cared for him, how we loved him. How he could trust us with his darkest secrets, when he withdrew, and left."

"He left."

"He left."

Warren kept his tone professional and reflective when he said, "And you didn't stop him? You didn't call for the orderly? You didn't ask the guard to hold him until I got here?" He sounded as benign as a written report.

"It would have—" Sarge sought the proper words—"engendered resentment. It would have impaired his future treatment. Not to mention that I didn't have the legal or moral authority."

"There may not be any future treatment now, though, isn't that right, Sarge?"

"Oh no, Cary, don't worry about that."

"Why shouldn't I?"

"He gave me his word he'd be back."

"Gave you his word."

"You'd have to be a vet to understand, Cary."

Dr. Cary Warren looked down the hallway, let his gaze pass over the polished red walls, the highly buffed concrete floors. He looked at the orderly who was now standing at near attention outside the gate, looked at the guards who were sitting at their station on either side of the electronically controlled door. He smelled stale cigarette smoke on Sarge's hair and in his clothing.

"It's not James's fault," Sarge said, misreading Warren, thinking that the orderly might be in trouble for letting Eddie leave. "I take responsibility for this, Cary. It was a judgment call."

Warren looked back at Sarge, nearly amused, but not showing it. He nodded several times, the consulting psychiatrist confirming an associate's difficult diagnosis.

"It's getting upward of one-thirty, Sarge."

"We usually wrap things up around two."

"The meetings are unauthorized." Sarge said nothing, though his mouth dropped open. He closed it quickly, looked hurt. Warren inwardly smiled.

"You may refer to me, in the future, as Dr. Warren. You are never again to refer to me by my first name." In spite of the harshness of his words, Warren's manner was casual. Confident, in control of the situation, merely giving Sarge informational notice rather than a cruel rebuke.

"I thought, seeing as we were all alone . . ." Sarge's eyes had grown wet. Warren watched him lick his lips, then swipe at them with the back of his hand. Sarge's wet eyes betrayed his fright; his submissive posture, his insecurities.

"Even alone, I'm still the doctor, Sarge. Informality's one thing, disrespect's another."

"I didn't mean to—"

Warren placed his hand on Sarge's shoulder, and the larger,

older man leaped. But Warren only squeezed the shoulder gently, reassuringly. "I know you didn't mean any disrespect, Sarge. I just wanted to make sure the parameters were in place."

"You—" Sarge stopped, and swallowed hard before continuing. "You're not gonna close down the midnight meeting, are you, Doctor?"

"Come on, Sarge, I wouldn't think of it." Dr. Warren slapped Sarge's shoulder in a comradely gesture, shook his head at Sarge's silliness. Dr. Cary Warren smiled.

"But if I thought you were undermining me, Sarge, diagnosing my patients? Well, I might have to recommend you for discharge." Warren looked around, as if ensuring their privacy. "Some of the other doctors have been remarking on your recovery, wondering if it would be better for you to be in an outpatient program. What with the budget cuts, the need for beds."

Sarge was drooling now, blinking rapidly. He shook his head from side to side, too terrified to speak.

Warren said, "I've stood up for you so far, Sarge . . ."

"Thank-thank-thank-thank you, D-D-Doctor."

"Calm yourself down, Sarge. That's it, close your eyes, take deep breaths." Warren paused, smiling. "Think happy thoughts."

Eyes closed, Sarge said, "I couldn't make it out there, you know that."

"Some of the other doctors think you could. They think you should, that you're just using this place to hide."

"Will you talk to them for me? Will you let them know how it is?"

"I'm doing my best, Sarge, but it's not easy." Warren waited until Sarge opened his eyes before he said, "Dr. Moran doesn't think you should be taking up space here. Those are his words, not mine."

"Dr. *Moran!* After all I just—" Sarge stopped, rethought his position. "Some people got no sense of gratitude, you know it? He turned to me for help! I gave it to him. I didn't expect him to kiss my ass, you know. But I gave him my confidence, and what does he do? He stabs me in the fucking back." Warren hid his pleasure over the bitterness in Sarge's tone.

"Now don't get excited again, Sarge. For the time being, I've got it under control. I just thought you should know. As you should know that you made a mistake tonight."

"I'm sorry, Dr. Warren, Jesus Christ, I should have just sat on the guy, fed him bullshit until you got here.

"If he comes back, Sarge, at night, that's exactly what I'll need you to do for me. I have to see this man again, in a therapeutic setting."

"I get you. Anything other than that, and—"

"You get me, Sarge."

"Can I go back to my meeting now, Doctor?"

"You can go back to your meeting now, Sarge."

Sarge turned, began to walk away, then stopped, stood stock still for a second. Warren watched his back, smiling at the man's emotional instability.

He used to debate passionately with a professor of psychiatry at Stanford who'd argued that psychiatry treatment could not help some patients. Now, more than ten years later, he agreed with the professor, but with a caveat: some people didn't want help, they simply wanted to be taken care of. Sarge—who now seemed to think better of speaking again, and continued on into the meeting room—was just such a man.

Warren put the idiot out of his mind as he turned, hurried to the gate, and ignored the orderly as he rushed past him, then the guards, his frustration mounting with every step. How often do you have the opportunity? he asked himself. How often in your entire career does a chance like this come along?

He blamed himself more than Sarge. He should have asked the man where he was when he'd called Warren at home an hour ago, seeking help, seeking treatment. Should have picked him up on a street corner, brought him here directly. The man—calling himself Eddie this time around; Dr. Warren knew why—had walked away from treatment last time, checked himself out one night while Dr. Warren was off duty.

And there was nobody for Warren to blame for that but himself, because none of the other doctors had been aware of what the man's true worth had been.

Warren could never have told them, because one of them would have no doubt gone berserk, and turned him in. Turned in Warren, as well as the patient.

Confidentiality only went so far.

But he had a contingency plan in effect this time. A plan that should cover him, should the truth come out. And he had devised a drug-treatment plan that shoud keep his patient not only in the hospital, but quite compliant, as well, and more than receptive to Warren's plan for treatment.

Warren had a paper written, ready for publication, one that would blow the minds of the stodgy old men at the *Journal of Clinical Psychiatry*. He had 370 pages of a book written, as well. It was while writing the book that the idea had come to him, how to deflect the blame that would come his way once his patient became a famous man, and was taken away from him forever.

Warren would say that he'd believed it all to be fantasy, that he'd discovered the truth only after the killer had been arrested. After all, what psychiatrist would ever believe they were treating a living, breathing, ambulatory, free, progressional killer? The organizations would have to back him up. Never in the history of psychiatry had such a killer ever turned himself over for treatment.

Until his jewel had come waltzing through the doors of the hospital—what was it?—four and a half years ago.

And then disappeared for four years, terrifying Dr. Warren.

But he was back now, and the final chapter could be written.

Warren would win a Pulitzer Prize.

All he needed were the finishing touches, the final chapters. Tonight he had thought that he would have those chapters, thought that he would speak to the man, gain his confidence again, talk him into checking himself in, and then probe him for the details of the final murder. At which point he would go to the police. The one deed would be evidence enough; the authorities would not have to know that Warren knew about more than one.

They could wait until the book came out, like everybody else.

Warren turned the car radio on to try and stop himself from thinking. His spirits plummeted as he tore out of the lot and drove east, heading the few blocks down to Lake Shore Drive, which he would take to his Hyde Park home. The music irritated him, compositions written by "artists" racked with pain that they would never understand they had brought down upon themselves. With their constant, thoughtless fucking, their search for enlightenment while using neither intelligence nor education as illumination through the darkened path, believing drugs to be their mind-expanders, while completely unaware that they were using them as a painkiller. Everything was *me, my, pain, suffering, blame,* without a single thought as to the work it would take to alleviate that pain.

It was all Elvis Presley's fault. No, that wasn't fair; Presley had never been bright enough to write his own songs. Lennon and McCartney, though, and their army of imitators, had to take some of the blame for what society had become.

Warren switched the station, punched the preset buttons until he came to an all-news station. He was calming down, secure in the knowledge that he was brighter than anyone else on the road this night, better educated, more informed. That his ideas were, to use Sarge's term, breakthroughs, rather than the rehashed theories of others. And the entire world would know it soon.

If his prized patient ever came back.

Something the radio reporter said caught Warren's attention, and he frowned. A familiar name? What? He focused on the newscast, a puzzled expression on his face. He listened, then flipped to another news-only station, got the story with just a few differences, straight from the top this time.

He felt himself grow excited; Warren's eyes were bright, his hands tight on the wheel. Butterflies danced in his stomach. This couldn't be happening, this couldn't be true. He had worked for everything he had in his life, it wasn't expected that anything this good would ever just drop into his lap.

But perhaps this was the time. Perhaps he, a man of science, who didn't believe in luck, would now have luck proven to be a quantitative fact. Because if this body they were talking about, the one found in the alley, had been put there by his patient . . .

Pulitzer his ass; Warren was looking at the Nobel.

CHAPTER

7

"So what do you want me to do?" She was sitting in the wooden chair beside DiGrazia's desk. Constantine didn't know how to behave, she'd never had anyone go to bat for her like this. Especially not someone like DiGrazia, who—along with Tony Tulio and Jake Phillips—was a legend in the annals of the Homicide division. Tulio was dead now, as was Phillips. A corrupt cop had shot Tony down; Jake had become a paranoid drunk after his wife had betrayed him while he was wheelchair-bound after a job-related shooting. He wound up eating his own weapon. There was a price to be paid when you dealt in death, and sometimes that price was high.

Still, it was Homicide. Constantine couldn't believe she was a part of it, even temporarily. She had silently witnessed the intrigue and political machinations that had surrounded the elite group when it had been reactivated after many years of absence; Violent Crimes had become the catchall term, until just a couple of years ago. Constantine had been as stunned as anyone by the unit's success, in a department filled with petty jealousies and bureaucratic infighting.

This guy beside her was pretty good at infighting, this Dominick DiGrazia. Rumors swirled around DiGrazia the way smoke swirls around ice. He refused to work with a partner, and got away with it; he was supposed to be vicious and cold and pragmatic and violent, but Constantine had never seen that side of him, had in fact seen quite a different DiGrazia than the one that was discussed by other officers when he wasn't around.

She watched him now, wondering about him. Why would a man like this want a cop like *her* for a partner, temporary or not? It didn't make sense, but then again, it didn't have to. This was Dominick DiGrazia, and he always got what he wanted, and would continue to get what he wanted, as no case of his had ever been thrown out of court. Prosecutors had screwed some of his cases up, had lost them on technicalities in the courtroom, or later on appeal, but not one of DiGrazia's arrests had ever been declared invalid by a sitting judge. Costantine wondered how he managed that, tried to think of another copper who had done that, and couldn't come up with a name.

The more superstitious coppers had spread the word that he had the Vision, the ability to look at a suspect and automatically estimate guilt. Tony Tulio had been known for the same thing when he'd been working the street. DiGrazia would hit upon a guilty suspect, and would work his case from there, gather the evidence, make the case, and it would always, always stand up.

Why had he picked her? For the first time in years, Constantine felt self-conscious, nervous around another officer. She knew she was a good cop, knew that since she'd quit drinking eleven years ago, her evaluations had all been nearly perfect. But still, this was *Homicide*. The bureau had grown until there were now over a hundred detectives assigned to it, working out of various district station houses, with a waiting list a mile long. Highly politically connected detectives—officers already in plainclothes—couldn't make the cut; so why had DiGrazia chosen her? Time, Constantine knew, would tell, as it always did.

She sat there looking at DiGrazia, wondering about him as he sat staring down at the top of his desk. She said, "You got the answer written there on the blotter?"

"What?" DiGrazia said, looking up.

"You want me to do anything?"

"How tired are you?"

"You kidding me? I'm on midnights, and I got three kids."

DiGrazia hadn't known that.

"Well, only two of them are still at home, and they're both in high school. But I always say three."

DiGrazia reached for his phone and punched in a number. Then slammed it down when he heard the buzz of a busy signal. "God*damn*it."

"That's three times. Who you trying to call?"

"Mike Schmidt. He used to be my partner."

"I remember Schmidt. Didn't know you were partnered with him."

"He retired before I transferred over here."

"I didn't know you ever worked with a partner."

"After being partnered with Schmidt, you don't."

"How you pull this lone-wolf shit off, Nick? You that well connected?"

"I'm that well connected—but I'm not a lone wolf. Wolves are pack animals, the lone wolf dies."

"Or gets shunned."

"I don't get shunned, either."

"That's what I gather. Don't lose cases either. I heard you've never had a case thrown out due to procedure, that true?" DiGrazia nodded, once. Constantine, watching him rub thoughtfully at his stomach, thought she should change the subject. "What's Mike Schmidt got to do with any of this?"

DiGrazia looked around. There were too many people in the room pretending not to pay attention.

"You feel like a cup of coffee?"

"Coffee, yeah. No food, though. First time I can remember I'm not real hungry."

"Me neither."

They walked together down the stairs, and on into the cafeteria. It was still early in the shift. There were only two other officers in the cafeteria, sitting together on the other side of the large room. Constantine got change from the machine, and dropped it into the coffee machine. When she was done, DiGrazia put his own quarters in, waited for his hot chocolate. He stayed away from caffeine, as well as any other stimulant. DiGrazia sat down at the table farthest from the other officers, and opened the conversation with care.

"Lieutenant Matthews is clearing it with your sergeant. You don't have to check out, or even talk to him if you don't want to." DiGrazia lowered his voice and leaned forward, as if trying to cajole a confession from a suspect.

"What you saw tonight, it's going to be big news."

"No shit—"

"No, I don't mean just from what happened. I mean it's a pattern. It's happened before. If the connection is made at all, it'll be the press that'll figure it out, probably faster than the brass does. The press investigates; the brass are administrators, they like to shuffle papers, they don't like to get their hands dirty. Matthews didn't even ask me what had happened to the girl in the alley, and he doesn't *want* to know. But that'll work to our advantage if we can keep them out of our hair."

"By *them,* do you mean the brass, or the press?"

"They're of equal significance to us, Janice."

"You said you'd seen something like it."

"I saw something almost ex*act*ly like it, but only in pictures. I was a senior in high school when the murder occurred."

"Which tells me Schmidt got the case." Constantine was now whispering, too. DiGrazia was happy that she had picked up on his reason for reaching out to Schmidt as quickly as she had; it proved that he'd made the right choice by getting her out of patrol.

"That's right. It was his personal crusade for the rest of his career, until the day he—retired." He didn't add that the case had destroyed his partner's life.

"And *he* couldn't solve it? Jesus Christ, the guy was a legend."

"That's right."

"And what makes you think you can?"

"Mike's got the largest personal file on this case that exists. He's not only got all the department documents, he's got the state and county crime commission's reports, every picture ever taken, the FBI files—"

"How'd he get *those*—"

"And his own personal notes and God knows how much other stuff he's picked up or stolen out of the department over the years. I think he'll hand it all over to me, if I approach him in the right way. And we already have a couple of suspects."

"We *do?*" Constantine spoke loudly, and the two other officers in the room looked over at her. DiGrazia nodded his head. Constantine lowered her voice. "Why don't we go grab them, then?"

DiGrazia made her wait. "I checked a few things out tonight, before we came upstairs."

"You *are* connected."

"The most important thing I found out, Janice, was who the downtown Undercover Community Policing walker was tonight."

Constantine closed her eyes and thought a second. "The UCP walker was . . ." She opened her eyes, wide. Looked at DiGrazia with dawning horror. "The Vampire. Terry Moran was walking downtown tonight. On overtime, too. I heard the request come over the radio on the citywide band right before we hit the street."

DiGrazia nodded again. Constantine put her hand to her mouth, then quickly lowered it. She took a sip of her coffee. She put the coffee cup down. She lit a cigarette and took a long, deep drag. Exhaling, she said, "I was in the academy with him, I remember when that happened."

"Long time ago."

"The thing, it changed him. He was a different guy in the academy."

"Getting questioned for murder'd change anyone."

"I know the wife, too, Nick. The doctor's new wife, I mean. She works at Northwestern Memorial, in the emergency room." Constantine thought for a second. "She used to be the chief administrator for the rape crisis center."

"Why 'used to be'?"

"I don't remember, but I can find out."

"Do that. If the second wife works at Northwestern, then she'd see Terry Moran—her brother-in-law—from time to time."

Constantine shook her head. "He doesn't get over there. *He's* a lone wolf. Someone needs emergency assistance, he might call the ambulance. He doesn't follow up, he's the walker, that's it." She paused. "You got any idea why they call him the Vampire?"

DiGrazia lied easily. "I don't have a clue."

"They've called him that for as long as I can remember. He was a different guy in the academy," she stressed the point again.

"I see him now, he doesn't even say hello. I'm not sure he even remembers me."

DiGrazia changed the subject. "Moran didn't answer his radio call when they tried to summon him to the scene. Nobody knows where he is, or what he's doing. I want to know those things. I want to find out what his brother was doing tonight, too."

"You think this is the same as . . . ?"

"I know it's the same as. It's almost the exact same crime scene, Janice, right down to the way the victim was holding her purse." He stared at Constantine, hard. "There're a couple of things that aren't the same, that don't make sense . . ."

DiGrazia paused in thought, looking over at the wall. Constantine didn't interrupt him. He shook his head, then turned back to her.

"It's two different killers. I'd bet my ass it is."

"But if it's the same—"

DiGrazia cut her off. "Nobody waits twenty years to kill again. They taught us a rhyme at the FBI training academy, we took an entire course on serial killers: They get the need, they do the deed."

"But—"

"And I'll tell you something else that's strange; the original murder occurred on May eighteenth. Twenty years ago tomorrow; or today, rather, it's after midnight."

"This can't be happening, Nick, not again, not after twenty years."

"We're looking at almost the identical crime, with a different victim. I saw some of the pictures, read some of the reports a dozen times, Janice. Mike never let it go, always worked it every spare second he had. He could never get it out of his head that the husband was guilty, and he told me straight out himself that he lost it altogether after Moran not only wasn't charged, but won a settlement from the city."

"Do you think Schmidt will turn over his files to us?"

"Are you sure you want it to be 'us'?" DiGrazia was watching her closely. "You sure this is what you want to do? Once the brass finds out what this is—and figures out that I didn't tell them about it on purpose—they'll go ballistic. There'll be a lot of heat."

"Maybe by then we'll have an arrest."

"And if we don't?"

Constantine waved a hand. "Fuck 'em. What'd they ever do for me? And what are they going to do to me, bust me back down to patrol?" Janice smiled.

"I thought that's what you'd say."

"Which is why you picked me."

"One of the lesser reasons. I knew I was going to need someone I could trust to do some of the footwork on her own, someone who wouldn't be cowed by a phone call from some big shot over at headquarters, or by the media. It might be a waste of time, but I'm going to have to go through hundreds, maybe thousands of pages of files. Tonight, if I can ever get Schmidt to answer his phone. We have most of what we need, but we still need to get that purse, along with all the victim's other personal effects.

"I'll need you to get the rest of the crime-scene reports from the techies as soon as you can. I want to know about any fingerprints, shoeprints, fibers, hairs, blood samples, sperm, *everything*, before I bring in either of the Moran brothers. I'm going to need you to fingerprint the victim at the medical examiner's office, then run them for a sheet. Anyone gives you a word out of line there, you beep me. I'll be over at Schmidt's, if I can't raise his ass on the phone. He's ten minutes away from there."

"I wouldn't want to be the one to wake up Mike Schmidt."

"He'll be glad to see me, believe me." He didn't tell Constantine that he'd been doing everything he could to avoid his ex-partner for more than a year.

"If you get back here before me, Janice, you run a check on the Moran brothers. Not on the Vampire, we can check on him easily enough, just the other two.

"There're three of them? I thought there was only two: the Vampire, and the medical student."

"The student's a doctor now, but there's another one." DiGrazia thought for a moment. "Frank. He was a busboy at a downtown restaurant when it happened . . . On second thought, strike the check, there are too many star fuckers around here locked into the computer. We don't want anyone going on-line and figuring out what we're doing, then calling some writer with stars in his eyes, hoping to be seen in public having dinner with a local TV news reporter. I'll try to get the license plate numbers from Mike, then have a uniform run them from the car deck, see if there's anything about them Mike doesn't know. I know a guy speeds on the Internet; he can hack his way in and see if either of the civilian brothers has any arrests."

"I'm still wearing my uniform. How'll I get anyone to believe I'm working with you?"

"We've been out of the office five minutes, away from the scene for twenty. The word that you're working the case with me was out before the squad room door closed behind our backs. By the time you get out to your squad car, the whole department will know we're a team."

"I got to admit, you're quite a step up from my last partner."

"You check on him?"

"They took him to Mercy for observation. Let's hope he isn't giving interviews."

"I think I've got that covered."

Constantine looked at him, but didn't say anything.

DiGrazia said, "If there're any questions, tell them to call your sergeant. He'll tell them you're working this with me."

"Taking Mike *Schmidt's* place, Christ." There was a touch of wonder in her tone. Constantine, as uncomfortable with wonder as she was with praise, grinned impishly at DiGrazia. The smile made her look much younger. "The lieutenant ask you if we were screwing each other?"

"Don't be ridiculous." DiGrazia paused, then said, "Just so you're absolutely clear, I didn't even tell the lieutenant, or anyone else, that this is the Moran thing all over again. Nor do I intend to tell anyone. At this point, you and I are the only ones who know."

"I figured that out on my own." Constantine rose to leave. That hadn't been the only thing she'd figured out on her own: She knew that the big Homicide detective had put his neck on the block for her, and had probably fought with the lieutenant to get her assigned to the case. She appreciated DiGrazia's circumspection, as he was the first officer in the entire department who'd ever done anything for her, and then acted as if he hadn't.

In Constantine's experience, the reverse was generally the case, and in spades.

Now she only said, "I appreciate it, your faith in me." She stopped right there, it didn't ring right in her ears. She said, "I'll get over to the lab right away, then down to the medical examiner's." DiGrazia sat back, watching her closely with an expression she couldn't read. Constantine turned to leave, and he called her name. She looked back at him.

"That was one goddamn fine piece of police work you pulled off tonight, Janice."

Constantine was about to open her mouth and spout one of her usual wiseass comments, but she stopped, looked at DiGrazia, nodded, and turned away.

"Thanks, Nick," Janice Constantine said over her shoulder, in an uncharacteristically gentle voice.

CHAPTER 8

The phone rang and Ellen jumped, felt a spasm in her back, then frowned angrily, settled back down on the bed, and composed herself before answering. It had to be Tom. Who else would be calling at this hour? She did not want to behave like an anxious child when she answered. Nor did she want to subject him to her anger.

What if it was the clinic, or one of his patients? What would she tell them? That her husband, their psychiatrist or colleague, had had a nightmare some two hours ago, and then had stormed out of the house to get some fresh air to clear his head? The explanation seemed hollow even to Ellen, and she knew that it was the truth. Still upset over his having left, Ellen reached out and picked up the phone.

"Hello?"

A slurred male voice said, "Hi there, toots. Hope I didn't wake you . . . Is *Doctor* Moran in, by any chance?" There was a chuckle in her ear; the caller was clearly enjoying himself. It was obvious to Ellen that whoever it was on the other end of the line had been drinking, and drinking heavily.

"Who is this!" Ellen's voice was smoking ice.

"Put him on, toots, come on. I ain't got all fucking night."

"Do you know what time it is?! How dare you call here at this hour?"

"You gonna let me talk to him, or not?"

"I am not!"

There was a pause, then the caller took a chance on speculation.

"He's not even home, is he?" His tone told Ellen that the question was rhetorical. She kept waiting for someone—even Tom—to tell her he was only joking. This couldn't be for real. The man chuckled again. "Got him a little sweet thing on the side, does he?"

"Stop it! I'm tracing this call!"

"Oh, bullshit. Listen, do me a favor, sweetheart, just wish that deviate motherfucker you're married to a happy twentieth anniversary for me, would you?"

Ellen felt cold fear take a spin up and down her spine as the line was disconnected. She took the phone away from her ear, and looked at it, aghast. She depressed the button with a trembling finger, then dialed *69, Automatic Call-Back; there was a pause, a click, then a recorded message informed Ellen that the number she had called was busy; if it became free within the next half hour, her phone would alert her with a distinctive ring. Please hang up.

Ellen did.

She leaned forward, her elbows on her knees, her head in her hands, in the position she'd been sitting in when the phone had disrupted her thoughts. She didn't feel the pain in her back when she was leaning forward like this.

Goddamn Tom. God*damn* him! She'd wanted Caller ID, and he'd said Automatic Call-Back was good enough. They lived in a half-million-dollar home, they had a combined income into six figures, and now his desire to not spend an extra ten dollars a month was causing her anxiety.

The phone rang again, startling Ellen. She looked over at it, fearfully. There was, however, no "distinctive ring," just the regular jangle, same as the last time.

Which didn't mean that the man wasn't calling back.

Was it him again? Or Tom? *"Damn* it," Ellen said, shaking

her head at her own uncustomary weakness. Decisively, she grabbed the phone, and nearly shouted into it.

"Hello!"

"Uh—Ellen?"

"Where are you, Tom?"

"I'm at my office. This is the only time of day I can be here without Warren sticking a knife in my back." Ellen didn't respond to Tom's feeble attempt at humor. He said, "I just walked over to the hospital; I needed to be alone, I needed a place to think."

"You have a den with a lock on the door, and a basement right here at home. And Dr. Cary Warren couldn't get past me with a machine gun, let alone his knife."

There was a staggered pause before Tom spoke. "Ellen . . . I'm sorry if I upset you."

"Sorry? You're *sorry?*" You storm out of the house in the middle of the night after scaring the hell out of me again with one of your nightmares, then you call me two hours later and tell me you're *sorry? That's it?* Oh, forgive my density, Tom. Am I being obtuse? Could you be trying to tell me that because *you* say so, everything's ok*ay?*"

The concern in his voice was the false concern that he sometimes displayed with overwrought patients; apprehension, with just a touch of superior levity. She'd heard him use it before. "Ellen, come on, you're overreacting."

"*One* of us is," Ellen said, then slammed the phone down and sat looking at it, frightened at her own outburst.

What was wrong with her? She was a thirty-seven-year-old intensive-care triage nurse with almost thirteen years on the job—she was tougher than this, stronger. She certainly wasn't the type to go all to pieces over Tom leaving the house late at night; it happened all the time, he was a psychiatrist, for heaven's sake.

Ellen slammed the heels of her hands into her forehead, just once, as if trying to knock some sense into her own head.

She could do with a Xanax, a Valium; she could sure use some damn thing to calm her down. But she knew she wouldn't take a drug, even though—as was the case in most doctors' households—there were prescriptions for both of these medications and more, in the medicine cabinet of the private bath that was attached to the master bedroom. Drugs were for emergencies only, and as much as she hated to admit it, Tom had been right, she'd been overreacting. This was not an emergency. Even if it had been she wouldn't have taken a drug tonight. As she wouldn't be taking any for at least the next seven months.

Ellen could make the distinction, because she'd had plenty of practice in identifying true emergencies, she'd worked through major crises many times before. When little babies were brought into the emergency room, having been dropped into boiling water by the very human beings who were charged with protecting them, their tiny bodies twisted in pain, most of the flesh boiled from their bodies. After working a shift like that? Okay, some sort of sedative, a tranquilizer, could be excused. *That* was an emergency.

This was only Ellen overreacting.

Wasn't it?

Then why was she so angry? And afraid? The phone call from the stranger had shaken her, Ellen had to admit that. She cursed herself for not having had the presence of mind to just immediately hang up on the caller, then consoled herself with the thought that the call would have shaken Tom even more, if he'd been here sleeping and the call had awakened him. She wouldn't tell him about it, either. He was under enough pressure as it was right now. She should never have hung up on him, Ellen knew now.

As always, her personal insights came too late to do her any good.

Ellen looked at the clock. There were twenty minutes left in the half hour her telephone company allotted. If the phone rang strangely—dis*tinct*ively—she'd have him, the phone company would have records of any calls made to this number.

Then she could get his number, and, once she had that, she could get any one of a hundred cops she knew to identify him by name and address, she could find out everything about him before she called him back, would have more than enough ammunition for her counterattack. Or, better yet, she could maybe even have one of her police acquaintances call the drunken son of a bitch for her, put the fear of God into him for making harassing, late-night phone calls to the home of a stranger he'd no doubt read about at one time or another in the newspapers during the course of his drunken and useless life. Yes, that's what she would do; get a big, gravelly voiced cop to give him a taste of his own medicine.

She gingerly lay back on the bed, roughly washed her face with her hands, and stared at the ceiling, suddenly drained, and wondered where she had gone wrong, how she had managed to fail her husband.

CHAPTER
9

DiGrazia drove through Bridgeport, one of the most solidly white, middle-class neighborhoods in the city, as well as one of its most racially divided. Schmidt lived less than a block away from a viaduct that divided two of Chicago's seventy-seven neighborhoods, an overpass which led into a black section of the city. For many years this viaduct had been barricaded with heavy steel fencing, until outraged black groups had brought it to the media's attention, which had brought political pressures to bear, which in turn had finally caused the fence to be torn down at city expense.

The crime rate in the area had begun to rise immediately, further eroding any chances that Bridgeport might have had for peaceful integration.

Mayor Richard J. Daley had been born, lived his entire life, and had died in the neighborhood; his widow still lived there, guarded around the clock by a contingent of uniformed police officers. Until recently their son, Mayor Richard M. Daley, had lived just a few blocks from the spot where DiGrazia now parked his car. A large number of powerful Irish politicians had come out of this neighborhood. Due to the city's residency ordinance, a large number of cops lived there too, and, unlike the mayor—

who had moved into the ritzy Central Station area, a stone's throw from the home of Tom and Ellen Moran—the cops had stayed.

Schmidt's house was a two-story brown brick bungalow, situated in the middle of the block. Either Schmidt's car was in the garage, or he wasn't home. DiGrazia hoped that Schmidt wasn't out at this time of night. Schmidt's drinking problem had been one of the reasons he'd been forced into retirement before the once great detective had been ready to go; that, and his attitude, his absolute refusal to believe that a young premed student named Thomas Moran hadn't killed his wife. He had a right to believe what he chose, but when he took city time to try to prove his theory, when he allowed the case to turn him into a vicious, hate-filled drunkard, it became time for him to retire.

Constantine needed to know none of these things. As she didn't need to know that DiGrazia had risked his own career by lying at Schmidt's departmental disciplinary hearing. Although DiGrazia had by now stopped respecting the man, he still—for his own personal reasons—did all that he could to keep the memory of the legend alive. At one time, Schmidt had been the single best detective in the police department, and he had trained DiGrazia well, without prejudice or jealousy.

DiGrazia could see lights on inside the bungalow. There was a Cyclone fence that did not extend around the lawn, as most fences in this neighborhood did, but which began, rather, at the porch. It afforded meager protection to the side of the house and the backyard. The fence ended at the alley. A low-watt porch light burned next to Schmidt's front door. DiGrazia saw silhouetted movement behind drawn, dirty curtains. Staggering movement? It was past two in the morning; it was a given that Schmidt would be drunk. DiGrazia stood there a moment, on the sidewalk, steeling himself for the uncomfortable spectacle that was about to play itself out.

He would have to pretend to be friendly, would have to pretend he didn't notice the further physical deterioration that Schmidt would no doubt display. A dog barked from somewhere behind a nearby fence, not Schmidt's. DiGrazia winced as a feeling of great sadness came over him. Determinedly, he fought it off.

He told himself that we all make choices; Schmidt chose to become obsessed with a case that had cost him everything that had ever mattered to him. What that obsession had been doing to him had been pointed out to him many times: First by his wife, before she finally left him; then by his three grown children, who had eventually turned their backs on him, and at last, by his superior officers, who could no longer allow his drinking, his chronic lateness, his disrespect, and his constant, repeated, loud public proclamations over the Case to embarrass the entire department. Not even all of his own and DiGrazia's combined connections could, in the end, save Mike Schmidt's career.

Still, it bothered DiGrazia to think about the man Mike Schmidt had once been, the man who had trained DiGrazia in the fine art of detecting in a manner that no training course or academy could ever come close to equaling. When he'd first been partnered with Schmidt, some twelve years back, the detective had been forty-one, and he had carried it well. When Schmidt had been forced into retirement three years previously he'd looked closer to seventy than the fifty he'd actually been.

There was sudden, quick movement behind the curtains, then the porch light went out, the door was thrown open, and Schmidt staggered out onto the porch, a cigarette dangling from his lips, a pistol in his hand. Schmidt yelled loudly, "Who's out there! Who the hell is it!"

DiGrazia shook his head as his ex-partner debased himself. Standing directly under the street light, it should have been easy for Schmidt to recognize him. Mindful of the neighbors, ready to leap out of harm's way if he had to, DiGrazia loudly whispered, "It's me, Mike, Dominick DiGrazia." Schmidt lowered the gun, peering at him drunkenly.

"That you, kid? Dominick?" The dog was barking wildly now; lights were coming on in other houses.

Schmidt said loudly, "Fuck me. I heard the dog barking, I thought it was another gang of niggers. They been running around wild lately. Come on in. Jesus, what are you doing standing out there in the middle of the night?"

Schmidt put the gun in a kitchen drawer, for which DiGrazia was grateful. He looked around the place as Schmidt self-consciously settled himself in. He could not believe what had happened to the place since his last visit.

The house reeked of booze, stale sweat, garbage, and cigarette smoke. There were piles of old, yellowing newspapers everywhere. Green plastic garbage bags were stacked one on top of the other, in a large pile against the back door. The carpet hadn't been cleaned in years; the curtains were rotting. DiGrazia remembered a time when the house had been so clean that you could have eaten off the floor in the kitchen. Back before Florence had finally decided that she had no choice but to leave. Schmidt had continued to fool the department for several years after that.

Schmidt himself had weathered the years with even less success than the house. He was wearing a filthy sleeveless undershirt. His chest was sunken, his once-tight belly soft and bulging obscenely over beltless, unzipped workman's pants. DiGrazia recognized the early stages of cirrhosis of the liver. Schmidt's skin was sallow, the whites of his eyes were yellow and red. There was a heavy rasp in his voice that DiGrazia didn't recall him having the last time the two men had spoken.

They sat at the kitchen table, in good wooden chairs. Something tacky that had come off the yellow floor tile was sticking to the bottom of DiGrazia's shoes. He kept his expression benign, wondering how to broach the subject. Schmidt seemed more than slightly embarrassed, ashamed of something, or perhaps he was frightened. DiGrazia believed it was caused by his humiliation in exposing how badly he'd decayed to a man who remembered him when he'd been close to his prime. Schmidt was breathing heavily, as if he'd just run a quick mile.

There was an overflowing ashtray on the table, next to a nearly empty bottle of Canadian Club whiskey. DiGrazia noticed that there were two different types of butts in the tray, Schmidt's nonfiltered Camels, and the filters from smoked-down Kools. Did Schmidt have company? Was there a woman hiding upstairs? There was no lipstick on the butts, and the type of woman who would come home with Schmidt would be older, the sort who still used lipstick before going out for the night. Or maybe she was like Schmidt; too wasted and hateful to care about how she looked. There wasn't a glass on the table—Schmidt was no doubt drinking from the bottle—but that didn't mean much; the woman would without question have taken her drink upstairs with her, if she was using a glass at all.

Dirty dishes were stacked in the sink; the receiver of what had once been a white wall phone lay upon them. The phone was now smudged nearly black. The cord was tangled beyond straightening. Used paper plates and other trash flowed out of the plastic garbage can, down onto the floor. DiGrazia wondered where the roaches were hiding. He said a silent prayer that the Nancy Moran files weren't in the attic, or, worse, down in the basement; if they were, rats might have destroyed them—he imagined that he could hear them scurrying around inside the walls.

"You want a drink?" Schmidt asked, then took a sip of whiskey out of the bottle. When he brought it down, his eyes were closed, and he sighed softly, as if in rapture. When he opened his eyes, however, he was glaring at DiGrazia.

DiGrazia calmly held his stare; Schmidt gave him an ugly grin, then offered the bottle. DiGrazia took it, tilted it to his lips, allowed a few drops to trickle down his throat. When he brought the bottle down and looked over at Schmidt, the older man was smiling at him with a look of triumph that said all that needed to be said about the relationship between them.

No matter what had happened, no matter how far he'd fallen, he was still in control here in his own home, and now the two of them knew it. DiGrazia allowed him his pitiful moment of triumph. He had come here seeking favors, and he knew he would have to pay in return, the drink had merely been the security deposit. Schmidt's pathetic, hollow victory seemed to open the door.

DiGrazia said, "You have company?" and Schmidt reacted as if the detective had slapped him.

"What do you mean!"

DiGrazia immediately backed off, afraid he'd lost the ground he'd gained by taking the sip of whiskey. A hooker, upstairs, would account for Schmidt's sense of shame, his obvious discomfort.

DiGrazia shrugged elaborately, opened his hands in a gesture of friendship.

"I was just hoping that I wasn't interrupting anything."

Schmidt surprised DiGrazia by laughing; there was something about it DiGrazia didn't like. The laugh deteriorated into a spasm of coughing. Schmidt pounded himself on the back, and DiGrazia looked away.

When he could, Schmidt said, "You're here on business?"

"I'm here on business."

Schmidt grunted indignantly. "I figured as much." He took another pull from the bottle. There was a twinkle in his eye this time as he offered the bottle to DiGrazia. DiGrazia had already played the game, and now he shook his head. Schmidt, still smiling, put the bottle down on the table. He left the tiny butt of his cigarette smoldering in the ashtray, and lit yet another one from a crumpled pack that he dug out of his front pants pocket.

"Whiskey almost gone, smokes almost gone; that means it's about time for bed."

"You got to give up those cigarettes, Mike."

"I remember what you went through when you quit," Schmidt said. There was a glimmer of pleasure in his expression as he recalled happier times.

Encouraged, DiGrazia said, "They wouldn't let me smoke in class, or at the library. I didn't smoke during the four hours a night that I was sleeping back in those days. And the daily withdrawal kept screwing up my concentration. I'd have never completed graduate school if I hadn't been able to give them up for good."

Schmidt's expression had grown more sullen with every word. DiGrazia decided it would be wise to shut his mouth.

"You don't tell a man what to do in his house, though, do you, Dom? I mean, even a *doctor* can't come into a guy's house, ask him about his personal life, if he's alone. Tell him what the fuck to do, order him around, right?"

"I've got a degree, I'm not a doctor."

"Sure you're a doctor. I danced at your graduation party, remember? I seen your fuckin' diploma. I got pictures around here somewhere, if the bitch didn't steal them on me when she took off. I got pretty drunk at the party we all threw for you, remember? We had some happy times, Dominick. These days though, you ain't got time to waste with me." DiGrazia didn't answer.

"You got shot last year, I called, I come over, they wouldn't let me in to see you. You never called me back. I called every day, for two weeks, Dom. The guys who answered your phone wouldn't let me talk to you. Until you went home, I called every day."

There was no answer DiGrazia could give to that, he couldn't tell the truth. The hurt on Schmidt's face was alive, twisting him.

"I was hoping you had a few minutes to talk tonight."

Schmidt gave the impression that he thought DiGrazia was squirming. He had a look on his face DiGrazia had seen many times before, when the older man had talked a suspect into the place Schmidt wanted him to be.

It was just as obvious that the ex-detective was enjoying himself when he said, "I don't know, kiddo, it's getting late, and I'm kind of tired. You should have called before you come over, too, I could have shot you outside, there."

"You almost did shoot me. And I tried to call; your phone's off the hook."

Schmidt looked over at the phone. "Yeah, looks like it is," he said, and he dropped the superior expression; the sheepish, embarrassed look returned. "I forgot about that."

DiGrazia took a shot in the dark. "You called someone tonight, didn't you? One of the department big shots. Got into another beef." He knew he'd guessed wrong the moment he spoke; the relieved expression that crossed Schmidt's face left DiGrazia puzzled.

"That's why you're here? The bosses you love so much send you over to straighten me out?" The resentment in his tone made DiGrazia sit back. He fought to keep his face impassive.

Schmidt said, "You tell them for me, they got any evidence against me, bring it to a court of law."

"Evidence of what?"

Schmidt leaned forward and slammed his fist down on the table. Crushed cigarette butts flew everywhere, the nearly empty bottle did a shaky dance before settling down. "Fuck 'em all, and fuck you, too, if you're here to bust my balls."

"I'm here for your help, Mike."

Slowly, Schmidt's anger subsided. His breathing grew calm, eyes slitted by hatred slowly rounded. DiGrazia had been afraid

81

that his statement might send Schmidt over the edge, drive him into further rage: You come around quick enough when you want something, don't you? He'd heard Schmidt shout those exact words at one of his sons. But now he seemed somewhat relieved. DiGrazia had no idea as to what Schmidt thought he was doing there. He decided not to ask. Schmidt was fragile enough, there was no good to come from antagonizing the man any further.

There was bitter outrage in Schmidt's tone when he said, "I even thought you might have come over to congratulate me."

"Congratulate you for what?"

"You didn't see the early edition of the *Sun-Tribune*, yet? Look on the front page."

"I've been working all night. What's in the *Sun-Tribune?*"

Schmidt ignored him. "Midnights. Jesus Christ, what'd an ass kisser like *you* ever do to wind up on midnights?"

DiGrazia ignored the insult. "I'm on afternoons, as always." He flashed a gentle smile. "That's when everything happens. I'm working over on a case."

Schmidt leaned forward now, his anger forgotten. His elbows were on the table. He swallowed a burp. DiGrazia had to once again fight to keep his expression impartial; he was nauseated by the stench of stale human sweat that wafted over to him with Schmidt's movements.

He said, "I should have waited for morning."

"You'll tell me now, if you want my help."

"It's the Moran thing, Mike." Schmidt's eyes widened. "We've got another one a lot like it, a second killing."

CHAPTER
10

The tension had been building for a couple of months now, increasing so gradually that she'd barely noticed it occurring until just these past few weeks. Ellen could see that now, in hindsight. She actually could have seen it coming, if she'd been paying strict attention, and now, as was her way, she took the blame. She told herself that she should have been much better prepared.

Sometime in mid-to-late March, Tom had begun to grow moody, eventually working later, then even later hours, staying up past midnight in the den writing his papers, or talking on the phone—the den was directly beneath the bedroom, Ellen could clearly hear every word he spoke when the bedroom vent was open—or going down into the basement after supper to work out—again—on the weight machines.

Ellen, lying back on the bed, dropped her hands to her hips, felt the slight pad of extra flesh that was spreading out onto the bed. Clothed, it was unnoticeable, but she knew it was there, and Tom did, too. He would grasp it during the infrequent love-making they'd engaged in during the last eight or nine weeks, and squeeze it lightly, not hurting her, but enough to make her aware of it, embarrassing her so that she lost any enjoyment of the act. How had that happened? Until all this confusion had

begun to happen in their lives, their lovemaking had been frequent, and, if not always exceptional, at least it was always
enjoyable.

Ellen snorted contemptuously at what she'd thought of as
"lovemaking." She was almost ashamed of what it had done
to her.

She had an unexpected and peculiar thought, and frowned
up at the ceiling.

Had he been doing it on purpose? Ellen wondered now.
Squeezing her extra flesh? She'd thought it an unconscious act,
but now she had to wonder.

He'd been acting so very strangely these past couple of
months—but did he have that sort of cruelty in him? If her suspicion was true, Tom would no doubt think of it as subtlety. Silently giving her the message that perhaps Ellen should spend a
little more time down in the basement, playing with his infer-
nal machines.

At forty, Tom didn't have an extra ounce of fat on his body,
anywhere. He walked the nearly two and a half miles to one of
the two hospitals every day, or to his private office, wherever he
was heading, carrying his jogging clothes and shoes in a leather
knapsack so he could change clothes later, and run at lunch time,
or after work. Every other day or so he would walk back home
to retrieve "forgotten" papers, or to have a late lunch, or just to
relax in his den when a patient canceled and he had the chance.

And even before the bad time began in the last couple of
months, he always set aside at least an hour every morning to
work out downstairs, often two or three hours, depending on
how early he got up. His time was truly managed; he slept and
ate less—and still worked harder—than any of the doctors at the
hospital where Ellen worked.

Ellen shook herself, climbed under the covers, pulled them to
her neck and closed her eyes. She'd wait past the allotted time
that the telephone company had given her. The phone hadn't
rung, distinctively or normally. She couldn't try the *69 bit again,
either, because Tom had called after the drunk had, she would
only get her husband's office at the VA hospital.

If that's where he'd really been calling from.

Ellen felt herself trembling; she felt her stomach cramping up, and she took deep breaths until the pain went away. She absently rubbed her stomach, patting it softly, and whispered a prayer.

She wondered how it had ever come to this between them. She'd done everything she could to be a supporting, loving partner—since the first day she'd met him, and on through all the years of their marriage, too, not only in the last two months.

Ellen was devoted to Tom, and until recently, he'd seemed totally devoted to her. It was remarked upon with frequency by everyone who knew them, and by plenty of people who didn't, such as waiters and waitresses, salespeople in department stores. They were often asked if they were newlyweds. They'd smile their secret smile at each other, squeeze each other's hand.

It was important to Ellen's self-image that her husband was always happy, that everything was taken care of, that all of his needs were met. Ellen would do anything for Tom. Equal distribution of labor was, in her opinion, a joke. The woman always had to do more, the wife was always the caretaker. She accepted this, and lived up to it. She'd set her personal standards high.

And then suddenly Tom was unhappy. Ellen felt that she had to take the weight for that. At least in her mind; at least for right now; at least for tonight, she would suffer.

Although it wasn't a topic of conversation between them, she'd been aware that this year would mark the twentieth anniversary of Nancy's murder. Ellen had decided that they'd needed a change, that a change of scenery, a new home, a fresh beginning would make the day pass with hardly a thought of the horror.

She'd taken it upon herself to house-hunt, to find just the proper place in the city (the suburbs were out of the question), working with the real estate agent, not even telling Tom she was looking until she'd found this glorious home.

Thirty-five hundred square feet of detached, single-family housing in the South Loop, a beautiful, two-story gray brick house with an attic and full basement, just fifteen minutes by foot from the very heart of the city. The school that the children they were now planning to have would attend was directly across the street. On the rare occasions when they'd been home at the same time during the day, Ellen would watch as Tom stood at the window and looked wistfully out at the school, as if regretting that they hadn't had children sooner, and he smiled out at the children playing in the schoolyard or walking home after classes were through for the day.

It was heaven for her, and although Tom had professed to love their Near North Side condominium, loved the convenience of apartment living, he'd immediately taken to the house the first time he'd seen it. He'd even given up two of his three gym memberships (keeping only the Racquet Club), and had person-ally supervised the installation of his weight machines in the basement.

That had been right after Christmas, in the week before the New Year; the house had been their Christmas present to each other.

Nearly three months then passed, and to Ellen, they'd been blissful. They'd entertained, they'd had parties that were much larger than any that could have been thrown in their cramped, one-bedroom apartment. Tom had increased his private client workload somewhat in order to ensure that the percentage of their savings never went down, but it hadn't made that much of a difference in their lives; Ellen barely noticed his absence, and actually enjoyed her now frequent moments of solitude, when her shift was such that she had the large house completely to herself.

It was a walled little community, with one road in and one road out, a guard standing lonely duty in a small shack, to raise the black-and-white electric gate when the cars with the proper stickers in the windshields approached on the blacktopped road. The same private security firm that supplied the guard had cars that patrolled the grounds twenty-four hours a day, on immedi-ate call to any resident. The infrequent homeless person or gang member who climbed the wall—whether out of curiosity or with other, uglier agendas—were immediately, and sometimes vio-lently, escorted out of the area. There were no graffiti, anywhere.

They had an alarm system. The homes were close together, and their neighbors were all professionals; who else could afford to live here? For Ellen, raised in the Far South Side community of Hegewisch, this was heaven on earth, and she worked hard, as the weeks passed and they settled into their new home, to make certain that Tom knew he was loved and supported, and that he felt strong enough to handle whatever pain the eighteenth of May might bring him.

But even Ellen, with her formidable strength and her towering love, couldn't prevent him from falling into the depression which she'd sworn she wouldn't allow to descend upon him.

You'd have to know him intimately to even be aware that it had happened, Ellen told herself now. That's how good he was, how well Tom covered it up. Although he'd hardly been aware that she existed, Ellen had known Tom since college, and he always seemed the most levelheaded, even-tempered, and humble premed student at the school. A great many of the students from the school had attended Nancy's funeral—some of them for the chance to get on television, some of them for a good excuse to miss their morning's classes, some of them even attending just to observe or participate in the freak show. Although her husband had been popular, hardly anyone had even met the quiet, mousy, suburban-born-and-raised young woman who'd married him during the summer, then joined him on campus at the beginning of his second year of studies—and it was the first time that Ellen had ever seen Tom express deep emotion.

It was one of the things she admired about him, the way he kept his secrets.

Ellen and Tom had been married for more than seven years when the tenth anniversary of Nancy's death had passed, and she hadn't been aware that it had bothered him much at all. She knew that the newspaper article about Nancy's unsolved murder had disturbed him to a degree, but she'd had to pay attention to notice it.

But that had been nothing at all like this, with the nightmares, the late hours, the mood changes. The way he'd begun to ignore her. The way he was neglecting his friends.

Ellen wondered briefly if Tom was having an affair. The ugly seed the caller had planted struggled to bear fruit, then she rejected the notion out of hand; she'd know; she believed in her heart that she'd know. There was evidence that he was having some sort of emotional trouble, but none that he was cheating.

He had begun to wheedle hs way out of social engagements by claiming fatigue or overwork, and everyone that knew Tom knew how hard he worked, how nearly every hour of every day was planned out by him weeks in advance. So he'd gotten away with it with them. She often spoke to his colleagues, his underlings and superiors, and often to his patients, when they called the house looking for him. None of them gave Ellen any hint that they thought there was anything wrong. He would wear his facade of polite distance, and none of them were any the wiser.

But he couldn't fool Ellen, who loved him.

"Shit."

Ellen was tired of feeling guilty; she knew that whatever was wrong with Tom, she was neither the cause nor the cure. But she couldn't overcome the feeling that she'd somehow personally failed him. That she'd let him down. Though she had gone to him more than once, tried to talk to him while he'd been working in his den, or down in the basement working out, she'd asked him how he'd felt, if he wanted to talk about anything, and she'd been rebuffed; Tom had always insisted that he was just fine. Smiling, shaking his head at her concern.

Wasn't that just like a shrink?

She knew that his dislike for his colleague at the VA hospital, Dr. Cary Warren, had grown into a nearpathological hatred. Warren was on the full-time staff of the hospital, Tom worked there two days a week. Still, Tom was Warren's nominal superior. They hadn't gotten along from the first. When Tom did talk about his work at the VA hospital, it was only to disparage Warren.

"I have to be at work in six hours; this is an emergency," Ellen said aloud, in an exasperated voice.

She threw the covers off and got out of the king-sized bed, walked over to the bathroom and slapped at the light switch. Squinting in the sudden light, Ellen padded past the sunken bathtub, which had a built-in Jacuzzi attachment, past the His-and-Hers designer commodes, past the two black sinks that stood on swan's-neck pedestals.

Her dream house, and Tom only had nightmares.

Ellen slid the mirrored cabinet open, looked at the bottles of prescription medicines, trying to find a nonnarcotic tranquilizer. She looked at the vials on the shelf, puzzled, then her eyes widened as she realized that several of the bottles were from differing pharmacies. Ellen had known more than a few nurses—and doctors—who'd become hooked on prescription drugs. Some who'd recovered, others who'd lost their jobs, their homes, their families . . .

She cursed herself for her paranoia, but still, drug usage could go a long way toward explaining her husband's mood swings, his distant behavior . . .

Ellen reached for the small, plastic bottle of Halcion, then drew her hand back. The last time she herself had taken one, she'd taken it with .05 mg of Xanax. She knew that if she couldn't sleep then, it was because God hadn't wanted her to. She saw that both prescriptions had been refilled. With dawning horror, Ellen again reached for the bottle.

She knew something was wrong the second her fingers touched it. She lifted the bottle, shook it. The bottle was nearly empty.

Ellen held the bottle to the light, read the date of the prescription. It was a new bottle, the prescription having been filled by a pharmacy on South Dearborn, right down the street. The last time Ellen had medicated herself—last February, was it?—there had been a half-full bottle of twenty-five Halcion capsules from the old pharmacy where they used to have their prescriptions filled, at the drugstore that had been just across the street from their apartment.

Ellen read the label. This bottle had once held twenty-five pills, too.

And it was nearly empty.

Which meant that Tom had to be ingesting at least one capsule every night, sometimes even more. A minimum of one strong, habituating sleeping pill every night. She shivered at the thought, then wondered how long Tom had been having his nightmares.

Ellen put the bottle down, and picked up the Xanax and the Valium. The tranquilizer, Valium, was from the old pharmacy, thank God. She didn't know how many might have been in there when Tom began to abuse them, but the bottle was still half full. The bottle of Xanax, however, the antianxiety drug, was from the new pharmacy, had been filled out for a hundred pills, and was now less than half full.

The prescription had been filled on the twenty-third of March.

She put the tranquilizer and the antidepressant back on the

shelf. She opened the Halcion, counted the four pills that were inside, then she screwed the lid back down tight, put it back in the medicine cabinet, then closed the cabinet, firmly.

Ellen stood looking at herself in the mirror, at her still-youthful face, at a body that was strong and, for the most part, toned. The new weight wasn't much, just stress poundage at this point, Ellen was certain of that. Her breasts sagged only slightly. Her legs had always been good, her best feature, she'd always thought. Everything else would change and grow, and spread, and that would all happen soon.

She hadn't taken a Halcion because she knew that the sleeping pill could cause defects in the baby that was developing within her.

Ellen studied her body carefully, trying desperately to avert her mind from the thought that her husband was probably a junkie. From the thought that the father of her child was more than likely addicted to drugs. Had he impregnated her since he'd been taking the pills? That was almost certainly so. Was the child in danger? Ellen felt her hands turn into fists.

She had planned to keep the pregnancy secret, just until this awful anniversary had passed. She hadn't wanted Tom to connect their greatest personal joy to his most horrid personal tragedy. Now Ellen wondered if she should tell Tom at all. Now she wondered if she should even have the baby.

Ellen averted her eyes from the mirror.

She heard the high-pitched whine of the alarm system warning, and she jumped, then hurried from the bathroom, turning the light off behind herself. She left the bathroom door open. She walked over to the bed. The small alarm light at the top of the keypad next to the bedroom door was flashing red, then turned a steady green as Tom punched in the numbers on the downstairs unit. Ellen saw the light change to a steady red as he rearmed it. She got into bed, and waited. She heard Tom's footfalls on the stairway, heavy at first, then lighter, as he must have understood what time it was, thought that Ellen might have fallen asleep, and he might awaken her.

Tom opened the door slowly and entered the room. She knew he was holding his breath. It was her call—she could pretend she was asleep.

Instead, she said, "I'm awake." Her voice was, thankfully, calm.

Tom said, "Watch your eyes," and Ellen averted her head as he flipped the switch that turned on the overhead track lighting. He hurried past her, on into the bathroom. Ellen listened carefully, trying to hear if he were sliding open the mirrored medicine cabinet, but all she heard was the sound of him urinating, then the toilet flushed, she heard the faucet come on as Tom washed his hands, and then he was walking toward the bed. Ellen kept her head averted, looking away from Tom, toward the door.

She felt the bedsprings sag as he sat down on his side of the bed, with his back to her. When Ellen turned back to him, squinting as if the alarm had awakened her, she could see that he was holding a newspaper in his hand. His shoulders sagged heavily.

He had spread the newspaper open, held it in both hands now, was sitting in almost the exact same position that Ellen had been in when the phone had rung, earlier. When the drunk had called and frightened her.

"I'm sorry, Ellen, I shouldn't have taken off like that, I should have stayed here with you."

She was listening to the sound of his voice as well as to his words; was he slurring? Were there changes in his normal speech patterns? Ellen couldn't tell. Tom was speaking in a low, soft voice, speaking slowly and carefully, as if choosing each word with great caution. Ellen was too stunned at the moment to detect any more than the most blatant of slurring. She would know if he was drunk; she had a long and ugly experience with the species. Ellen thought of her brother, what he would do to her when he was drunk, and she shivered. This was not the moment to be walking down *that* particular path. Ellen forced the disgusting memories from her mind, and turned her full attention back to Tom.

She could tell that he was as depressed as she'd ever seen him during their marriage, that much was obvious. She felt her heart going out to him, and forced herself to hold back on her compassionate instincts, at least for the moment.

"I'm sorry, too, Tom. I shouldn't have snapped at you when you called."

Tom only nodded his head.

91

Ellen wanted a look at his eyes. She wanted to see his pupils. She sat up in bed, moved over until she was at his back. Hating herself, she knelt behind him, held him. She smelled the faint scent of alcohol at the same moment that she noticed that his body was shaking, realized he was silently sobbing. She worked her hands around to Tom's front, felt something wet, and pulled her hands back in shock.

Her hands were covered with blood.

"Tom?" As concerned by Tom's uncustomary show of emotion as she was frightened by the blood, Ellen moved rapidly, climbed out of bed and stood in front of him, holding her hands out in front of him. She said his name again, softly, but with tension.

"Tom!"

Tears were streaming silently down Tom's face, marking it, dropping like tiny waterfalls onto the paper he held in his hands. The front of his shirt was covered with blood. He looked up at her, and she saw the slow trickle that was still dripping from both nostrils.

Ellen didn't even think to check his eyes now, she didn't care that he'd been drinking, none of that mattered anymore. Ellen sank down to her knees and held Tom's arms, looked up at him. He pulled one arm free and swiped the blood away from his nose.

In a breaking voice, Tom said, "See what they've done to me? They'll never let me alone. No matter what I do, no matter how many people I help, no matter how much I accomplish." Tom inhaled a quivering breath. "They'll fucking *never* let me alone Ellen, never!"

Tom held the paper out to her. It was the early Friday edition of the *Chicago Sun-Tribune*, the front page of the Metro section. Tom's sad, youthful face stared out at Ellen in black and white. It was the mug shot picture taken twenty years ago to the day.

"I saw myself looking at me from the news box down on Dearborn . . ."

A large headline above the picture read: CULT SLAYING STILL UNSOLVED TWENTY YEARS LATER! Under this, in smaller type: RETIRED NOW, DOGGED DETECTIVE HAS NEVER GIVEN UP. There was a smaller color picture of an older man sitting in a recliner and staring momentously into the camera. He was holding a pile of what

Ellen recognized to be evidence folders in both hands. Ellen could picture this man, drunk, closing one eye for clarity, stabbing at the numbers on the telephone as he made hateful midnight phone calls.

"The bastards!"

"I saw it, and my nose just started flowing blood . . . That hasn't happened in—" Tom paused, as if remembering the exact night his last spontaneous nosebleed had occurred. "—I don't know how many years. I didn't even realize it was happening until I saw my blood all over the newspaper."

Tom looked up at her, his emotions raw, right on the surface. His nose, she saw, had at last stopped dripping. In spite of her concern, Ellen felt a rush of pride at the thought that Tom was finally allowing her insight into his emotions, had dropped his stoic facade. She forgot about the pills, even forgot about the hateful caller.

All Ellen could think of was that she had been waiting for this moment to arrive for more than twenty years.

She'd been waiting for Tom to need her since she'd been seventeen years old.

Tom crushed the paper in his hands, then lowered his head into it.

Ellen gently pulled Tom's head to her breast and comforted him as he cried.

CHAPTER
11

A slow, knowing smile crossed Mike Schmidt's lips.

"What'd he do? Kill his second wife? I told you he wasn't through. I told all of you assholes for years and years that that prick'd kill again. It was the wife, wasn't it? The new old lady?"

"No. At least, I'm not sure. The remains haven't been printed yet, but she doesn't look to be out of her teens. It's the same thing all over again, though, I can tell you that. I stumbled into a murder tonight that's almost exactly the same as your Moran case; the eviscerated chest cavity held open with a pressure vice, blood drained, the organs removed and positioned in a diagram around the corpse, the way the woman was holding the purse, everything's the same."

DiGrazia was laying it on thick, trying to win the older man's cooperation. The truth was, he didn't believe a word that he'd spoken. But still, it intrigued him, Schmidt's expression didn't waver. DiGrazia looked at him, startled by the nonreaction. DiGrazia's reopening of the case that had brought the man to his present condition should have caused some change in the man's expression, if only a look of glee.

Yet it hadn't. Schmidt was giving him a flat, closed look, as if he hadn't heard him, or didn't understand what he'd heard.

"I need your files, Mike."

"Did you pick up the doctor?"

"Not yet. My partner's still working the scene."

"He know you're suspicions?"

"She knows. I told her. She's the only one who does. I didn't even tell my lieutenant."

"Why the hell *not?*" Schmidt's anger was out front again. "It's fucking *ob*vious the doctor's at it again!" Schmidt was glaring. DiGrazia didn't know what was wrong. He put it down to the man's condition. Over the course of the years, DiGrazia had had many contacts with chronic alcoholics. He knew their mood swings, knew how any little thing could set them off without warning.

Soon, DiGrazia would hate himself for this immediate dismissal, his blatant misdiagnosis of the reasons for Schmidt's temperament.

But for now, he calmly said, "I thought you'd approve. I did the very same thing you did, the last time. I didn't tell anyone because I want this kept quiet for as long as I can. I don't want the brass in on it, I don't want any political pressure. The way the faces change on TV, as young as they all are, they might not even remember it. I slapped a wall of silence around it—the same way you did—but I don't know how long that'll last.

"If it breaks within the media, it'll come from Royko, or one of the other old-timers who remembers what happened last time." Schmidt laughed shortly, then caught himself, sat smirking. Puzzled, DiGrazia continued. "If it's what it looks like, I don't need the AMA, the media, any high-priced lawyers, or anyone else coming down on my head during the investigation."

"That don't tell me why you didn't pick up the doctor, Dom."

DiGrazia shook his head. "I didn't even call in his brother, the cop, Terry, for an interview yet. I'll sweep him up soon, though. It's an interesting angle, that's one of the things I wanted to talk to you about. Moran was working UCP. He never responded to repeated radio commands to report to the scene. And he's not answering his beeper." DiGrazia shrugged. "There's uniforms out looking for him right now, they've been ordered to bring him in quietly. They just think he's being disciplined for having his radio and beeper off."

"No shit."

"He's paranoid, and a drunk." DiGrazia immediately regretted his word choice. He hurriedly added, "He thinks everybody's out to get him, thinks everybody remembers what happened, and is holding it against him. He can't accept the fact that he's just a drun—a loser. You say hello to him, he bites your head off."

"You know where he drinks?"

"I'll check it out." He said it as if he hadn't had the thought hours before.

"Find out. Nine'll get you ten that he's been barred from half the joints in the city, and all he does in the ones that let him in is cry in his beer about the bum break he got twenty years ago."

Schmidt would have experience with such a mindset. DiGrazia said, "Twenty years ago tonight."

"You got him talking about it all the time, you might have him talking about his brother cracking under the pressure of med school."

"I'll check it out." DiGrazia paused, then, still trying to win Schmidt over, said, "Do you think the brother, the cop, might have done it?"

"Never happen, the doctor's the one you want." Schmidt didn't elaborate. Instead, he returned to what was becoming his favorite topic. "Dom, answer me straight out, without the running around, the diplomacy, or the fear that you'll offend a sensitive drunk and he won't let you see his files: Why the hell didn't you pick up the doctor?"

It was the way Schmidt had always referred to Thomas Moran, even before he'd officially become a doctor. To Schmidt, the title itself was an indictment. DiGrazia had answered the question a number of times; Schmidt was beginning to get on what was left of his nerves. DiGrazia decided to lie to the man, see if he could shut him up, get the files, and get out of there without another display of the old man's temper.

He said, "Because I don't have any evidence, Mike. What's my probable cause? That he was arrested twenty years ago, and walked? Besides, he's twenty years older, he's a psychiatrist, he's got another wife, he's got prestige, he's got money. I call him in, he shuts his mouth, calls his lawyer, and the next time I want to talk to him, when I *might* have something, it's harassment. I don't want to talk to him until I know what questions to ask."

"Questions? What *questions?*" DiGrazia thought Schmidt was about to explode again, but he only squinted his eyes, looked scornfully at DiGrazia. "You've got the same crime, on the twentieth anniversary of the first one, and you tell me you don't know what fucking *questions* to ask the guy?"

DiGrazia's tone was low and careful when he said, "In the first place, it's not the exact same crime. And remember, he walked on the last one, Mike. There's no MO here, no prior. The charges were dropped—and he won a lawsuit against the city."

DiGrazia hurriedly added, "Besides, the scene isn't even officially closed down yet; I made sure the body was gone before I left, but I've got a couple crime-scene techs I can trust still working the area. There might be some other evidence that I missed, something I can put together before I bring anyone in. My partner's stalking the techies right now, making sure she gets everything they get."

"That'll piss 'em off."

"They're not the only ones pissed off, and they'll all have to live with that. What I'm praying for is a print, what I'm hoping for is a partial. What I'll settle for is a single fiber from a man's suit, or from the trunk of a car. I have to have more against him before I pick him up."

"Did you at least call the state's attorney, ask for their considered *legal* opinion about snatching the doctor up before you decided not to?"

DiGrazia took a deep breath before saying, "Not yet. They'd never approve charges at this point, and no judge would give me a warrant. I don't want to stir up any trouble until I have to. Hell, I'm worried that one of the cops on the scene might remember what happened twenty years ago, and try to get in tight with one of the pretty young TV reporters by giving her the story."

"Forget about it. It's old news. That's not where the attention's gonna come from." Schmidt grunted, then smiled a drunk's secretive, self-satisfied smile. "Shit, there aren't twenty people still in the department ever laid eyes on those pictures. It's all bullshit now, every veteran cop in the city *saying* they saw them, or were there, or their father was. I locked that scene down so tight, there's hardly anyone *alive* ever saw what that cocksucker did to Nancy." Schmidt grunted.

He said, "That murder's got more myths floating around it than the Kennedy assassination. What you got to worry about is what my *Sun-Tribune* story does to the case. Before you get back to headquarters, the media's gonna be all over this, and I ain't just talking about Royko."

What was he saying? It was the second time Schmidt had referred to the *Sun-Tribune*. DiGrazia let it go this time, it would be easy enough to pick up a paper when he left. He'd wasted enough time here already, letting Schmidt pretend he was still a working cop.

He said, "We can cut through the myths, Mike, right now. This is the same thing as before." DiGrazia told this lie quite easily, but was honest when he said, "And you could help me solve it. Give me your files."

"Files." Schmidt snorted the word. "All you smart guys think I got every shred of paper ever written about this thing."

"Mike, I know what you've got, I've seen some of it."

"You check with the department? Why don't you use *their* files?"

"Come on, they don't have anything; you've got it all. You know that better than I do, there isn't even a blurred copy of one of the reports left downtown. Even the negatives for the pictures are missing from the crime lab."

"Yeah, and I got railroaded out of the department because of that same thinking. I stole it all, huh? You believe that? Can't be the bureaucrat's mistake, gotta be the old, drunk, crazy man, Mike Schmidt, stole everything."

DiGrazia took another deep breath. He fought a sudden, irrational urge to beat the resentment-ridden drunk into senselessness, then search the house until he found what he wanted. He couldn't look at Schmidt's maddening smirk for another second. He closed his eyes and thought about the man Schmidt used to be. He thought about what Schmidt had lost. Not only his wife and grown children, but the long-dead first-born daughter, whose death must still haunt Schmidt's every waking hour, and who had most definitely been part of what had driven Schmidt in his obsession to arrest Tom Moran for his wife's murder. DiGrazia thought about how much he personally owed him, how much Schmidt had taught him.

But none of it did him any good, as there was nothing he could do to bring that man back, and even with his eyes closed, he could still smell Schmidt's scent, and it disgusted him.

DiGrazia tried one last time. He said, "You going to let me have the files?"

"You pick up the doctor, you can have the files." Schmidt's mouth was set in a determined line, his eyebrows beetlelike over hard, squinty eyes.

"I came here to ask you for a favor, not to enter into negotiations."

"Where you been the last three years? Where the hell have *any* of you been? Dropped me like a nigger bitch drops babies the second I couldn't do you any good anymore." Schmidt's voice was rising with every word; DiGrazia got to his feet. He'd had enough, and knew he had to get out of there. Schmidt's accusing eyes followed him.

"I have to go now, Mike."

"Yeah, you go and blow my case. Kiss the doctor's ass. Prick." Schmidt slapped the ashtray in DiGrazia's direction, and DiGrazia sidestepped it, but ashes and butts showered the lower part of his body. "Don't even give me your home number. Me! Go on, get your backstabbing ass out of my house!"

DiGrazia's eyes narrowed.

Schmidt laughed at him. "What am I, supposed to be intimidated by a badass *look?* You forget who it was that taught it to you. You son of a bitch, I treated you like a *son!*"

DiGrazia felt the need to strike back, and he did it in a manner that would have more effect on Schmidt than a beating: He gave him his honest opinion. "We've got two different killers here, Schmidt. Two. It's a copycat. It's not the doctor, it's someone else who knows the case as well as anyone."

"So you're saying I'm a suspect instead of the doctor!"

"No. You're a washed-up old drunk. You couldn't even kill yourself."

Schmidt's face grew red. He leaped to his feet and pointed a trembling finger at DiGrazia's face. "You cocksucker, you arrest that doctor, and I mean tonight, or I'll—"

DiGrazia moved quickly. He raced toward Schmidt and didn't break stride as he grabbed Schmidt by the throat, pushed him back and lifted at the same time as he ran toward the wall. The chair behind the older man fell over as Schmidt panicked, making choking sounds. DiGrazia slammed Schmidt into the wall, then held him there with one hand, and put his face in close. He spoke in a malevolent whisper.

"You self-centered, hateful, ignorant old cock*suck*er." DiGrazia's breath came easily; under the horrid body odor, he could smell Schmidt's wriggling fear. "You wrecked your life over that case! You turned into a bitter, morbid, hateful piece of human garbage over it. I come here asking for your help, and you hand me insults? You fucking curse at me? You *threaten* me?"

DiGrazia smacked Schmidt's head into the wall, hard. Schmidt had partially regained his senses, was now pulling feebly at DiGrazia's hand with both of his own. DiGrazia squeezed a little harder.

"You throw an *ash*tray at me? When I'm giving you a chance to put some kind of meaning back into your world?" He smacked Schmidt's head against the wall again.

Schmidt was wheezing, his face was turning blue. His eyes were wide with fear. DiGrazia looked deep into Schmidt's eyes, and Schmidt looked away. DiGrazia didn't whisper now; he shouted. His anger was dissipating—Schmidt knew DiGrazia's reactions as well as anyone alive, was relieved to hear him shout.

"I just told you I was looking for a favor to soothe your *pride!* You think I can't get the state's attorney on the phone and have a warrant for those files in five minutes flat? To obtain stolen police property that could help solve the high-profile, downtown murder of a young white woman? You're as fucking crazy as they said you were when they bounced you out of the department!"

DiGrazia let go of Schmidt and stepped back in disgust. Schmidt crumpled slowly to the floor, both hands at his throat. He was wheezing. DiGrazia searched himself for pity, could find none.

In a very soft, derisive tone, DiGrazia said, "I was trying to give you your manhood back, trying to prove that everyone had been wrong about you all these years. Whoever did this knew all about Nancy Moran. And you could have helped me solve it."

Schmidt had one hand over his eyes; his head was down. He waved DiGrazia away with his other hand.

"All you had to do was help me, and I'd have made you a god to the media, I'd have given you all the credit when I broke the case, told anyone who'd listen that all I did was ask you for help, and you did the rest yourself. The city would have forgiven your stupidity over Moran. A book, Movie of the Week, you could have had it all."

There was a harsh scratchiness in Schmidt's voice when he said, "Get out, goddamn you! This is still my house!"

"And you live in it all alone, wallowing in self-pity. I would have fucking *absolved* you. But you don't want that, do you, Mike?" Schmidt now looked up at him, impotent frustration alive in his eyes. His lower lip quivered as his body shook with unrelieved rage.

"You just love being the poor, broken down ex-cop."

Schmidt looked down, tried to rise to his feet, but DiGrazia pushed him back with a foot.

"Stay where you are. Where you fucking belong. You used to be the best cop in the department, but now you're just another piece of garbage, flowing out of the can.

"I'm leaving now, Schmidt, but I'm going to do you one last favor. I'm not going to take your gun; I'm not even going to take the bullets. I'm going to turn my back on you, go outside, walk over to my car, get in and drive away. I'm going to give you a chance to have the courage you used to have. I can't remember anyone ever slapping Mike Schmidt around and getting away with it, but I just did. You got any pride left? Let's see. 'Cause if you do, if that front door opens, if you come out again like you did the last time, you'll be committing suicide by DiGrazia. I'll give you that opportunity, for old time's sake. And while Homicide's processing the scene, I'll find your files and take them."

DiGrazia made a quick move forward, as if he were going to kick Schmidt. Schmidt cowered away, banging his head on the wall as he did so. Some sort of change came over DiGrazia, even Schmidt could see it happening. The tension drained from him, he seemed almost surprised at what he'd done. His fists unclenched, and he stepped back. He took a hesitant step forward, as if to help Schmidt to his feet, and Schmidt misconstrued the

101

movement and slunk away, whining in fear, bringing one hand up to protect his face.

DiGrazia stumbled back, looked in shock at what he'd done to Schmidt, then turned quickly and walked out of the room. He slammed the front door behind him as he left the house, took the concrete stairs in one leap, ran to his car, and—less conscious now of the neighbors than he'd been when Schmidt had been waving a pistol in his direction—tore away from the curb with a long peel of rubber, and he didn't slow down until he pulled to the curb in front of the 28th District station house.

The swarming hordes of reporters outside the station house door had already fallen upon him before DiGrazia understood that they'd been specifically awaiting his arrival. Schmidt's prediction had come true: DiGrazia's shroud of silence had been pierced. They thought they knew what had happened in the Chicago Avenue alley, and the party, DiGrazia realized, as he walked quickly toward the building—coldly and professionally, stone-faced and without comment—was about to get truly interesting.

It was only then that he remembered that Schmidt hadn't bothered to ask him where the body had been found.

CHAPTER
12

The killer sat in the room and stared at the curtains that covered the windows, as shadows from the television set danced across his vision. The volume was turned down low. The killer wanted to know what was going on, but he didn't want to attract attention to himself, didn't want anyone wondering what he was doing.

What he wanted was forgiveness. He wanted someone to tell him that it was all right. That *he* would be all right.

There was no thought for his victim, past or present, no compassion for the dead, nor pity, nor contrition over the lives he had taken. He felt no remorse over what he'd done to the woman's body earlier that night. The only pain he was capable of feeling was his own personal suffering. He felt that pain now, and felt it strongly.

He took a drink of beer, then closed his eyes for a moment. He bit down very hard on his tongue. He felt the pain, he tasted the blood. Yes, he was awake. You didn't feel physical pain in dreams, you could not taste. This was not good news for him, as being awake also meant that he had indeed killed the girl, had—

The beginning of a scream originated from somewhere deep within him. He cut it off before it could reach his throat. He put his beer down on the table, put his head in his hands, and, once again, began to harshly, silently, sob. "What did you *do?*" he whimpered, in a voice he thought could not be heard outside the room. The walls were thin, and the weather nice. Neither heat nor air conditioning were needed at this time of year. He wondered if, due to this, the vents carried sound from one room to another. Startled at the thought, but needing to hear his voice, he whispered.

"Oh, my God, what did you do? How could you do that to that girl?"

At times such as these, he liked to think of himself as somebody else, liked to use a false name, to pretend that he was someone other than who he really was. It was a practice he'd begun when he'd been a child, his mind's escape. It gave him someone he could blame, and that, to him, was of the utmost importance. The pain was easier for him to handle when he did that; when he could blame someone else, his alter ego, and cast an unblinking eye on what somebody else had done.

He was so good at it. At times, entire periods of his life would pass him by as he lived another man's existence, in a world inside his mind. He would come back to himself and wonder in panic at what he might have done in the past few days.

He'd been through this before, he told himself now. The suffering, the tremendous urge—almost a need—to confess; he'd felt it before, at other times.

But the pain then hadn't been as strong as it was this time, he was sure of that. He'd *never* felt as horrible as he felt at this very minute. The stomach pains were getting stronger. He wondered if he had cancer.

He stood and went to the place where he'd hidden his pills. He took them out, washed the last two down with his beer, and dropped the empty bottle beside him.

There were ways to deal with it, the guilt would go away. It had before and it would again. He repeated this to himself in a whisper, over and over again. He could return to his normal existence, which was actually abnormal, and actually not much more than an existence.

But it was better than what he had now, and infinitely better than being locked inside a cage.

As he would have been if the cops were as smart as they were in the movies, in the TV shows, in the books that he had read. He tried to smile at the thought of police incompetence, and found that he could not. He settled for a small sense of satisfaction instead, convinced there was nothing to worry about; the police weren't smart enough to catch him, not now, not ever.

Except for Mike Schmidt. Cop or not, Schmidt could still put him away. He thought about that, wondered if he should kill the old man. Nothing fancy, nothing that could set a pattern that would bring the FBI into the case. He could not have that. The FBI were a lot more sophisticated than the Chicago Police Department—if they came into this thing, they could find him. So he wouldn't eviscerate Schmidt, wouldn't lay his organs out in a pattern around his body, or make any other fancy moves. He would just shoot him. Or stab him. Strangle him, if he wanted to. Schmidt was an old man, a drunk, and would be unable to defend himself. He'd be sleeping now, it would be easy.

He had a key to the house.

He didn't trust Schmidt, didn't like him. He had never before killed anyone he had known even casually, but he might have to make an exception now, he might have to stop the only man alive who could get him locked up.

He suddenly slapped himself across the face, hard. He leaned forward in the chair, trying to force Schmidt out of his mind. He wouldn't kill again, he wouldn't. He was looking at eternity in hell already, and the entire objective of his life—at least at the moment—was to seek forgiveness.

"God, forgive me," he whispered, then sobbed. He thought of Schmidt, dead. He slapped himself again. He looked at the clock. Had he slept at all? He could not remember. The pills were taking effect, and he fought to keep awake. He did not want to pass out, not yet. There was someone he had to see, someone he had to speak with. Someone who could help him, who could lead him to the road that led to forgiveness.

He had to talk to him. He could help him.

He laughed once, bitterly and aloud, then leaned back in the chair. Outside somewhere, a siren blared. Police? Fire? Car alarm? Were they coming for him? He did not know, and did not care, as sleep overwhelmed him.

CHAPTER
13

The tears had dried and a joint shower had been taken, and Tom and Ellen had fallen asleep in each other's arms. At daybreak she'd felt her husband jerk, and Ellen came fully awake, expecting the worst, another nightmare. But what had awakened Tom seemed to be an emotional need rather than a bad dream. He made a strange, strangled sound, and reached for Ellen, held her tight. She stroked the back of his neck, his head on her chest, Tom taking deep breaths and letting them out harshly through his nose. Ellen felt him stiffen against her leg. She felt him lick her neck.

They were making rather sorrowful love when the bedside telephone surprised them. Ellen, thinking it was the drunken cop who'd dredged everything up for the newspaper, immediately warned Tom not to answer it, but he'd gone soft within her at the sound of the first ring, his body had tensed up, and he had immediately pulled away, grabbed the phone and shouted an angry hello. Ellen had watched as Tom's strong shoulders slumped; she'd heard his surprised, monosyllabic response.

That had been the first call.

A half-dozen calls later they'd taken the phone off the hook. Tom was now sitting in semidarkness at the kitchen table as daylight lightened the side windows, tossing a sliver of brightness across the table, illuminating Tom's hands. The crystal face of his watch made a prism of light dance on the ceiling. Tom was dressed in a suit, drinking coffee, awaiting the arrival of his older brother, Terry. Ellen had already called off work, now she wondered if Tom was going to do the same.

He'd told her that he'd wanted to be alone, but she'd be damned if she'd let that happen. She had given him his space while she'd done what she thought she had to do. Ellen had burned the clothing Tom had worn the night before, along with the bloodstained bedsheets. She'd used the *Star-Tribune* for kindling. She'd scrubbed the hardwood floors on her hands and knees—from the front door, all the way up the stairs, on into the bedroom, and she'd scrubbed the tile in the bathroom—until there wasn't a drop of blood visible anywhere in her home. The pain in her back forced her into the whirlpool the second she'd completed her task.

Ellen came into the kitchen now, dressed, her makeup on, her hair combed, her hands in the pockets of her snug-fitting jeans. In spite of everything that happened, Ellen felt nearly composed, somewhat in command of herself. The lack of sleep was somehow relaxing her, Tom's crisis, his need for her, calming. She wondered how long her tranquility would last.

She could almost feel the child growing inside her.

Ellen thanked God that she hadn't taken the Halcion. She decided that she wouldn't say anything to Tom about the baby, not until this crisis was resolved. How long would that take, a few days? Perhaps a week?

Ellen waited until she was sure that Tom wasn't going to acknowledge her presence before she said, "Tom? Are you all right?"

Tom looked up at her. It was immediately apparent that the lack of sleep and the horrible news was affecting him badly; he looked drained, exhausted. Ellen couldn't let him go to work. She had to get him through this day.

"Tom, don't do this. Talk to me."

He opened his mouth, as if he really wanted to speak to her, but then he shut it softly, shook his head, and turned away.

Ellen, suddenly enraged, stormed over to him, grabbed his head in her hands and forced him to face her.

"Don't you even pretend that this doesn't concern me!" She let go of him, and he stared up at her in surprise. She tried to calm herself down. "I'm your *wife! I* was mentioned in that article, too! What I do, where I work, where my parents live, *every*thing!"

"We should have moved. We should have moved out of state when we had the chance."

"Since when do we run and hide?!" Tom tried to look away, but Ellen touched his head again, and he obediently turned back to her. "We talked about this years ago! We talked about it before we bought the house! We don't run away, goddamnit, we haven't done anything to run away from!"

"I thought it would be different. I thought I could prove myself, at least prove my innocence through my work. Jesus Christ, I thought I *had!* Ellen don't you see? They'll never let me alone."

"It's not just *you,* goddamnit Tom, it's *us!*"

"I'm sorry you got mentioned, I'm sorry you got dragged down into this mess."

"I was 'dragged down into this mess' the day I fell in love with you, and it's not your fault what some drunken retired cop says about us in the papers, so don't you dare apologize for him."

"That's not what I was—oh hell, what's the point!" Tom angrily slurped his coffee, then looked around as if seeking more.

The morning sun was seeping in around the edges of the blackout curtains when the phone rang, and Capt. John Parker came immediately awake. He snatched the phone up before it rang a second time, but he knew that it had awakened his wife; Donna stirred beside him, as used to the late-night or early morning calls as Parker was himself. Parker held the receiver to his chest while he rapidly blinked his eyes.

He put the phone to his ear, and was mentally alert when he grunted his name. He cleared his throat of its sleep-huskiness as Lieutenant Matthews identified himself, and Parker was sitting on the side of the bed by the time his subordinate's initial words sank in.

Parker's voice betrayed none of his apprehension as he said,

"Don't take him off the case." The mattress moved as Donna, alert to his tone as well as the tenseness in his body, sat up in bed and listened in on his side of the conversation. Parker snapped on the bedside lamp, raised his voice and cut Matthews off in midsentence.

"I'm telling you, Matthews, don't take him off the case. That is not a fucking request, that is an order. Do you understand me? . . . Put him on the line." Parker shook his head in exasperation. "Never mind, I'll run him down myself . . . No, you listen to *me*, Lieutenant, I want DiGrazia on this case, and I don't care who he lied to . . . Don't you try it. I'm on my way. Don't make any *command decisions* until I assess the situation." Parker slammed the phone down and got to his feet.

"What is it?" Donna asked, and Parker turned to look at her. His anger dissipated at the sight of her sleepy face, the puffiness under her cheeks. He would never tell her that from time to time he would just sit up on his side of the bed and watch her as she slept. The year that they'd been married had convinced him that happiness was not an illusion, nor was it held in exclusive title by the young.

Parker shook his head now, in frustration more than anger, trying to see through all the games that could be played by a man such as Matthews, trying to see the truth. "I swear to God, the way things are getting in this department, I'm ready to turn it in and retire."

"You can't do that. What else are you going to do? Clean house and watch soap operas until I get home to tell you about my exciting day on the job?"

"DiGrazia went off on his own on a big-time media case."

"Aren't they all these days? What happened, another football player kill his wife?"

"It looks like we might have a serial killer in town, Donna."

"Oh, God." They were both veteran police detectives, and as such were aware of how rarely serial killings occur; as such, they were also aware of how the smothering media coverage of such cases could paralyze an entire city.

"DiGrazia tried to hide it from the media, threw up a wall of silence, he didn't even tell Matthews what he suspected."

"Good for him. Surly as he is, I'd take DiGrazia over Matthews any day."

"As a partner, you mean?"

"As a human being."

Parker was throwing underclothing onto the bed. "Matthews is a ladder-climbing politician."

"And DiGrazia's not."

"That's my point." Parker sat down on his side of the bed, looked at the phone, then picked it up and dialed in a number. "I'd bet my star DiGrazia shut his beeper off." Parker spoke in a near whisper, as if to himself. He dialed in his home number, added 911 so DiGrazia would know the call was urgent. He turned to face Donna.

"The good news is, DiGrazia has the clout, and the know-how, and doesn't give a damn about what happens. He's a doctor, for God's sake, he could go to work anywhere, and make more money. We got a repeater in this city? I want DiGrazia on it." Parker grunted. "If I had ten more cops like DiGrazia, I could fire half the dicks in the city, save the taxpayers millions. He's that good. And that proud. And he commands respect, superior pain in the ass or not." Parker rose, walked into the bathroom, and roughly washed his face. He was slathering on shaving lotion when Donna came and stood in the doorway. He looked at her in the mirror, smiled inwardly at her artless, unstudied pose, her brown hair disheveled, and he thought, not for the first or the ten-thousandth time, that he'd gotten very, very lucky.

Even before things had gone sour between them, Parker could not have turned his back toward his first wife without her feeling the need to remind him that his bald spot was growing ever wider. Donna had never mentioned it. He wondered if she even noticed it.

"Pride goeth before a fall," Donna said now.

Parker began to shave, wearing the flag-patterned silk pajama bottoms she had found for him at Filene's basement, his chest bare, speaking to her as he shaved.

"I hardly ever talk about him, and don't have to watch him. He's so damn good he's just sort of *there*, and he's there like electricity's there—try living without it. You remember when he got shot last year?"

"Remember? I didn't see you for three days."

"He was investigating Tonce Alberti."

"Alberti shot him in Little Italy, I remember that."

"And DiGrazia, with a bullet in his belly, took the gun away from Alberti and emptied it into Alberti's skull. That was in the papers, on TV."

"But there's more to it, right?"

"He was investigating Alberti on the first hit the old man had done personally in something like twenty years. It was some sort of stupid, Old Country bullshit thing those guys pretend they live for. Alberti gets scared when he hears DiGrazia's looking into it, and then naturally transforms that into anger, and comes charging into a candy store in Little Italy, where DiGrazia's interviewing maybe the only old woman in the whole neighborhood who isn't afraid of big, bad Tonce Alberti. He starts shouting and yelling, waving his arms around: 'You're Italian, I'm Italian, whatsamatta you?' the usual shit these guys spiel, like sharing nation of origin means you're supposed to turn your back or wink at a small, little, fraternal thing like murder. Anyway, there's DiGrazia, seven feet tall, whatever he is, and he backs the little outfit guy into the corner, never raises his voice, and Alberti starts getting terrified, asks DiGrazia if he knows who he is, how powerful he is.

"DiGrazia tells him he knows exactly who he is; a swamp-guinea, low-life, piece of shit peasant who's been feeding off his own people since he was old enough to hold a baseball bat."

"That's when Alberti shot him."

"Well, yeah, but there's a little more to it than that." Parker turned on the sink, purposely making Donna wait for the punch line. He washed his face again, rubbed his wet hands through his hair. Since marrying Donna, he'd stopped using Rogaine, stopped trying to comb his hair creatively. He wore it short enough so he could comb it in thirty seconds and not think about it again until he shampooed the city off it at the end of the working day.

Donna handed him the towel, and he thanked her, wiped his face, and said, "While he was talking to Alberti, he emphasized his words with slaps. Got him in the corner and slapped him with every word. What he did was, he left the guy no choice:

Alberti would either draw down on him, or he'd lose any respect he had on the street."

"DiGrazia could have got bounced for that one."

"Should have, maybe, seeing that it was on tape."

"The store was *wired?*"

"Not by us, the old woman had a security camera. Now, get this." Parker shot deodorant under his arms, spread toothpaste on his brush, and held it while he finished his story, his head turned a little to the side so his breath wouldn't offend Donna. "There's maybe forty, fifty cops milling around—I don't have to tell you what it's like when a cop gets shot."

"And they saw the tape?"

"Most of them."

"John, how did that not turn up on the *NBC Nightly News?*"

"I'll tell you how. One of the cops got up, took the tape out of the VCR, walked into the bathroom, and a bunch of *other* cops stood around him for protection while he unspooled it and flushed it down the toilet, foot by foot."

"What about the woman?"

"The store owner? She was guarding the bathroom door."

"That's what you mean by commanding respect."

"As dishy, jealous, egotistical and miserable as most cops can be, let me ask you a question: did you ever hear that story before?"

"How can you cover him on something like this?"

"I won't have to. He'll cover himself. I'll just do whatever I can to make sure that Matthews doesn't get in his way."

Donna was wearing the top half of the silk pajamas, fingering the top button, leaning against the doorway. She said, "Be careful, John."

Parker, understanding what she meant, said, "Always."

CHAPTER
14

Ellen closed her eyes, took a deep breath, and forced herself to calm down. They were not connecting here, and her shouting at Tom wouldn't make that connection happen. She pulled out a chair and sat down across from him, leaned on her elbows, looked her husband in the eye and spoke to him in as calm a tone as she could manage.

"Don't you understand what I'm saying to you, Tom? We're in this together, you and me. It's not your problem, it's *ours*. Like always, just the two of us. Husband and wife."

"Till death do us part . . ."

"That's not funny."

"Neither is what happened to some poor young woman in an alley. Or what was in the paper, *that* wasn't very funny, either. My God, I hate to sound self-centered at a time like this, but how many private clients do you think I'll have left by this afternoon? How long do you think the hospitals will keep me on staff after what happened last night, not to mention after what was in the paper? Christ, now that there's been *another* killing, who do you think they're going to focus on, who do you think they'll blame? You didn't hear the reporters, Ellen. They weren't seeking quotes, they were asking me if I did it!"

"It'll go away, Tom, the same way it did before. You won't lose any patients, and you don't want the type of patients who'd leave you over something like this, anyway." Ellen paused.

"Besides," she said, "this sort of ugliness might double your client load. You know how people are; there are plenty who'll want to know you, want to say they go to you for treatment. You'll get every emotional lightweight neurotic in the city."

"*Those* aren't the type of patients I want."

"Their checks will clear."

"Oh, Ellen, you don't understand. The entire city will think I'm Hannibal Lecter now."

"They will not. You underestimate your clients, how they bond with you. They trust you, Tom, they rely on you, some of them love you, for God's sake!"

Tom grunted.

"They won't believe you had anything to do with any of this."

"They will after the police come sniffing around. I'm amazed they haven't shown up already. What do you think will happen when I can't prove where I was or what I was doing when the body was found?"

"That's ludicrous; you were here with me!"

"I have a two-hour gap I can't account for!"

"The hell you have." Ellen stared at him, and when she spoke, she spoke firmly. "Tom, listen to me: You were here with me."

The softness—and strength—in Ellen's tone made Tom's eyes narrow. As soon as he understood what she was saying, he shook his head.

"No, that's not possible. We can't do that, we can't lie to the police."

"Why not?"

Tom shook his head. "They'll find out."

"No, they won't."

"I made a call from my office, remember? I called you, Ellen."

"You called me from an office in the mental ward of a veteran's hospital. The calls are automatically blocked from Caller ID, they may even be untraceable—at least you can't use Automatic Call-Back with them—it's all done from inside. You tell them

114

you were with me, and I'll back you up. If the police call us on it, if somehow they *can* check the calls made from your office number, all we tell them is that we got . . . two obscene calls last night, one right after the other. One will turn out to have been made from your office phone. It's not as if you have the only key to the room."

Tom looked at her. "What do you mean, two calls?"

Ellen backed up quickly. "Some drunk called last night, a few minutes before you did."

"An obscene call, you said?"

"Just a wrong number," Ellen lied. "But nobody has to know that."

"Ellen, they'll insist on polygraphs, at the least." Tom's face fell. "My God, I bled all over the *house!*"

Ellen waved the comment off. "I took care of that hours ago, when you were making calls in the den. As for the police, if they even ask permission to speak with you, we tell them to talk to our attorney. One of those calls you made *was* to Chris, wasn't it?"

"Of course it was. There's not much he could do at that point; he hadn't read the article yet—he was sleeping when I called— he hadn't even heard about the second murder. He's going to consult with a First Amendment expert to see if we were libeled by Schmidt and the newspaper. He told me to call him the second I see a squad car."

"Did he tell you not to make any statements to anyone in the media?"

"He didn't have to—"

"Did he tell you to tell the police to go to hell when they come around?"

"Ellen . . ."

"Don't you condescend to me, Tom. I've been through too much with you to get shut out now. I know you didn't kill anyone, not Nancy, not whoever it was they found in the alley last night. And I'm not going to let anyone accuse you of either murder."

Tom sat silently, looking down at the table.

"I've been with you all the way for more than seventeen years, buddy. Don't think I made it that long by being weak."

Tom looked up. Ellen nodded once. She maintained direct eye contact.

"That's right, you heard me. I was with you through the toughest part of your training. I put up with the twenty- and thirty- and forty-hour shifts without breaks, with hardly ever seeing you for two straight years on end. I left you alone when you had to study, and helped you with your studies whenever you needed me to. I dropped out of college and worked two jobs to help put you through medical school—before the city settled your lawsuit—and I paid my own way through nursing school even after you got your settlement." Ellen leaned further toward him, reached out and grabbed one of Tom's hands, then squeezed it.

"Now it's *our* turn, Tom. Finally. The last four years have been the best in our lives. Lately I've had to stand up to your silences, and I've always lived with the emotional walls you built up around yourself. And I've lived with some pretty strong mood swings these past few months. I put up with it all and never complained. I kept my mouth shut, because I love you.

"But I won't let you shut me out, not now, not after all we've been through together." She squeezed his hand again for emphasis. "You're everything to me, Tom. I won't allow anything to change that."

Tom looked at her as if he'd never seen her before. He finally said, "Don't you see, Ellen? Can't you see what a dream world we've been living in?"

"Dream world?" Ellen withdrew her hand. She sat up straight. Tom waved his hand around the room.

"Look at us! We buy this house, we're going to fill it with kids now, we're going to be an old-fashioned Mom and Pop. Ward-and-June-fucking-Cleaver. As if our children won't ever find out, as if they won't be hounded at school, made fun of and rejected as soon as the other kids' parents find out who their father is."

"Tom, don't do this, don't say those things."

"It's the truth. You think Warren isn't going to milk this for all it's worth? And God knows how many others? I've never been able to live this down, and I won't be able to now. I thought I'd be able to, but I can't."

"So what do we do?"

"There's not a month goes by that I'm not offered a position somewhere else in the country. For even more money, more prestige. I'd be working fewer hours. We'd be in a better climate."

"You love Chicago as much as I do."

"It's starting to lose its allure."

"I'll go wherever you are, Tom. You know that. But wouldn't taking off now look more damning than if we stayed?"

"Don't think I haven't thought about it."

"So what do we do?"

"First, we have to get a few things straight between us, and at the top of the list is this: There will be no lying to the police." Tom held his hand up to stop her expected protest. "Ellen, we have nothing to hide. Besides, I went to my office in the VA hospital, not to Northwestern, or to my private office. I had to sign in with the door guard. People saw me at the clinic, half a dozen guards, orderlies, patients who couldn't sleep."

He didn't mention the fact that he'd stopped off somewhere for at least one drink. Ellen didn't mention it, either.

Instead, she said, "Then they can give you an alibi."

"Oh, I'm certain their names will come up, wherever confidentiality isn't involved. But again, that's not the point. Ellen, even if we *could* get away with lying to the police, I wouldn't do it."

"Why not?" Ellen bit off a sarcastic statement concerning his moral superiority.

"Because a dead woman was found in an alley last night, that's why not. And my lying to them could impede the investigation."

"I'm as sorry as you about that woman, but let me tell you something: You're a lot more important to me than she is."

"Jesus Christ, I hope so." Tom searched her face for a moment, and she stared back at him, her eyes hard. His face fell as he at last said, "My God, what have I done to you . . . ?"

Ellen didn't even have to think about it.

"Done to me? What have you *done* to me? How long a list do you want? You took a life of probable futility and gave it real meaning. You took a sex-scared, frightened young girl and helped turn her into a mature woman. When my brother killed himself, who got me through that? My parents? No, *you* did! You helped me to break away from everyone who was hurting me, and taught me how it was only by leaving them that I could help myself. You taught me to laugh. You taught me it was okay to cry . . .''

Speaking the last word called forth the deed, and Ellen angrily swiped at her eyes with the back of her hands, then put her elbows on the table, buried her head in her hands, and let the tears flow.

CHAPTER
15

The two men and one woman were locked behind a steel door, in the basement, with only the light from a single, bare, low-wattage bulb that was hanging from a wire illuminating them in a room where the walls were cinder blocks painted blue. The door had been painted the same color, and was made of very heavy steel. No one would hear their conversation. They were on one side of an old boxing ring, standing in shadows and speaking in low voices.

Constantine took it all in, and was surprised; the intrigue, the hiding out like this, was more than she had expected. What *had* she expected? Constantine didn't know. But she realized that she was on the inside for once, and was grateful.

John Parker was everything she had expected him to be. Tall, handsome, muscular, and self-possessed. He questioned DiGrazia and DiGrazia answered without ego or hostility, two professionals getting their stories straight, masters of a profession in which secrecy had become the most cherished asset anyone could possess. Constantine remembered a time when favors were all, were the coin of the realm, but that had been before the media had become a rapacious beast, before police officers had to be trained in how to deal with journalists in an eight-hour Police Academy class, with videotaped quizzes, and role-playing scenarios.

Parker didn't seem angry that DiGrazia had brought her onto the team, either. She didn't know if that was a sign of his respect for her abilities, or if it was a sign of his respect for DiGrazia's personal judgment. But he'd made it easy on her, and when he spoke to her now, he spoke in the same tone he'd been using with DiGrazia, not resorting to the careful, special voice most commanders hold in reserve for the occasions when they were forced to address lower-ranking female officers.

"You're sure you've got everything there is to get? Your reports are accurate and up to date?"

"I just got back in when you called for Detective DiGrazia to come down here, sir. Most of my report's from the medical examiner's office, and the crime lab. It doesn't get any more up to date than that. Everything else's off the computer, scanned out of newspaper articles." She looked at DiGrazia. "You were right. There isn't one single report on the Nancy Moran murder anywhere, not in the computer, at least, and not in any of the downtown files, I checked through boxes that have been down there since the fifties, even the ones that were scanned into the computers."

"You didn't have to waste time on that," Parker said to her. "Schmidt stole everything there was long before he retired."

"Sorry, sir."

"Call me John, it makes things easier all the way around."

Constantine did not think this was the time to tell him that she'd worked with Donna Bonaventure before Donna had made detective, met John Parker, and married him.

Neither man had engaged in any small talk, nor had any of them shaken hands when Parker had called them down here. He'd simply nodded acknowledgment of her when DiGrazia had introduced them.

"How much interference can I expect?" DiGrazia asked.

"I don't know. I can talk to the superintendent, if you want. He's got two messages waiting for me upstairs."

"I've got his man coming to the meeting, John, you should know that." Constantine didn't know what meeting he was referring to.

"Don't worry about it," Parker said. "You should have all the help for your side that you can get. He'll try and stack the deck, you know, Matthews will."

"Can you stop him?"

Parker nodded. "There are ways. When you can, I'll need a written report of the meeting. If he makes one false move, I'll get rid of him. And don't lose your temper if he runs any games on you in the meeting. We'll all be better off if he hangs himself in there. But I want to clear everyone on your team as you pick them, Dom. No publicity whores, or outsiders." He turned to Constantine. "No offense intended."

Constantine, not understanding most of what they were talking about, nodded at him. She wanted to get DiGrazia alone, wanted to find out what the hell was going on.

DiGrazia said, "I asked one crime-lab criminalist to come in. Dr. Eberhardt. You know him?" Parker nodded.

"Eberhardt's good, and you'll need access to what he can get you. Everyone else's one of ours?"

"Yes."

"If your man can't square any beef, if Matthews is slick enough to pull an end run around you, and somehow doesn't step on his dick in the process, I'll drag *him* off it, and reassign the case to myself. You run it for me from there."

DiGrazia nodded, thoughtfully.

"No media access, either. No matter what they say in the meeting today—in their ass-covering hindsight—you had the right idea last night, Dominick."

"You see the *Sun-Tribune?* I might have gotten away with it if Schmidt hadn't come out for one last, twentieth-anniversary turn at the batter's cage."

Parker was smiling when he said, "Not hardly what you thought it was going to be when you were writing your doctoral thesis, is it?"

"I should have gotten the degree in political science." DiGrazia turned to Constantine.

"Do me a favor, Janice. We've got a team coming in; I'll brief you when we're done here. We'll need five—" he looked at Parker "—make that *six* copies of everything you have. Go up and run them yourself, and don't let a single page of that report out of your sight. I'll want two copies immediately.'' Constantine cursed inwardly, there went her chance of getting DiGrazia alone. She had turned to leave when DiGrazia snapped his fingers and called her name.

"When you're done, run down to Dunkin' Donuts. Get a dozen of whatever doughnuts, and a dozen large cups of coffee." He was reaching into his pocket for some cash, was walking toward her, holding a bill out toward her.

Constantine stood looking at him for a second, awkwardly. Both DiGrazia and Parker were looking at her oddly. She closed her mouth, took the bill, and nodded, part of a team now, then she turned to the door, wondering if either one of them even understood the magnitude of the insult.

CHAPTER
16

Tom never made a comforting move toward her. Ellen tried to understand; after all, he was under a considerable amount of stress. Rather than reveal her disappointment, when her tears had stopped, she said, "That's just great, on top of everything else, now my makeup's ruined." Tom looked at her for a moment, then, implausibly, he laughed. Ellen realized how she sounded, and laughed a bit herself, sniffling. She shook her head. "I sound like a real emotional powerhouse, don't I?"

"Actually, what you said made me feel better than I've felt in—a while."

Ellen sobered immediately. "You should have come to me, Tom. You should have talked to me about it."

Now Tom reached over and took Ellen's hands, held them tightly in his own. Two sets of searching eyes met, Tom's seeking forgiveness, Ellen's seeking understanding.

"I was here for you all along; all you ever had to do was come to me."

"Is it too late?" Tom asked, and Ellen shook her head.

"Never. I'm in this for the duration."

"Then I have to help the police in their investigation, Ellen."

"After what happened last time? After what the paper said this morning?" Ellen tried to pull her hands away, but Tom held her firmly.

"He's a discredited cop, and he was forced to retire, that was in the article, too, how Nancy's case became the fixation that destroyed him. The article was as much about how crazy he is as it was about what happened to Nancy; how I was cleared, and I won a large lawsuit against the city for false arrest and malicious prosecution. He's lucky I didn't take his house. Who else is he going to blame?" Tom took a deep breath, blew it out, and tried to smile.

"Let me tell you something. Last night, after I came home, after I—when you held me? It was the first time I cried in front of anybody since Nancy's funeral."

"Oh, Tom . . ."

"You know me better than anyone, better than Nancy ever did, better than she ever got a chance to, anyway. And I was just a kid then myself, trying to find my personality."

"You were—"

"Let me finish, please." Tom waited, and Ellen nodded. "I've always tried to not be a burden on anyone. I know I should have told you a lot of things that I kept inside, I knew you'd help me. But I thought it would pass, I put it all down to this anniversary thing, Ellen, and I thought it would go away with the day." Tom shook his head in surprise.

Ellen's heart was breaking. The earnestness in his eyes, the sincerity in his expression melted her. He was speaking slowly, having a hard time saying the words. She didn't think she'd ever loved him more than she did this minute.

He said, "I've been having such horrible *night*mares. There's a man at the clinic with the same problem, maybe he brought it on, I don't know. Things I hadn't thought of in years, Ellen, my father, my brothers, it's all happening again, just as it happened then, in living color, at night." Tom looked down, as if wondering if he should continue. Ellen squeezed his hands, encouragingly. He looked up at her, and Ellen knew before he spoke that he was about to make a confession.

"I've been medicating myself, honey. Taking too many sleeping pills, antianxiety pills, mood elevators. I told myself it would only be until I got through today, until this anniversary passed. Then I saw my picture in the paper last night at the newsstand, and my whole world seemed to fall apart. If you hadn't been here for me, I don't know—I don't know what I might have done."

"Tom, don't say that, I'll always be here for you."

"I know it." He took a second to collect himself. "Don't take this the wrong way, but after I, after I *cried*, I felt more relieved, and closer to you, than I had in a long time. And I wasn't manipulating you, but I wanted you to come into the shower with me to keep me away from the pills as much as just to have you in there with me."

"Do you want me to—"

"I'm not finished." Ellen didn't get angry at his curtness; he'd spoken more words to her this morning than he had in the past week, and more words of substance than he had in months, maybe years. She waited patiently.

"I didn't mean to cut you off, but my stream of thought isn't running straight, I want to say this before Terry gets here, or before I start thinking about something else, or forget it altogether." He smiled ruefully. "That's been happening a lot lately. A side effect of the medication, I think."

"I don't know how the reporters got our number—"

"Schmidt—"

"—but the media doesn't know much. I wouldn't make a statement to them after Nancy's death, but from what they know, from what they said on the phone, they don't know much more beside the fact that it was a similar type of murder. Nancy was killed in a church, not an alley, but it seems there were some similarities that can't be ignored. And that son of a bitch Schmidt's probably calling a press conference right now, to demand my arrest." Tom sighed. "I—*we'll*—cross that bridge when we come to it." He paused, and Ellen sensed that he had indeed lost his train of thought, that it would be all right for her to speak.

"You want to take it to them, don't you, Tom."

"I want to make a statement. If not on camera, then at least a written statement. I don't want to hide from them this time. Nor do I want to impede the police investigation."

"Why would you want to go to them?"

"I want to help them."

"But why? They never did anything but hound you."

"First, if they find whoever did this, it'll clear my name."

"What's second?"

"There was a woman murdered last night, Ellen. She has to get the justice that Nancy never got."

"Is that it? I can tell, there's more you're not telling me."

"Let me say something else, first." Ellen nodded, waiting. "This is hard for me."

"Nothing should be too hard for you to tell me."

"I know." He forced another smile. "You're tough. You told me that already."

Tom looked away, squinted into the sliver of sunlight that had risen until it now fell across his face. He leaned back, away from it, and turned back to face Ellen.

"All my life, since I was a little kid, I had to hide what I was feeling. You know why I went into psychiatry?"

"I thought you did it to understand what had happened to Nancy."

"I did it so I could try to understand my father. You never met him, but he was, well, he wasn't normal." Tom stopped, lost in thought, and Ellen didn't prompt him. She had never heard Tom discuss his father in depth before, nor had the man been a topic of discussion in the home of Tom's mother, before the woman had died last year. It was as if the man had never existed. All Tom had told her was that his mother had divorced his father when he'd still been just a child. Ellen understood his secrecy; she had her own deep-seated problems concerning the area of biological families.

Tom said, "Anyway, I've been hiding in my head ever since I was a little boy. I've known for years how much you loved me. I never even doubt your feelings. I know how you supported me, and I appreciated it. I always knew, back then, years ago, when you were bringing in all of our money, that I'd be successful someday, that your faith in me wasn't misplaced. But I didn't really know, didn't fully *know* until last night, how you could really support me, and how much I need that support." Tom swallowed hard, and once more looked away. "Jesus, I'm half ashamed to even admit it."

"But you were the one who told *me* that it was all right to cry. You always told me that it was good to cry, to let your feelings out. My God, when my brother killed himself, I thought the conflicting feelings, grief and gratitude, then guilt, were going to kill me, until you made it better, until you helped me work through my grief."

"I tell my patients the same thing. Preaching and practicing are often different things."

"Tom, I only wish you had done it sooner."

"Me too."

"I want to flush the pills down the toilet, all of them."

Tom paused, and a haunted look passed across his face before he said, "Let me taper off. Stopping cold might do more damage than good."

"Would you mind if I count them?"

"You can dole them out."

"All right, then. After all our years together, you've finally come to the understanding that you can trust me, that you can count on me for emotional support." Ellen smiled to take the bitterness out of her words. "Fine, Doc. Now that you've established your keen analytical skills, what else was there?"

Tom was half smiling. Ellen could tell what an effort it took out of him. He said, "What?"

"The other thing, or things. The things you were going to tell me, but you had to talk to me about how you felt last night before you did." Ellen's look was level.

Tom shook his head. "*You* should have been the shrink."

"Tom."

"There're two things, really. First, Ellen, if the media isn't just overreacting—which has been known to happen—if this *is* the same thing as Nancy's murder, then it could be that whoever killed Nancy is back. In twenty years, not a peep, until last night. That just doesn't happen."

"Could it be his cycle? Could it take that long for the compulsion to build up?"

"Not a chance in the world. No serial killer in history has been able to quit for twenty years. And I'd know if similar murders were occurring anywhere else." Tom caught himself, then hurriedly said, "They'd come around to question me if a similar murder occurred in Bosnia. I can't figure out what happened.

127

But if it *is* him, and it won't take the police long to find that out for sure, then Nancy can get justice.''

"You want to cooperate with the police. All right, I can understand that.''

"You sure?''

"I'm sure. What's the other thing?''

"If he's back, Ellen. If he's back?'' Tom squeezed Ellen's hands, leaned over and stared into her eyes. "Dear God in heaven forgive me for saying this, but he might come after you.''

Ellen hadn't even considered that possibility. She began to tremble. She pulled her hands away, sat back, put the tips of her fingers of her right hand to her mouth, and stared at Tom in shock. "Dear God.''

"I had to tell you that, I had to warn you. We've got the guards here, we've got the alarm system, but until the killer's found, you can't live as you have been. You can't have the same patterns. For all we know, he didn't come after you because you were difficult to find. He might have done this first murder to drive us into the public eye, so he could find you.''

"But that would mean that the killer was after *you* instead of Nancy.''

"There're worse things than dying, Ellen. If you were a psychopath, and really wanted to hurt someone, would you kill them? Or would you kill someone they loved, so they'd have to live with that the rest of their lives?''

Ellen didn't know how to answer that. It was the first time that such a possibility had ever been presented to her. She couldn't even consider such a thing. She looked at Tom, puzzled and afraid.

At last she said, "How will you know if it's him?''

"I'll know.''

"How? Say what you want, there were months of publicity over Nancy's death, it was in the media every day, details, exclusive interviews with family, friends, and cops. Then there was the whole business with Terry's suspension. It was always something. Now this article in the *Sun-Trbune*. What if this is a copycat? Someone trying to set you up?''

"Then there's even more cause to worry. Ellen, my first wife was murdered that way, a copycat would want my second wife to die the same way. And if it *is* the same killer, and he's just beginning the game again . . ."

"Tom, I want a gun." Ellen didn't even try to hide her anxiety.

"We can get you one."

"More than one. I want one in every room, hidden, where I can get at them if I need them."

"All right."

"How will you know, Tom? How will you know if it's the original killer or if it's a copycat?"

"I'll know," Tom said, seeming to already consider himself a part of the investigation.

"How can you be so sure?"

"In spite of all the publicity, there were still things that were never released to the public, never discovered by the press. Things that even the most enterprising reporters never found out about."

"Like what."

"Ellen . . ."

"Goddamnit, Tom, it's my life in danger here! Tell me what they were!"

"Nancy's body had her purse—propped onto her lap. Her hands were wired to it."

"Oh, God."

"You sure you want to hear the rest?" Ellen didn't trust herself to speak. She swallowed, and nodded.

"The killer took the fetus of our unborn child out of Nancy's body. It was inside the purse."

Ellen felt herself getting lightheaded, felt herself swooning. She didn't know that she was falling off the chair until she felt Tom's strong arms stopping her from falling, holding her up, steadying her.

"Oh, Jesus, Ellen, I'm sorry, I shouldn't have said anything, I should have kept my mouth shut." He waited until her dizziness passed, holding her shoulders, hugging her. "You want some water?"

"I want some Xanax. I want some Valium. I want to take some pills and sleep until this whole nightmare is over. I want to—I don't know what I want to do."

Tom went over to the sink and got Ellen a glass of water.

Ellen said, "I already called off work."

"Good. I'll stay here with you."

Ellen now didn't want him to do that. She had too much to think about, too much to consider, and too much to do.

"No, don't do that. I'll be all right. I'll keep the alarm on, and I'll stay five feet from a phone. I'll call my father and have him bring me a gun. He can take me out to a gun shop in the suburbs. We'll use his Federal Officer ID to arm me."

"I finally reached Terry, he's coming over. I'll ask him to get you a weapon."

"Tom, do you trust him?"

"I don't know. Terry's always been—unstable. I *do* know that he didn't have anything to do with either of the murders."

"How?"

"He never showed any fear of being arrested, he pretended to grieve, but all he cared about was his job, how Nancy's death would affect his career. When he got suspended, he was devastated, all he'd ever wanted to do with his life was be a cop. He got his job back, but he's been getting more and more paranoid over the years. The truth is, if he was the killer, Terry could never have waited this long. He'd have done it long before now."

"Are you sure you want him in our *home?*"

"Can I ask you a question?"

Ellen nodded. She was expecting a question about Terry, so she was surprised at Tom's next statement.

"After Nancy died, my own mother asked me if I did it. Sat me down in her living room, handed me a drink, looked me in the eye, and asked me. You know what the cops did, and we know at least one of them who still thinks I'm guilty. And there's been a stigma on me ever since, for twenty years now, people always wanting to drop it into conversation, pretending to empathize with me when all they really want to do is talk about it, as if they're trying to find out what I know, as if I'll slip up and confess." Tom paused.

"You said you knew that I didn't have anything to do with either murder. You didn't know me twenty years ago—"

"I knew you."

Tom waved a hand, dismissing her words.

"I was your teacher's assistant, that's all. You didn't really know anything about me. You were just the young U of C whiz kid who followed everyone around, taking their picture. And you didn't know where I was last night, or what I'd done before I called." Tom stopped and stared at her, a confused expression on his face. "How can you be so sure? You never asked me a question about it, never expressed any doubt."

"I know."

"How?"

"Tom, I just know." He waited. Her answer hadn't been good enough. "I love you, you know that?" Tom nodded. "And I trust you. I *know* you're a good man, I have miles of evidence of that, Tom. You said to me earlier, you told me not to take something the wrong way. Now I ask the same thing of you.

"You want to know how I know you didn't do it? Because if you did, *you* wouldn't have been able to wait this long either, would you?"

The back doorbell rang, and Tom jumped, frightened. It could be Terry, it could be the police, it could even be reporters. Still, he seemed relieved, because now he didn't have to answer Ellen's question. She watched him walk to the back door, heard him speak his brother's name in greeting, heard them walk through the dining room, talking to each other in low, tense voices. Ellen waited until the door to the den closed before she got up and hurried upstairs to call her father, and to count the pills that were stacked in the medicine cabinet.

She was at the top step when she stopped dead, one foot on the carpet of the hallway, the other on the stair.

So much had happened, so much new information had to be processed. Ellen knew that she had to be careful here, couldn't jump to conclusions, or get paranoid. But once she was out of his orbit, free from his sight, once the bond of her love wasn't blinding her from rational thought, it seemed clear to her that Tom, after all these weeks of silence and denial and nightmares and withheld anger, was now, all of a sudden, out of a clear blue sky, going out of his way to be nice. Disclosing his drug abuse. Telling her he loved her. Saying he was going to help the police in their investigation.

Ellen stood there, thinking. He'd said he'd wanted her in the

131

shower with him because he was afraid he'd take drugs if he'd been in there all alone. Yet he had been, when he'd first come home. He'd gone into the bathroom by himself, when she'd been lying in bed.

Had he found out that she knew? Had he somehow rigged the medicine cabinet? Tom's sudden revelations began to take on a darker cast. He'd been endearing, holding her hands—but not when she'd been crying.

It seemed almost as if he were just trying to make certain that she was still on his side. As if he was making sure that she didn't suspect him of—anything. And now he was locked inside a small room with a man whose persona alone had frightened Ellen since the first day they'd met. What was *that* little family reunion all about?

"This is stupidity," Ellen said, and shook her head at her own suspicions. She hurried down the hallway. She had to call her father.

From the bedroom, where she could open the vent and listen in on Tom and his brother.

CHAPTER
17

The team that Dominick DiGrazia had been forced to command met at six that morning in the captain's office, in a corner of the upstairs Homicide squad room located in the 28th Police District station house. Lieutenant Matthews was not in attendance, nor was John Parker. DiGrazia was not looking forward to the meeting that was scheduled to take place in the lieutenant's office in less than forty-five minutes.

DiGrazia had handpicked the other four people who were in the room with him and Constantine:

James McMillan, a tall, middle-aged, black Violent Crimes detective, who'd been chosen because of his expertise on the unit's state-of-the-art computer; Vernon Hill, also black, a slender, tightly muscled detective who worked out of the Harrison District, and who—with the exception of DiGrazia himself—had more connections on the street and in the department than any cop DiGrazia knew; Kristina Stefaniak, a uniformed sergeant whose previous assignment in Youth Crimes had brought her into daily contact with more teenage hookers and criminals than the average Chicagoan would like to believe existed; and the only non-Violent Crimes officer in the room, Thomas Eberhardt, who worked in the police laboratory, and who was not only an expert at collating evidence from a scene, but who also held a doctorate in the delicate, controversial art of forensic sciences.

With the exception of Constantine, all of the officers had received a call from DiGrazia around 3:00 A.M., and were requested without further explanation to report to him at 5:45 at the Chicago Avenue station. With the exception of Constantine, they were all veterans whom DiGrazia had worked with before on difficult cases. Along with Constantine, every other officer in the room had Dominick DiGrazia's respect.

DiGrazia had told them a partial truth: that due to the high media involvement of this case, he'd been ordered to put together a string of specialists who would work in a completely covert capacity. He'd also told them that he'd picked each of them for this special assignment due to their intelligence, savvy, experience, and expertise in their individual fields. Although that was all true, he didn't tell them about the shouting match that he and Matthews had had in the squad room after DiGrazia had returned from his visit to Schmidt's, although he knew that each of them would more than likely hear about it soon enough. He didn't tell them what leverage he had used to keep the lieutenant from taking him off the case, and that they would *not* hear about, as it had been said in private discussion, behind the closed door of the lieutenant's office.

Although DiGrazia wasn't happy about having been forced to use a string, he knew that they would come in handy, particularly if there wasn't an immediate break in the case. They would most certainly perform a lot of the footwork for him and Constantine, save them a lot of time. They were a good group, and even though he was not pleased at having been forced to use their services, he would indeed now use them for all he could get out of them.

As the situation had been somewhat explained to them, each of them had agreed to their personal involvement in the assignment. Everyone knew what this was: a once-in-a-lifetime opportunity, a detective's dream come true.

Now, with cream and sugar added to the coffee that Constantine had delivered, doughnuts in hand, they listened as Constantine told them what she'd discovered during the long night.

"There's almost no doubt that the killings are the same, even if we're not certain that it's the same perp. There is *nothing* in the files—" There were a number of snickers as Constantine said this, and someone muttered Schmidt's name in union with a curse—"I had a clerk go through the morgues at both newspapers, asked her to do a Lexis and Nexis search—there are copies of everything printed off that in your files—and from what we got, this is not only one disturboid son of a bitch, but everything else matches, too, right down to the 'message' in the purse." Constantine paused, patted the jacket of her suit, trying to locate her cigarettes. She remembered where she was, and stopped. The captain would have her ass if he found out she'd smoked in his office.

"What message was that?" Stefaniak asked.

"There was a fetus in it."

"Hers?"

"Yes. And that was never reported to the press. Schmidt somehow managed to keep that completely in-house."

Hill put his doughnut down on the captain's desk. DiGrazia waited, but nobody asked if the murder could have been done by some radical pro-lifer. He'd picked his string carefully.

"Her name's Veronica Davene." Constantine spelled it out. "AKA Ronnie Day, AKA Roni Divine. Seventeen years old, with eleven arrests for prostitution since she came up here from Biloxi a little under two years ago."

"She living in Uptown?"

"Last known address. Off Sheridan Road, up in the Fifties. Exact address's in my report. The file's long—Detective DiGrazia has requisitioned interview room three for you for one and a half hours after this meeting, so you'll all have the chance to sit down, read it, and talk it over between you before you leave the station. Our phone and pager numbers are on the last page of the report, in case something's unclear and you need to ask us any questions."

DiGrazia said to Stefaniak, "Veronica will have been gone for two or three days, maybe longer. Get a handle on who's been hanging around, any specific john she'd grown inordinately close to; see if anyone'd promised to marry her—" He waved his arm in a magnanimous gesture—"to take her away from all this."

Stefaniak nodded, while Constantine looked over at DiGrazia, surprised. He said, "I'll give you a grand to grease whatever snitches you think deserve it. I'll get it authorized and be reimbursed later."

"What is this Nexis-Lexis shit? Can't we just get the fucking files away from Schmidt?" Vernon Hill asked.

"I'm working on it," DiGrazia said without explanation, then nodded for Constantine to continue.

"She was murdered somewhere else, her body dropped four blocks away from here, in the dead-end alley next to the Blockbuster."

DiGrazia interrupted her. "Vernon? I want you over there the second you've finished reading your file, see what you can find out. That alley's used as a parking lot from the time they open until they close, people picking up and dropping off videos. I know it's a long shot, but I want a list of everybody who rented videos after 5:00 P.M. last night. Name, address, and phone number." He didn't insult Hill by telling him to ask if one of the customers might have mentioned anything strange happening in the alley.

"What if they cite confidentiality?"

"Bring the manager's confidential ass in here, and he can wait until I have time to question him.

"I'm meeting with representatives from the mayor's office, the state's attorney's office, and some guy from the corporation counsel in the lieutenant's office in," he checked his watch, "thirty-five minutes. I don't think we're going to have a lot of trouble getting warrants, or any other legal permissions."

Hill nodded, and Constantine continued.

"Dropping the girl in the alley was a reckless act. A crazy act. As Detective DiGrazia said, that alley's well used. But the killer wasn't stupid about it, he'd broken the lights earlier." Hill began taking furious notes. Constantine said, "There were four of them altogether, we're operating under the assumption that they were smashed, shot out with a high-powered pellet pistol, though we haven't found any pellets, or somehow otherwise deactivated sometime before nightfall, say before eight o'clock. The perp would have backed his car up in there, all the way back, blocking the view from the street. He could have done almost everything before he got to the alley, the positioning of the corpse could have been done inside of a minute or two."

"We got pictures?" Eberhardt asked. "I can get them copied at the lab in ten minutes."

"We've got pictures. Can you keep a lid on them?" DiGrazia asked. Eberhardt nodded his head.

"Oh, yes. Could have had it done already, I'd have known what this was about. We have to number and mark each proof these days, and we initial the envelopes going out and coming in. No pictures go out without authorization. I personally trained the kid who worked the lab last night. If she isn't in a mental ward by now, she'll tell me what's been going on, and who's been asking for copies."

"We don't have to worry about that, we took all the pictures ourselves; stills and video."

Stefaniak said, "To cut down the risk of anyone selling some to the press?"

"Opportunistic cops are the least of our worries now. The lid was taken off several hours ago. Now, we're just trying a little damage control. You know the drill, the less they know, the better."

Constantine said, "And we allow Veronica her dignity."

"Eberhardt?" Stefaniak said. She wouldn't let it go; the victim was the sort of girl she had worked with every day, before her elevation to Violent Crimes. "You make copies, who'll have access to them?"

"Nobody. Not a chance. This isn't public access information. Anyone who gives them out will be on the unemployment line before the day shift's over."

"That's a relief," DiGrazia admitted. "Which brings me to the press. They've been told to go to the media public-relations room at headquarters and await a statement from the department spokesperson. We know that's not going to be taken seriously. Any reporter asking around downstairs is to be immediately directed to one of the lieutenants, who'll show them the telephone banks, and let them interview whomever they want to showcase for promotion.

"*This* group will operate in total secrecy; we do not officially exist. All the media's been told so far is that there are certain distinct similarities between this murder and a twenty-year-old, open homicide. That's all they're *going* to be told, until we crack this." There was no response. DiGrazia nodded at Constantine.

"That's just about all I have, Detective. Except that the medical examiner's people are playing it as closely as we are. They're not as tightly secure as us, but still, they got a sheet over Veronica's body, and they put her on the top stack. A reporter who sneaks in there with a forklift could get a picture of her, maybe. It's getting warm out, so murders are up. They won't be doing the autopsy until sometime later this morning, or early afternoon."

"Autopsy report *is* public access," McMillan said.

"The press is already speculating, and besides, with any luck, by the time they get it we'll have a written confession." All eyes turned to DiGrazia, as if trying to see if he were kidding. He was not widely known as a kidder. He looked at McMillan.

"All right, Jimmy, after you leave the interview room, I want you working that computer. Punch into the Department of Corrections. I want the names of every felon released in the last three months—"

"What?"

"Who's been incarcerated for the last, say, nineteen years." McMillan's face lost its look of disbelief. "If our killer's the same guy who did Nancy Moran, he seems to have been away somewhere. I was hoping he'd killed himself, but now, my money says he was in a penitentiary."

McMillan said, "You want mental institutions?"

DiGrazia raised his eyebrows. "Can that be accessed?"

"The one at Pontiac can be, for violent felons. I can check on the state joints, but you're right, we probably won't have much luck there."

"That's great, Pontiac'll be good enough. I don't think our killer'll be a guy whose been in outpatient therapy with some private hospital. See if anybody's been in there for the last—let's check it for nineteen years, or however far back the computer records go." McMillan nodded.

"Kristina, I need you in Uptown. Find out anything you can about Veronica Davene. There are two officers on the way over to Biloxi, to work with her parents, look for letters, dig into them about anything she might have told them on the phone. On this end, I want to know everything you can discover about her from the day she hit town. Particularly who her pimp is, who she's been set up with, if she had any steady freaks, specifically men over forty. You don't need me telling you the rest."

"I didn't need you telling me *that*." The anger in her tone was evident. DiGrazia ignored it.

"When's the FBI going to take over?" Eberhardt wasn't smiling.

"As soon as they can link it to another crime in another state. Don't think they're not working on it, they want a VICAP sheet yesterday."

"Fuck 'em," Stefaniak said.

DiGrazia said, "We're in agreement. As far as public help and response, we have the names, addresses, and phone numbers of some dozen people who're willing to give us statements, who were in the area of the crime scene last night. We've also got several amateur videos that're being analyzed. They've got still shots of the white male who originally found the body, though I don't think he'll do us a lot of good, even if we find him.

"All the witnesses will be interviewed by detectives from Matthew's and Bailey's units, hopefully today, and Officer Constantine will get copies of all these reports. She'll go through every one, looking for any out-of-the-ordinary similarities. We'll also have an eight-hundred number hotline set up for tips, AT&T promised it'd be on-line by eight. We all know how much good these usually do, but at this point, nothing can be overlooked. Uniformed officers will staff the phones, and others will check out every tip. They find anything of value—and I'll personally be going over the reports from every call that comes in—and they'll pass it on to me or Constantine. We'll decide who to call to check out what." Stunned by DiGrazia's statement, Constantine turned quickly toward him, her mouth open, before she caught herself.

Eberhardt saved her further embarrassment by asking, "You want me at the lab, Dominick?"

"Absolutely. I want an analysis on every fiber, every hair, every piece of soot vacuumed off Veronica's body or her clothing. I want her eyes checked, her finger and toenails. I want her teeth printed, Tom, for partials. Her upper teeth aren't hers; I want you to print the bridge, the killer might have taken them out so she couldn't commit suicide by swallowing them, and then put them back in later, before he dumped her body. Whatever hasn't already been done, I want done before the autopsy.

"Now, after you make the copies, I want the original pictures locked in a vault, and I want the negatives destroyed. I want DNA samples taken from Veronica *and* the fetus. *And* I want a lid on this death like this city hasn't seen since Harold Washington died. The media can speculate all they want, and they can report whatever they want, but not one word of it will come from this team. Lieutenant Matthews has—" DiGrazia smiled, "—*agreed* to be the spokesman who'll discuss any breakthroughs we might have with the media."

There was a general smattering of laughter, and DiGrazia caught Constantine staring at him. She rolled her eyes.

Hill said, "What else?"

"Read the files, people, even the boring pages. I want this killer pinched. We might get lucky and catch a break at the lab, but you all know as well as I do how most cases get broken. We need a break from somewhere, we need a break from some*one*."

"Nobody caught any breaks twenty years ago," Stefaniak said.

"I wasn't working the case twenty years ago," DiGrazia replied. "Now dump *every*thing in the trash, coffee cups, Dunkin' Donuts box, crumbs, the whole works. I'll take it out myself before the captain comes back in here."

"He doesn't know we're in here?" Hill was incredulous.

"He isn't a part of this. Now listen up. We will be working out of the basement, in the old gym, it's all being set up right now, so everything should be in place for us before nine. We'll have six temporary phone lines down there, one for each of us, the numbers are in your reports. Our desk will be set up against the outside wall, in the corner, on the other side of the boxing ring. We'll work closely together on this, word of mouth and field notes *only*, written reports only when there's time, and there won't *be* a lot of time.

"I've cleared overtime, so sleep when you can, catch a few hours at home, and don't worry about it. It'll all be covered until this thing is put to bed." DiGrazia paused, and looked each member of the string in the eye, slowly, from left to right.

"At this time, there are over a hundred officers involved in this case. We are six of them, and the *only* officers who are working out of the public eye. Nobody knows about us, and as far as I'm concerned, nobody's going to find out about us.

"Still, as usual, there's talk. Most of it's bullshit, but there's gonna be a lot of indignation against us out there from the other detectives, in particular—and unfortunately—from our colleagues in Violent Crimes. Don't let it bother you. And don't let it get in the way of your work.

"We'll meet in the basement at," he checked his watch, "say, five, just to compare notes, see if anything gels. If you're in the middle of something, don't worry, but call in around then, leave a message so we'll know. We have a job to do, let's do it."

He watched them dump their trash and file out of the room, a group of dedicated police officers, flattered and impressed with the enormity of their assignment. Constantine waited with Di-Grazia, anxiously. When the last officer was out of the room, she went over and closed the door.

"You want *me* to pass assignments on to *this* group of heavy hitters?"

"They're all professionals, and they can all take orders as well as they give them. I didn't pick any bitchers or moaners, Janice, I don't ever deal with personalities."

"Right. That's why you chose police work as your profession."

Constantine was wearing a baggy, wrinkled suit. She'd combed her hair and applied makeup to her face when she'd stopped off at her home to change. She seemed alert and awake. DiGrazia didn't ask her if she'd gotten any sleep.

"Here I come back and see the press, see the lieutenant and you inside the prick's office, I said to myself, 'Janice, you're out of plainclothes before you ever got *into* them.' The lieutenant's going nuts, going to—" Constantine lowered her voice in a pale imitation of an angry male's—" 'have your balls this time.' Next thing I know, we're in a basement meeting with Parker, and you're commanding a detail." She paused, waiting for a response, but DiGrazia just stood looking at her.

"What the hell did you *do*, Nicky?"

"I compromised." That was all he intended to give her. He said, "I didn't want a team. Unlimited use of patrol officers would

141

have been enough. I thought you and I were all the job needed. The lieutenant and his masters thought differently."

"Just us, right? You to do the detective work, me to run for coffee." DiGrazia's eyes narrowed, and Constantine added hurriedly, "But Matthews, he's still pissed off?"

"Let's just say the two of us aren't on speaking terms."

"What about what you said at the meeting? What makes you think Roni's been gone for two or three days?"

"I don't think she was a random victim." DiGrazia did not elaborate. Constantine looked at him, thoughtfully.

"Nicky, can I talk freely here?"

"It's the captain's office; if it's bugged, I didn't do it."

"Well, if we're partners, I need to know everything that happens. I'm not asking you to tell me the names of your rabbis, and I'm not asking you to give up any street informants. But if I'm working on this with you, my ass is right next to yours, and if that's the way it's going to be, I have to know what happened with the lieutenant."

"He wanted to take me off the case."

"No kidding. Got any more surprises?"

"I convinced him that wouldn't be prudent."

"Goddamnit, Nick, quit playing games. How?"

"He found out I lied to him, found out what the murder was. Found out from the *press* mind you, Janice." DiGrazia gave her a fake shudder. "When I got back from Schmidt's, we had a little argument in the squad room, and it spilled over into his office. When I finally calmed him down, I told him that if he took us off the case, we were taking everything with us, that we'd destroy everything we had. He wouldn't get any pictures, any notes, the crime-scene sketches, we wouldn't even give up the fingerprints taken from Veronica's corpse."

"You were serious?"

"Oh, yes."

"You spoke for me, too. Put my neck on the chopping block, Nick. Twenty years I been on this job, and I ain't got no *doc*-to-rate to fall back on if I get canned."

"We're working together, aren't we?" His tone was cold, and he stared at her as he spoke.

Constantine shrugged. "Ah, shit. You hadn't done it, I'd be in a patrol car right this minute, counting the minutes 'till eight."

"You sure you're all right with it?"

Constantine had to think for a moment before she said, "Use my name as freely as you want. Especially if it's to get under a lieutenant's flesh. So what was the compromise; we give him what we have, and we get to stay on the case?"

"He demanded a high-profile crew. He wanted twenty officers; I talked him down to the six of us and several—let me just say specialists—that you *don't* need to know about. Parker backed me up with Matthews. So here's the deal: All the public detectives and uniforms on the case can come out of his group of personal pets, and he'll be the liaison with the press, so he's happy, and he and the rest of them will get to bask in the glory when we crack the case."

"If we crack it." Constantine paused. DiGrazia looked at his watch, and made a short, impatient motion with his hand. Reluctantly, Constantine said, "I don't think the doctor did it, Nick."

"I don't think so either."

Constantine looked at him oddly, then nodded. "Just so we're clear on that. I read the *Sun-Tribune* article." Constantine hesitated, and DiGrazia inclined his head, indicating that she continue. Still, she hesitated.

DiGrazia impatiently said, "I didn't snatch you out of patrol to stifle your personality, Janice."

"I just don't want to step too hard here."

"Stomp, Janice. You're the senior member of the team."

"Well I'm glad *that* bullshit's out of the way." Constantine looked at him steadily, and said, "I read the article, and I asked around. I think your ex-partner's as much of a paranoid drunk as the Vampire."

"You think right."

"He was trying to railroad the doctor. He went nuts when he was ordered to leave the guy alone."

"That was even before the city settled the suit. Before I partnered up with him. You're right again, he couldn't handle it. Mike didn't believe that anyone could order him away from a suspect."

Constantine said, "My money, off the top of my head, says it's the Vampire, or Frank."

"We'll be checking everyone out, but I don't know that it's either one of them. I don't think the two killers are the same."

"You mentioned that earlier. Why not?"

"Two reasons, mostly." DiGrazia looked away, collecting his thoughts.

Constantine prompted him by saying, "What you were referring to before, in the cafeteria. The things that weren't the same."

"Right. First, if it was one of the Morans, why didn't he commit the *exact* same crime, with the exact same sort of victim? Why did he choose a prostitute this time, instead of a medical student's wife, or a doctor's wife, or even Dr. Moran's wife? The newspaper article said he's been married again for almost eighteen years.

"Second, Veronica wasn't found in a church. Why didn't the killer re-create the scene exactly? Why didn't he kill her in the chapel at the University of Chicago, where Nancy Moran was found, or at any other church? Why do it somewhere else, and bring the body downtown? How hard would it be to break into a church? If it was the same killer, I think he'd have done that."

"So you think it's a copycat?" Constantine shook her head, defeatedly. "Then we're at square one."

"We've still got suspects, I could be wrong."

"There were no sperm samples or evidence of sexual assault, Nick, and yet you keep saying 'he.' Have you excluded a female suspect?"

DiGrazia hadn't ever considered the possibility. He looked hard at Constantine, shook his head. "You think a woman could have done this?"

"I think a woman's capable of every form of conduct a man's capable of."

Constantine walked over to the captain's desk, saying over her shoulder, "You want me at the meeting, too?"

"You bet your ass I do. I want backup as to everything that's said. They'll leave me hanging if they can, even with Deputy— what are you doing?"

Constantine had picked up the trash can. She looked at Di-

Grazia, then back down at the can. "Dumping the trash." DiGrazia walked over and snatched the can away from her.

"Give me that. You'll be catching enough shit without those people out there seeing you dumping garbage. We've got a few minutes before the meeting. Go have a cigarette. But go outside, the brass'll be here anytime. Meet me in Matthews's office at six-thirty sharp." DiGrazia was walking to the door with the wastepaper basket in his hand when it was pushed open by a uniformed officer who stuck his head inside and informed DiGrazia that Mike Schmidt, the former sergeant, was on line three, saying it was of the utmost importance that he speak with DiGrazia immediately.

CHAPTER
18

The events of the previous night had caught up with Ellen Moran. She could not, absolutely could *not* believe what she was now doing.

Yet she couldn't stop herself from doing it.

Alone in the bedroom, leaning directly in front of the vent, sitting in a small chair which she'd taken from in front of her bathroom makeup mirror, Ellen felt on edge, nervous, ashamed, and more than a little guilty, as she listened in on her husband's conversation with his brother, Terry.

Their opening conversational gambits only seemed to have reestablished the fact that Terry was still nothing more than a miserable, small-time, self-obsessed loser.

"You've been drinking, Terry." Tom's voice was strongly accusatory.

"I had a couple." Terry was mumbling, his tone apologetic. "Jesus Christ, who wouldn't? Man, I read the paper, read what Schmidt said. That was bad enough. Then I listened in on the talk over my radio. They were out looking for *me*, Tom! I heard the pickup order come over my own radio." Terry repeated himself, as if he disbelieved his own statement. "They were out looking for *me* . . ."

"I'm lost, Terry, wait a second. You have to back up a little bit—"

Terry continued, seemingly uninterested in backing up.

"Soon as I heard that, I went underground. Everything else I know, I picked up from watching TV in a room at the Avenue Motel. I passed out watching TV, trying to see if they had a citywide alert out for me yet." Ellen heard Terry grunt. "You're damn right I had a few drinks."

"You should have come straight over here."

"I tried to call you for an hour straight, your phone was off the hook. The TV was doing live remotes all night, dredging everything up as soon as they got wind that it was a possible repeat of—of what happened to Nancy. I kept waiting to see if they were going to blame me, convict me without a trial."

"Nobody's blaming you—"

"I don't know how long I slept, but it couldn't have been much after five when I called you. Your line was busy. I don't know what I'd have done if you hadn't finally put your phone back on the hook."

"Going 'underground' wasn't a good idea, Terry."

Tom's voice was cautious. Was he finally beginning to understand that his older brother Terry was dangerous?

"I'm in a lot of trouble, Tom, I think they're gonna nail me to the wall for this. I've been afraid to go anywhere near my apartment. Right after I left you, when I went and . . ." Terry's voice trailed off. Ellen could picture him looking around, wondering if his own brother had bugged the room. Or perhaps he thought the police had. She imagined him looking at the roses on the wallpaper, at the prints on Tom's walls. She had a sense that he was looking up, had an image of Terry spotting her, and Ellen inadvertently leaned back. She shook her head and leaned forward again.

Terry said, "You know, what we talked about when I met you at the bar? I turned off my pager, left my radio, gun, wallet, beeper, and shield in a locker at Water Tower Place. Then after I returned to duty—"

"Returned to *duty?!*" Ellen flinched as Tom half shouted. "Returned to *what* duty? You told me you were getting off at midnight! When I left you, we had a plan worked out, you said you were going to—"

"I was almost back at the station when I got ordered to work overtime."

"Oh, *Christ*, Terry, why didn't you call me and let me know?"

"For what? It happens all the time. Besides, I didn't even know where you were, and you had enough on your mind last night. I figured you'd come straight home, and I don't like to call you here. I know how your old lady feels about me. And then, after everything fell apart, your line was busy . . ."

"Ellen doesn't—"

"The hell she doesn't."

"Terry, I called you over and over this morning. I paged you, and I left four messages for you before you finally called me back."

"And I returned your call after you put your phone back on the hook!" Terry shouted it, then composed himself. "Now I'm sorry I even called in and checked the messages. You got any idea how many people been trying to call me since midnight? And tried to beep me? I listened to that little motherfucker until it almost drove me *nuts*. I put it on vibrate, then heard it shifting around in the drawer. I finally just shut it off."

"Terry, does your answering machine have cassettes, or digital microchips?"

"How the hell would I know?"

"Did you at least try and erase your messages?"

"I don't know how! It took me six months to figure out how to answer it from a different phone, for God's sake."

Ellen heard her husband mumble something, but she couldn't make out what it was. Had Tom put his hands over his face? Was his mouth covered? And where had Terry been last night, when had he met with Tom? And how could he talk in such a droning manner about something that quite possibly could destroy all of their lives?

What was going on? They were obviously in far closer contact than Ellen had been led to believe. Tom almost never spoke his brother's name. Terry's statement implied that he kept in close contact with Tom, but he never called him here at home. So he obviously called him at one of Tom's offices. Tom certainly had enough opportunities to meet with whomever he wanted without Ellen ever finding out about it. She fought down a sense of betrayal. She told herself that Tom just didn't want to upset her; he knew how she felt about his brother.

And who could blame her? Terry's end of the conversation was a textbook example of narcissistic behavior. Tom's picture was on the front page of the paper, next to an article that nearly convicted him of killing his first wife, and his own brother was talking about it as if it were ancient history.

Tom wasn't taking it dispassionately, though. Ellen couldn't remember the last time he had spoken with such animated intensity. Then again, she couldn't remember the last time she'd heard him speak with Terry. At their father's funeral, she guessed it was. Ten, eleven years ago. Terry hadn't bothered to even show up when Ellen's brother, Todd, had died. She had never forgiven him for that.

Tom was still mumbling. Ellen, frustrated, stood up carefully, hoping the polished wood beneath her feet didn't squeak and give her away to the men sitting directly below her. Just as carefully, she lowered herself to her knees, grimacing in pain and anger as the wrenched muscle in her back screamed. She lowered herself to the floor, stretched out, and the pain lessened. She lifted herself onto her elbows, with one on either side of the vent, lying with her face directly above the outlet.

She could hear Tom clearly now as he said, "You didn't answer your beeper, and you shut down your radio and had it inside a locker at Water Tower Place. The mall would have been closed down by the time you got there—"

"I go in anytime I want. It's one of the places I use for toilet breaks—"

"—which means the security guards there can make a statement to that effect."

"Water Tower Place's two blocks away from where the body was found. A statement from a rent-a-cop won't do me a whole lot of good, Tom. It'll only make things worse."

Ellen heard Tom groan, heard a pounding noise, as if one of them had slammed their fist down on Tom's desk.

Tom said, "If we knew the definite time frame, if we knew exactly when they found the body, we could work around it.

TV's for shit, I watched TV and listened to the radio on and off since the first reporter called me. They only said the body was found sometime after midnight. Is there *any*one in the department you can trust, Terry? Is there anyone you can call who can tell you anything?"

"No one."

"You're telling me that not one officer out of all those thousands of—"

"That's what I'm telling you." Terry's voice lost its monotonous tone, became as accusatory as Tom's. "I lost out on any chance to have friends in this department twenty years ago, I shouldn't have to tell *you* that."

"Nancy's death cost all of us a lot."

"You seem to be doing all right."

"You son of a bitch."

"I didn't mean—"

"The hell you didn't mean it, Terry. You listen to me, goddamn you." Ellen could picture him leaning forward, pointing a finger at Terry. "I'm the only one in this family who's ever been able to have a long-term relationship. I'm the only one in this family who went on to college and didn't run away to the service as soon as I was old enough. Whatever I've got, I earned."

"From a lawsuit."

"I put myself through medical school—"

"You were the youngest kid! You don't even *know* what we had to live through."

"I remember it all! I remember every goddamn fucking incident! I caught my share."

"You weren't the one he did it to, you were the baby! He *loved* you! Ma took you with her when she left! *We* were stuck with him, not you!"

"I was eleven years old when she left him! You think I don't remember?"

Ellen pulled her head back as the two men shouted at each other. She heard a chair scrape back; one of them had risen to his feet.

Terry, underground or not, would still be armed.

"Sit down, Tom."

Terry's voice stopped Ellen from racing downstairs to try and protect her husband. She wished there was a gun in the house. She wished she had one in her hands this very moment. She closed her eyes and fought back her hatred as Tom's voice floated up to her, powerful and strong.

"I remember that man just as well as you do. I still have nightmares, too." Tom's tone had been bitter; now it turned cold. "You and Frank both used him as your excuse for every failure either one of you ever had. I didn't. I went on to college, I did something with my life."

"You sure did." Was that said sarcastically? Ellen couldn't tell. She wished she could see Terry's face.

"*I* didn't kill Nancy, Terry."

"Did I say you did?"

Ellen was now certain that Terry was being cute. She had to once again literally stop herself from leaping to her feet, running down there, and ordering that son of a bitch out of her house. She heard Tom sigh.

"Before we get back to last night, let me ask you one question. Where did Schmidt get all the information he talked about in that article? How did he get the idea that Nancy was about to leave me when she got killed?" Tom raised his voice sharply. "Don't light that, we don't allow smoking in the house." Ellen heard Terry take in a deep breath of air, then expel it. He'd obviously lighted his cigarette anyway. She'd be able to smell it in a minute. She heard Tom's steel trash can being dragged across the hardwood floor. She winced.

"Looks like I'm not the only one who had a few drinks last night."

"There's one beer can in there. Use it as an ashtray."

"How about I use the pill bottle?" Pill bottle? What pill bottle?

Terry said, "You got bigger problems to worry about than secondhand smoke, brother." Ellen heard Terry pull in another drag, rubbing it in.

Terry said, "Schmidt probably got it all from Nancy's family. Remember how they acted when you got married again so soon after Nancy was killed. They probably never forgave you for that. Or Schmidt might have made it up. You read the article, it made more out of his personal crusade against you than it did about the killing. She wrote—that reporter—about all the empty whiskey bottles and beer cans all over his house, how filthy the place is, the way Schmidt kept disappearing from the living room during the interviews, then came back smelling of booze."

Tom used a psychiatric trick: Without advance warning, he abruptly changed the subject on his brother. "You're acting awfully calmly for somebody who's worried about getting 'nailed to the wall,' Terry."

"You have a calming effect on me, broham; shrinks always do."

"Maybe it's because you weren't mentioned in the article this time."

"Didn't have my picture either, a mug shot of me on the front page." There was a long pause. Ellen could imagine her husband raising his eyes and looking up at her, staring at the ceiling as he tried to calm himself down. He would have understood by now that when dealing with Terry, exposing anger was a mistake.

Tom's voice seemed filled with compassion now as it filtered up through the vent.

"Terry, listen to me. Listen to me carefully. I'm not analyzing you, I'm not saying this to insult you. I'm not even mad at you. But you need help. We talked about all this last night, before any of this even came out, and we made a plan. You should never have gone off and done what you did."

"What else was I supposed to do? They had my ass cold! I was out of communication for over two hours, and they were out looking for me!"

"You should have changed the plan. As soon as you got called for overtime, you should have revised it, you should have done *something* rather than taking the risk of throwing away the only thing you have left."

"I ain't got nothing left."

CHAPTER
19

Janice Constantine stood around the corner from the station house door, in front of the parking lot, out of sight of the brass that were beginning to make their way into the building. She felt a little like a schoolgirl, sneaking a cigarette outside, between classes.

The day-shift captains and lieutenants would be inside the station by now, getting their reports from their midnight counterparts, preparing themselves for the day. The Chicago Avenue station was one of the premier assignments in the city, and nobody wanted to lose that duty, not the patrol officers, not the sergeants, not even the lieutenants or captains and commanders.

Which was why nobody dared smoke inside the building during the daytime.

Janice had plenty of company. Several other smokers were out here with her, in the coolness of the early morning. Uniformed officers and plainclothes patrol officers, TAC team members and Homicide and Burglary detectives mingled freely, without any arrogance, unseparated by their status. Minority bonding, the shunned smokers thrust into a guilty union with each other. The early morning traffic whirled around them; horns and sirens blared around the corner on Chicago Avenue.

The early night shift—working eleven to seven, the late night shift worked twelve to eight; there were six staggered shifts throughout the day, to ensure that there would always be plenty of officers on the street at any given time to handle whatever came up—would soon be ending, and the smokers among the early day shift workers were getting in their last few puffs before going in to change into their uniforms or to otherwise prepare themselves before the 6:45 A.M. roll call.

Constantine stood alone, though, purposely stood apart from the other officers. She was thinking, with her back to the small crowd. She had done nothing more than wish them a good morning whenever one of them caught her eye. They wanted to talk to her, she could tell, wanted to find out what she knew. Gossip traveled as quickly within the department as it did in the penitentiary; everyone wanted to know about the killing, and about Constantine's sudden promotion.

She didn't plan to give them the opportunity to find out anything, as there was still too much she had to discover for herself.

Constantine heard quick, light footsteps behind her, but did not turn around. She lit another cigarette from the butt of her last, tossed the filter into the street. Detective Tina Rosen of Violent Crimes was now standing directly in front of her. It would be Rosen, Constantine thought. She was nosy enough to be a reporter. Pushy enough to be one, too.

"Hi, Connie!" Rosen was smiling broadly. Constantine hated it when people called her Connie.

"Tina."

"Got a promotion, I heard?"

Constantine smiled ruefully. "Some promotion. Temporary assignment."

"Yeah, but it's Homicide." Rosen paused, lording her position over Constantine for a moment, before saying, "Working with DiGrazia?"

Constantine nodded cautiously.

Rosen shivered. "He's a creepy guy, but a hunk." She yawned. "Long night." Rosen looked away casually, then back at Constantine. "I heard he shut down the crime scene last night. Heard he wouldn't let but one other criminalist inside." Rosen

154

laughed and shook her head at what she saw as DiGrazia's arrogance. "College guys . . . You catch any hell over that?"

Constantine looked at her. Rosen waited. Constantine let her wait.

Undeterred, Rosen said, "You should have heard the fight they had while you were gone. DiGrazia and Matthews, I mean. They had a real blowout." Rosen paused again, as Constantine figured out her program.

Rosen was giving a little, hoping for a little something back in return. The way she was condescending to Constantine, Rosen could have put a curling iron to her cheek and Constantine wouldn't tell her anything about the case.

"I heard," was all she said. Rosen raised her eyebrows and waited, expecting more. Constantine looked away, trying to appear deep in thought.

"Oh, shit," Rosen said, and the tone of dread in her voice made Constantine look back at her. "Well, take a look at who's here *now.*"

A black Lincoln Town Car was pulling to the curb. A plainclothes officer was driving it, a woman. The back door opened and a short, dark man in a well-tailored suit—the second most powerful man in the Chicago Police Department—stepped out. He leaned back in to say a few words to the driver. Constantine dropped her cigarette and stepped on it as First Deputy Police Superintendent Louis Alvarez turned toward the building. She remembered DiGrazia's statement to Parker, down in the basement less than an hour ago: "I've got his man coming to the meeting, John." Referring to the superintendent's man. Nobody was closer to the chief than Louis Alvarez.

"Morning," he said, giving the crowd a brief, bright smile. Of the dozen or so officers now on the sidewalk, only one still held a lit cigarette in the presence of the vehemently antismoking crusader, the man who had instituted the no-smoking policy within the department. Detective Tina Rosen made a point of taking a deep drag as the boss passed them.

"Fuck it, I'm off duty," she said.

Most of the officers smiled and returned his greeting formally, stiffly, while two officers ignored him completely, and one brazenly walked over and tried to begin a conversation. Alvarez held his hand up and walked hurriedly away from the man. Constantine heard him tell the officer to take his complaint through the proper channels.

The rebuffed officer stood, insulted and humiliated, on the sidewalk, and waited until the deputy superintendent was out of earshot before whispering, "Fuckin' spic."

Constantine lit a final cigarette, and took several deep puffs. DiGrazia hadn't told her that the deputy superintendent would be at the meeting.

"That's your hunk's secret weapon."

Constantine ignored Rosen's statement.

Rosen wouldn't let it go. "Gotta be in some pretty heavy-duty trouble this time, to have to call in the biggest gun in his arsenal to get him out of it."

"He's got it under control. Alvarez's probably just showing up for a briefing." Constantine felt that saying this much alone wouldn't break any confidences, or compromise her loyalty.

"He's queer as a three-dollar bill, you know."

"*Alvarez?* He's been married to the same woman since he was still in the academy. See his license plate? CPD 35. That's the number of years since he joined the department, and got married."

"Not him; DiGrazia."

Constantine took a last, deep drag on her cigarette, then flicked it into the gutter. She turned her entire body so she confronted Rosen straight on. She took two steps, got right into Rosen's face, towering over the smaller detective, outweighing her by forty pounds.

Constantine said, "How'd you figure that out, he try to suck your dick?" Rosen flinched at the insult, but said nothing. Constantine shook her head, and began to walk toward the front of the building. Tina Rosen did a little side step and moved hurriedly out of her way. Their shoulders brushed. Constantine put some muscle into it. Rosen didn't say anything, at least not while Constantine was within the sound of her voice.

CHAPTER
20

"I ain't got nothing left." Terry spoke the words, and Ellen felt her face twist into a hateful grimace. The two of them had been plotting—had Tom's nightmare been a sham? A ruse he'd conceived in order to get out of the house and meet his brother? No, Ellen decided, that just couldn't be true. Nobody could have acted out a nightmare as well as Tom had last night.

As always, Ellen was unable to blame the man she loved, so she turned her anger toward Terry.

Ellen unconsciously shook her head in loathing of her brother-in-law. A second ago, he'd been breezily accusing her husband of murder, and now here he was, thinking only of himself again, as he sent Tom the message that his own life's losses were somehow Tom's fault. As if Tom hadn't lost enough in his lifetime, as if Terry's lack of career advancement somehow stacked up with the life that had been torn away from Tom. As if Tom's courage, his refusal to quit or to run, were signs of weakness rather than proof of his bravery.

"Terry, you said that you were hiding out. Do you have any real evidence to believe that the police have gone to your apartment?"

"Evidence? How about repeated demands over the police

radio to pick my ass up on sight? How about the shift commander on the phone, leaving a dozen messages?"

Tom didn't answer, he was obviously waiting for more. After a time, Terry continued.

"Oh, God, I don't know. I move around so much, I don't even tell them about it anymore. But I fill out change of address cards at the post office, and the shift commanders all have my phone number. I got gas and electricity under my own name. I wouldn't be hard to find if someone was really looking."

"Has it ever occurred to you that perhaps you're *not* a suspect?"

"Come on, Tom."

"No, I'm serious. A couple of hours away from a post isn't the end of the world, and it isn't evidence of a crime. Maybe they're only wondering what happened to you. Maybe they're just planning to discipline you for abandoning your post. Maybe they're *worried* about you."

Now Tom paused. To Ellen, listening, every moment was eternal.

Tom said, "Did it ever occur to you to tell your—bosses—where you really were last night? Not earlier, but during the time they were looking for you? They don't know we were together, and they don't seem worried about the time you were away, when we were together. They don't have to know about that. But you could explain it to them. You wouldn't be the first cop who—"

Terry cut Tom with an immediate response.

"Uh-uh. Forget about it, Tom. Fuck that. You remember what happened out in L.A., to that Mark Fuhrman guy, after it came out that he talked to a—"

"We're not discussing Fuhrman."

"No, we're discussing what they'd do to *me!* Not to you, to *me!*"

Tom waited. Ellen was trying to anticipate his next comments, wondering how he'd choose the words that would nail his brother's hide to the wall, but, once again, Tom changed the subject without warning.

"If they *did* go to your apartment, they'd have found your medications."

"Yeah? So what? It ain't illegal to take medicine. Even when they're prescribed by your own brother."

Ellen heard Tom sigh heavily once again. She assumed that it was finally dawning on her husband that—as was the case with all psychopaths—there was no reasoning with Terry.

Tom said, "I was gone for most of the time that you can't account for, myself. I could tell the police that we were together."

"*There's* a ringing endorsement."

"I'm serious, Terry. You told me last night you could retire anytime you want to, that you had the three months you lost twenty years ago, while you were being investigated, backed up in sick leave and vacation time."

"I won't let them run me out of the department!"

"You're planning to retire in September anyway."

"That's my decision, my choice, Not theirs, and not yours! The department's all that's kept me going through all these years, the fact that they weren't able to take my work away from me!"

"What work!" Tom shouted back. "Walking fucking *State* Street, cracking down on vandals?"

"Don't you belittle me! It's important work, it's police work!" Ellen heard Terry's heavy breathing as he threw his temper tantrum. "You owe me, goddamn you! Frank and me, we saved your ass, you don't know how many times!"

"Anything I owed either one of you was repaid a long time ago."

"How? With a few loans? By writing me 'scripts? Seen Frank lately, bro? Think about him, then take a good, hard look at me. *This* is what we saved you from!"

"Frank's a high-grade mental defective, for Christ's sake. He's got brain damage from being a chronic alcoholic and drug abuser. Even if he is still alive, he won't be for a whole lot longer."

"And what's left for me? I can't afford a lawyer—"

"You haven't even been questioned yet."

"They're looking for me, aren't you paying attention? There was a pickup order out for me last night!"

"I can afford a lawyer for you, if it comes to that. Which it won't. The police haven't come around here yet, and I'm a lot easier to find than you are, and probably a lot more likely suspect. If they were going to try and blame anyone, they'd blame me."

"Don't think they're not planning to. There's a squad car out front right now, that's why I came around back. All you got to do is flash a badge at those rent-a-cops at the gate, and they'll let you in." Terry laughed. "Scared you, did I? Don't worry, they'll be careful. You won a lawsuit against the city the last time they accused you of something, don't think they don't have that in mind. They're going to be very careful before they come sniffing around you."

"You didn't mention that I was wrongfully arrested last time."

"Strange how it works, isn't it? Twenty years ago, you get arrested and wind up rich from it. Me, I only get *questioned*, then cleared, and I wind up being blackballed in the department for the rest of my career."

Ellen's hands had turned into fists, which were now tight against her forehead. Her eyes were squeezed shut. She was processing information, and hating Terry's blindness, his stupidity. She was trying to not blame her husband, but that wasn't getting any easier as the downstairs conversation progressed. Her loyalty to her husband allowed her to rationalize even this.

But she could not rationalize away the fact that Tom wouldn't lie to the police in order to protect himself, but he'd lie to them to try and help Terry. Ellen told herself now that that was only more proof of Tom's selflessness, of his loyalty. And in the meantime, all that man could do was sit there and condemn Tom and feel sorry for himself? My God, Ellen herself had lost more in her life than Terry ever had, entire years of her childhood wasted in a ten-year reign of terror perpetrated upon her by her psychopathic brother. And look what she'd done, look at the life she'd built for herself, she and Tom, together.

"Don't put that out in the beer can. It'll stink up the room. Use the toilet down the hall."

Ellen heard footsteps, then heard the door to the den open. She heard her husband curse softly. She realized that she'd been holding her breath. She opened her eyes, then let the breath out slowly.

She no longer felt guilty or ashamed, nor was she nervous.

She felt enervated, completely dissipated. She took shallow breaths and tried to think things through.

As much as she hated Terry, she was gaining insight into her husband through him. No wonder Tom had kept putting off having children. She'd always thought it was because of what had happened to Nancy, and because she'd been pregnant when she'd been murdered. Now Ellen thought she knew better.

Tom hadn't wanted children because of the way he himself had been raised. Even if he wasn't afraid that he would be an abuser—as his own father no doubt had been, judging by Terry's words—all he had to do to turn against fatherhood was to take Terry's advice. To look at Terry and Frank. Both of whom were, thank God, childless.

No wonder Tom wanted the Moran bloodline to end with himself.

She decided that after he left, after Terry was gone, she would go to Tom and tell him. She would tell him that she was pregnant. And that she was going to have the baby. She heard heavy footsteps, heard her brother-in-law moan as he sat down, as if he were now in pain. Ellen wished that he was, she wished him cancer.

"You said, earlier, that you were gone for a couple of hours, that you couldn't account for them." Terry paused, but Tom did not answer. He would have used the time that Terry had been gone to compose himself, to put on his shrink's face, to think through what Terry had said, and try to find a way to deal with his brother's persecution complex.

Terry seemed to have taken the time to compose himself, as well. He sounded like an entirely different man now, like a TV cop, when he said, "Let me ask you a couple of questions, Tom: What did you do with that time? Where were you, and what were you doing?"

"Why?"

"Why? Because you seemed so worked up about our *plan*, that's why. Mentioned it—what?—half a dozen times since I been sitting here."

"And?" Terry didn't answer. "Where does that take you, Terry, where do you go from there?"

"Where does it take me?" Terry laughed. "Like it's all made

161

up, right, Tom? The dumbass, paranoid patient being asked what sick conclusion he's drawn this time by the all-knowing shrink."

"That's not what I'm doing."

"It's not? All right, let's take your word for that. But I was thinking, Tom, that maybe the entire plan was set up so I'd be out of the way, out of contact with what was really going on. If I'd stuck with the plan, with what *you* decided I should do, I wouldn't have known about the search for me, now, would I? If I'd have stuck with the plan, I'd have been gone, in-commun-i-cado, right?"

"Terry, don't do this to yourself, don't let your mind run away from reality."

Ellen flinched as the sharp sound of a hand slapping the desk rang up through the vent again.

"Don't you pull that reality shit on me! I'm in touch with reality! Frank's a drunk, and you live in an ivory tower, with guards and walls and a fucking seven-foot wrought-iron gate to keep reality away from you! And when you're not here, you're locked in some office, listening to spoiled, rich, socialite whiners. Reality. I'm the only one out of the three of us who knows what reality *is*, who isn't hiding from it!"

"Sit down, Terry, relax." Tom's voice held fear as well as warning.

"What's the matter, little brother, am I getting too close to the truth?"

Tom said, "Did you—happen to open the medicine cabinet when you were in the bathroom?" Terry didn't answer. "Here, take a couple of these, Terry, they'll make you feel better." Tom must have had some medication hidden in a drawer. Tom's voice was wheedling, cajoling. Downstairs, there was a moment of silence.

The fabric of Ellen's world, already rent, now tore wide open. Her hands were trembling. She closed her eyes and lowered her head to the vent, felt its coolness on her forehead. She had to stifle a sob.

"Got any water?" Terry's voice was resigned, yet still belligerent.

"Dry swallow them, or go down the hall. Don't take more than two; you've been drinking."

"Three won't kill me." Terry's voice was muffled. He must have had the pills in his mouth.

"I want you to go back to the original plan, Terry. I want you to act as if none of this ever happened, as if you never found out about any of it."

"I can't do that. How do I get past the bosses? How do I make it okay with the department?"

"I'll make a phone call. They'll take you as an inpatient, right now, as soon as you can get over there." Tom paused. He blew out his breath. "Tell me you didn't use a credit card at the motel."

"Are you nuts? With the cops out looking for me? I used cash, and a false name."

"Thank God."

Tom paused. He took another labored breath, let it out slowly.

"I could lose my license for doing this, but I can fix this for you. I have access to the files. I can change the dates on the intake papers. Change your check-in by twelve hours, whatever you need."

Ellen slowly pushed herself to her feet. She stood above the vent, swaying, her face to the ceiling, her eyes closed. Tears streamed down her face. Her husband's voice wafted up to her as if through a long, deep, metal tunnel.

"I can put you in there hours before they found the girl. I can deflect it all away from you."

"Let me ask you a question . ." Terry's tone was pleading. Tom didn't respond. Terry asked, "What's the deal with this confidentiality? Whatever I tell them, it stays with them, right, no matter what it is?"

Ellen didn't hear Tom's reply; there was a sudden, insistent pounding on their front door. Ellen, shocked at the sound, jumped, then quickly turned toward the door.

Her world spun.

Ellen literally felt the blood draining from her head, felt herself losing control. She tried to make it to the bed before her legs gave out, and she fainted.

CHAPTER
21

"Dr. DiGrazia was within his rights. He's got the qualifications, and he's done it before." Alvarez spoke the words as Constantine came through the door of the lieutenant's office. DiGrazia looked up at her, she couldn't tell if he was angry. She smiled at him sweetly.

She said, "Sorry I'm late," to the deputy superintendent, as she walked toward him, her hand out. "I'm Janice Constantine, Dr. DiGrazia's partner." She'd thrown in the "Dr." for good measure, having heard Alvarez use the term. Alvarez, taken aback, sitting in Matthews's chair, half stood and shook Constantine's hand.

"Good to meet you," he said shortly. Constantine thought that politicians were all the same.

Constantine turned to the lieutenant, nodded briefly. Two of the other three men in the room had stood as she'd shaken the deputy superintendent's hand: the corporation counsel for the city of Chicago—the city's top lawyer—and a young, little, well-dressed, greasy-haired turd who was one of the mayor's aides. The third man, the state's attorney himself, didn't bother to rise.

DiGrazia had said representatives from their offices would be coming to the meeting. He hadn't told her that the men themselves would be in attendance. He hadn't told her that the deputy superintendent was showing up. These things bothered her, and she looked over at him. He gazed impassively back at her.

Constantine ignored the two men, left them standing, and they sat down awkwardly as she walked over to the only chair in the room that wasn't already taken. The argument that had begun before she'd gotten there continued as she sat down.

Jack Gheritty, the Cook County state's attorney, leaned far forward in his leather chair. He pushed his glasses up. "Legally, Louie, you're right."

"So what is the problem—morally?" Alvarez smiled at the lawyer, as if to tell him what he thought of the man's personal morals. Alvarez spoke in clear, distinct, cultured tones, with the sweeping gestures of a second-generation Hispanic who had been raised in America by well-educated parents.

Gheritty had been raised on Chicago's Southwest Side.

He said, "The problem is that this is a media circle jerk. My office, the attorney general's, the mayor's," Gheritty nodded his head at the other men in expensive suits who were seated around the room, "have been inundated with calls already. Headquarters looks like Camp O.J. Satellite dishes, vans, they got trailers set up. They're all excited, the killing and the goddamn *Sun-Tribune* story got them all smelling blood, and they don't care whose veins they suck it out of."

Constantine could tell that Gheritty was Matthews's man. Or, more likely, it was the other way around. The two men shot furtive looks at each other every few seconds, as if the others in the room weren't bright enough to be able to spot their male bonding. It told her that they were both pretty stupid men.

Her opinion of Alvarez kept going up, however.

He was backing up DiGrazia in front of a hostile crowd; not the sort of behavior one expected from a career politician. Then again, he was a thirty-five-year department veteran, he'd know which side of the bread the butter was on, and that would always be with the smartest, best connected detective. Constantine had known for years that DiGrazia was very smart. She was just today discovering how connected he was, and how devious.

Gheritty said, "Louie, come on. This kind of secrecy, this total lack of disclosure, it's an insult to all of us, and it makes us all look bad to the media. Including you."

"Would cracking the case quickly make us all look *good* in the media?"

Gheritty was somewhat taken aback by the question. Constantine hid a smile as his mouth worked, seeking words. She had never liked men who parted their hair down the middle. The young man from the mayor's office was as slick as the hair that was pasted down on his skull, and faster on his feet. He stepped into the silence.

"You're damn right it would."

Alvarez pursed his lips, nodded, then turned to DiGrazia, seeming almost amused.

"Will you be able to solve this case, Dr. DiGrazia?"

DiGrazia's answer was immediate and assured. "Yes."

The deputy superintendent shrugged broadly, held his hands out to Gheritty. "Then what's the problem?"

"When?" Gheritty had found his voice. "How?" He turned to DiGrazia. "Even with the way you tried to hide all the crime-scene data, you at least covered your ass by letting another criminalist in there—"

"Only because it's the law."

"—and he tells me that there's not one particle of evidence from the scene."

"If he told you that, he's wrong. There's evidence. Every time. There's always, always something." DiGrazia said it as if he were a teacher, and the state's attorney one of his slower students. He shook his head slightly, in disapproval of the man. "I shouldn't have to tell you that, Mr. State's Attorney."

"Don't step too far, *Doctor*." Matthews spoke for the first time since Constantine had come into the room.

Alvarez waved the argument off. "I'm not here to watch you guys get into a pissing contest. Dr. DiGrazia says he can solve the case, that's good enough for me."

"So just how do you intend to do that, Doctor?" The mayor's aide was smiling at the detective. DiGrazia smiled back. He was able to convey a lot in that smile; disdain, arrogance . . . he gave the impression that he was doing the mayor's man a favor by deigning to answer him. The corporation counsel hadn't said a word, but was busy scribbling furiously on a legal pad held on his lap. No wonder DiGrazia had wanted Constantine to sit in on the meeting.

"First, I'll process whatever material was gathered at the scene. I'll have the lab test everything we vacuumed up, everything we shook loose from Ms. Davene's body—"

Alvarez broke in. "And don't worry about politics on this one, Doctor, it's too big for that. The superintendent has personally spoken with Director Freeh, we'll receive full federal cooperation. We've already got some banked, through the Latent Descriptor Index." DiGrazia sat forward, slightly arching his eyebrows.

"And?"

Alvarez shook his head. "No good. There's been nothing like it at all since Nancy Moran's murder, at least that their computer can come up with. And I don't have to tell you what their computer can do. For the sake of reciprocity, I've got a team working up a VICAP—"

"Wait a minute, wait a second, what the hell is this Index thing?" Matthews's voice seemed pained, Constantine saw the look on his face, as if he were just now understanding that he was only in the room as a courtesy.

Alvarez ignored him, and said to DiGrazia, "They've got the full resources of the Quantico lab standing by for us, in the event our own lab isn't sophisticated enough to handle whatever evidence is found."

Constantine broke in with, "Dr. Anna Lee Chen, who worked the scene with Dr. DiGrazia, has agreed to stay on duty and follow it through, until all the evidence is processed. She's following strict procedure, and is never without her assistant for backup if she needs it. You know how those lawyers can get." Constantine saw three sets of angry eyes turn toward her, the state's attorney, the corporation counsel, and the mayoral aide were all lawyers. "Present company excepted," she said, and smiled at the three of them.

"Our lab can handle whatever comes up." Matthews was demanding inclusion.

Alvarez looked over at him. Constantine saw the semiamused gleam that came into his eye. He spoke to DiGrazia while looking at the lieutenant. "We get to cut through the protocol and other parliamentary red-tape bullshit because I have access through a section chief who taught one of my classes when I went through their academy." His stare bored right through Matthews's studied air of indignation. Constantine saw the cruel look that passed briefly across Alvarez's face as he said, "I was in class two-oh-one. Which cycle were you in, Doctor?"

"Two-seventy-three."

"Lieutenant?"

Matthews started in his chair, he had not been expecting the question. He glared at Alvarez for a second, then softened his look when Alvarez smiled at him.

"I've never been there."

"Never been sent to the FBI Training Academy?" Alvarez asked in broad, false wonder. Constantine was aware that Alvarez would have known all along. He was in charge of submitting to the superintendent of police the names of the seven or eight highly qualified candidates who were sent each year from the 14,000-member Chicago Police Department to the FBI Academy's three-month training course for regular police officers. It was considered a primer course for officers being groomed for high command; only the best and the brightest were allowed to go to Quantico, and they were encouraged, in their orientation there, to spend a third of their free time studying, a third seeing the sights, and the last third doing what Alvarez had done when he'd called his friend, the section chief: networking. Any officer in the city who had been through the training would know who else had been through it, and would be able to count on them for help if they needed them. Conversely, the FBI would feel free to call upon any officers who had trained at Quantico for help when they needed it. As far as Constantine was concerned, the whole thing was an FBI public-relations ploy: free food, lodging, and education, in return for being on call should the government ever need your services.

Still and all, Constantine—as well as everyone else in the room—realized that Alvarez had only asked the question in order to humiliate Matthews. His stock rose higher still in Constantine's eyes.

Now Alvarez grunted, as if in sudden comprehension. Constantine saw the lieutenant's face redden. Alvarez turned away

from the lieutenant, dismissing him, and spoke directly to Di-
Grazia again.

"They'll process whatever we need, as soon as we need it.
They're as intrigued as you are. And by the way, they don't think
it's the same killer, either." Several eyebrows shot up at this.
DiGrazia wasn't the type to have discussed his misgiving with
any of the other men in the room. "They've never known a
serial killer to wait this long between murders, either."

"What makes all of you so certain that it's *not* a serial killer?"
Matthews asked. Constantine decided that he either didn't have
the intelligence to figure out how he'd been snookered, or his
ego was too large to accept it.

DiGrazia merely looked over at him, seeming surprised by the
interruption.

"I'll explain it to you later," Alvarez said, and Constantine
laughed straight out. All five men in the room were suddenly
looking at her.

"Sorry," she said.

Matthews spoke loudly. "What will you be *sending* to the FBI?
Do you *have* anything, Doctor? How do you plan to solve this
case? You've evaded the question twice now." Matthews looked
at Alvarez, then looked away. Still, he had to comment. "Or been
saved by the bell."

"For starters, I'll be sending copies of every report, picture,
and newspaper story about both murders."

"How'd you get . . . ? That's right, you were Mike Schmidt's
partner, weren't you?"

"Schmidt called right before this meeting. He had his lawyer
on a three-way; they claim they're having everything sent over
here." DiGrazia turned to the state's attorney. "How are we set
for warrants?"

Gheritty looked sheepish for some reason, seemed startled by
the question. He immediately passed the buck. "Marty better
handle that one."

The corporation counsel stopped writing, surprised to have
been addressed. He was older than the mayor's rep, going bald
in front, pudgy. He pushed his glasses up before he spoke. "We
can get what we need, within reason."

"Can we get a court order for a list of all calls made from

Schmidt's phone between, say, eight last night, and six this morning?"

"Case like this, we can probably get his phone tapped. We've got enough judges who want to see this case closed as soon as possible."

"Friendly to the mayor," the mayor's rep said. "What makes him happy, makes them happy."

The state's attorney now found his nerve. "What's your probable cause?"

"I suspect he made some drunken phone calls last night, maybe to someone in the department. I'd like to know who he called, then I can ask *them* what the conversations were about. I went over there early this morning, he wouldn't give up his files. He even threatened me with a gun."

"Why didn't you arrest him on the spot? You'd have had probable cause to search the place," Gheritty said.

"I don't want a search, I want a list of his phone calls, and I didn't arrest him because I need those files. Pinching him wouldn't give me any probable cause to impound them." He turned back to the lawyer. "His phone was off the hook. He was drunk. I asked him who he was avoiding."

"No law against having your phone off the hook." Constantine was puzzled, wondering why Gheritty was doing this, what game the man was playing. DiGrazia and the deputy superintendent were looking at him oddly, too.

Alvarez broke the silence by saying, "Get him the list, Marty."

"Ameritech won't do it without a court order." Alvarez looked over at him. Marty obviously was not a decision maker. He would want to check with someone before proceeding. He shot Gheritty a filthy look.

Alvarez said, "I thought the judges wanted to make the mayor happy."

The mayoral aide said, "Get him the list, Marty." A conspiratorial look passed between the corporation counsel and the state's attorney. Gheritty looked quickly at Matthews, and Constantine followed the look, but the lieutenant was gazing at the wall, as if none of this concerned him. The counsel finally nodded, then cleared his throat, as if awaiting permission to speak. Alvarez slowly nodded that permission toward him.

"You should all be aware that we've got a somewhat sticky situation here, with this Dr. Moran." The lieutenant shifted in his chair, leaned forward.

"He nailed us for a half a million in a lawsuit the last time."

"The mayor does not want a repeat performance," the mayor's man said.

Gheritty said, "So we have to proceed carefully." He turned to DiGrazia. "Have you approached him yet, called him? Asked him to come in for questioning?"

"I'm waiting."

"Why?" Matthews demanded.

"He'll be coming to us."

"*What?*"

Alvarez said, "What about the brother?"

Matthews answered. "We've got a squad outside his apartment house."

"Moran isn't inside. We've called, we've beeped, he's been out of touch since the killing. The day shift throughout the city will be alerted to bring him in, all the sergeants will be mentioning it at their various roll calls. We'll have him before lunch."

"You think he did it?" the mayor's rep said.

"Seems like guilty behavior to me."

Alvarez said, "*Excuse* me," then turned to DiGrazia again. "Dr. DiGrazia, I was referring to the second brother, the eldest one, Frank."

DiGrazia nodded, as if he'd understood whom the deputy superintendent had been speaking of all along.

"We've got a series of vagrant arrests on him, disorderly conducts, public intoxication, some panhandling, all in the last three months. I didn't pull any farther back than that, the sheet would have run from here to Evanston. I scanned it for violent crimes, there are none. I ran a line through the map; the last pinch was three days ago, in Calumet City, Public Intoxication. He refused treatment, was held over in a cell, and was released the next morning on his own recognizance. He's heading home, if he's not here already."

"You have an APB out on him?"

"Better than that," DiGrazia said, but didn't elaborate. He spoke to Alvarez before any of the other men in the room could ask him what he meant.

"The lieutenant and I have put together a team of five people, including Constantine, here. All specialists, they've all got their assignments." Constantine saw Matthews look impatiently at his watch, then over at the phone. The man pursed his lips angrily.

DiGrazia said, "As soon as the boxes are delivered from Schmidt, I'd like someone on a plane, headed to Washington with copies. I'd like one transport a day; the courier can drop off what I send, and bring back their results."

"I don't know, Nick, you know they like it all FedExed; that way, it's inventoried."

"Doesn't get any more inventoried than when it's delivered by special courier."

Alvarez turned to the corporation counsel, Marty. "Can you get the funds cleared?"

For once Marty was confident of his position. "Money's no problem. As long as there's a payoff at the end." He turned to DiGrazia. "And as long as the fare's coach, and there aren't too many days involved."

"Excuse me, Chief?" Matthews's impatience was palpable now. Constantine realized that the man was afraid of something. She wondered what it was. Alvarez turned to him as if he'd forgotten the lieutenant was even in the room.

"What is it?"

"We seem to be forgetting something, here."

Nobody responded to his overt bid for a prompt. Matthews continued without one. "The doctor might be innocent, and his wife might be in danger. It was his first wife who caught it last time, remember."

Alvarez sat back in the lieutenant's swivel chair and entwined his fingers over his tight belly. He rocked, twice, watching the lieutenant. He said, "And I'll just bet you have a contingency plan in place for her protection, haven't you, Lieutenant Matthews?"

"I've got a one-man—" he looked at Constantine, gave her a tight smile, "—one-*person* squad in front of their home, I just wanted you all to know that." Constantine saw DiGrazia's quick look of hatred, directed at Matthews. He was good, though, he covered it up quickly and replaced it with a disinterested, superior look; something approaching disgust.

"Why the full disclosure now?" Matthews didn't answer. Alvarez turned back to DiGrazia. "Are you worried about the wife?"

"It's a consideration Constantine mentioned last night, and one of the reasons I don't think it's the same killer. But I don't think she's in immediate danger, no."

"Why?" Gheritty asked.

"As far as we know, she isn't pregnant."

That quieted them down.

After a time, Gheritty spoke. "So it's clear, you don't want my investigators in on this." Gheritty sounded hurt. He slapped his knees with both hands, in anticipation of closing the meeting. "Now, is all your infighting over with? DiGrazia runs the case, downstairs, with his crew, in secret, and Matthews here will take care of the PR business."

"And you'll do the prosecuting. You'll get your chance to shine in the spotlight as soon as there's an arrest," Alvarez said.

"And there'd better *be* an arrest," the mayor's aide said. DiGrazia's expression remained dispassionate.

Alvarez rose to his feet. "There are only five people in this meeting. If there're any leaks to the press, it won't be hard to find out where they came from." He glared around the room with his olive eyes. Nobody answered him.

Gheritty changed the subject.

"Speaking of the five of us in this room, if we're working together on this, we'll need copies of your reports, DiGrazia, the pictures, whatever. We need copies of all the stuff you refused to turn over to your superiors last night."

DiGrazia said, "No," simply and quietly. Gheritty turned bright red, but before he could open his mouth, the phone on the lieutenant's desk rang. Matthews leaped out of his chair to answer it, smiling embarrassedly at the foul look that the deputy superintendent gave him.

"I only authorized one call to come through, sir, it's urgent."

He picked up the phone and growled his name. Nodded to himself. Waited, listened some more. He said, "He was sure it was blood? Positive?" Matthews listened. "All right. Tell him I said good work. I want to see him as soon as he's processed his suspect." Matthews hung up, and turned solemnly toward the deputy superintendent.

"As soon as it got light out, my man watching guard over the Moran house noticed blood drops on the sidewalk, leading up the steps, into the doctor's house. There was an even larger blood sample—a pool of blood—in front of the door. The officer was let inside by the doctor himself, after he knocked and announced himself. He noticed a freshly washed patch of floor, leading up to the staircase that leads to the bedroom. At that point, he advised the doctor of his rights, and he placed him under arrest."

DiGrazia slowly rose to his feet, glaring at Matthews. Alvarez said his name, held a hand out toward him, and it stopped him. Constantine watched DiGrazia's face, and he seemed a stranger to her now, someone who looked like DiGrazia, but wasn't. She'd heard the stories about his violent nature, the rumors about his tendencies, but this was the first time she'd ever witnessed his anger in person. It wasn't something she wanted to see again.

DiGrazia was seething, the veins in his neck bulging, his hands balled into fists. She watched him take in two deep breaths, almost *felt* him stomp down hard on his anger. She watched his hands relax, saw him shrug his shoulders slowly, saw him rotate his neck, roll it around like a boxer does just before the opening bell.

And then she recognized him again, he was DiGrazia again, no longer an imitator. He crossed his hands in front of himself and stood there, awaiting instructions from Alvarez.

Alvarez was also angry, but he hid it far better than DiGrazia. Softly, he said to Matthews, "Don't tell me, let me guess: you also just happened to have a team of detectives waiting to question him." Alvarez's tone was almost as frightening as DiGrazia's anger. Matthews's actions would cost him. Alvarez continued. "And I'd guess, for public relations reasons, they're both black?"

Matthews did not try to hide his smile. "Hispanic," he said.

Alvarez nodded thoughtfully. Constantine turned her head along with the deputy superintendent of police as he turned and spoke to DiGrazia.

"Get on this, Dominick, make sure none of the lieutenant's sycophants screws this thing up."

"I suspect they already have," DiGrazia said. He waved a hand for Constantine to follow as he stalked out of the room without looking at the lieutenant, as if he did not trust himself to do so.

CHAPTER
22

Frank Moran's own moaning awoke him in his room at the transient hotel flophouse. He realized he was groaning aloud at the same time that he understood he was holding his head in both his hands, and he didn't remember raising them. He felt a momentary sense of hysteria—what else might he have done in his sleep and not now remember doing? The pain tore him away from his frightening self-examination. He took a short inward breath, groaned it away. His head and stomach were on fire. In a few minutes, the moaning stopped. Frank had to piss desperately, and the toilet was down the hall. If he'd only taken the room for the night, he would have pissed right there in the bed. But he had paid in advance, for a week. For his visit. He knew he had to pull himself together enough to get down the hall to the bathroom.

Frank lay there, in his lonely bed holding his head, assessing the damages and knowing that this was going to be a bad one. As if any of them were good ones. He hadn't saved himself an eye-opener, as usual. Every morning he vowed that he would, and every night he greedily drank the bottle empty. His prescription bottle was empty, lidless, lying on its side on the floor. One of these days, he suspected, the combination of drugs and alcohol would kill him.

Had he eaten anything last night? he wondered. He'd planned to get a hot dog, but he hadn't. Scattered, selective memories came to him as he lay there, shuddering in pain and self-pity over his suffering. He'd done something last night, what had he done . . . ?

Jesus Christ Almighty in Heaven, what had he done?!

Frank moaned aloud as he recalled the memory of later events. In an attempt to calm himself, he remembered sitting on the bed in the room alone and drinking himself into oblivion with the cheap television set that was bolted to the floor turned down low.

The usual morning remorse attacked Frank with its customary, dark vigor as the past night's occurrences came flooding back in Technicolor. Another night of begging, of drinking on the sly, then the alley, then the wino, then, as he'd left Chicago Avenue, the overwhelming physical pain that had made him stop and lean against a building until it passed. Thankfully, as always, Frank had been able to drink it away.

Frank took a deep breath, then took a quick physical inventory. It wasn't difficult to diagnose, he was in the throes of a horrendous hangover.

He was nauseous, with a terrible case of heartburn, and his head felt as if it were in the grip of a vise; a vise that squeezed, greatened, then lessened in intensity with each beat of his heart. His entire body was shaking. He felt almost as if he were lying there, somehow outside of himself, as if his brain had somehow died and moved on, leaving him only his damaged nerve endings. Those nerves felt sunburned.

Frank closed his eyes and breathed through his mouth, trying desperately to prevent himself from throwing up all over the bed.

After a time he was able to reach a shaking hand out over the side of the bed and feel around for the cheap, plastic wastepaper basket that he had filled with an entire package of ice last night, and placed by the side of the bed. There were two sixteen-ounce plastic bottles of Pepsi-Cola floating around in the melted ice. He had gotten the ice and the Pepsis at the Amoco station across the street. This was one of the things he'd learned to do whenever he had a bed to sleep in; when he was on the street, when things got really bad, he'd just sleep with a liter bottle of

Pepsi inside his coat, when he could afford one. Frank felt a stab of anger mixed with his shame and with the morbid, self-absorbed pity that he almost always felt for himself lately. He shook it off. He was too old for anger. And even if he wasn't, this was just a dim anger, nothing at all to bother with, a mere shell of the rage that had driven him in his youth.

Frank grabbed one of the Pepsis, lifted it to his forehead, and held it there for a second, sighing, gaining relief even from its tepid touch. He shivered. It didn't do much for the pain. He held the bottle to his head with his left hand, then reached his right into the bucket, searching vainly for ice. Frank brought the bottle down to his chest, still not having opened his eyes, and with a great force of will somehow found the strength to twist the top off the plastic bottle with his weak, trembling fingers. The physical exertion exhausted him, and he gave out with a little sigh of relief when the task was finally done.

He let the cap fall onto the bed, then brought the bottle to his lips—spilling an ounce or so onto his chest—and downed the entire Pepsi in several greedy gulps without taking it away from his mouth. He let the empty bottle drop to the bed and then gasped, lay there breathing heavily through his mouth once again. He forced himself to burp. The expulsion of gas made him feel slightly better.

When he was almost certain that he could move without throwing up, he lowered his legs over the side of the bed, held onto the thin filthy mattress for support, then just sat there for a time, smelling his own stink, a drunk's stink, evaporated alcohol and sweat, mixed with the stale smoke from the cigarettes he'd chain-smoked the night before. Frank's face twisted into an unconscious mask of pain and self-hatred.

His cigarettes were on the stained night table beside the bed. Frank reached for them, managed to get one out. It took him a while to tear a match from the book, longer still to strike it alive on the back of the cover. He finally got the cigarette going and dropped the spent match to the floor, left the cigarette dangling between his lips. Frank knew that he wouldn't have been able to hold the cigarette in his hand without shaking the ember off it, without it falling on him, without it burning him. He took drags and let them out around the filter. He coughed, heavily.

When he could move without dizziness, Frank dropped the spent cigarette into the empty Pepsi bottle, then let it fall to the floor. He reached down, grabbed, opened, and drank the other Pepsi. He reached under his mattress and took out a single sock, his money was inside it. He staggered to his feet and, carrying the sock with him, moved slowly toward the door, using everything there was on the way to it for physical and emotional support; leaning on the bed, then on the shabby dresser, then making a falling movement toward the doorway, and hanging onto the molding. He leaned away from that and nearly fell. He fumbled with the small, flimsy, eyehook lock, got it free of its circular metal container, tore the door open and staggered naked down the hall. He left his door wide open. He held the wall all the way down, one hand over the other, using his shoulder, spinning once when he thought he was going to fall. At last, he was at the bathroom door. Thankfully, nobody was using it.

But somebody had, and hadn't bothered flushing behind himself.

Frank turned away from the disgusting mess, breathing through his mouth as he latched the bathroom door, deciding that the toilet might be plugged. He couldn't looked at it, couldn't bring himself to flush it. He couldn't have that mess floating around his feet or he'd die. He would use the bathtub, kill two birds with one stone. Frank put his sock on the toilet tank, leaned onto the sink, reached out with one hand and pulled back the grimy, fungus-covered shower curtain, then pushed himself off the sink and carefully lifted one leg at a time over the rim of the tub, holding onto the tiled wall so he wouldn't fall down and break his neck.

He had a sudden instant of severe white pain in his head as he reached down to turn on the water, and he leaned his head against the filthy, yellow tiles, gasping, until the moment—and the fierce panic that came with it—passed. He turned on the water and pushed himself away from the wall, let the weak pressure of the water hit him as he wondered darkly about the pounding within his chest.

He knew that his father had died of a heart attack, and he'd been a drinking man, too. His father had died in his own kitchen, more than likely in terror, panicked, knowing what was happening, terrified because it was happening at all, but terrified most of all because he'd died all alone, with nobody there to see him off, to hold his hand, to lie to him and tell him that he was going to be all right.

Frank was glaringly, achingly aware of the fact that he could die right here and now, fall over in this tub, and his body would not be found for hours, maybe not even for days.

And if he did die, he wondered, would anyone mourn his loss? Tommy, maybe. Tommy had always liked him. But Tommy wouldn't spend any time suffering over Frank's death. No one would do that. Maybe his mother, if she was still alive.

"Fuck me," Frank Moran managed to say, pissing into a grimy clawfoot tub, while icy cold water rained down upon his body.

Frank leaned back, stood wobbling in the center of the tub, with colors flashing before his eyes. He forced himself to breathe through his mouth, slowly, evenly, until he had himself somewhat under control. If he moved that suddenly again, he thought, he would never get out of the shower, his head would explode, he would die.

Although he was feeling a little better now. Just a little bit better. He needed something to eat, a few more cigarettes. He needed to brush his teeth. Get dressed. Go out and get a bottle. Two sips, maybe three, and he'd be all right, he could make it.

Frank managed to turn the water off, pushed the curtain away from the tub, and slowly, carefully, stepped out onto the grubby bathroom floor. He dripped water all the way back to his room, carrying his stocking, smelling the room long before he got to it. It reeked of stale cigarette smoke, cheap alcohol, and stale sweat.

Frank stepped into the room gingerly, avoiding the dead cigarette butts that he'd crushed underfoot as he'd chain-smoked and drunk himself into oblivion the previous night. He dried himself with the sticky, stained sheet from the bed. He was able to light a cigarette more easily, now. He stood there taking deep drags, the door still open, to air the room out. He nodded at an inner decision, and plodded over to the window, somehow managed to push it open. He leaned out into the cool morning air, leaned his elbows on the sill, taking deep breaths. He was facing a weed-infested parking lot; there were black men down there, sleeping on pieces of cardboard. Car noises rose up to greet him; horns honking, the loud, rude burps of broken mufflers.

Frank looked down at the lot, wondering why he couldn't sleep more than three or four hours at a time anymore, wondering why he lived the way he did, wondering why his life was what it was.

He decided that he didn't want to really know any of the answers.

"You all right there, buddy?" Frank jumped at the sound of the voice, banging his head on the top of the window, then turned angrily toward the intruder, breathing harshly, cursing himself for leaving the door wide open in an unfamiliar place in a city he could no longer call his home.

A skinny, short, black man was standing in the doorway, looking at Frank with sympathy. He was wearing a Bulls T-shirt and shorts that had been cut off from stone-washed blue jeans. The pants hung very low on the man's hips, and extended well past his knees, frazzled ends where scissors had chopped hanging down a few inches farther. The man was wearing a cheap gold chain around his neck. He said, "Didn't mean to scare you."

"You didn't scare me." Fear was alive in Frank's voice, betraying him. The man was leaning against the doorway. Frank couldn't see the man's right hand, it was out in the hallway, maybe holding the wall, maybe holding a knife. "What do you want?"

"Heard you coming down the hall after your shower." The man squinted. "You don't look too good."

"I'm all right." Frank was aware of his nakedness. He was tall, and, when dressed, could project an attitude of strength. He knew what he looked like naked, knew what this stranger was seeing. His ribs protruded, his arms had no muscle tone. His legs were like sticks. His dick was tiny, his scrotum shrunken. The man pushed off the door, and Frank started. He brought his right hand into view.

It was holding a six-pack of Schlitz. Frost was still on the cans; water dripped down onto the floor. Frank licked his lips, looking at the beers with longing.

"My name's Barry, I just checked in last night. Why don't you get yourself dressed, and come on next door, have a cold one with me? You look like you could use one."

Frank licked his lips again, and nodded gratefully. "Give me a minute, Barry." The man nodded agreeably, and turned away, and Frank tossed his cigarette out the window and reached hurriedly for his pants.

CHAPTER
23

"**W**hat the hell was *that* all about?" Constantine demanded. She was hurrying to keep up with DiGrazia's long strides as he marched down the hallway, heading for the stairs.

"They're playing games," DiGrazia told her. His voice seemed normal, if tight, but his body looked coiled, every muscle tensed. He reminded Constantine of a cobra, just before it struck.

"Nick, did you get any sleep last night?"

"You see the way they were looking at each other? Like little kids in school, hoping the teacher doesn't catch them passing notes." They were on the stairs now, DiGrazia striding down them two at a time, Constantine holding the railing, puffing, cursing the Marlboro company. "It's all a game to them, but they don't even know the rules. And something's going on between Gheritty, Matthews, and the lawyer that they don't want us to know about."

"Think they're trying to steal the case?"

"Make one, maybe." DiGrazia moved against the wall so that three uniformed officers on their way up could pass him. Constantine was losing ground. She passed the officers as the last one turned to look at DiGrazia, as if he were insane. "Gheritty can use his own investigators, and he'll probably prosecute himself. That way the city's off the hook, and that'd make the mayor happy."

"*He's* in on it?"

"His aide isn't, you can bet on that, even though it's all political." DiGrazia had reached the bottom step. Constantine noted that he wasn't even breathing hard as he stood there, hands on his hips, waiting for her, or so she thought.

Absently, as if it weren't really important, he said, "Matthews is the odd man out. They used him, and they'll cut him loose. Parker was right, he stepped on his dick. Now Parker can get him out of his hair, and Alvarez'll castrate him, and he's too dumb to have even seen it coming. Alvarez won't forget whoever sides with Matthews, either."

"What's there to castrate?" Constantine stood next to him, positioning herself so that she did not block the stairway. She looked through the crowded first floor lobby, past the desk, to the door, and understood that DiGrazia hadn't been extending her any courtesy, hadn't been waiting for her to catch her breath.

He'd been watching an obviously terrified Mike Schmidt, who was being ushered into the building by a tall, older, silver-haired man. Schmidt was in dirty clothing, the lawyer was dressed impeccably in a thousand-dollar suit that hung elegantly from his thin frame. Behind them, two workmen pushed tall hand-dollies that were stacked to the top with cardboard boxes.

Schmidt was literally shaking, Constantine saw it in his hands, the jerk of his head. He walked unsteadily, allowing himself to be guided by the lawyer, who was leaning over and speaking confidentially into Schmidt's ear.

"He got Parkinson's?" Constantine asked, and DiGrazia shook his head.

"He didn't as of last night."

"Either that's the worst case of alcohol withdrawal I've ever seen, or the guy's absolutely terrified."

DiGrazia said, "Or pretending to be." He looked around, saw something, then nodded to himself.

"What?"

His voice was a whisper. "It's a setup. Don't look at the cameras when they come on, keep your face impassive." Constantine looked around, but did not spot any reporters she recognized.

Officers throughout the first floor had stopped to watch Schmidt as he slowly made his way past them; Constantine could see the older officers explaining who Schmidt was to their younger counterparts. Heads were together, voices low, the veterans speaking quietly, as if watching a fallen colleague's funeral procession passing by them, rather than his still-living, breathing image.

The lawyer looked up and spotted DiGrazia, and stopped. Schmidt saw him and whimpered. The lawyer linked his arm through Schmidt's, patted Schmidt's forearm with his free hand, as if to calm him.

"Detective DiGrazia, I suggest you move aside." Constantine noticed that the room was suddenly silent as every police officer, lawyer, civilian worker, complainant, and the relatives of arrested detainees watched the standoff—a whole roomful of people— while DiGrazia calmly remained where he was. Constantine looked from one man to the other, then caught herself, and stared at the lawyer. She heard the shuffle of feet, heard the front door slam hard against the wall, then bright lights suddenly cloaked them. She was getting a little tired of DiGrazia always being right. Distantly, Constantine registered the fact that at least one TV Minicam had come alive. She heard a whirring that she would later recognize as the peculiar noise made by expensive still-shot cameras. Schmidt had hung his head, and was now staring at the floor.

DiGrazia's voice was only for the lawyer. "I was supposed to be gone already, wasn't I, Counselor?"

The lawyer did not answer, except by his expression.

DiGrazia said, "Are those boxes for me?"

The lawyer raised his voice. "I won't ask you again, Detective!"

DiGrazia seemed totally relaxed, did not even glance over at the cameras. Constantine willed herself not to look at them, either. DiGrazia smiled softly as he said, "What's going on, Mr. Silverman?" Constantine heard fast, heavy footfalls on the steps behind her, and turned to see Gheritty hurrying down toward them.

"I called you from the car phone; where have you been?" Silverman said.

"You want to watch that, Harold," Gheritty whispered. He was out of breath, from excitement, Constantine thought, rather than from having raced down three flights of stairs. His gaze flitted briefly toward the cameras, then he pulled down the hem of his suit coat. "Is this the complainant?"

"It is. Detective Sergeant Michael Schmidt. Retired." Silverman said this loudly, then backed away from his previous arrogance. "And I appreciate your taking the time to deal with this yourself, sir."

"I've got a man upstairs standing by to take the complaint, we'll talk after that's out of the way."

"But you'll approve the charges?"

Gheritty paused. His gaze flicked to the cameras again, then back to the lawyer. DiGrazia turned to face him, his visage now carved from stone, giving away nothing, but Constantine nevertheless still sensed the coiled cobra within him, awaiting its opportunity. Gheritty looked away from him as Capt. John Parker came around the bend in the stairs, took in all that was happening, almost stopped, then slowly came down the last flight of stairs as Constantine, watching from the sidelines, admired him and DiGrazia at the same moment that she began to understand what was really going on.

Gheritty said, "The county supersedes in this case, Captain, it's a matter of a complaint."

"Against whom?" Parker said, and DiGrazia moved in close to Gheritty, spoke directly into his ear.

"Against *whom*, Jack?"

"Against—against no one, at this point. There hasn't even been a formal charge leveled, let alone an investigation begun." Gheritty was withering under Parker's harsh stare. He nervously said, "We'll take the statement, and then we'll decide if any charges should be filed." He looked over at the crowd in the lobby. "You want to shut off those cameras, please?" His plea was ignored.

"Against *whom*," DiGrazia said again, more forcefully. He seemed to be almost enjoying himself. Gheritty turned to face him, and DiGrazia stood still, their faces inches apart, DiGrazia's dark eyes burning into the state's attorney's glasses. Gheritty backed away a single step, and the statement it made for the camera had the same affect as a mile.

"Against *you*, you son of a bitch!" Schmidt spoke his first words since he'd entered the station. Everyone turned to look at him: Parker with unhidden contempt, DiGrazia with indifference, Gheritty with relief. Constantine saw the ex-cop pull down on the collar of the T-shirt he was wearing, saw the maroon, purple and yellow handprints that colored his unshaven neck.

"Look!" Schmidt seemed to have regained some of his strength. He was glaring at DiGrazia now, as he raised his head and thrust himself forward so everyone could get a better look. "Look what he did to me!"

Schmidt turned to the room, playing to the crowd, to the reporters, the cameras, his head still bobbing feebly in time with his heartbeat, his fingers ripping the fabric of his shirt as he pulled down on its collar.

"Do you see? Do you see what he did to me?" He'd torn his arm out of Silverman's grasp, and the lawyer, now perturbed over his loss of control of the situation, grabbed at Schmidt, attempting to stop him.

Schmidt hollered out, "Do you see what he did to an old man? He tried to kill me, and I got witnesses!"

"Mr. *Schmidt!*" Silverman grabbed at him, got hold of his arm, and turned him toward the stairway. The workmen with the dollies were smirking, having fun, momentary celebrities trapped in a promotional and marketing activity that had nothing to do with them, but one which they would nevertheless videotape from the news, after they got off work. The lawyer had one long arm firmly around Schmidt's shoulders now, and began to lead him up the steps, slowly, carefully, as if he feared breakage. Parker held his ground, and turned to watch them as they ascended. The reporters moved closer, vultures ready to settle in now that the drama seemed to have played itself out, ready to ask questions for which there could be no answers.

Activity resumed around them, as people went about their business. Constantine looked at DiGrazia, who hadn't moved an inch, was still right in Gheritty's face.

"I told you not ten minutes ago that the man waved a weapon at me." DiGrazia said it in a reasonable voice, as if he were puzzled. He was playing to the same cameras Schmidt, Silverman, and Gheritty had, but with far more subtlety.

"And I asked you why you didn't arrest him on the spot." Gheritty, no doubt mindful of the reporters he had called to memorialize his political ascension, had regained his composure, and now added a touch of indignation to his tone as he said, "You're excused, Detective DiGrazia. We'll call you in if we need you."

DiGrazia turned to the workmen. "And these?" he waved a hand at the boxes of files. Gheritty turned to Parker.

"Captain Parker, I'd like these files delivered directly to Lieutenant Matthews's office, for perusal and disbursement relevant to the investigation of the murder of Veronica Davene."

In a very calm, controlled, and reasonable voice, John Parker said, "No."

CHAPTER
24

Ellen subconsciously registered the smell of familiar scents before she even opened her eyes, and knew immediately that she wasn't at home, that she was in the hospital. Full awareness came with a jolt, she remembered what had happened, and she gave a short scream as she bolted up in the elevated bed. Dizziness attacked with fury, then arms encircled her, and a male voice she recognized spoke reassuringly in her ear.

"It's all right, sweetheart, it's all right, Daddy's here." Daddy. Ellen loosened her hold on him as she realized how tightly she was holding on.

"Tom . . ."

Her father spoke hurried, reassuring words. "His lawyer's on the way over to him, he's safe, now you've got to calm down, sweetheart, you've got to—"

"I've got to get to *Tom!*" The dizziness had passed. Ellen spoke the words without releasing her grip on her father, but her eyes darted around the room, taking in images, seeking reassurance as much as information. She saw the familiar NWM logo—the letters displayed in the pattern common to the monogrammed shirt of a rich man—stitched into the sheet that was half-covering her. The buildings outside the window were familiar, well known to her, she saw them every day. She'd been admitted to the hospital in the medical complex where she worked. Ellen thanked God. She even knew the building she was in, and the floor she was on, by the view. She could get out of here in a second if she had to, if they wouldn't discharge her.

She fought off a wave of nausea, and a strong feeling of panic. Her husband was in trouble, they'd arrested Tom. She remembered that, remembered being weak and dizzy and too feeble to stop the paramedics as they pushed her, strapped to a gurney, out her own front door. Tom had been in handcuffs, in the backseat of a patrol car, she'd seen his plaintive face watching her as she'd been pushed past, heard his muffled screams for her through the closed window of the squad car. Neighbors had stood watching as the melodrama played itself out, neighbors who were probably still gawking as they stood together gossiping behind yellow crime-scene tape, watching the police and the FBI agents as they tore Ellen's house apart, top to bottom, looking for evidence they'd never find.

"It was Tom's blood!"

"He told them, he told them that, Ellen," Daddy tightened his hug briefly, then pulled back so he could look at her. He gave her a slight, wan smile, all that the present circumstances allowed him. Ellen smelled the cigarette smoke on his breath, the coffee, and that particular old person's smell that attacked the breath of people over seventy. She felt, strangely, relieved, better than she had when he'd been holding her. A wave of memories flooded into her, and she fought them off. This was here, this was now. She was no longer a child. The past was long behind her.

Daddy said, "Momsy's waiting by the phone at home right now, hon, waiting for Tom or the lawyer to call. That's why she ain't here."

"He didn't do anything."

"We know that, sweetie." Ellen looked at his wispy white hair, at the heavy fringe above his ears. The stems of his glasses were wedged somewhere inside that tangle of white. Ellen saw that her father's glasses needed cleaning. She looked at him sitting there. He'd always been so skinny, yet so strong. When had her father gone fat? He had been devastated when his only son had committed suicide, had gone downhill since then. Age—and life—hadn't been kind to Ellen's father.

"Ow." The needle in the crook of her arm was pinching her, tore her out of her reverie. Ellen took a deep breath, and let it out slowly. She pulled gently away from her father, and he slowly, reluctantly allowed it, his hand trailing along her arm, her hand, her fingers, before he unwillingly relinquished contact. Ellen lay back, looking at him.

"They charged him, though, didn't they?" Her father closed his eyes, lowered his head, and nodded, once, then lifted his head and looked at her again. Daddy's shamed admission. With an expert, practiced movement, Ellen reached over and plucked the needle from her arm. She tore off the tape that had held it secure.

"Where are my clothes?"

"You can't leave, Ellen, you have to stay here for observation."

"Either you're with me or you're against me, Daddy." Ellen sat up in the bed, sat still, put her hand on her father's shoulder and squeezed the soft flesh firmly. She said, "I'm leaving here, right now. I need my clothes. I need a car. I need a weapon for protection. You can give me all of those things, or none of them, but whatever you decide, know this: The worst you can do is slow me down, you won't be able to stop me."

"I won't put a gun in your hands, not in the condition you're in."

Ellen squeezed her hands into fists so she wouldn't snap sarcastically at his judgment of her. She told herself not to take it personally, it meant she'd get two out of three. Carefully, she said, "Are my clothes in the closet?" Her father nodded. "Bring them here, then go out front and have a cigarette." Ellen swung her legs over the side of the bed, holding onto her father's shoulder for support. "Call Momsy from the lobby if you want to, so she won't worry." She stood, steadied herself, let go of him, then, when she was sure she wouldn't grow faint, nodded for her father to go and fetch her her clothes. Ellen would wait until he was out of the room before removing the thin hospital johnny.

"I'll meet you on the front steps in five minutes," she said.

Her father walked over to the closet, and pulled out the folded clothing she'd been wearing when she'd been admitted. Ellen knew that it was still morning by the way the light filtered into the room through the miniblinds.

"The doctor said—" her father paused, turned to Ellen with her folded clothes in his hands, his eyes cast downward out of respect for Ellen's modesty. Ellen stood staring at him. She stiffened, automatically lifting one hand toward her belly.

"The doctor said what?" Her voice, to her own ear, was steel. Her father looked up at her, then back at the floor.

"He said the baby's all right. You just passed out from exhaustion, or fear." He lowered his eyes again and shuffled across the room, dropped the clothing on the bed next to Ellen. "He said you were dehydrated, too."

Ellen didn't feel the need to indulge his hurt feelings. She only looked at her father, until he turned away and left the room.

Barry said, "Go ahead, man, have another one. You sure look like you could use it." His teeth, Frank noticed, were very white, very shiny. Barry smelled clean in a building filled with stenches, Barry smelled of deodorant, of soap, of toothpaste. Frank thought that he had to be some kind of hustler, but he didn't care, the man's beer was ice-cold, and he was being generous with the six-pack.

"Thank you," Frank said, and reached for his second beer. The bedsprings squealed under him. Barry was sitting on a rickety chair, with three or four feet between them. Frank's hands were shaking less than they had been, and the first beer had gone down quickly, smoothly, blessedly, disappearing down his throat with his having barely a conscious sense of swallowing. The burp that followed had been delicious.

Frank managed to open the second can, drank half of it, and closed his eyes in relief. There was an ashtray on Barry's nightstand, and one of Frank's cigarettes was smoldering in it. He opened his eyes and reached for it, took in a welcome drag. Barry laughed.

"Did I do something funny?" Frank asked it without attitude, as if he really wanted to know. His crossed legs looked like a mannequin's, his pants draped over them, around them, fell into a small pile around them.

"Naw, man, I was just thinking of all the mornings I been

191

exactly where you are right now." Barry, Frank noticed, was not drinking his own beer. He had an intuitive flash, wondered if he were being readied for a pitch. He didn't care, he almost welcomed it, be it AA or redemption through the Lord Jesus Christ, Frank would buy whatever Barry might be selling. Or at least he'd pretend to, for as long as the beer held out.

Frank decided to expedite matters, wanting to get the man talking, and keep him talking. Frank was an excellent listener, as listening gave him more time to drink. "I got a hangover you wouldn't believe."

"Frank, I'd believe it." Barry was studying him now. Frank smiled slightly, encouragingly, and Barry said, "All you got to do is look at you, man, it's obvious as sin."

"Well, I guess I *am* a sinner." Wasn't Barry going to rise to the bait? Frank finished off half of what was left in the can. "I can pay you for these beers. I got some money."

"That's all right, the company's worth it," Barry said.

"I just want you to know I'm not freeloading, I can pay my way."

Barry seemed amused as he considered this, and Frank immediately felt self-conscious, aware of himself and what he was. He was unaccustomed to drinking with another person. In their company, perhaps, but rarely with them.

Frank drained the can, placed it in the small, plastic wastepaper basket that Barry had set at his feet. He looked around the room, saw the toiletries lined up in a row on Barry's tiny dresser, the can of Lysol, the tin of foot powder. Barry was wearing clean white Nikes on his feet, and they looked new. Frank heard the *whoosh* as a beer can was popped open, and he looked up, expecting to find that Barry had finally decided to join him, and was therefore surprised to discover that Barry was holding the can out to Frank. Barry waved it toward him, seductively.

"Go ahead, take it."

"Barry . . ." Something about this didn't make sense. Barry waved the can. Frank forgot his misgivings and took it, nodded his thanks.

After a time, Barry said, "You mind some advice, Frank?" Frank shrugged. It didn't matter to him one way or the other, he'd been on the receiving end of many things far worse than advice. "Stay away from Chicago Avenue." Frank, startled, looked up so quickly that his vision blurred.

"What?" His voice was a croak. He was breathing heavily. He felt his hangover come back with all its fierceness. Barry looked at him, puzzled.

"I said, stay away from Chicago Avenue, man. Some girl got killed there last night, in a alley. They right away saying some homeless guy did it." Barry tilted his head as Frank drained his beer. Frank looked back at him, desperately. He squeezed the can between his fingers.

"Christ."

"What's the matter? Something wrong, partner?" Frank hurriedly shook his head. Barry leaned down and picked up the three remaining beers, holding them in his hand by one of the empty plastic rings. Frank watched water drip onto the floor. He stared at the cans, the answer to his famine, as Barry stood and walked to his window, looked down at the street, the cans hanging from one finger.

"Sure wouldn't have wanted to have been around there, around Chicago Avenue. I just lost my old lady, my kids, my house, a couple weeks ago. I ain't been questioned by the police since I was a teenager."

"It ain't so bad," Frank said, in an effort to get Barry to turn around. "They question me all the time." Frank tried to think of some way to get that beer back over to this side of the room. He said, "What you do is, you play dumb. Don't answer them, but don't get out of line with them, either. You do that, and they'll slap you around, because they know they can get away with it." Frank paused, looking at Barry.

"They pick you up and start asking questions, you have to show them respect, no matter what you're feeling inside. Act—" Frank searched for the proper word, then got it. "—pathetic. And humble. Sometimes they'll feel sorry for you if you do it good enough." Frank stopped himself, realizing that he not only was nervously rambling, but that he'd just spoken more words to Barry than he had spoken to any individual at one time for as long as he could remember.

"That what you do, Frank?"

"That's what I'm saying you should do." That was better. One sentence. He didn't get too mixed up when he kept things clean and simple.

"I'll be out there begging soon, too." Frank watched Barry shrug. "I'm damn near broke. My credit card was cut off, I had to move into this shithouse.

"Where can I go? Where can *I* go to beg, Frank? I can throw these cans out this window and hit a millionaire's condo, and here I am, sleeping with roaches. Where you go to beg in this city? Rich white man walks by you like you don't ex*ist*. I seen 'em." Barry turned quickly, startling Frank. "Chicago Avenue, Michigan Avenue, they all the same to me. Filled with white guys ignoring guys like me." Barry paused. Frank couldn't think of anything to say.

"Where you beg money at, Frank?"

"I just got into town yesterday."

"You come in with money? You bring some cash with you?"

The question made Frank nervous. He decided to give Barry some pointers. "Stay downtown, and don't stand in anyone's way. Step aside if they barge into you, the young guys do that sometimes, to try and show you how tough they are. You let them, they'll embarrass the shit out of you." Frank confirmed this with a hard little nod. "But stay downtown. Anywhere else, you get arrested a lot. Disorderly Conduct, Drunk and Disorderly. Public Intoxication. They made a lot of new laws out in the sub-urbs, just so they can arrest you and run you out of town. It ain't so bad if you stay downtown. It's good duty, the cops down there don't want to do anything to draw attention to themselves, something that could get them transferred to a—a neighborhood that ain't so nice."

"How you know that, you just got into town yesterday?"

"I been here before." Frank didn't look at Barry; he couldn't take his eyes away from the beer cans. He nervously fanned his legs. Barry swung the cans, and Frank winced as they hit his legs. Now they'd probably spray when he opened them. If he got another chance to open them.

"Where you beg money from last night?"

"You won't tell anyone?" Frank was desperate. The beer cans were a hypnotist's watch as they swayed, so far away, all the way over by the window.

But now the beer cans were coming toward him, closer, closer, until they were just in front of Frank's face. Barry held them up a foot away from Frank's face, swung them cruelly back and forth. Why was he acting like this? Frank stole a look at him. Was it some racial thing? Had Barry used the beer just to get him into this room? Was Barry going to hurt him? Frank looked up at him, his mouth working silently. Barry waved the cans, moved them directly in front of Frank's face.

"Where you beg last night, Frank?"

Frank said, "On Chicago Avenue."

"You got to be shitting me." Barry lowered the cans into Frank's lap, and Frank sighed in relief. He tore one out of the ring, remembered that they'd hit Barry's leg, so wrapped his mouth around the opening as he pulled at the tab. He sucked most of the foam up into his mouth, sucked at it until it stopped foaming, then took a long drink of the beer. He ignored the foam that had sprayed onto his face, dripped down onto the front of his shirt and pants. Frank licked at the top of the can, ran his finger around it, then licked that, too.

"Man, watching you's getting me thirsty. I'm about ready to join you," Barry said. "Think I'll go down and pick me up a case. You hold down the fort okay?"

"I can wait in my own room, if you want."

"You one accommodating motherfucker, ain't you, Frank?" Frank looked at him blankly. He held the beer tightly in his hand. Barry's voice carried suspicion when he said, "You happen to see anything out there last night, Frank? When you was begging on Chicago Avenue? You happen to know anything about that girl?"

Frank nodded conspiratorially. "I seen something."

"What'd you see, Frank?"

"I think it's time for me to go." Barry moved in close, not in a threatening manner, but in a way that blocked Frank from getting to his feet.

"What'd you *see?*"

Frank looked up at him. At times such as these, he thought he'd been born afraid. "A drunk guy, a crazy guy. He came out of the alley, scared to death." Frank spoke quickly, trying to make Barry happy, but Barry was leaning over him now, shouting into Frank's face.

"That all you seen, Frank?!"

Frank cringed away, held his hands up to his face. "That's all I seen!"

"You know what? I don't believe you." Frank didn't care what Barry believed, he only cared that Barry didn't seem mad at him anymore. Barry backed off, was now looking at him, studying him. All Frank wanted was to just make Barry happy, and somehow get the hell out of this room. He lifted the beer to his lips, but it was suddenly gone, slapped out of his hand. He shrank back, trapped and snarling. Barry pushed him on the bed, and Frank hollered, "No!" as loudly as he could as Barry tossed him over, onto his belly. He yelled the word again, as Barry's intention became clear to Frank. Frank had been sexually assaulted before, in an East Texas jailhouse.

"Help!" Frank screamed, despairing that help would arrive. *"HELP!"* Frank thought his lungs would burst, felt a soreness in his throat, as if screaming had torn his flesh. He felt handcuffs ratchet down hard upon both wrists.

He heard Barry say, "Shut up, would you? I ain't fucking you, I'm taking you in. I'm a cop."

"You're arrest—arrest—arresting me? For what?" Barry pulled Frank to his feet by the chain that separated the handcuffs. He pushed Frank into the hall.

Barry said, "You're not under arrest. We just need to talk to you."

"About what?"

"About first-degree murder, that's about what."

CHAPTER
25

"Any statements, Detective, any statements, Detective?" Constantine had raised her voice into a squeaky imitation of a television reporter as DiGrazia drove them quickly down State Street, barely pausing at the morning red lights, hitting the siren a lick and inching through the busier of the intersections. The wind rushing in from the open window blew his hair around, causing it to slap against his forehead, as if chastising him for a secret sin that only the wind and DiGrazia knew of.

Constantine examined him carefully while he had his guard down, feeling a small sense of pride in the fact that he let it down in her presence at all. She was gaining an ever growing, keener appreciation for DiGrazia's feverish intelligence, appreciating it more because—even though he never tried to hide his intellect from anyone—there was so much more of it there that he *didn't* let anyone see.

Watching him, Constantine decided that at the moment he looked more like a reflective college professor than a cop. In the room, earlier, he'd seemed to be a wild animal, ready to attack, but now he appeared to be calm, relaxed. At least while he was seated, with his size hidden, his weapon and badge concealed by his jacket. For some reason that she couldn't quite understand, her awareness of his intelligence presented her with the desire to mask her own.

She said, "I got a statement for them: blow me; that's my statement." DiGrazia didn't laugh, he didn't even smile. He just drove and thought, staring out the windshield. "What a bunch of ignoramuses. I think that's how they get hired. Give them a reverse IQ test, the dumbest one gets the job." DiGrazia nodded in distant agreement.

She said, "Where do we go from here, *Doctor?*"

DiGrazia smiled a small smile at that one as he said, "You picked up on that, did you?"

"I've seen screaming, wide-eyed, knife-wielding maniacs with more subtlety than Alvarez."

"You saw what he was trying to do, though? You understood Matthews's agenda?"

"I—"

"Catch that on the radio, Janice, that's us."

"What if it's Gheritty?"

DiGrazia didn't seem concerned, he even grunted what she'd come to think of as his personal, single-syllable laugh. DiGrazia did that frequently, almost as if he were embarrassed to laugh full out. "He can't use our frequency."

Constantine had the microphone in her hand. "Nick . . ."

"If it's him, it's him. Besides, he doesn't have the power to suspend me. If they want to cover their asses, they better wake Bailey up and have him call me in."

"They could suspend you on the word of a drunk?"

"It could go either way. We'll know soon enough." He looked over at her, then back out the windshield. "Answer the call, Janice."

"What's our number?"

"Five-one-two-nine."

She depressed the lever and spoke the identifying numbers in the microphone, and listened as the dispatcher spoke the call letters that said DiGrazia had an urgent message from someone named Barry Jenks.

"Advise dispatch to assign Jenks my cell phone number."

Thirty seconds later, the cell phone rang. Constantine watched DiGrazia fumble with it as he drove, first yanking it out of the pocket of his suit jacket, then trying to unfold it, finally getting it open, and hitting the button to take the call. She did not offer to help him out, as he had only given her his beeper number last night; she didn't know he carried a cellular.

Although, even angry, Constantine realized it was a smart move to have Jenks (whoever he was) call DiGrazia on the cellular number; the media monitored all police transmission, and they'd need a lot more sophisticated equipment than a RadioShack police scanner to listen in on a call transmitted over a digital cellular phone.

He spoke his last name, then he listened, and a slow, sly smile spread across his face.

His smile disappeared as he hurriedly asked, "Where are you, Barry?" Constantine watched him shake his head. "No, don't do that, don't go there, that's too hot right now." He thought for a second, seemed to come to a decision.

"Take him to State Street. Bring him in through the prisoner door. I'll talk to him there, I'll be there in half an hour." He handed the phone to Constantine. "Shut that damn thing off and close it up for me, would you?"

"Half an hour? We're two minutes away."

"No, we're not," DiGrazia said, as he turned right on Van Buren, drove west down several blocks, then turned into the parking lot of a tavern on the corner of Van Buren and Clark Street.

The Lincoln Town Car Constantine had seen earlier that morning as she'd been having her cigarette was already in the lot, idling, tinted windows rolled up against the cruelty of its surroundings.

As DiGrazia pulled up next to it, the Lincoln's back door opened, and Alvarez stepped into the lot, crushing multicolored glass under his well-shod feet. He closed the door behind him, cutting his driver off from sound, folded his arms and leaned against the car, nodding at DiGrazia, his brown face impassive as he waited.

DiGrazia shut off the car, but left his window open when he got out. Constantine did not believe that he'd done that accidentally.

"Which way'd it go?"

"For us, this time."

DiGrazia made a happy little boxing move, and punched Alvarez lightly on the shoulder. "This time, hell. When'd you ever lose one?" The relief in his voice was obvious, as was the fact that the two men had a far more familiar relationship than they'd appeared to have when they'd been back in the lieutenant's office.

Alvarez said, "Matthews is out. Parker cut him off cold, and I backed his decision. I won't be able to fire him, but by the time I get through with him he'll be answering phones in the Wentworth District." He looked away, as if ashamed to have DiGrazia witness his anger. "I may not be able to fire him, but I can make him wish I had."

"Gheritty?"

"He gets voted into office, there's nothing I can do about him. At least not until March." He flashed a smile. "Next year's election time again, believe it or not." Alvarez looked through the open window, and Constantine had to fight the urge to hastily look away. She told herself that she was DiGrazia's partner, she told herself she was a twenty-year veteran, and as good as anyone on the department. She told herself these things as Alvarez made some inner decision, then his eyes seemed to go out of focus, as if Constantine wasn't there. He looked away from her, back to DiGrazia.

"But don't be surprised if you get a formal letter of apology from him, one that'll exclude him from all culpability while he kisses your ass." Alvarez shrugged in a broad Mexican gesture. "He knows he blew it, and he's a professional, I think he'll accept it and move on."

"As long as he stays out of my way."

"He'll do more than that, he'll extend you every courtesy throughout the course of your investigation." Alvarez gave DiGrazia a hard stare. "Unless he has to push for an indictment."

"What about the files?"

"I had them transferred to your temporary basement headquarters. I didn't have the locks changed. The phone lines Parker requested are connected. The eight-hundred number's up, by the way—the phones are ringing off the hook already."

"Every moron with a resentment'll be calling in reporting his boss, his coworkers, some guy who's screwing his wife . . ."

Alvarez shrugged again. "It's good public relations."

"Who do you want to bow down before the press, now that Matthews is out?"

"Parker won't do it. He's beside himself, he wanted Matthews disciplined." Alvarez leaned over and tapped DiGrazia on the shoulder with his index finger. "He thought you did the right thing last night, by trying to keep it quiet. I agree with him, you know."

"It all works its way back to Schmidt, somehow."

Alvarez said, "I woke Bailey up, we'll let him handle it." He flashed a brief, bright, ironic smile. "It will endear you to him. Do you ever wonder how much you'd get done if you didn't have to play these games all the time?"

"Every day." DiGrazia said, then blew out his breath, put his hands in his pockets, and leaned against the front fender of the car, crossing his ankles, looking at Alvarez.

"I appreciate this, sir."

"Think I was cunning enough?" Alvarez was smiling. DiGrazia grunted his little laugh.

"I should have called you earlier. Thank God you saw it coming."

"Parker was the one who saw it coming. And besides, professional publicity whores aren't all that hard to anticipate." Alvarez lowered his voice. "You might have a problem with the Schmidt thing, though. He was on the front page of the paper today, Dominick, he won't just go away. And you *know* he'll be on every afternoon newscast, trembling, showing off those fingermarks on his neck."

"I didn't think he had it in him."

"Did you do it?" Constantine watched as DiGrazia nodded his head. She heard Alvarez's long sigh.

"That temper of yours is all that's standing between you and magnificence, you know that?"

"He threw an ashtray at me."

"Maybe you should file a complaint. Waving a gun at you on the street's a felony." Alvarez stopped to consider this. "It might deflect some of the attention away from you and the investigation. Have his weapon impounded, make him put up his house as bond, a man like him doesn't have any money. You can be an inconvenience to him, let him know it's not worth the trouble it'd take to follow up on his little amusement."

"He's got an agenda. I just can't figure out what it is yet."

"His agenda seems to be to hurt you, and get attention for himself."

"I don't think so, I think it's what it's always been: to get the doctor locked up. He doesn't have any witnesses, he doesn't have any friends close enough to lie for him anymore, either. And Gheritty won't dare bring charges against me after what happened."

"He may not have any choice. We're dealing with a celebrity now."

"Another reason for me to not file charges against him. He can call a press conference easily enough, now that he's a star. Talk about how we're hounding him. Make us all look bad while we're trying to run the bad guy to ground."

"TV screwed up everything," Alvarez said. "Makes people want simple solutions to complicated crimes. The public wants everything solved right now, because they saw Quincy do it in an hour on a rerun last night, between ads for soap."

Alvarez pushed off the car, looked up at the morning sky, as if for guidance.

"In the meantime, you and I have to meet in saloon parking lots, like thieves, so that reporters don't pick up our conversation with distance mikes." Alvarez shook his head.

He squinted at DiGrazia, and there was weight in his voice when he said, "What you said in the office, was that for real, or were you just blowing smoke, following my lead. Can you solve this one, Dominick?"

DiGrazia shook his head. "I'm not sure." It was the first and last time Constantine would ever hear DiGrazia admit to even a shred of self-doubt.

"How do you want to play it?"

"How far can I take it?"

"As far as you want to go."

"As far as I want to go?"

"You heard me." There was only a slight hint of reprimand

in the deputy superintendent's tone, but DiGrazia pushed away from the car and stood up straight at the words. He looked down, thought for a moment, nodded to himself, twice, then looked up at Alvarez and told him exactly how far he wanted to take it.

Chapter
26

The plainclothes policeman had introduced himself as Detective Muñoz, and his partner as Detective Chacón. They insisted on being referred to in that manner, while casually calling Tom by his first name. Tom understood it was one of the tricks detectives used to diminish their suspects. He knew about the Stockholm syndrome. He'd read hundreds—and written dozens—of papers about the effects of stress, oppression, and fear on the human mind and body, but he'd had no idea—until this very moment he hadn't really had a clue.

"Now you got *two* of them, you motherfucker! Two innocent women!" Chacón screamed it in his face, and Tom flinched. The detective's voice dripped with sarcasm and revulsion when he said, "I'll bet that makes you feel like some kind of fucking tough guy. First your old lady, now a teenaged kid." Tom said nothing, trying to live in his head, sitting in there in his business suit, trying to maintain his dignity, trying to simply survive until his lawyer arrived. Muñoz was pacing, smoking, blowing the smoke toward Tom.

"We leaked a report to the press that we already got a signed confession out on you, asshole. They'll print it, put it on the TV news, on the radio. It'll taint the jury pool. We own you. All you're doing with this closed-mouth shit is buying yourself a little time. That's *all* you're doing!"

Tom closed his eyes, willed himself not to listen to the condemning words.

They'd dragged him out of his house, would not let him attend to his wife. He'd had to sit handcuffed in the back seat of a squad car as they'd rolled her out past him and into the ambulance, Ellen strapped down to a wheeled stretcher. Tom had always thought the worst day of his life had occurred twenty years ago, today. Now that had been replaced, topped by this horror. Happy anniversary.

Muñoz said, "Look at him. Pussy." He turned his voice into a WASPy whine. " 'I want my lawyer, I want my lawyer.' Lawyer won't stop the shines from turning you into a jailhouse bitch tonight in the county jail, *Tommy.* It won't take them long to figure your whitebread ass out."

"You ain't got no idea what they do to guys like you. They *live* for guys like you." Chacón looked over at his partner. "You imagine this guy, tonight, what he'll look like? Mascara and Maybelline, have him wearing a little white negligee before lights out."

Tom's eyes were wide open, but he'd shut them out.

There were a number of reasons why this was worse than the last time.

The first reason being that he'd been married to Ellen for almost all of his adult life, and to see her helpless, strapped to the gurney, had been as painful to him as anything he'd ever witnessed. He had never seen Nancy's body, at least not until after it had been cleaned up.

"*We* can help you with that. But you won't let us," Chacón said. "You'd rather be an asshole gonna wait for his fucking *law*yer."

What hurt most was that Tom was older now, had turned himself into something, a man of prominence, through his hard work and dedication. He'd still been just a kid when Nancy had been killed, and although the terror seemed just as strong now as it had been then—if not more so—one of the major differences between the two times was that twenty years ago the detectives had been older than he, he himself had merely been a student.

Today he was a doctor, a doctor who'd spent the past three hours being insulted, humiliated and embarrassed by men younger than he, with less education, with less intelligence.

But with far more power.

Tom had to bite at the inside of his cheek to stop himself from telling them these exact things, especially now, as Muñoz stopped pacing, joined his partner at the little bolted-down table, leaned on it, and screamed in Tom's face.

"We got you cold, motherfucker! Ain't no lawyer gonna stop us from locking your ass up!"

"I want my lawyer!"

Chacón mimicked him. *"I want my lawyer, I want my lawyer!"* He dry-spat on the table. *"Bitch!"* The detective shouted the word into Tom's face.

At first he'd kept asking about his wife, as well as for his attorney, and they were slick, he had to hand that to them. They told him he could call the hospital just as soon as he answered a few of their questions. As for his lawyer, well, the last they'd heard, he was on his way.

That had been more than an hour ago.

They had been badgering him since then, without tapes running, without video, without any other witnesses. Chacón jotted things down in his leather notepad from time to time, but Tom couldn't imagine what he was writing down. He hadn't spoken a word to them in the three hours he'd been there, except to repeatedly ask about his wife, and for his lawyer.

Tom felt a momentary panic. He closed his eyes, tried to regulate his breathing. He would *not* let them see that they had hurt him. He would die first.

"Let me tell you what the Supreme Court says, Tom. It says we gotta stop questioning you as soon as you request a lawyer. It doesn't mean we can't *talk* to you until he gets here." Muñoz came around behind him and grabbed Tom by his hair, pulled his head back, leaned down and shouted in his ear. "What's the matter, you don't like me? You too good to have a conversation with me, Tom?"

"Gimme a square, Ray," Chacón said to Muñoz, and Muñoz dropped Tom's head, made a disgusted sound, and Tom opened his eyes. A package of Kools sailed over his head. Tom clenched his hands together in front of him, fighting to keep his face blank. There were other ways to fight these men. He couldn't handle them physically, he couldn't even say anything that would make them feel disrespected. There were ways they could hurt him without leaving marks. Tom knew about such ways, had studied them. He put his tongue on the roof of his mouth, unclenched his toes, then tried to clear his mind again, tried to escape into his head. It was harder now, more difficult than it had been. If they kept at him for a few more hours, he knew, they'd defeat him.

Chacón shook a cigarette out of the pack, lit it, and grunted at Tom. "Look at him. Pretending to be cool. We know what's going on inside you though, Tom. We know how scared you are." He exhaled a double stream of smoke through his nostrils.

Tom saw the smoke, heard the words, but on a distant level, as if he were watching a TV show while absorbed in something else.

He needed his medication, particularly the Xanax. He was having the sort of inward anxiety attack that even the patients in the mental ward would marvel over. How was Ellen? Where was Chris?

They'd said she'd only fainted. He didn't expect these half-trained, high-school-educated troglodytes to understand it, but he knew that she might have a blood clot, a subdural hematoma that had been brought on by the fall. Men like Muñoz and Chacón, you could hit them in the head with baseball bats and get nothing more than a blank stare. They could never understand.

Muñoz was in front of Tom again. "You're a pretty stupid guy, for a doctor. We can get you protective custody. We can save your ass from lethal injection." He looked at Chacón. "This genius, he'd rather sit through a year of detention in Division One, getting fucked up his asshole and in his mouth every night."

"Not to mention he'll be found guilty, get strapped down to the stretcher. Catching the needle instead of pitchin' them." Chacón smiled at Tom. "And we'll be there, front row, Tommy, watching. We'll blow you a kiss goodbye."

"Save the state some money, Tom." Muñoz's voice was reasonable. He acted this way from time to time, after they'd shouted for a while.

"We got the blood, we got the clothes. This is the big time, it ain't like it was twenty years ago, with drunks running the case and an ID section which still had fingerprints on index cards, a lab that couldn't type blood for three days. We got stuff now makes the technology from those days look like Fred Flintstone shit. We get blood typing done in hours, we got DNA, we spray Super Glue in to find fingerprints, we got all kinds of shit you never thought about twenty years ago."

Just as reasonably, Chacón added, "It's over for you, Tom. You killed that little girl. We know it and you know it. Your lawyer's gonna know it. The guilt's written all over your face. Think of the alternatives, and you'll know talking to us is the right thing for you to do."

Tom felt himself being dragged out of his head, fought it as hard as he could, but he couldn't stay inside, he found himself right there, right then, facing a year in jail before trial, and a death sentence after conviction. He clenched his hands more tightly together, hoped his panic wasn't reflected in his eyes. He thought about what they'd told him, what would happen to him in the county jail.

"We'll try you at Twenty-sixth and Cal, you won't be in no safe white neighborhood there, with guards at a gate keeping out the big bad gangbangers so they don't drive by your house with their radios up high. We'll try you right in front of the place where you'll be living the next year or so, with a jury made up of about 85 percent minorities, who ain't exactly widely known for their liberal attitudes toward rich white motherfuckers like you. They send 'em off to the death chamber every day, Ace."

The detectives would not let up. The small interrogation room Tom was in stank of their cigarettes, their constant smoking was yet another indication of the control they had over not only Tom's life, but his environment as well. Tom's cheeks burned with shame.

Although there was no mirror on the wall, he wondered if others were watching. The large round clock on the wall in front of him could conceal a recording device, and listening bugs could be put anywhere. He was suddenly certain that they were. He could picture them, a bunch of cops giggling together as they watched Tom's hands shake.

"We can save you from that," Muñoz said, wheedling now, pretending to be an advocate. "Just tell us what happened, that's all you got to do. We're your last hope. We'll make sure you don't get injected, we'll get you a life sentence. Doctors make out all right in the pen, believe me, if the way's paved for them right. Shit, you let us help you, and everybody'll protect you, the gangs, the guards, on account of you'll be the guy plugging the holes they stick in each other every day."

"And that *happens* every day, Tom, shankings, rapes. You don't hear about it on the outside, on account of nobody gives a shit."

"Let me turn a tape on, get the recorder going." Tom closed his eyes and took in a long, deep, shuddering breath. Muñoz took this as a sign of his breaking down.

"Tell you what, Tom. Let me tell you what else we can do for you. The thing with Nancy, a guy can understand that. A guy's in school, under a shitload of pressure, stress, to begin with, meanwhile, the old lady won't stop harping on him. It happens all the time. Guy explodes, kills her. Ain't a married man walking the earth wouldn't understand that, couldn't relate to it. You were smarter than most, you made it look like some sort of cult killing, and you got away with it. All right, that's old business."

Tom slowly opened his eyes and looked at Muñoz, hard. Muñoz did not seem impressed.

He said, "All we want you for is the girl, for what you did last night. She was a hooker, for Christ's sake, who gives a shit? It ain't like it's your wife, or a woman with a respectable job. We'll forget about Nancy, we won't even talk to you about that. I can talk to the state's attorney for you, we'll let that twenty-year-old business go. You cop to the hooker, just tell us what happened last night, that's all we want out of you."

Chacón said, "We'll get you anyway, it's just a matter of a couple of hours before all the tests are in."

Muñoz said, "You do that, and we'll make sure you're looked after right. Special Division at the county, protective custody, special meals, the whole works. Plead guilty and we'll make sure you go to a medium-security penitentiary, just for a couple years. Then we'll get you transferred to a minimum, some place like Vandalia, where you can sit in the sun, birdwatch all day when you ain't pickin' cherries off the trees. Ten, twelve years from now, you walk.''

"Don't confess, and God as my witness, you go to Menard until your appeals run out, then you get the needle.''

"Come on, Tom, what do you say?''

"I want my lawyer.''

"You cock*sucker!*'' Muñoz lunged for him, had Tom by the shirtfront with his fist cocked before Chacón managed to pull him away. The two men struggled for a moment, then Muñoz stopped fighting. He was breathing hard, sweating. He glared at Tom, and Tom avoided his eyes. Without another word, Muñoz spun and stalked out of the room.

"You're a real shithead, you know it?'' Chacón said, then followed his partner.

Tom took in several deep, grateful breaths, let them out slowly, his eyes closed, his head thrown back in the chair. He wouldn't break down, he wouldn't. He'd sit there, shaking, unti his lawyer showed up. His lawyer had once been a judge. He could get Tom out of this place. He would have to get Tom out of this place, or Tom would lose his mind.

Tom was almost calm a few minutes later when the door opened, and two different detectives walked in. This time it was a man-woman team, neither of them young, the man around Tom's age, the woman somewhat older than the man. She was short and heavy; the man was very tall, and appeared to be quite strong. Big-boned, but without a lot of beef on him, a boxer, rather than a weightlifter. The sort of man you see on cable late at night, fighting in winner-take-all Tough-Guy competitions.

Although his expression was pleasant enough. The woman, on the other hand, was looking at Tom the same way Muñoz and Chacón had: as a suspect to be grilled. Tom knew that he did not want to be alone in the room with this woman.

"Dr. Moran, my name's Dominick DiGrazia, and this is my partner, Janice Constantine.'' The woman nodded at the mention of her name. He looked at her, noted her pursed, bloodless lips, her grim expression. He looked back at the tall man.

"Are you detectives?''

"Yes, we are.''

Tom made sure that his voice was level when he said, ''Would you please find out how my wife is doing? Please? She fainted when the policeman pounded on the—"

"Your wife is fine, she's checked herself out of the hospital, we believe she's on her way over here."

Tom closed his eyes and leaned back in the chair, feeling half the tension drain from him. "Thank God," he sighed.

"We have a few . . . problems, but now we're just waiting for Judge Haney to arrive before we release you."

Tom shot forward in the chair. "Re*lease* me?"

"Officer Battenmeyer—who arrested you—and Detectives Muñoz and Chacón will be administratively restrained, and relieved of all police responsibilities until we can get them in front of a disciplinary committee. Battenmeyer should never have arrested you. Muñoz and Chacón did not allow you to call your lawyer." The detective lowered his head and voice fractionally as he said, "Muñoz lied to you when he said the judge was on the way."

"They said they called—"

"They lied to buy themselves some time with you. It's happened before. It won't happen again, at least not to you, not today, and not by them. The judge was not pleased when I called him."

Tom said nothing, just sat open-mouthed in the chair. They hadn't called Chris? They hadn't . . . ?

"The lieutenant who ordered the arrest has already been relieved of duty, pending departmental correction." Detective DiGrazia smiled. "That means he'll be walking a beat in South Chicago, if he isn't smart enough to retire."

"Then I'm not—"

The detective raised a hand, said, "Doctor, please, listen to me." He had grown somewhat colder, it was there in his expression, in the way he held himself. He had disclosed things that Tom had never expected, opened the department up to a lawsuit, in front of a witness. Tom now understood that the other shoe was about to drop.

"Doctor, there was blood all over the sidewalk in front of your house, there were hot ashes in a fireplace in the middle of May—"

The woman said, "Somebody have a weenie-roast?" and the

tall detective cut her off with a glance. Tom wondered if this was a game, good-cop bad-cop refined to a higher degree. He felt his elation desert him, felt the depression once more descending. Maybe they were lying, too. Maybe Chris still didn't know that he'd been arrested.

"—There were fresh scrub marks leading in a direct line from just inside your front door, across the hallway, up your steps, down the upstairs hallway, through your bedroom, and on into the bathroom. Blood has been found in the cracks of the wood in your floors. Samples have been taken, are being analyzed right this minute."

"It's my blood, my nose was bleeding!"

"What about the fire?" the woman asked. Tom looked over at her. He thought about that, thought about what she would think if he told her what had really happened, and knew that he didn't have a chance of convincing her of the truth.

He turned to the man and said, "Excuse me, can I ask you a question? Weren't you telling me I'm free to go?"

"I'm telling you that you were wrongly arrested, and, under the circumstances, I shouldn't have to tell you that you're free to have Judge Haney file a lawsuit against the city, and the police officers involved."

The detective pulled one of the molded plastic chairs toward him, removed his jacket, and placed it on the back of the chair. He was wearing a short-sleeve shirt. Tom saw the furious, re-strained power in his arms, saw his muscles dance with his every move. The detective sat down in the chair, not across from Tom, but beside him. The woman detective took her cue from her partner, and moved the third and last chair in the room directly across from Tom's. Now he could see them both without moving his head, would not have questions coming at him in stereo. Neither detective was armed. Tom wondered if that, too, was part of a well-planned ruse.

The woman, Constantine, said, "We're telling you that evidence seems to be mounting against you, Doctor. We're telling you that your brother's in custody, and he's scared to death, too afraid to even talk to us." Tom closed his eyes again, thinking that they'd caught Terry before he could check himself into the clinic.

Constantine said, "And we're *both* telling you that neither one of us thinks you're guilty."

Tom's eyes snapped open. "You're *what?*"

DiGrazia said, "Now, you can wait on Judge Haney to effect your release—say the word, and we're out of here, Doctor. We'll even stand guard at the door until he gets here, make sure that nobody else gets in this room and bothers you."

Constantine said, "But if you clam up, Doctor, you'll be our number-one suspect. We won't have any choice but to focus on you."

"But the cop, what's his name, the guy who arrested me and the other two, Muñoz and Chacón, they're in trouble. I don't understand. How could that be if you two aren't sure I'm not guilty?"

"They should have just brought you in for questioning, Doctor, you should never have been placed under arrest."

"This is about Schmidt, isn't it? He's pulling strings, he's—"

"He has no strings to pull, Doctor," DiGrazia said, and Tom believed him. "He's a drunk, a burnout. The newspaper story was a joke."

"Except that a woman was killed in an alley the night before that joke got told, and I've been arrested for it."

"You've been *un*-arrested." DiGrazia leaned forward in the chair.

"Explain it to us, Doctor. Can you do that? Free us up, let us loose to go after whoever really did this. If you can't do that, if you refuse to—which is your absolute right—then we have no other choice than to focus strictly on you, and we all know that means that a killer's running around free." DiGrazia leaned forward still, his eyes intense, burning into Tom's. Tom held his gaze, then nodded his head.

There was a note of bitter irony in Tom's voice when he said, "I was going to call and offer to help."

"I know."

Tom looked at him, but the detective did not elaborate.

Tom said, "Chris is gonna kill me . . ."

"But you'll help us anyway?"

"I'll tell you what you need to know, but I want to wait for Chris, and I want it all on tape, and on camera, every word. No notes." Tom saw Constantine smiling at him, in appreciation, he thought. She seemed to have lost the edge of her anger. DiGrazia's eyes were smiling, as if he completely understood what Tom had said. He reached around, dug into his jacket pocket, and took out a card. He took a pen out of his shirt pocket, scribbled something on the back, then pushed the card over to Tom.

He said, "If for some reason you want to talk off the record, Doctor, feel free to call me. That's my home telephone number on the back."

Tom put the card in his wallet, thinking quickly, wanting to phrase his next statement as carefully, as respectfully as he could. "Please understand that I'm not putting any conditions on you, but I would like to see Terry first, if that's possible, while we're waiting for Chris."

"Terry?" Constantine said. "We haven't found him yet. Nobody knows where he is."

"He isn't . . . ?" The truth struck Tom and he sat up straight in his chair. He looked from one detective to the other, shaking his head in disbelief. "Not Frank, it's not Frank. Don't tell me you arrested Frank."

"Frank's being held for questioning, that's all. He's not under arrest."

"Mr. DiGrazia, you have to believe me, Frank's a mental defective. He's alcohol and drug dependent, he's brain-damaged. He was mistreated so badly for so long that all he wants now is to get high, and to please anyone who can help him do that. A good interrogator could get him to confess to the Crucifixion in about thirty seconds."

"There's videotape of him panhandling right outside the Chicago Avenue alley."

"Sweet Christ."

"He's admitted that he was there. He's made—other admissions—too, Doctor, you should be aware of that."

Tom leaned forward and grabbed DiGrazia's forearm. It felt like the leg of a racehorse. "Frank *does not know* what he's saying to you, Detective! He'll walk into any trap you people set."

"Nobody's trying to tra—"

"Please let me see him, please. Detective. You don't know what he's going through, you don't know how his mind works.

214

Let me just talk to him for five minutes, *please.*" Tom felt the burning sting of tears behind his eyes, breaking for freedom. He desperately fought them back. He let go of DiGrazia, turned his head away, and blinked several times, and felt the urge to weep lessen. He turned back to the detective, who was watching him closely, watching impassively.

At last, DiGrazia took in a breath, blew it out in near disgust. "You think Judge Haney's going to kill you?" He said. "Wait until you see what happens when my boss finds out about *this.*" He turned to Constantine.

"Go get Frank, Janice, and bring him in here while we wait for the judge."

CHAPTER
27

Ellen had to look away as the guard inside the cute little pipe-roof shack came out and wrote down her father's license plate number on a paper attached to his clipboard. The guard sauntered over to the driver's side, squinting in to look at them. Her father rolled down the window, letting out his cigarette smoke. He dropped the half-smoked butt at the guard's feet.

"You're visiting who?"

"I've got Mrs. Moran with me, for God's sake!" Her father's frustration was bubbling over. Ellen turned to glare at the guard, and he was clearly stunned at the sight of her.

"Mrs. Mor—"

"May we proceed, Kenneth?" Her voice was crystalline, icy.

"Ma'am, I'm real sorry about—"

"Kenneth!"

He disappeared into the shack, the gate went up, and Kenneth's arm appeared in the doorframe, waving them through. Ellen felt her father watching her as he rolled over the first speed bump, and she turned her head away again, looked out her side window. She had to say something though, had to deal with her anger and deal with it right away, or she would let the frustration bake inside of her until it burned into a full-fledged rage.

216

"Do you think that rent-a-cop moron asked the *reporters* who they were visiting?" Her voice was high and shrill, but if her father noticed it, he didn't comment.

He just said, calmly, "You could ask them, there's sure enough of them."

Ellen turned to look through the windshield, saw the vans with the satellite dishes atop them, their call letters stenciled on the side, the vans lined up from one end of her block to the other, double-parked, blocking in the squads and unmarked police cars, while the camera crews, the directors, the producers, the van's drivers, all of them were standing around as the talent interviewed Ellen's neighbors.

She said, "Daddy, just keep—"

"I'm way ahead of you, honey, just look back out your window, don't look at them."

Ellen turned her head away. "Is my door open?"

Her father didn't answer at first. The short silence nearly drove Ellen mad.

"Yeah, the door's open."

"Those sons of—"

"Popped the garage door, too. The connecting door to the house's open, so's both your car doors. Got reporters milling around in it, that, or they're really well-dressed cops, with a lot of slick shit in their hair."

"Goddamn sons of *bitches!*" Those motherfu—"

"Ellen!"

Ellen bit off her anger, bit down on it hard and willed away the incredible sense of personal violation; they were inside her house, snooping around, there was nothing she could do to change that now. Alienating her father would not help her, she needed him.

"I'll have to take your car, Daddy." Ellen sensed his reluctance. "I can drop you off at the train station, or you can drop me off at a car rental agency." Ellen saw the end of the schoolyard, it was okay to turn forward again.

"You going to see Tom?"

"Yes."

"Radio said they were holding him at Eleventh and State. That's two blocks away."

"I need a car, Dad. I'm not looking for a cab ride, or worrying about distance. Tom will need things, I'll have to meet with his lawyer, there are other things I have to do . . ."

"Can't you drop me off at home, first?"

Ellen turned to look at him. For a moment he was no longer old and fat, for just an instant he was trim and strong, had a full head of brown hair, the arrogance glimpsed through his profile had turned him into his son, Todd, dead all these years. Todd, who didn't care about anyone but himself, who only cared about filling his own needs, having his selfish, personal desires immediately fulfilled.

At least that's what everyone had thought, until Todd committed suicide. After that, people had their own theories concerning his past behavior. Only Ellen knew the truth, what Todd had really done. She knew because he had done it to her.

Her father said, "You guys can stay with us, if you want." Ellen had made herself look away, and when she looked back, her father was driving. Todd was gone. Ellen thanked God for small favors.

"Just drop me off at the police station, would you please?" Ellen said, and she was happy at the humble yet manipulative sound of her voice in her ears.

Tom could remember the very first time that he realized his brother was crazy. He'd been six or seven, which would have made Frank ten or eleven, and on that day Frank had been wearing their father's self-hatred all over him. He'd been standing by the window, their father still at work, Frank fat then, overweight, withdrawn, and shy; their mother out at the Laundromat; Frank babysitting Tom and Terry, music playing on the radio. A Beatles tune, Tom recalled, as he visualized Frank trying to dance, the radio up loud, Frank's body jiggling as he shook it in time to the beat, waving his arms around, his eyes wide open, staring off into space with a panicky look, thick blood blisters under both eyes, swelling them. Frank had moved, swayed, singing unintelligibly, his voice high pitched, girlish; Frank gyrating and pretending to fit in in a world that had already abandoned him; Frank's nose smashed over to the right, one ear already cauliflowered; Frank only ten and yet already filled with the knowledge that he would never, ever fit in, while fitting in was all he wanted. He looked out over the swelling, not seeing much more than red, as the realization dawned upon him that he would never dance with a young girl at the high-school homecoming ball, would never fumble with a bra in the back seat of a car, parked behind the IGA, late at night. Would never be touched, talked about in whispers, admired the next day at school. He would never run a touchdown pass through the goal posts, or catch the final out in a baseball game, working center field. Tom saw all that in Frank's eyes, as his brother desperately pretended he could dance, and he saw Frank's shoulders droop, and the defeat come into Frank's face, the knowledge that it was over for him before it ever had a chance to begin. And then he watched his brother as Frank tried to fight it, as he began to dance more wildly, more excitedly, with more abandon, moving his feet, waving his arms, thrusting out his torso like Tom Jones on the TV show. And then it was over, Frank was out of breath, looking over at his younger brother, exhausted and destroyed, and Tom looked into those beaten, crying, puppy-dog eyes, and he knew, he knew his brother was crazy.

Although that was not a term he would use now, not after twelve years of medical training. Though the look was still there, that bewildered look; Frank would never be a man who'd understand that life had dropped on him in much the same manner that an anvil drops on an egg. Frank was no longer fat; he was skinny. But it was the thinness of the ill, rather than that of the fit. The nose was gone now, flat, against Frank's cheek. Several teeth were missing, scars crisscrossed his face. And the look in his eye was flatter now, the self-knowledge no longer a new thing, but very old, ancient.

But the look was still there, panic, now mixed with acceptance.

Tom looked at his brother and remembered, and tried to keep his face impassive while the detectives were still in the room.

Which they weren't for very long, the tall man, DiGrazia, excusing them both moments after Constantine had led Frank into the room.

As soon as they were gone, the two men embraced.

"Tommy, I didn't do it, I didn't do it, I didn't do it—"

"Sh, sh, I know you didn't Frank, I know you didn't, it's all right."

"Tommy! They're going to lock me up! I was just begging, that's all, I was just begging on the sidewalk!"

"There's a lawyer on the way, Frank, he's coming, he'll get us both out of here."

Frank stiffened in Tom's arms.

"Both of us?" Tom smelled Frank's breath as his brother asked it in his ear. Frank leaned back, sniffling, wild-eyes wide. "Both?" Tom cursed himself for wincing. He led Frank to one of the chairs, sat him down, and kept one arm around Frank's shoulders as he pulled a chair close enough to sit right beside him.

"They're questioning me, too, Frank, that's all this is. Nobody's under arrest, nobody's going away. We're going to get out of here, and you're going to come live with me." Frank looked away.

"I got a room this time, Tommy, I got a place to stay."

Eighth-graders had, on average, higher intelligence, but Frank's pride was still in place.

"With me and Ellen, Frank. We want you there, we talk about you all the time. We miss you. You can pack your clothes and get out of your room, and you come back to live with me, all right?" Frank nodded, as pleased as he was afraid.

"They're not going to lock me up? You promise?"

Tom leaned in very close, put his mouth directly next to his brother's ear, and spoke in a whisper that even Frank had to strain to hear.

"They made some big mistakes today, Frank. They did bad, and they'll have to pay for it." Tom closed his eyes for an instant as his brother winced at the words. Tom hadn't the time for diplomacy, he'd gone for the vein right off, knowing just which buttons to push. "If you do what I tell you to do, *exactly* what I tell you, we'll be eating steak tonight in my new, big house."

"Will Mom be there?"

"Ssh." Frank's voice had rung in the room. He obviously hadn't found out that their mother had died two years ago. Tom did not think that right now was the time to tell him.

"Sorry." Tom smelled his brother's fear-sweat. He felt the warmth that followed terror, it radiated off Frank.

Tom whispered, "Say nothing. Not one word. Act—" it broke Tom's heart to say it: "—act dumb . . ."

Frank nodded, then pulled away, placed his own mouth next to Tom's ear.

"That's the problem, Tommy, that's the problem. I told a cop—when I thought he was my next-door neighbor—I told a cop that the way to get the cops to leave you alone was to act dumb. I told him that if you wanted to get the cops to feel sorry for you, you had to act pathetic." Tom winced again at the word; Frank was an emotional thesaurus, one which had just matched Tom's most forceful impression toward him.

They switched positions again.

Tom said, "So they're treating you as if you're just playacting with them?" Frank nodded, smart enough not to go through the entire procedure just to confirm Tom's words. "If they're watching us, they'll ask you what we were talking about in here. You tell them nothing, tell them I just told you how much I love you, can you remember that, Frank?"

Frank nodded again. Tom was surprised to hear him whisper, "I love you, too, Tommy." He hadn't thought Frank had that in him. He frowned.

"You want to come to my house, you want to come live with me, don't you?" He continued before Frank nodded. "Then you have to listen to me, you have to do exactly as I tell you, Frank." Several rapid nods of compliance. Tom said, "Don't say another word to them. I don't care what you've already said: you're not under arrest, which means you haven't been advised of your rights, which means—"

"I know." Frank's voice rang in the empty interrogation room. Tom winced, then realized that Frank hadn't said anything that could be used against him when they took him away.

"Then you know that we're both all right so far. No matter how scared you get, no matter how badly they threaten you, no matter what they say they'll do, whatever, all you have to do is say, 'I want my attorney,' you understand that, Frank?"

"I want—" Tom shook him to stop him from repeating the phrase. Frank stiffened as he realized his error.

"Your lip has to be zipped, Frank." Tom's voice was stern. He had pushed another button, and the sudden tension in Frank's shoulders assured him that his brother clearly understood the message.

Tom leaned away from Frank's ear, looked sadly into his face. He mouthed the words, *I love you,* and took both of Frank's hands in his own and squeezed them as his brother wiped at his eyes with the back of his forearm, and said the words back to him, out loud.

"There's nothing in the room? Not a blood-stained T-shirt, nothing?"

"Nada." Barry looked disappointed.

DiGrazia spoke to Constantine without looking away from the closed-circuit monitor. "He'd have needed a basement."

"Frank?"

"The killer. A basement. Maybe just a bathtub. It could have been done in an apartment, but I doubt it."

Constantine said, "Larry Eyler did all right in an apartment."

"But never in a rented room, with a toilet down the hall. You couldn't do this in a flophouse."

The room was small, and Barry was tired, and more than a little depressed. Twenty-nine men had been assigned to DiGrazia's experiment, and he'd hit the jackpot, and now his pinch appeared to be useless. They stood around the small monitor and watched Tom as he whispered into his brother's ear. Tom's arm never left Frank's shoulder; every now and then Frank's body would go rigid.

DiGrazia said, "Cut Frank loose."

"Oh, for . . ."

"We can't justify holding him, Barry, not after the way Matthews fucked up. We'll be lucky if Haney doesn't file a multimillion dollar lawsuit this afternoon."

"He's too smart, he'll wait," Constantine said.

Distractedly, DiGrazia said, "I wonder what he's telling him?"

"You want me to try and find out?" Barry said. DiGrazia shook his head without looking away from the screen.

"No point in it. We've got several citizen videos showing the guy outside the alley, panhandling, right after the wino found

222

what was left of Veronica. All the news stations have copies, they're running them during the commercial breaks, as teasers for the four o'clock news.

"We've got the clothes he was wearing, we've had the entire flophouse searched. The guy never owned a car in his life, never even had a driver's license. We know he spent the night before last in Calumet City, and the two previous nights cleaning up in a biker dive in Cedar Lake, Indiana. He slept on a cot in the back." DiGrazia shook his head again.

"What about the pill bottle?"

"What about it?" DiGrazia said. "So his prints were on it. There was no label, no doctor's name, no pharmacy, nothing to connect it to Frank. Even if there was, taking medication proves nothing; half the country takes something these days."

"I think he's part of it, DiGrazia."

DiGrazia pursed his lips. "He's no part of this; cut him loose."

"Want me to at least follow him?"

"He'll be wherever the doctor is."

Constantine looked at him. She said, "We've got to find Terry."

"I'm heading home," Barry said.

"Good work, Barry, sorry it didn't work out." The last word sounded as Barry shut the door behind him.

"How do you know he'll be with the doctor?" Constantine wanted to know, and DiGrazia, staring at the screen, answered her in a voice that told her it was obvious to anyone paying attention.

"That's what he's telling him, that's what he's saying to Frank right this minute."

"You want me to follow Tom?"

"After we question him, we'll assign a team, tell him it's for his own protection, if the judge doesn't file a motion prohibiting it. Haney's top-notch, and he's pissed off. You should have heard him when I called him, it was like having a conversation with a glacier. He'll have all his bases covered before he even gets here.

"What I want you to do, Janice, as soon as the doctor leaves with the judge, is run down Ellen Moran. Stick to her like glue."

"You think she's in danger?"

DiGrazia did not answer her. There was a knock on the door,

and a uniformed officer stuck her head in when DiGrazia grunted loudly.

The woman said, "Judge Christopher J. Haney is waiting for you, Detective," and DiGrazia reluctantly looked away from the monitor, and nodded that he'd heard her.

Behind them, Frank told Tom that he loved him.

CHAPTER
28

The civilian who worked at the lobby desk had a sheaf of papers that had been messengered, officer-delivered, or faxed there for DiGrazia, and the detective didn't even look at them as he took them and handed them off to Constantine, walking quickly toward Judge Haney. Haney was a large man who'd played college football and whose only form of exercise in the past twenty years had been golf.

"You find out why Ellen Moran resigned from the rape crisis center?" DiGrazia asked Constantine, as they walked toward the judge. Constantine was surprised by the question, but ready for it.

"They started letting men work as counselors, she didn't agree with that."

"I don't either," DiGrazia said, as they closed in on the judge.

The judge had a stern look on his face, one DiGrazia remembered from the days when Haney had been sitting on the bench; it was the look he'd use just before he ordered sanctions and leveled fines upon attorneys; the look he cast upon police officers he suspected were being less than truthful under oath; the look he leveled upon child molesters at sentencing hearings.

Haney pointed his chin at DiGrazia, raising it higher as Di-

Grazia got closer, so that by the time DiGrazia stood directly in front of him, he was looking up Haney's nostrils. Haney shoved a tri-folded paper into DiGrazia's hand.

"You know what this is?"

"A writ."

"Where's my client?"

"Judge, calm down. I called you, I was the one who blew the whistle, remember?"

"And you can sleep all the better tonight for having done it." DiGrazia wasn't used to having to look up at other men. "And you can do the rest of your civic duty by testifying honestly when you're called to the civil trial."

"Judge—"

"I'd like to see my client now, if you don't mind. I'll be escorting him to—a safe place. He can't go home because of the media encampment outside his house." There goes police coverage, DiGrazia thought.

Haney's tone had been sarcastic, now it grew caustic. "His wife is downstairs, DiGrazia, hysterical, locked into an interrogation room because some nitwit pretty-boy reporter from Channel Seven recognized her on her way in."

Haney paused, dissected DiGrazia with a glance, then said, "If I were you, Detective DiGrazia, I'd bring my client out here, right this second. And, just so you're aware of it, there will be an investigator staying with them to document any further police abuses."

"Judge Haney, would you listen to me for just one minute? Please?"

The former judge stood stone-faced, eyes burning righteously, a man who had wanted in his lifetime, who'd fought in Vietnam. He'd scrabbled for everything he'd ever gotten, he wasn't seeing dollar signs.

"Your client has expressed a willingness to discuss where he was last night with—"

"Who wouldn't? How long have you had him, four hours now? Without counsel? You think I don't know what kind of damage you people can do with that much time?"

You people? DiGrazia's eyes narrowed at the words. He fought down the urge to lash out.

"A young woman's been murdered—"

"And it's your job to find the killer. It's my job to ensure my client's constitutional rights. You have the writ, now I suggest you either escort me to Dr. Moran, or bring him out here to me, right now."

"Let us eliminate him, Judge. Please."

"Let you badger him while you wait for blood tests from the body, for your results from the lab, is what you mean. Pull your stunts on some kid fresh out of John Marshall, DiGrazia, don't try and pull them on me."

"I'm not pulling any stunts."

Haney looked at his watch. "Every minute that passes from right—*now*—" He looked back at DiGrazia. "—will be another million added to the lawsuit."

DiGrazia, aware that the man was serious, immediately turned and began to walk down the hall. He heard the judge's footsteps behind him, slowed, and waited for the man to catch up, then walked next to him, shoulder to shoulder, as he spoke, Constantine not far behind.

"Can I at least *ask* him if he'll cooperate?"

"You can ask him whatever you want." The judge's tone was brusque. "If he gives you any answers, he'll have to seek other representation."

"You've been a lawyer since right after the war, then a judge for what? Ten years? You have a vested interest in the truth, sir, you have more reason than most to seek it out." DiGrazia stopped outside the door, his hand on the knob.

"Dr. Moran's brother was in there with him, his name is Frank."

"I expect he'll be leaving with us."

"I said 'was.' He might have left. We've cut him loose."

"Good for you." Judge Christopher J. Haney tried to reach around DiGrazia, tried to grab the door handle. DiGrazia stepped into his path, blocking him. The judge was taller, but DiGrazia did far more strenuous exercise than golf. The two men stood there, looking at each other.

"Judge . . . Let me just ask him for his help."

"No. Now get out of my way." DiGrazia wondered if the lawyer would actually try to get physical; it wasn't something he could let happen, no matter how much he might welcome it at the moment. He nodded, then pushed the door open so the judge could enter first.

There were two men in the room, Tom Moran and his brother, Frank.

"Chris, thank God you're here."

DiGrazia heard Constantine come into the room with them, close the door, and move up behind him. She was covering up the embarrassment she was feeling for him by looking through the papers he'd handed her. He looked at Frank Moran, whose eyes were now red-rimmed. The man's lower lip was trembling; the experience had been hard on him. DiGrazia closed his heart off. He heard Constantine stop, heard a sharp intake of breath, heard her flip back rapidly through several other pages.

Judge Haney said to his client, "And God is the only person you speak to until we're out of this room, and you'll speak to Him silently, understood, Doctor Moran?"

Tom looked at his lawyer in near bewilderment.

"Nick?" Constantine said. DiGrazia did not answer. He was staring at Doctor Moran, pleading with his eyes.

Dr. Moran said, "I thought—" and DiGrazia nodded his encouragement, but the attorney cut Moran off.

"So did Detective DiGrazia. You both thought wrong. Now, please keep quiet until we're out of this room." Tom noded, and the judge turned to Frank. "Frank Moran?"

Constantine said, "Nick!" more urgently.

DiGrazia didn't look at her, just held a hand up in a *wait-a-minute* gesture.

Frank Moran said, "They told me I could go home, but I wanted to stay with Tommy."

"This must be my lucky day, I'm meeting all sorts of admirable people." Haney made a beckoning motion with his hand, and Tom stood slowly, puzzled, and motioned for Frank to join him.

"Goddamn you, DiGrazia, look at me!"

Everyone in the room stopped, turned, and looked at Janice Constantine. DiGrazia raised his eyebrows, casually, but the warning was in his eyes, he was close to an explosion. Constantine looked around the room, then back at DiGrazia, as if seeking his assistance.

She said, "Could I speak to you outside the room for just a second?"

"If it concerns my client . . ." the judge warned.

"Bag it, shit-heel."

DiGrazia's eyes closed for a second, then before the judge could respond, he said, "If it concerns his client, he'll get it anyway."

"It's Dr. Chen's report from the lab, Nick." Constantine's voice was grave. "There were two types of blood found on Dr. Moran's front porch; his own, and a type that matches Veronica Davene."

"That's not . . ." Dr. Tom Moran said, then had the presence of mind to shut his mouth as he dropped back down into his chair. Judge Haney, having less to lose, did not surrender his composure.

"Are you placing my client under arrest at this time?" He was issuing an ultimatum rather than asking a question.

DiGrazia looked over at Dr. Moran, at his brother, Frank, whose mouth was now working slowly, soundlessly. There was a string of spit connecting Frank's lip to his T-shirt.

He said, "You knew about the report when you came in here, didn't you, Judge?" There was no hiding his admiration, DiGrazia displayed it openly, with a half-smile of appreciation.

Haney wasn't buying it. "I asked you if you were placing my client—"

Constantine said, "And I told you to bag it, you—"

DiGrazia raised a hand to her, his head now lowered. His mind was racing furiously, reaching for more than the obvious conclusions, rejecting each one as it came to him, reaching, grabbing frantically for the next.

His head jerked up toward Constantine, and he quickly said, "What about *inside* the house? The blood they got out of the cracks?"

Constantine, nervous now, searched quickly through the papers, grateful that DiGrazia allowed her to, that he hadn't snatched them out of her hands. She scanned the report, shaking her head, saved face by turning sideways so DiGrazia could read beside her.

Judge Haney said, "Come on, Dr. Moran. You too, Mr. Moran—Frank."

DiGrazia snapped at him. "Just one moment, Judge." He turned back a page, then flipped forward two pages, hard eyes cutting into the paper like sun through a glass.

"I'll ask you only one more time, Detective DiGrazia: are you placing my client under arrest at this time?!"

DiGrazia let go of the paper, Constantine was holding them now. Several papers, exclusive of the report, fluttered slowly to the floor. DiGrazia stood looking at Dr. Moran, head tilted, eyes slitted, trying to see through him, trying to figure him out.

The doctor looked back at DiGrazia as he said, "I didn't—"

"Doctor!" The attorney shouted the title.

DiGrazia studied him for what seemed like a long time. At last he said, almost formally, "No sir, I am not." He turned to the doctor. "You're free to go," he said, and a look passed between them that neither Judge Haney nor Constantine could fathom, a look that Frank didn't even notice. It was an acknowledgement between them, a bond forged quickly, like those shaped on a battlefield. Dr. Moran nodded at DiGrazia, then followed Haney out the door.

DiGrazia bent down and picked up the pages that had fallen to the floor. He straightened, frowning down at a fax.

Constantine said, "Look, Nick, I don't understand what just went on here, but as far as I'm concerned, this is *all* bullshit . . ."

DiGrazia looked up at her, and she fell silent at the sight of his face.

"You want me to go follow the wife now, right?"

"I want you to come with me, first, as a witness."

"Again? What am I, your official witness? As long as we're talking, why didn't you bother to tell me that the state's attorney, the deputy supe, and God only knew who else were going to be at that meeting this morning?"

DiGrazia looked over at her. "Is this a sign of sleep deprivation or what?"

Constantine sighed. "Where are we going?"

"Bridgeport," DiGrazia said.

CHAPTER
29

But they couldn't go to Bridgeport, at least not right away, because a commander, two captains, a lieutenant, and a sergeant were waiting for them in the lobby, courteously but firmly demanding explanations for their actions of the day, wanting to know their plans, as they led DiGrazia and Constantine into an interrogation room where a stenographer had already been set up at a desk, a stenographer who took down the same words that were automatically recorded as soon as DiGrazia spoke them in the small, bugged room. DiGrazia spoke those words hurriedly, too, well aware of what could happen in a case such as this one, how if he didn't resolve it quickly he would be replaced, no matter who he was connected to. He'd been aware from the beginning that all John Parker and the assistant superintendent had bought him was a little time. Perhaps a day, perhaps a week, but the media pressure was heavy, the public was aroused, the tide was rolling in at full force, and DiGrazia could drown in the waves if he wasn't very careful.

Constantine knew enough to keep her mouth shut and let DiGrazia do the talking, although she watched him, keeping her face impassive at even the most outrageous lie, secure in the knowledge that what he told them could not come back to haunt

231

either one of them in the future. She admired the way DiGrazia cajoled and wheedled, though she hated the need for him to have to do it, and she thought she was gaining an understanding of the thin line that separates genius from madness.

She wondered which side of the fence DiGrazia would fall on, if he toppled off the fence of diplomacy, and vented his rage.

She watched him work them, play them, giving them small hints of things he had already figured out, making promises that he already knew he could keep, and Constantine wanted to smile, but didn't.

DiGrazia was still speaking to his superiors as Tom and Ellen had a tearful and—at first—joyful reunion in the lobby, with cameras rolling, recording their every move and word. The cameras captured Ellen hugging her brother-in-law, and would, in a few short hours, when the edited tape was broadcast on the early evening news, show Ellen turning up her nose at the smell of Frank's body odor, her lips turned down in distaste at the stench of his breath.

Neither DiGrazia nor Constantine witnessed Frank being put into a cab, neither of them saw the twenty-dollar bill change from Tom's hand to Frank's, they did not see the cab pull away from the front of the station. They wouldn't see, until much later, film of Ellen, Tom, and the judge walking hastily, refusing to answer any questions as they hurried around the corner and into the parking lot, the camera's last view of them the taillights blinking as Haney braked quickly at the mouth of the alley before turning onto Roosevelt Road. They did not hear Haney shouting angrily that his client had not made a confession, that whoever had told them that was a goddamned fascist liar. They had no idea as to the savagery of the argument that ensued in the back seat of the judge's car, as Tom and Ellen loudly bickered about what they should do next, what their next immediate moves should be, while the judge drove impassively, pretending to be a sightless, deaf chauffeur, until Ellen said that she wanted to make a statement to the press, and only then did the judge speak up.

"You can't Ellen, you don't understand what's going on."

"What's going on?" Ellen was looking at the back of his head as if he were a cab driver who'd butted in on a private conversation. "I know my husband's been falsely accused of a crime! I know there are fucking reporters, cops, neighbors, and God knows what else tromping through our home! *Through our home!*"

"The media will convict Tom in a minute if you give them a chance."

"You think they haven't—"

"Remember the Dowaliby case?"

Ellen did. The thought of it made her close her mouth, made her lean her head back against the seat and stare at the car's upholstered roof. The judge spoke as if Ellen had never heard of the case.

"Both of the Dowalibys appealed to the press, Ellen, seeking help in finding their daughter's killer. When they stopped talking to the media at the demand of their attorneys, the cops stepped into the void, told the media they both refused to take polygraph tests, went on about how their stories didn't fit. The press ate it up along with the spoon they'd been fed it with, the public fell for it, as usual, and David wound up doing a couple years in Joliet before the state supreme court overturned his conviction."

Ellen looked over at Tom, wondering what "a couple years in Joliet" would do to him. His face was bloodless, frozen. He had his hands on his knees, was squeezing them.

He said, "I told Frank to come to the house, I gave him our address."

Ellen exploded. "Do you *want* to be prey? Do you *enjoy* the idea of having them out there with their cameras, waiting for one of us to peek out the window?"

"As your attorney, I advise you not to—"

"You're not my attorney!"

"He's mine!" Tom, who had more to lose, shouted it at his wife. His words slapped Ellen across the face, made her shrink back at the very thought of Tom taking sides with anyone over her.

The last eighteen hours caught up with her; Ellen shouted back.

"My father's car is in that lot, I'm not leaving it overnight. I won't have it towed away. Stop this car, right now! Goddamnit mister, I said pull over." Sighing, Haney did so.

Then the judge protested her actions. "I want you to try and understand what the media will do to you, the conjectures they will assign to your going back to the police station alone, without your husband at your side." His voice was calm and low, he knew her mind was made up, he was simply telling her what he thought.

Ellen answered him by slamming the car door behind her.

The judge turned his attention to Tom, raised his eyebrows at the look of utter remorse on his client's face.

"We have a lot to talk about, Tom."

"Tomorrow."

"Tomorrow could be too late."

Tom's voice held defeat. "Would you please just drop me off at the VA hospital? I need someplace to think, I want to sort this out in my mind."

"They can still come back for you, you know. They probably will, soon."

"I know," Tom said. It was all he had been thinking about.

They were in the interrogation room for just over an hour, it only seemed longer to both DiGrazia and Constantine. Both of them were surprised when they checked their watches as they left. DiGrazia's expression was sullen as they finally got into the car. He waited until it was started, had his seat belt strapped on, before he muttered, *"Shit!"*

"They all report to somebody, and everyone wants some of the glory, right?"

DiGrazia didn't answer her until they'd pulled out of the alley onto Roosevelt Road. "But none of the pressure. A case like this attracts worldwide attention. Nobody wants to be remembered as the cop who fucked it up."

But you didn't have to take the case, you wanted *it.* Constantine didn't verbalize her thoughts, saying instead, "How much more time do we have before they pull the rug out from under us?"

"God only knows. When a case like this goes public, the pressure comes from everywhere. Usually, the FBI catches these guys, charges them with a single murder, and they go down for the count, and the public's none the wiser."

"Serial *killers?*"

DiGrazia looked over at her as if he'd never seen her before.

"Come on, Janice. They don't want to have to deal with the media any more than you or I do. And the killers, they can't *wait* to become famous, get called by all three of their names, get money, love letters, attention for the first time in their miserable fucking lives. I can think of a half-dozen cases just off the top of my head where the FBI nailed one of these guys, quietly locked them away for the rest of their lives, with nobody getting wise. Without books being written, the media camping out on the courthouse steps, or any of the other attention that comes along as part of the baggage."

Constantine had to think about that. It was a pretty slick move on the FBI's part. Get them off the street, as DiGrazia said, "Down for the count," without having to deal with an intrusive press, and without their ever becoming celebrities. Which meant that they would also be in the general prison population, where knowledge of their crime would get them the exact opposite of the fascination the public was greedy to get. It would become a badge of honor to slap such a man around, to force him into sexual acts.

Maybe the FBI wasn't as bad as Constantine had thought.

DiGrazia said, "Parker has the greatest pull within Violent Crimes. Even his superiors will do what he wants, for a while, but he'll have to watch himself, too, because there are plenty of people who're out to get him. Alvarez has the superintendent's ear, and the chief of detectives'll generally do what Alvarez tells him. I know a few people at City Hall myself." She could sense DiGrazia's bitterness at having to waste his thoughts on this. He used his free hand to rub his stomach. Constantine wondered if he were scratching his scar.

"A lot of it depends on who's pulling the strings behind the scenes for Matthews, and all the others. There're plenty of detectives with more pull than I have, even with Alvarez. But he'll do what's in his own best interests first. Matthews won't forget about how we showed him up, either. We'll have the rest of today, at least. They'll need that much time just to find us."

"I didn't know we'd be hiding."

"We won't be in another police station unless we have a suspect with us, I can tell you that. Unless we're in the basement headquarters—I have to go over those files and find the connection between the two killers. We'll double-lock the door as soon as we go in." DiGrazia turned left on State.

"Maybe we should have a secret knock for the team. Thump, thump-*thump*."

It was almost noon, and DiGrazia thought that they could get to Bridgeport more quickly if he took the Dan Ryan Expressway. He drove quickly down State Street, the light in the rear window flashing red.

"What a waste of *time* . . ." He muttered it, shaking his head.

"They were pretty hard. More courteous than I thought they'd be, but hard," Constantine said.

"We only got the courtesy because the videotape was running."

"Covering them while it condemns us."

"It won't condemn us."

"You sound awfully sure." Constantine was thinking of the many times DiGrazia had lied to them. It also could mean he trusted her. She wondered now if he did.

"Wait, let me throw up my hands, cry out in despair." DiGrazia glanced over at her. "Would that work better for you?"

"He can tell a joke, Christ, listen to him."

DiGrazia had to stop at a red light on Twenty-Second Street, and he looked over to his left, had to wait for a bevy of oncoming traffic that was working its horn-crashing way down the single westbound lane that hadn't been closed due to construction. He had forgotten about the lane closures. DiGrazia sighed. He kept his foot on the brake, and turned to face Constantine.

"What's your problem, Janice? What's going on?"

Constantine bit her lips together, and for a split second, DiGrazia was transported back to his childhood; his mother used to do that after she applied her lipstick. Afterward, she would check her teeth to make sure no lipstick stained them.

Constantine thought for a second, then shook her head.

"Let it go, Nick," she said softly. "I'm a big girl, and I threw in with you. I knew what I was doing, nobody twisted my arm."

"But?" Constantine fell silent. "Look, if we're working together on this, I have to know what it is, if it's about this case. If it is, it could affect your judgment."

"I've been a cop longer than you have, but I never saw it this way before, how bad it is. I can't get over how fucking political it all is at this level. Jesus Christ, first they made you put together a team of people you didn't want, then Matthews tried to take all the credit for himself, then they tried to get Schmidt to file charges against you, now you're lying on video, immortalized for all the bosses—Jesus Christ, we got more to worry about from *inside* than we do from *outside*."

"It's all just part of the deal, Janice." DiGrazia didn't seem overly concerned.

"And the doctor wrapping himself in the Constitution? Is that part of the deal, too?"

DiGrazia didn't tell her that that was his favorite *part* of the deal, beating them at their own game, within the confines of the Constitution, as defined by the Supreme Court. Stretching it when he had to, but not breaking it, never stomping on it. Any lesser effort, to DiGrazia, wasn't worth the challenge. In spite of his temper, he didn't view himself as a brute. Nor did he tell Constantine what he thought of cops who took constitutional "shortcuts" with suspects.

All he said was, "Of course it is."

"Let me tell you something. I'm starting to feel mighty sorry you got me out of patrol."

"Come *on*."

"No, I'm serious, listen to me. I've pinched a couple thousand people over the years, easy. We take them in, write the reports, go to court, whatever, you know? I've only had the screws turned on me maybe eight times in twenty years. You catch some big shot's kid driving drunk, or doing a burglary for drug money. One time it was the wife, caught in the act in a park with some guy she wasn't married to. She was crying, hysterical. Guy tells me she begged him to do it in the park, said it turned her on, the thought of getting caught. Husband wanted it all hushed up, didn't want to be publicly humiliated. Shit like that, nothing deep, nobody ever told me specifically, straight out, that I had to drop a pinch."

"You've blown reports, though, and don't tell me you haven't."

Constantine knew exactly what he was saying; DiGrazia wasn't commenting on her penmanship.

"Sure, who hasn't?" She grunted. "Right. *You* probably haven't. You got some guy cuffed, already in the squad for attempted murder, you find out he was beating the shit out of the guy who raped his daughter. What are you gonna do? You got to blow the pinch some way, detail the report or screw up the arrest so a first-year public defender can get it thrown out."

"Or don't show up in court."

Constantine seemed surprised to find herself saying, "You know how much time you've wasted just having to suck up, explain stuff to people? I had no clue. Lawyers everywhere, the media. Even the bosses want your ass. And all *they* really want is to get their faces on TV, use the exposure from that to score another promotion. You paying attention to them, what they're saying? Not a single *one* of them asked squat about the girl. Doesn't anybody care about Veronica?"

"We do."

"Yeah, we do." Constantine did not sound convinced.

"That's not it, Janice." Now DiGrazia's voice was persuasive. "That's part of it, but it's not what's bothering you."

"What are you, my father?" The two of them looked at each other until Constantine looked away.

She was a woman used to speaking her mind, but now she tried to stop herself from doing just that. Now she had to think about it, wanted more time, but he was right there, in her face, looming over her, and the climate inside the car was heavy. DiGrazia wouldn't take no for an answer.

In front of them, a double-length tractor-trailer truck was blocking the intersection, air horn trumpeting. They had the green light, but couldn't get through because of the truck.

"I've been watching you, Nick." Constantine did not look at him as she spoke, and DiGrazia did not respond. "Seeing how you operate." She could feel his eyes, those dark eyes, scalding the side of her head. "You don't have partners, everybody knows that. You just don't. And you have to be in control of things. I wish there'd been a mirror around when Matthews dropped the bomb about the doctor's arrest, I thought for a minute you were going to kill him.

"Still, you're the smartest copper I've ever seen. You don't make many mistakes, and no lazy errors."

Constantine turned to him, face to face, and did not blink when she said, "Did you set this all up this way, Nick, right from the beginning? You didn't know this was going to go over big in the media, nobody knew what Schmidt had pulled."

"What?"

Constantine screwed up her courage and said, "Did you pick an old lady with nothing to lose, drag her out of patrol to work a ballbuster case like this? What the hell, if it goes wrong, I got my time in, I can retire, right? You can go teach, go to a laboratory somewhere, and make a lot more money doing it, and there won't be some fine, young police officer gets his career ruined over any of it."

"You—" DiGrazia blurted out the single syllable, and Constantine flinched, sorry now that she'd spoken. She found herself rushing to explain her doubts about him, to make them fully clear to DiGrazia.

"You don't make a lot of false moves, Nick. I was there, I saw you close down the scene, and I've been working with you since. You need control. You need to always know what you're doing. Guys like you, you try to orchestrate everything you're gonna do in a given day before you even leave your house in the morning."

"Do you believe that?" DiGrazia said. "Do you think that's what I'm doing? Do you think I'd do that to you?" He did not seem hurt, he did not seem angry. He wasn't even bemused. He just seemed curious.

"I think you wanted me to do the work that the rest of the team's doing, now that some damn lieutenant made you work with one. I think now that you've got them doing it, you don't need me for anything."

"So what do you think you are to me now, an appendage? Is that what you think?"

"I think you can turn now," Constantine said, looking through the windshield, wanting to avoid his gaze.

The rest of the short ride had been silent as Constantine cursed herself for her honesty, as DiGrazia wondered about her, thought about what she'd said. He didn't speak to her again until they were mounting Schmidt's stone stairway.

"Did it ever cross your mind that maybe I did it to try and help you out?" he said it as he pushed on Schmidt's buzzer, as they heard the old-fashioned, deep, single bong inside the house, the noise that comes from heavy depending pendulum chimes.

DiGrazia was holding a hard copy of a fax in his hand, and he looked down at it now, at the check mark that he'd placed next to Dr. Thomas Moran's home telephone number. The number had been called from Michael Schmidt's phone, early this morning, around the time that DiGrazia had been pointing his Mag-lite at Veronica Davene's organs.

He wanted to ask Schmidt about a lot more than that. He naturally wanted to know what he'd been doing talking to the doctor, but he wanted him alone, without a lawyer or the media around, to press him hard while he still had the chance to ask him questions that he would not have been able to ask if Silverman was in the vicinity.

In other words, DiGrazia wanted to squeeze Schmidt like a grape, see what sort of juice flowed out. The phone call to Moran was just his legal excuse for being here. And he didn't care if the old drunk called a press conference in protest after he left.

Constantine looked at DiGrazia, seeming somewhat hurt but managing it. Her professional demeanor did not dim for even an instant.

DiGrazia muttered, "Wake up, you drunken son of a bitch."

"I'll go around back. We'll get him in surround-sound."

"Careful." The word passed over DiGrazia's lips easily and automatically, it was what one partner said to another when circumstances forced them apart while they were working a dangerous case. Constantine, aware of this, looked at him, opened her mouth, then closed it and nodded once.

DiGrazia depressed the buzzer again, cursing under his breath. The curtains were closed, the small window in the front door was useless to him. It was an older house, the front door led onto a foyer, with another door leading into the home itself. In happier times, DiGrazia would leave his shoes in that foyer, between the two doors, snow dripping off them, joining the puddles formed by the children's galoshes.

DiGrazia leaned far over the railing and pounded hard on the picture window.

He heard Constantine's voice calling his name, excitedly. DiGrazia almost fell over the railing, caught his balance, took two quick steps and jumped over the railing on the other side. He ran around the back to his partner, his weapon drawn as he turned the corner, all of him coming around at once, gun first, DiGrazia crouching.

Constantine was standing at the back door, her own weapon held in both hands, up close to her cheek. Her face was white and grim. She motioned her head for him to join her. He bounded up the steps as Constantine pointed her weapon at the door, ready to blast through it if she saw even a shadow move through the dirty torn lace curtains covering the window.

"He's in the kitchen." DiGrazia could see that, but said nothing, as his eyes looked past Schmidt's body with the halo of blood surrounding it, as he looked frantically around the room, searching for a killer. He saw no one. He stepped away from the window, turned to Constantine. Who said, "Want me to get your equipment out of the trunk?"

DiGrazia was impatient with her. "Wait a minute. We have to check it out first."

DiGrazia opened the screen door, and Constantine didn't have to be told to take the handle. She held it open for him as he stepped back, put his weight into his leg, and kicked the door hard at the lock.

It would have opened with half the effort.

The window shattered on impact, the door flew back against the wall. Before it could swing shut again DiGrazia was inside, crouching, weapon out, going to his left as Constantine came in on the right, Constantine breathing heavily, backing him up superbly. They covered each other as they'd been trained, going from room to room, from door to door, starting in the kitchen and working their way up: open door, one inside low to the right, the other inside and to the left, behind the door, quick to the closet, under beds or anywhere else where a human being might be hiding.

One of the three upstairs bedrooms was spotlessly clean, the floor scrubbed, a new white shade covering the window. There was a steel filing cabinet against the wall. What was it, an office? No, there was no desk, just a bed. Constantine looked under it, weapon out to the side so no one hiding under the bed could snatch it from her hand.

"Clear," she said, and DiGrazia closed the closet door, looking around the room, puzzled.

She followed him quickly back downstairs, where there were four closets, a living room and a dining room, a couch to look behind.

It took them less than five minutes to ascertain that nobody else—living—was in the first two floors of the house.

Still, they neither dropped their guards nor relaxed when they had to go back into the kitchen to get to the door that led down into the basement. The door had a lock, and a second, higher, barrel-bolt lock, one that children couldn't reach. The bolt was thrown, but that didn't mean that somebody wasn't down there, a hostage, a participant—stranger incidents than either of these had occurred in both their careers. DiGrazia looked at Schmidt's body as Constantine fumbled with the locks.

It was lying on its back, its face flat but unmarked, eyes wide open, as if in surprise. The bullet had entered through the right temple, at the side of the head, had exited hugely through the top of Schmidt's skull. The .38—the same pistol Schmidt had waved at DiGrazia just the night before—was clenched tightly in Schmidt's right hand.

He had to fight the urge to check the body, to feel it for warmth. His thermometer was in the trunk of his car; he could calculate the time of death later, if the basement was clear. He had to get Schmidt's hands wrapped . . .

Constantine touched his shoulder, and he got into position beside the door, then threw it open as she crouched and pointed her weapon down the stairs. This would be harder than going upstairs, more dangerous. There were openings, gaps between the wooden steps, a hand could grab at ankles. DiGrazia elbowed the light switch upward as he stepped onto the first stair, then went down them two at a time in case someone was hiding beneath them. Constantine waited until he was standing on the cracked concrete floor, weapon in front of him, pointing it around the basement, before she hurriedly followed him down.

It took only a quick glance around to establish that there was nobody down there with them. It took only a quick glance around to establish that, until very recently, somebody else had been.

The basement reeked of slaughter. The gray concrete was darker around the floor drain, had been stained with blood, the darker gray surrounded the drain in the center of the floor. It had been wiped up, washed, repeatedly, but it was still there, they could smell it.

As they could smell the fear, the terror Veronica Davene had felt as she'd waited for a monster to come downstairs and complete his business.

Constantine noted several boxes against one wall of the room, the same sort of cardboard boxes that Schmidt had brought to the Chicago Avenue police station. She was breathing in gasps as DiGrazia, breathing through his open mouth, walked close to the wall, away from the stain. He shone his Mag-lite on one of the thick concrete poles that supported the foundation beams, on the one closest to the drain.

The pole was scratched, marked, paint wiped off, steel chipped in places. The marks were recent. DiGrazia hugged the wall as he played the light around the room. A heavy chain lay under the stairway. DiGrazia held up a hand, motioned Constantine back up the stairs.

In the kitchen, he said to her, "You have Dr. Chen's beeper number, her home number, any way to reach her?" His voice, though soft, was surprisingly loud in the room where death had visited.

"I have her beeper number."

DiGrazia stored his weapon, handed Constantine his cellular phone. "Give her a call. I want her taking the samples from the basement herself, I want her to get some of the credit."

Constantine had to fight off the sudden urge for a cigarette. "He kept Roni down there, didn't he?" She searched through her wallet for Dr. Chen's card. "You knew that's what we'd find, but you didn't know where. It's why you told Stefaniak to find out if she'd been missing for a couple of days. You told me she wasn't a random victim."

DiGrazia, thinking, barely heard the words.

Constantine said, "Chained to the post, until he needed her. He couldn't be sure where she'd be on the night of the anniversary, so he grabbed her a few days early. You knew it all along, didn't you? He chained her down here so she'd be available when he needed her. He culled her out of the pack, he knew it would be Roni all along, *didn't he, DiGrazia?* He didn't just cut her out of the herd, he fucking *chose* her." DiGrazia nodded, just slightly. The two of them were now thinking the same thing.

He said, "You ever have the urge to kick a corpse?"

Constantine dialed in Dr. Chen's beeper number, then hurriedly handed the phone to DiGrazia; she still didn't know his cell phone number. DiGrazia punched in the digits, hit the pound sign to send it off, then shut the phone down, handed it back to Constantine.

She accepted it, and articulated what they'd been thinking. "She must have been terrified, so fucking scared. Pregnant and alone down there. Waiting." There was a catch in Constantine's voice.

They waited, but the phone didn't ring. The two of them stood there, looking at Schmidt.

"I always thought it was too convenient, him having his face splashed across the front page of the paper just when another body popped up. So the heat came on, you scared him, and he killed himself. He must have thought you'd be coming back here with a warrant."

DiGrazia looked at her, opened his mouth as he shook his head, then he closed his mouth, as if he'd thought better of enlightening her. Constantine forced her anger out through her nose, with a hard puff. She'd get used to him someday.

DiGrazia said, "I'm going to call Bailey, I want him over here, too. He can be the hero." His glare pinned Constantine. "And he can give you the credit for solving this."

"Don't do me any more fucking favors, DiGrazia."

"I've done all I plan to, but you can still do *me* a favor. After Chen calls back, go upstairs, and search the bedroom. Schmidt was a pack rat, that's where he'd most likely keep a diary or a journal. Look in the filing cabinet in the other bedroom, too, the one that was clean. We might get lucky, and if it's there, we want it before the rest of them arrive."

Constantine watched him walk wide around the body, stepping into the hallway to call from the phone in the living room. She was hurt, confused, angry at the way he'd treated her. And the worst thing about it was that she felt that she owed him an apology.

The phone rang in her hand, and she was grateful that Di-Grazia wasn't in the room to see her jump.

CHAPTER
30

Dr. Warren sighed in relief and gratitude as he hung up the phone. He closed his eyes, steepled his fingers under his chin, and tilted his head back, looking sightlessly at the ceiling, then contained himself and opened his eyes, put a warm, welcoming smile on his face. There was a small knock on the door.

"Come in."

Dr. Warren watched his prize patient step tentatively through the doorway, saw him turn, close the door, watched him lock it, as if doing so would somehow keep his secrets in there with them. Eddie was carrying a cream-colored manila folder in his right hand, holding it to his chest as if it were the only thing that prevented him from having a heart attack.

Dr. Warren made certain that both the cassette tape machine and the digital recording device were running; he would have the confession on both cassette and CD-ROM, he would be able to listen to it over and over again as he transcribed the statements for the book.

The killer shambled over to the couch, and, sighing heavily, lay down. He at last let go of the folder, placed it on the table beside Dr. Warren's couch. He had not looked Dr. Warren in the eye. Warren heard a muffled sob.

It was nowhere near as rare as the general public thought, this sort of situational guilt. Warren and his colleagues witnessed it over and over again. The FBI did, too, but they weren't telling the public about it, not even after they retired and wrote books about their careers.

But it was a fact, a known—established data proved it: repeat predatory killers such as this one often experienced deep feelings of guilt, guilt that spiraled as their body count swelled.

Not "guilt" in the manner that a normal person would feel it, but, rather, guilt they could switch on and off, depending on how close they'd come to getting caught, depending on how strongly they felt the inner urge to bond with others of their clan. Depending on how intelligent they were, and how purely psychopathic.

In other words, it depended on how much they wanted to pretend they were still human.

This one seemed to want to live in that fantasy forever.

"Hello, Doctor."

Warren had purposely made him squirm, made the killer speak first.

"So, Eddie, how bad is it this time?" The man on the couch grunted. Warren watched him shake his head piously, as if Warren would never understand.

"I know you've been back in Chicago. You've been refilling your prescriptions here again; the pharmacy checked with me because the 'scripts were written four years ago." Eddie nodded. Warren was angry, but he knew he couldn't push it, the only thing keeping Eddie on the couch was his own willingness to be there, and Warren couldn't make him stay, unless he was ready to disclose the truth. And he wouldn't do that, couldn't do that, because if he did, they'd take Eddie away in chains. So it was out of the question for now.

But until that time came, if it ever came, Dr. Warren wanted Eddie isolated, wanted him in his control, wanted to be able to study him without outside interference, or without Eddie coming and going at all.

But Eddie didn't seem to want to cooperate. Dr. Warren thought he had a way to finally gain that cooperation.

"Would you like some medication, Eddie?"

Eddie nodded again, but this time, Warren waited for an answer. It came in a tight little frightened voice.

"Yes."

Warren took the pill bottles out of the center drawer of his desk, shook what he believed to be the appropriate mix out into his hand, then rattled them back and forth in his palm—as if he were shaking dice, hoping for a seven—as he got up and walked over to the water cooler set up in one corner of the room, under Warren's diplomas. Warren took two paper cups out of the dark plastic chute, dropped the pills inside one of them, filled the other one with water. He stepped over to Eddie, and the man sat up quickly, frightened.

Warren was frightened, too, and rightfully so. The pills in the paper cup were combustible, they could send a man like Eddie into an enchanted, nonviolent dreamworld for the rest of his life. All of Eddie's urges would be suppressed, all his violent urges overwhelmed. The portions of his brain that allowed him to even think such thoughts would—if Warren's calculations were correct—be shut down, closed off to him. Eddie would—perhaps for the first time in his life—be at peace.

And he would no doubt have a compulsive urge to confess his varied sins.

Eddie was looking up at him hungrily, beseeching Warren for help. If Warren had a free hand, he would have smoothed Eddie's brow. He held out the cups, smiling with understanding.

"Thanks."

Eddie still did not look into Warren's eyes as he accepted both cups, greedily popped the pills into his mouth without even asking what they were or what they might do, then washed them down with the water.

Eddie wiped his lips with the back of his hand as Warren accepted the empty cups from him, put one inside the other, and was careful not to crush them as he dropped them both into the wastepaper basket beside the couch. He sat down on the edge, pulled a Kleenex from the box on the coffee table, within easy reach of the couch. A preparation that had been made due to the fact that patients often got emotional with Dr. Warren; he had the gift, and they knew it. He was the most popular staff doctor at the hospital, and he was well aware of that, worked hard at making it so, at winning the trust of his patients.

He handed the tissue to Eddie. Eddie seemed to take it as his cue, began to cry into it.

"Shh, it's all right, Eddie, it's going to be just fine." Dr. Warren's voice was soothing, his hand soft on Eddie's shoulder. "It's good to let it out, you know, I've told you that before."

"You-told-me-a-lot-of-things-I-should-have-listened-to!" Eddie was doing his penance, and Dr. Warren allowed it, encouraged it, pulled Eddie to him and held him in an embrace. Feeling the tears of a monster dribbling down his neck gave him a small, delicious thrill.

"You have to stay with me this time, Eddie. You can't go off again."

"I keep getting so *afraid,* so scared they'd—"

"They won't!" Warren's tone was harsh. "I won't let them, Eddie."

"You won't?" Eddie pushed away and looked up at Warren, eyes pleading. "You promise me!"

"I give you my word, Eddie, nobody's going to lock you up in a jail, nobody's going to put you away in some institution for the rest of your life. You're safe here, Eddie, don't you know that by now? I'll take care of you; don't you trust me?" Eddie nodded his head rapidly several times, trying to erase the Doctor's doubt.

"But you have to promise me something, too, Eddie. You have to do something for me."

The mix of psychedelic and psychotropic drugs were beginning to have their planned effect; Eddie literally felt them flowing through his bloodstream, felt them calming him, felt the demon within him fighting against them, felt it losing the battle. He closed his eyes as sedation overwhelmed him, as he felt the massive weight of his inner aching lifted from deep inside, torn from the depths of him and ascending up and out of him, through his nose, through his eyes, his ears, his ass. He thought that if he opened his eyes he'd be able to see it: evil, all black, curling out of his orifices like smoke from the devil's cigar.

Eddie kept his eyes tightly shut as he said, "I'll do whatever you want me to do this time, Dr. Warren." His voice was dreamy, distant. Eddie felt a sudden sense of great love for Dr. Warren. "I promise. I can't ever do it again." He smiled softly, then the smile widened. "I've burned all my bridges behind me."

What had he said? What did that mean? Dr. Warren let it go.

"You have to sign commitment papers, Eddie."

Eddie's eyes popped open wide, and he half sat up on the couch.

"I—" He looked around wildly, as if he'd been expecting to see something that wasn't there.

Dr. Warren's voice was gentle as he said, "You have to, Eddie, it's the only way. You have to trust me this time or we won't be able to find the cure in time to save you." Dr. Warren said this just before rising and going back to his chair, to become the floating, Godlike presence behind the confessing patient. Eddie settled back down on the couch.

As he strolled over to his desk, he said, "You know as well as I do what will happen to you if they catch you out there. Prison, or a state institution. They'll put you on a ward. Here, we can work together. You'll be safe, with a single roommate. We have medications now that can control your impulses—take away the *need*.

"You have to promise me you'll stay with me, Eddie, you have to promise me that you won't leave until I say that your therapy's complete."

In a near fog of delight, Eddie said, "You think that can happen? You think therapy can work with me?"

"Oh, I know it can," Dr. Warren said, as he thought of the bottles lined up in his desk's center drawer.

"I can't, I can't, I can't *talk* about it, yet."

Dr. Warren hid his disappointment, it was one of the risks he had taken when he'd given Eddie the pills. All right, let him have a taste of it, let Eddie know how good Warren could make him feel. Then withhold it, let him feel the pain. See if he felt like talking then.

Warren said, "But you will, Eddie, when you're ready. And I'll be here to listen to you."

He didn't tell Eddie about the machines he would hook him up to, didn't tell him how he'd study his brain waves. Eddie wasn't ready for that, yet. He wondered how Eddie would take to single-cell containment. First things first; get those papers signed.

"Stay in here." The way the words were spoken told Warren that Eddie didn't find the prospect completely unattractive. "There's only one way I can do that, Doctor."

Conditions? Did the man somehow understand that he was indeed in a position to make them? He was smarter than Warren thought.

"I'll stay here for as long as you want, if you put me in a room with Neal."

Dr. Warren was very careful when he said, "Neal, why of course. I can arrange that for you, Eddie. But you can't talk to him, you can't tell him, or Sarge—or anybody else—your business." It was a risk Warren had to take, he had to keep Eddie in this end of the hospital. If he were locked up with the psychotics or in the detox center, he would be under another doctor's care.

"If you talk to them, if you tell them anything, Eddie, you know what might happen, don't you?"

"The big cop will come for me."

"Big cop?" Warren thought this was delusional, soon found out that it wasn't.

"The big cop from TV. I saw him last night, heard what they said about him. DiGrazia." Eddie shivered. "He wouldn't talk to them, but they had enough to say about him. I know all about *him*, all right."

"How can he harm you, Eddie?" Warren knew the answer, he just wanted the answer on tape.

"He knows about—last night."

"The girl they found dead in the alley. That was your work wasn't it, Eddie?"

Eddie quickly covered his face with his hands and shrieked. "I don't want to talk about it!"

"It's all right, Eddie, you don't have to."

After a time, Eddie said, "Can you check me in then? Will you check me in, Doctor?" Warren almost smiled. The man had no idea how valuable he was to Warren. He tried to think of a way to keep him in this room for another hour. Maybe by then, he'd be ready to talk. Or he might be a vegetable. It was a terrible risk, but a risk Warren was willing to take to keep him.

"Of course I'll check you in. I drew up the necessary papers last night." Warren sat back in his chair when there was no response. "Which was, by the way, a chance you shouldn't have taken. You should have waited for me. You might have been caught."

"I had to—clean up some loose ends." Eddie's voice was drifting, he was nearly in a state of drug-induced catatonia.

"Let's sign the papers, Eddie, then we'll get you into your room. I want you to rest, I want you to relax. I want you to— decompress. Then, later, we can talk." He didn't tell Eddie that if he tried to leave again, or called a lawyer to help him in that pursuit, he would tell the authorities everything he knew. He would save that threat for later, if he needed it. At the moment, Eddie was entirely in his power, and for that Warren was grateful.

Dr. Warren wanted to keep him that way until he'd gotten everything he needed.

Ellen sat on the sofa in her parents' living room, eyes closed, the inner edge of her hand over her brow, as if she were shading her eyes from brutal sunlight. Her elbow was on her knee. This house did not hold kind memories for Ellen. She started at the sound of her mother's voice.

"He'll call, sweetie." Ellen looked at the woman, and prayed that she was not seeing herself in thirty years. Plump, wrinkled and soft, pompous and all-knowing, with swift, cruel opinions. Her mother thought that her age gave her the right to be openly discourteous. Ellen had to look away.

"If he's home, he's not picking up," she said.

"Did you leave a message?"

Ellen looked over at the hallway, toward her old bedroom, toward Todd's old bedroom . . . She forced the thoughts from her mind. Todd was dead. The brightest day in her life had been the day that he'd committed suicide. Until the day she'd married Tom. Then *that* had become her shining, brightest day.

Now, to her mother, Ellen said, "I can't. I don't know who's there, who might be listening in." Ellen rested her head on her hand again. "I don't know anything anymore." She could feel her mother's disapproval of her behavior, and was grateful for it—it was the only thing that kept her from breaking down.

"Machines." Her mother snorted. "Remember when you were a little girl? We had the heavy plastic phone with the round metal thing in the middle, you turned it with your finger."

"Rotary."

"Now everything's—what's it called?—*touch-tone*. We used to—"

"He call?" Ellen was saved by her father's voice, booming in front of him as he came in from the kitchen. He was holding a mug in either hand, coffee for himself, tea for Ellen. Ellen's mother hadn't wanted anything. Ellen thought she received most of her nourishment through her harsh judgments, the rest from her buried resentments. She was the one who had created Todd, Ellen thought, with her constant criticism, her beatings, her screaming, while their father was at work, blissfully unaware of the torture chamber his home became the second he walked out the door. Or at least he pretended to be unaware, Ellen thought. She stopped herself, forced herself calm. Tom had taught her that such thinking was dangerous for her, counterproductive. It was in the past, it had been dealt with. Still, she couldn't stay here long, or she'd go insane thinking about the ghosts that haunted this house.

Her father put Ellen's tea down on the small table in front of her, sat down in the soft chair that faced the television, just to the right of the sofa.

"Not yet," there was a hint of reproach in her mother's voice. It had been in every statement the woman had made since she'd discovered that Ellen hadn't told her parents she was pregnant.

They still had their old console TV, the type that had a record player and radio built into the top of the cabinet. It had been state of the art when Ellen had been in grade school. The TV was on, the sound turned off, some pudgy, middle-aged, male talk-show host was looming over a guest, waving a finger in his face, challenging him. To the right of the guest was another man, one decked out in full Ku Klux Klan regalia. Ellen and her parents were waiting for a newsbreak. The large metal channel-changer was on the arm of her father's chair. It had big buttons that literally clicked when they were depressed—when the channels were changed—but that's all it did, it did not have a volume control. When the news came on, someone would have to get up and twist the dial to turn up the sound. Ellen fought the urge to check her watch again.

"Did you try him at his office?" her father said, and Ellen looked over at him, then reached for the phone.

CHAPTER
31

Janice Constantine stood in the harsh glare of the television lights, trying to appear professional and humble, trying not to squint. Her part was over with for now, she had told them what she'd done, how they'd come upon the body. Several of the reporters, disbelieving her statement, tried to question her but Bailey had shouldered out of the way, and Constantine had been grateful for his interference.

Now Lieutenant Bailey was speaking into the microphones, extolling Constantine's courage and investigative ability in a tone that was just slightly officious. Constantine hadn't seen DiGrazia in hours, since he'd been huddled with Eberhardt, speaking to him rapidly before the media horde descended. She put her hands behind her back and sidled to her right as Bailey finished his extemporaneous remarks and began to take questions from the press.

Fortunately, the reporters decided not to risk his prematurely ending the impromptu press conference by shouting angry questions at him, as they'd tried to do with Constantine.

"Do you think Schmidt was the killer both times?" The voice was louder and more strident than the general shouts that assaulted the lieutenant, so he turned to the woman who'd screamed it and pointed at her, and the woman repeated her question.

Constantine had seen the woman before on TV, she had switched stations though, judging by the logo on her microphone. A sea of similar microphones were stuck in the lieutenant's face, along with hand-held Pearlcorders, and regular cassette recorders, but he was able to speak naturally and calmly, with the solemnity the occasion demanded.

The lieutenant paused, as if seeking the proper phrasing. He spoke slowly and carefully when he said, "Let me just say that we have no evidence—*at this time*—to support such a conclusion, but it's not something we're overlooking." His audience welcomed such ambiguity, it was what they were seeking; they could now fill in the blanks themselves, savage carnivores, devouring.

Constantine was aching for a cigarette, she had a slight headache from the glare of the lights. She went a little farther to her right, as if moving out of the way, then raised her eyebrows and pointed to her chest, as if someone just out of camera range had spoken to her, then she moved quickly away, following an imaginary order no one else but she had heard.

Around the corner, through the gate, and out back, and she was safe. Nobody could get back in this area unless they were wearing a badge. There were several male officers on Schmidt's back porch; none of them gave her more than a passing glance.

Constantine reached into her jacket pocket, took out her cigarettes, lit one, and sucked in a deep drag. She went to put them in her other pocket, and was surprised to discover that she still had DiGrazia's cellular phone. It wasn't like him to forget about such things; she decided that he must have been in a hurry to avoid the media frenzy.

She forgot about it, closed her eyes and enjoyed the nicotine buzz, the dizziness that overcame her after several hours without a cigarette.

She admitted to herself that she'd enjoyed her moment in the spotlight, even as she realized how much she was dreading the followup, one-on-one personal interviews she'd been told she'd have to do. She'd worry about that later, tonight, maybe tomorrow. She wondered if she had scored a permanent transfer out of patrol, wondered if she wanted one, now that she'd seen what could happen.

"So, are you a celebrity now?" The question was asked with a smile, Dr. AnnaLee Chen was teasing her. Constantine hadn't heard her come down the back steps. She watched as the young woman removed her surgeon's cap and swept her long, straight, brilliantly black hair away from her face in one small, narrow hand. Her hair fell nearly to her waist, shining in the afternoon sunlight. Dr. Chen nodded her head at the cigarette between Constantine's large, stubby fingers.

"Those are worse for your health than heroin or crack."

"All you doctors are alike. DiGrazia wouldn't let me smoke in the car with him, either."

"One of the captains was just looking for him." Chen looked very tired, looked suddenly small and frail. She shook it off, and lowered her voice and moved her shoulders in an exaggerated parody of a swagger. " 'Anybody seen DiGrazia? Somebody get me DiGrazia!' As if we were all supposed to race around in panic, searching for him."

"It's what they're used to. They don't deal with doctors very often, except at the country club, or when they go for their yearly prostate check." Constantine recognized the anger in her own voice, and shot a nervous glance over Chen's shoulder, saw the officers on the porch, saw one of them staring at Chen with open appraisal.

Chen stopped kidding around, looked off into the alley, and Constantine took a few steps toward the back fence; Chen naturally followed. Constantine positioned herself in a way that protected Chen from the male officer's scrutiny.

"You read my initial report?"

"Scanned it."

"Then you know the wounds were postmortem. He killed her first, before he cut her."

"Big of him."

Dr. Chen said, "Do you ever wonder how things like this happen, Janice? Can you imagine what she went through?"

"It's crossed my mind." Constantine looked off with her, at garbage cans, at the backs of garages, at nothing. Schmidt's garbage cans had been taken away hours ago, for analysis.

"The pole had been washed down, of course, but the chain was long enough to reach the laundry tub, so the girl could self-hydrate. There are partials on both the hot and cold water spigots. If they're hers, I think they'd be on the hot water valve because she might have tried to wash herself. There are also clear prints on the underside of the sink. Which indicates she may have tried to unscrew the pipe, perhaps to throw it through the basement window and attract some attention."

"Or maybe the prints are Schmidt's. He mopped the area pretty good, probably planned to do it every day for a month or so, until all the evidence was washed away."

"We have the mop, there'll be blood on it."

"They'll find a dish somewhere, too, he must have fed her. Maybe a plastic doggy bowl, nothing she could have used to hurt him or herself."

"I wonder why DiGrazia didn't want to do the scene himself this time?"

Constantine had been considering this same question for some time. She said, "Is the basement clear?"

"It'll be off limits in a little while, when they tear the gutter up, looking for evidence." Chen paused, and shivered. "There were skin samples under one end of the chain he used to keep her down there. He padlocked her around the right leg. It was in the report, the missing patches of skin, I mean. There were also hairs from her leg."

"Blood?"

"We luminoled the floor, it looks like somebody spilled a gallon of red paint on the concrete."

"There was more than the swatches around the grate, then?" Chen shook her head. "Not enough for samples?"

"Oh no, not from the floor. Even if there had been, the luminol would have destroyed it. There'll be plenty of samples for matches when they excavate the sewer line, take out the gutter trap."

"So it'll all be wrapped up in a pretty ribbon. Schmidt killed Roni, and tried to blame Dr. Moran."

"The other detectives—when they're not making basement jokes—are saying that he probably killed the first woman, too. Nancy, her name was. They're saying he had been having an affair with her, that he killed her in the heat of passion, then made his life's work out of blaming her husband, just to throw suspicion away from himself."

"That's why I skipped out on the end of the press briefing. Lieutenant Bailey was starting to imply the same thing, just planting the seed, but you know how the press is, they'll jump all over it, and think they solved the case, and the brass'll let 'em. I don't want my face on videotape, standing behind him, when the tape comes back later to bite him on the ass."

"You don't believe it, either?"

"You ever been in the throes of passion in a church?" Chen giggled. She covered her mouth with her hand.

"I don't go to church."

"Seen too much to believe in Jesus, Doctor?"

"I worship at temple."

"Excuse me, I'm sorry." Constantine was immediately contrite.

"Don't be. I almost wish I *didn't* believe," Dr. Chen said, "because then I wouldn't have to think about a man like Schmidt coming back."

Constantine didn't want to think about it, either. Or about the headlines in tomorrow's papers: DUNGEON OF DEATH in large bold type. The daytime talk shows would have a field day.

She said, "They let the media down there yet?"

"There's still too much work to do. Poor darlings, they'll just have to wait a few days." Dr. Chen sighed. "I'm going home, and I'm going to bed. It'll take a week or two for confirmation on the blood they find—we have to send those samples away—but we can match the skin and hair samples up pretty quick, by tomorrow, probably, or the next day." Chen turned to Constantine, lowered her voice again, and made an earnest face. " 'Well, King, this case is closed.' "

"*Sergeant Preston of the Yukon*," Constantine smiled. "You don't look old enough to remember that."

"Cable reruns," Dr. Chen said, then smiled, and touched Constantine's arm. "I appreciate your calling me in. There're half a dozen men working at the lab right this minute who would've been real happy to handle this."

Constantine looked up, at the men milling around on the

porch, at the men inside the house, their laughter booming out into the yard. DiGrazia had told her to call Chen. He would have known about the men at the lab; DiGrazia knew everything there was to know about his work.

She said, "Maybe we can both come out of this looking pretty good."

"And let it come back to bite just the men on their asses."

"From your lips to God's—to whoever's—ear."

"Good night, Janice."

"Doctor, you get some sleep."

Chen went out through the alley, in order to avoid the press. DiGrazia had made sure that both alley entryways had been sealed off before he'd left.

Down in the basement again, wanting to see it one last time, working her way slowly through a sea of broad backs, Constantine was aware that she was the only woman in the house, and that offended her. She barged through a couple of officers who were standing around the now open sewer, ignored their complaints as she stared down into a hole that held Veronica Davene's blood. She turned away from the smell, looked away, at the wall. One of the officers touched her arm. Constantine didn't look at him as she pulled away.

The cardboard boxes that had been against the wall were gone.

She thought about that as she left the basement, thought about it some more as she stood in front of the spot where they'd found Schmidt's body, Constantine deep in thought, wondering why DiGrazia hadn't told her that Schmidt hadn't killed himself. DiGrazia would have been disappointed that she hadn't figured it out for herself.

And she had, finally, back in the yard. She remembered the state she'd been in, how excited, how angry. DiGrazia had no goddamn right to allow her to make a fool of herself, he should have told her what he'd been thinking just as soon as she'd opened her mouth.

He could be one miserable son of a bitch when he wanted to be.

Constantine left the house through the back door, walked through the yard, and followed Chen's route through the alley.

DiGrazia had the vehicle. She would have to find a cab to take her downtown, where she had parked her car. That, or bum a ride from one of the squads working crowd control at the end of the block. Constantine didn't even know if she was officially off duty.

The kids would be home now, watching TV rather than doing their homework. Her husband, Luke, would not yet be home from work. They had to attend their weekly AA meeting later on tonight. A member of their home group was celebrating her first year without a drink, maybe the most vitally important anniversary she'd ever have.

What had DiGrazia done with the boxes? She knew he'd taken the filing cabinet, she'd seen him do it, had watched as he'd muscled it into the trunk of his car, just before the other officers had swarmed onto the block. He'd carefully put all his lab junk in the back seat first. He'd put white cotton gloves on his hands before he'd touched the cabinet. He hadn't tried to hide what he'd been doing.

So why had he sent her upstairs to look for a journal while he'd snatched the boxes? And what had DiGrazia and Eberhardt been whispering about?

The phone in her pocket rang, and Constantine didn't know what to do. It wasn't her phone; should she answer it? Hell. She pulled it out of her pocket angrily, barking her knuckle on the butt of her weapon in the process.

"Son of a *bitch!*" Constantine said, as she fumbled the thing open, pressed one of the buttons. "Where's the goddamn little thing at . . . ?"

"—not even going to ask you who you're talking to." She heard a man's voice, managed to get the phone up to her ear in time to hear just the last part of the sentence, but she didn't have time to recognize the voice.

She said, "I'm searching Bailey's underpants," and waited, heard a surprised pause where she'd expected DiGrazia's bark of a laugh. A sunspot slightly interrupted them, a small near-toneless beep, followed by a moment of white noise.

"May I speak with Detective DiGrazia, please."

She'd been certain this would have been DiGrazia, but now

Constantine recognized the voice as that of Deputy Superintendent Louis Alvarez.

"I'm sorry, sir, he can't come to the phone right now."

There was another surprised pause on the other end of the line. She could hear his wheels spinning, wondering how much DiGrazia may have told her, wondering if he could trust her.

Alvarez said, "Do you know who this is?" He didn't have to warn her about airwave monitoring.

"Yes, sir."

"Tell him to call me."

"Yes, sir. I certainly will."

There was another pause, then, "Where are you right this minute, Detective?"

Constantine didn't even have to think about it. "The basement on Chicago Avenue, where else?"

"Pretty good reception for an underground basement with cinder-block walls." Constantine cursed herself. She prayed that a car horn didn't honk, she might shoot the driver for totally giving her away.

"He'll be right back, sir, he's just—" She hit the red End button in the middle of her sentence, hoping Alvarez would think they'd been cut off by two much downtown air traffic. Or by the blue, cinder-block walls of the Chicago Avenue Station basement.

Constantine came out of the alley, turned onto the street, and walked up to several officers who were milling around, watching the circus down the block. A dozen squad cars were parked at the curb. She searched the crowd for a familiar face, found one.

"Nelligan, give me a ride down to Chicago Avenue, would you?" Cate Nelligan, working the afternoon shift, was surprised to see Constantine in civilian clothes.

"Sure," she said, seeming grateful to get away from the boredom of standing around and doing nothing, not having much in common with the men with whom she was working.

CHAPTER
32

Dr. Thomas Moran felt the medication controlling his raging emotions, and he sat back in his leather chair, relaxing for the first time since waking from the previous evening's nightmare. He took deep breaths, let them out slowly. The terror had been coming at him in waves for hours on end, and its diminishment was, for Tom, nearly glorious. He nodded in self-approval over the way that he'd dealt with the terror as the two detectives had verbally assaulted him, Tom thinking of other things, not letting them, or their threats, break through to his conscious thoughts.

It was something he had plenty of practice at, hiding his thoughts and feelings.

But they were getting to him now, those threats. They were all Tom could think about. The Penitentiary, what would happen to him in there. What would happen to Ellen without him. Would she wait for him? Did he want her to?

He should have never started taking the drugs. They were having an adverse affect on him, Tom knew that now. But who wouldn't have begun taking them, after what he'd learned, after discovering what he had discovered? He would wean himself off them after all this was over. It was what he'd been telling himself since sometime in early March. He had to get through this first, work through his problems and get out from under a murder charge before he even started thinking about detoxing from the medication.

Somewhere outside this room, Tom knew, Dr. Warren was plotting against him. Hiding his conspiracy behind a smarmy, satisfied smirk. He wanted Tom's job. He wanted Tom's acclaim, his life. He envied Tom his youth.

Tom had a mental image of Dr. Cary Warren, pictured him in his office, reading the papers and dry-washing his hands, chuckling.

But he couldn't think about that now. He had other issues to address, and he had to take care of them immediately, in accordance with their level of importance, as he was expecting Dr. Freeling's knock to come at his door at any time. Freeling was the hospital's chief of psychiatry, and the hospital wing administrator; Tom already knew the rehearsed speech the man would give him.

It would begin with lies and distortions of truth, as Freeling pretended to care about Tom's dilemma, then Freeling would find a subtle intro to the words: "In the best interests of the hospital . . ." and Tom would be relieved of his duties. He'd be paid, at least until the internal, federal investigation into his guilt or innocence was over, but even if he were cleared of all suspicion, the stigma would never leave him. His life, his work, would mean nothing.

There were memos all over Tom's desk, covering it, WHILE-YOU-WERE-OUT slips informing him of who had called him during his absence. Terry's intake file was on top of the stack of papers. Tom opened it now, nearly relaxed and free of panic, and carefully changed the report, changed the date and the time. He would now have to slip it back into the circular files without getting caught.

If the data had already been typed into the computer, it would be untouchable, Tom couldn't even consider changing that, as his own computer-terminal number and pass code would be locked on-line as soon as he accessed the confidential patient information. But that could easily be explained away by a human data-processing error, if it ever got to that point, if the police came around, checking, making their accusations. Tom knew that

Terry was in no better shape to handle interrogation than was Frank. Having just been through it himself, the terror of it was still fresh in his mind, despite the medication. He knew how they could scare you, what they could do to your faculties, how they could distort your self-image.

Tom closed his eyes and silently hoped it wouldn't get that far, that Terry wouldn't become a suspect. He hoped the assistants had been slow, had not yet data-processed Terry's intake record.

If it happened, if they came after Terry, Tom knew he would have no choice, he'd have to go to the police—to DiGrazia—and tell them who had killed Nancy.

DiGrazia might even understand. Tom had studied him closely as the two of them had spoken—it seemed like days ago to Tom now—in the small, smoke-filled interrogation room. The man had intelligence, it shouted out from his eyes.

The woman detective, Constantine, could never be allowed to find out, or she would talk. Tom felt certain about that. But DiGrazia might keep it out of the media, might not destroy innocent lives by going public with what he was told. Tom would do that for Terry, if he had to. He would even do it for Frank. No matter what the risks, no matter who got hurt, he had to protect his brothers' lives.

The only Moran he was not willing to do that for was himself.

Haney had already recused himself from the case, angry over Tom's refusal to be manipulated by him. Tom knew that they took classes in Controlling the Client in law school. Now Tom told himself that Haney should have known better than to attempt the technique with him.

Tom used the pencil eraser to push around the messages and memos on his desk.

He had to find another lawyer, and quickly, as he suspected that they'd be coming for him again once their other suspicions couldn't be confirmed, when other leads didn't pan out. He knew that he had to get up out of his chair, right *now*, and go get the yellow pages, find a familiar name. He couldn't let them question him without good legal counsel. He didn't have the energy. He knew he had to do it, but he didn't.

Tom was drained. He had used up all his energy reserves

when he'd been standing on the edge, looking over it and down, and he considered himself lucky that he'd been able to pull himself away from it before falling into the pit. And what had his first move been, after finding a safe harbor? Getting into an argument with his wife, with the only human being alive who had ever loved him without condition.

He had to make things right with Ellen. Poor, sad Ellen. He pitied her nearly as much as he loved her. What was she going through now, he wondered?

A pink telephone slip—the color signifying urgency—had been buried under the many requests for call-backs from various reporters. Tom squinted down at it, he'd need reading glasses soon.

CONGRATULATIONS, DAD! the message read, it was signed by an obstetrician he knew from Northwestern Memorial Hospital. Tom studied it, making connections. He vaulted back in his chair as if he'd been punched in the face when he realized what the message meant, when he understood that Ellen was pregnant.

Someone was knocking on his door. Tom saw the knob turn back and forth; he'd automatically locked it when he'd come in with Terry's file. He shoved Terry's intake report into one of his desk drawers, slammed the drawer shut with his leg as he rose. He stuck the pink phone memo into his pocket as he walked to the door.

Dr. Freeling stood in the hallway, tiny, ancient, bald, and ominous.

"Thank God they caught him," the old doctor said as he entered Tom's office. Tom stepped back automatically. Freeling closed the door behind him, Tom watched him twist the lock. Freeling turned to Tom, compassion and understanding distinct on his face. "We've been taking media calls all day. I can't *imagine* what you've been going through during the last sixteen hours."

"Wha—What?"

Freeling, internationally renowned in the psychiatric community for his intuitiveness, looked down, frowned, then looked up quickly. His eyes scanned the room, saw that the television wasn't on.

"It's all over the TV and radio." Freeling understood that Tom was hearing this for the first time. His expression was earnest, and he put a hand on Tom's arm as he said, "They caught the killer, Tom." Tom stood gasping. He felt faint, felt the urge to vomit. Felt the urge to grab the old man and shake the truth out of him without any of this pretentious, studied hesitation.

"It was the ex-cop, the one in the paper, the man who tried to frame you," Freeling said at last.

Tom said, "Schmidt?!"

"*Schmidt!* That's it, I couldn't remember his name."

Tom looked at the doctor, his mouth open, as the phone on his desk began to ring.

Freeling, having no more stunning revelations to share, said, "Your brother checked in a little while ago, you know. It was the right thing for you to do, sending him here, Tom. It was a little worrisome, I had to admit, the ethics of it, when I saw Terry's face on the news . . ."

Freeling paused, then said, "Are you going to answer your telephone?"

Constantine pounded on the basement door until the heel of her hand was red and stinging. The door was fireproof, made of layer upon layer of heavy-gauge steel. The outside of the door had recently been painted gray, and it reminded her of a door in a movie battleship. She thought of taking out her pistol and shooting it once or twice.

She heard the *click* as an inner bolt was thrown back, the double *snick* as two locks were opened. Thomas Eberhardt pulled the door toward himself and looked out at her, scowling.

"What do you want?"

She pushed past him as if he wasn't there.

DiGrazia sat at an old, large metal desk that had been set up in one corner of the room, on the south side of the old boxing ring that hadn't been used in years due to problems with the insurance company. Empty cardboard boxes surrounded him, hundreds of papers were strewn about, in haphazard piles on the desktop. DiGrazia flipped through these pages as he spoke into a phone that was pinched between his ear and one broad shoulder. He gave Constantine a look that made her feel like a mouse being eyed by a circling hawk.

"She went up to the bathroom, sir, maybe she was embarrassed to tell you that, hell, I don't know. She came back in about ten minutes ago, you want to talk to her . . . She *did* tell me that, yes, but I couldn't call you back right away, I've got four other people on hold . . .'' DiGrazia looked up at her impassively as Alvarez spoke to him, and Constantine fought down her anger and nodded, once.

But DiGrazia didn't see it; he was looking through papers again, now he was shaking his head. The file cabinet he'd taken from Schmidt's house was directly behind him, covered with fingerprint powder, inside and out. Both drawers were open, gaping, starving mouths awaiting feeding.

''No, no, that won't work, they'll have interviewed the neighbors by now, they'll know somebody else had been staying at the house . . . We've just got to find him before they break the story, and you've got to keep the politicians off our ass while we do it. And we need Terry . . .'' DiGrazia held up a paper as he listened, frowned at it, then placed it on his desk. Constantine read it upside down.

It was a memo from one of the officers who was manning the phones—it stated that Terry Moran had been spotted at a meeting of Alcoholics Anonymous early that morning, at a little after midnight.

DiGrazia was studying the paper as he said, ''Oh, don't worry, we'll find him soon enough.''

James McMillan, the tall, muscular, computer whiz, was sitting in front of a terminal on the north side of the boxing ring. He looked over at her with a smile of relief. ''Thank God you're here,'' he said, his voice ringing in the large, near-empty room. Constantine believed him.

DiGrazia's tone was slightly impatient as he said, ''I don't give a shit who comes out looking bad. They brought it on themselves. We're waiting on FedEx right now, we're sealing the file cabinet up, sending it off to Quantico for acid etching.'' He looked up again, surprised to find Constantine still standing in front of him.

''Sir, excuse me, could you hold on one second, please?'' DiGrazia punched a button on the phone, let the receiver drop into his lap. ''About time you found your way down here.'' He snapped his fingers. ''Give me the cell phone.''

Constantine ignored his outstretched hand, slammed the

phone down on a corner of the desk. "You left it with me on purpose, didn't you?"

"Janice, I've got Alvarez on hold. Go help Mac, right now. He'll tell you what he wants you to do." He paused, giving her a hard look. "That, or leave."

"Where's the rest of the team?"

"Dismissed," Eberhardt said from just behind her.

DiGrazia picked up the phone, took Alvarez off hold.

"Sorry . . ." Constantine watched him listening, then he said, "Bullshit. It was what those idiots wanted to believe. It was obvious, sir, even the recruits at the academy know a twenty-year copper wouldn't kill himself that way. There're too many things could go wrong, too many bones and teeth the bullet could deflect off . . . How many suicides you worked where the pistol stayed in the shooter's hand? I can't remember one."

She could still sense his gross impatience with the conversation, though his tone had calmed down considerably. He was scratching his stomach again. He looked up at Constantine, did a purposeful double take, opened his hand, raised his eyebrows, then waved her away.

He said, "This way, we can keep the crazies off the eight-hundred line, work without the media in our ass . . . You *can't* tell the bosses about this . . ." DiGrazia was pleading.

As she walked over to McMillan, she heard DiGrazia say, "The house was filthy, but one guest bedroom was spotless, it didn't make sense, somebody else had to have been staying there."

Constantine walked quickly over to McMillan, cursing herself for having missed the obvious signs. McMillan distractedly said, "Pull up a chair." She plunked down, lit a cigarette, ignored the way he curled up his nose at the smell.

"Where's Stefaniak and Hill?"

"Their precious little *feewings* got hurt because they didn't think DiGrazia was giving them a big enough piece of the pie—they left."

"Oh, Jesus, you think they went to the media? After all the trouble DiGrazia went through to pretend the case was wrapped?"

"They're pissed, they aren't stupid. They know Parker'd put them on patrol in Englewood if they went public."

There were four tall, near-even stacks of three-by-five-inch index file cards piled next to the computer. At least as many again were scattered all over the floor, around McMillan's chair.

"If we had a scanner, we wouldn't have to waste time with this. Take the top card, read me the name, last name first. Spell both names out, that's all I need."

Constantine did so.

"These Schmidt's cards?"

McMillan's fingers flew. Behind them, she heard Eberhardt speaking loudly into a phone.

"Next name." He typed it in. He stared at the screen as he said, "Asswipe thought he was smarter than us. It's one of the reasons why DiGrazia won't have partners anymore. Too many supersensitive assholes in this department, Janice. Everyone wants to know everything you're doing, keeps you from getting the job done."

Constantine was glad that McMillan had used the pronoun *he*.

"I've got a good taste of that today." She said, "You're talking about Schmidt, though, right?"

McMillan nodded. " 'Mong others I could mention." They had it down to a routine now; she read him a name, he typed it in. He spoke to her as he typed, confident in his abilities.

"How much you figure out?"

"I didn't pick up on how clean the other bedroom was, I noticed it, but didn't think it was important—I should have." She did not point out that they were searching a house at the time, weapons drawn, adrenaline spurting, wondering if a killer was lurking behind every door, or under one of the beds. Constantine spelled a name, not telling McMillan that she'd at first believed that Schmidt had killed himself.

Instead, she said, "I suspected right off that Schmidt didn't kill himself." She spelled another name. "And I thought right from the beginning that it was too convenient, Schmidt being on the front page of the paper at the same time Veronica's body was being found."

"You should have told DiGrazia that. Might have saved us a little trouble."

"I told him."

Constantine read him the names off ten more cards before

she said, "Schmidt didn't bring those boxes in because he was trying to help us out. He just didn't want DiGrazia coming back with a warrant. He did *not* want him in that basement."

"Don't think Gheritty isn't trying to use it against him already, now that he thinks the case is closed. Dickhead's making rumblings, said he *told* DiGrazia he should have arrested Schmidt last night. We get a hit, we'll show him who's in charge." McMillan typed silently for a moment. "Another few days, he'd have pulled it off, too. He'd'a got all the traces of the blood off the floor, bleached the drains, dumped the chain, the padlocks, and the mop, he'd have been home free."

"I'm surprised none of the bosses realized that he killed himself at an awfully convenient time."

"DiGrazia got Eberhardt to go over that room with a microscope; they didn't even get a partial, the walls, the doorknobs, the bedframe, even the file cabinet had been wiped down with Windex. Whoever killed the old man knew what he was doing."

"These are Schmidt's old arrest cards."

"From his last few years on duty; he made copies of everything. Thank God he was a paranoid bastard."

"And DiGrazia's got the rest of the reports, the ones about Nancy Moran."

"Take a look when we're done, the pictures are ex*act*ly alike, only the environment's different."

They had worked through one stack. Constantine was dropping the cards to the floor just as soon as she spelled out the names.

"You're looking for a match, right?" Constantine's pulse quickened. "Somebody who was in here, somebody Schmidt arrested."

"DiGrazia took a shot. We could either fingerprint every card, run it, hope for a partial match sometime tomorrow, maybe, or do it this way right now." McMillan shrugged his beefy shoulders and concentrated as Constantine spelled another name. "We got a partial off her upper plate, you know. It was put in after she died."

Constantine had to close her eyes for a second. An impatient snap from McMillan forced her to open them. She read him some names, then said, "Veronica's?"

"No, Mother Teresa's. The partial doesn't match Schmidt or Roni. It was what gave DiGrazia the idea Schmidt had an accomplice. We get a suspect, we can match it."

"He plays his fucking cards awfully close to his vest."

"You should talk, not saying anything about your suspicions." There was no malice in McMillan's tone. Constantine didn't argue with him this time, but she wondered what DiGrazia had said about her before she'd figured things out and come down here.

"They send the partials over to the feds?"

"They're checking it now, but that doesn't mean anything; our boy might never have been arrested." The thought chilled them both. "But when we catch him, we can use it to hang his ass." McMillan was now smiling as he rapidly typed in another name.

"Took a hundred clerks twelve goddamn years to get all the arrest records off file cards and onto computer. All that shit that was rotting away in the district basements all over the city."

"I remember. They were always bitching about the smell, getting mold on their fingers."

They were halfway through the second stack now, in a rhythm, Constantine making direct correlations between what she already knew, what she merely suspected, and what McMillan was telling her. She did not hear the knocking on the door, did not hear Eberhardt shouting out angry directions as he bullied the Federal Express pickup man.

She said, "Wait a minute, wait a minute," almost to herself.

"Spell the next *name* Constantine!" McMillan waited only a second before he grabbed the card from her hand.

"If we know there's a second killer, and we know he killed Schmidt, then we know the second killer went through the cards, through Schmidt's files. He'd have pulled his card out of there, there wouldn't *be* a file on him." She grabbed a card and spelled a name before McMillan could do it himself.

"You can't talk and chew gum at the same time, say so."

"Just punch in your names, Mac, I can spell just fine."

She heard DiGrazia behind her, shouting something at Eberhardt. Eberhardt responded in kind; although their voices were raised, neither man seemed angry.

They were caught up in the excitement of the intoxicating

moment, lost in the thrill of the hunt. Constantine found herself caught up in it herself, she smelled the scene for the first time in her life and found it to be exquisite.

"I'll be goddamned," she said. They were through the second stack.

"Got it, huh?"

"You're looking for the name that *doesn't* have a match."

"It's a shot," McMillan said.

CHAPTER
33

"I ain't seen a TV or a radio in the three weeks I been in here." Neal was sheepish about it, speaking to Eddie as he sat on the edge of a bunk that had been made tightly enough to please the most exacting Marine drill sergeant. Eddie was lying back on his own bed, hearing Neal through a pleasant cloud. Eddie was smiling dreamily, a near ecstatic expression dancing across his face. Eddie was snatching at the words Neal spoke, he could see them in the air, all around him. He felt Godlike at the sight of them, all-powerful and strong.

"Why didn't I stay last night?" Eddie watched the words leap out of his own mouth, laughed outright at the sight of them. Neal, as he'd been taught by the doctors, expressed his feelings, told Eddie that he should have done just that: stayed.

Eddie closed his eyes and thought back through his life as furiously as he could, but he held no memories of ever having felt this safe. He felt sleepy, and he struggled against it, he did not want to waste this sensation, would not let himself sleep it away. He wondered how long it would last, wondered if Dr. Warren had left orders for him to get more.

It seemed to take him a very long time to sit up. His legs seemed very long, he had yards and yards of legs. No TV, no radio, no newspapers, that's what Neal had said. They could watch approved movies on a VCR in the day room, but the TV the recorder was hooked up to was just a large monitor, it did not carry regular programming.

Sarge got to watch TV, Neal was telling Eddie now, and he got to read the papers, and he listened to the radio. Neal suspected he was granted such privileges because Sarge was the orderlies' pet.

Eddie put his hands on his thighs, heard his muscles relax, smelled the colors in the room. Neal was saying something else to him now, the young man's eyes were cast downward. He was shamed by what he was saying. Eddie, well acquainted with shame, snatched the words out of the air, pulled them to him, turned them over, arranged them in their proper context and looked at them. He read what Neal had said.

The poor kid. Eddie reached out the long arm of God and patted Neal's head. He felt the force of his own power being transferred to his roommate. He wondered if Neal knew what had happened, wondered if he felt the charge that had just passed between them.

Neal was looking up at him, his confession over, his deep, dark secret exposed.

"Your bad dreams are over now, you know," Eddie said, and Neal sniffled. Eddie wanted to kiss his tears away, wanted to catch them in a glass and drink them.

"Dr. Warren gave me some stuff that made them stop."

"You can stop taking it; the dreams are over." Eddie felt beneficent, he had bestowed greatness on poor young Neal.

"Doctor Warren told me that I shouldn't even talk to you tonight. He'll be watching you like a hawk, he said, and he said that I should too. I oughta leave."

He didn't really want to leave. And Eddie didn't want him to go.

"Dr. Warren doesn't—" Eddie searched around in his head for words that could express his anger, but, inexplicably, none would come. He giggled at the very idea. Eddie without rage was a tiger without stripes. Unrecognizable. What had Dr. Warren done for him? The man was a genius. "He'll understand," Eddie said.

"He told me he gave you medication that might make you

talk strange, that I had to report to him immediately if you said anything that sounded weird."

"Weird?" Eddie's smile vanished. He began to laugh aloud. *"Weird?"* Eddie held his sides, he couldn't stop laughing. Neal broke a smile for the first time in days, then laughed for the first time since his nightmares had begun. It seemed to Eddie that they were laughing forever, and then the laughter gradually subsided as Eddie remembered who he was, remembered what he'd done. The night before, now. For years now, without end. Since the beginning of time, perhaps, who knew?

"What you did to that woman who was reaching out to you in your dreams, are you sorry for that, Neal?"

"As sorry as any man could ever be." Neal was attentive now, staring at the wall. "But I ain't going to jail for it. I didn't check myself in here so I'd wind up in the pen." It was hard for Eddie to believe that they'd laughed together, hard to believe laughter existed in the world. Neal was carrying so much pain. Eddie wanted to make it go away, as his own pain had, wanted to make it float out of his friend in puffy black smoke.

He said, "Let me tell you something, Neal. Will you listen?"

"Yeah, yeah, I'll listen." Neal leaned forward, and revealed another secret. "I knew last night, as soon as I saw you, I knew we could talk to each other." Eddie was nodding solemnly. "As soon as you opened your mouth, I knew."

"I felt it too, Neal."

"You can tell me, Eddie. You can tell me anything."

"You can't tell anyone else, not even Sarge." The name "Sarge" came out colored black. Eddie immediately associated the man with the darkest of evils.

"I'd never tell *Sarge.* Sarge's just a big mouth, a fucking swaggering braggart. Don't ever tell Sarge anything you don't want the doctors to know."

"Seven years, he's been here, did you know that Neal?"

"He thinks he's a shrink." Neal's disgust filled the room. Eddie waved it away with one hand, watched it dissipate. Under Dr. Warren's magic spell, he could not relate to negativity.

They heard the toilet they shared with the two men who lived in the next room—Sarge and Alex—flush. Neal put his index finger in front of his lips. "Shh."

Eddie mimicked him. "Shh." He saw the "s"'s and "h"'s bounce off the walls, saw that the room understood what he wanted, saw it become enveloped in a veil of scarlet secrecy. He closed his eyes and heard the little lock on the bathroom door unlatch, heard Sarge or whoever it was who had been in there walk into his room and throw himself onto his bed. Eddie heard the bedsprings squeak, heard voices talking, and then there was quiet.

"We got supper in an hour."

"I'm not hungry, Neal, are you?"

"No."

"Then let me tell you something, all right? A story. Can I talk to you, Neal, like a brother?"

"I *am* your brother."

"I spent a long time looking for you, do you know that? My entire life, I've been seeking you."

"I'm fucking-A glad you found me," Neal said, and leaned forward so he could hear what Eddie was saying in his soft, drugged voice.

Alex said to Sarge, "You know what? Sometimes I don't know about you."

"It's enough to piss a man off, is all." Sarge wasn't trying to hide his anger; in the past seven years he'd learned that that had been a major part of his problem, ever since he'd been a child. Now, like the child he'd never had the opportunity to be, Sarge had a child's demands for forbearance, patience, and instant gratification.

"You do everything you can to help a man out, and he bad-mouths you as soon as your back is turned."

Alex said, "It's supposed to be Quiet Time, Sarge."

Alex had been committed for treatment of an obsessive-compulsive disorder. He now made a strange pattern with his fingers, waved them around in front of him, then he brought them together, joined them in a bizarre, formal, stylized move, then pointed the tips of his fingers at his feet. Alex's treatment was working already; he'd been making far more elaborate moves just a couple of days earlier. He had shared with Sarge his secret belief that if he didn't do it just right, one of his daughters would die of breast cancer.

Alex untwisted his hands, placed them calmly on his lap, then said, "It's human nature, Sarge. Everyone's like that. Gossipy, bitchy. Ungrateful. No matter what you do for them, it ain't enough. I know, I been married to enough bitches who were exactly like that."

Sarge let his resentment fester, watched Alex make his move again, as he made it twice in a row every half hour, then saw Alex sit back and relax. The guy was all right—even if he did jerk off two or three times every night when he thought Sarge was sleeping—he kept the room spotless. Sarge saw his roommate's eyes go blank. He'd be counting now, in his head. Sarge knew there was a name for what Alex was doing, a term. He'd read about it in the journals, but he just couldn't quite grasp it now. *Vegetable,* he thought.

Thinks he's a shrink, indeed.

Sarge got off the bed as quietly as he could, sat on the edge of it, leaned over and put his ear to the wall. Alex was looking off into a different world. All Sarge could hear were murmurs. Sarge stood, stretched, looked over at Alex. He'd be gone for a while, counting in his head. The man was a classic mixture of anxieties, fears, and neuroses.

Sarge tiptoed into the bathroom, left the door open behind him. He did not turn on the light. He leaned his ear against the door that led into Neal's room. Neal and Eddie's room now. He could hear clearly and well, heard Eddie speaking. At least Eddie hadn't said anything bad about him behind his back. Sarge wondered if he should lock the connecting door, decided that it would make too much noise, that he'd be found out if he tried. He would be able to hear if they stopped talking, would hear footsteps coming toward the shared toilet and would have time to escape.

Sarge breathed through his mouth, concentrated, and got taken on a field trip that descended straight into Hell.

CHAPTER
34

Ellen said, "I'm coming right over there."

"No, wait for the news. Let's see what happened first."

Freeling had had the sensitivity to leave, even though he hadn't wanted to. Tom spoke to his wife on a phone he was uncertain of, trying to think of ways to say the things he wanted to say without hurting Ellen any more than he already had. He asked after her parents, heard the coldness in her voice when she told him they were just fine. Tom understood it; she had told him everything early on. But it had only been in January when he had at last put all the pieces together.

Then there was a long silence, which neither of them was anxious to break.

"Haney quit, you know."

"He never argues with his wife?"

"I don't—"

"He'll be back soon enough, he'll want a third of the lawsuit."

"I'm sorry, Ellen . . ."

"Tom, don't . . ."

Their silence was apologetic this time, both of them feeling extremes of guilt over exterior stressors which they both now knew should have been fought against together. Rather than standing united, they'd torn into each other's throat.

After a time, Tom said, "I told Frank to meet me here, I'll wait until he gets here, we'll take a cab home."

"The media will still be out there."

"I don't care about the media anymore. If Freeling's right, we've been vindicated, and they'll know it. They'll be on our side because they'll feel guilty over how they tried to blame me."

"Who will they blame?"

"The cops, Schmidt, who knows? As long as it's not me."

"Is he going to stay with us?"

"Frank? I'd like him to."

There was another silence as Ellen processed this information. Tom heard her voice again, suddenly muffled, knew that she must have put the phone against her shoulder as she spoke to one of her parents. Then her voice was in his ear again, "I can borrow my father's car and be home in an hour, Tom."

"You can, or you're *going* to?"

"I want to know about the plan you had with Terry, Tom. I need to know what that was all about. Where you sent him. What he did last night. Why you were drinking with him."

Tom took in a quick breath. He closed his eyes. He did not answer.

"I need to know these things, Tom. Tonight."

"All right." It was all he could manage to say. "And Frank?"

"We'll talk about Frank when we're locked inside our house, once it's cleaned, with the alarm on and the lights out, after we've had a drink and a nice hot bath." Ellen's relief was obvious. She still loved him, wanted him to come home.

"I love you, Ellen." Tom's voice was shockingly soft. He sniffled, leaned far back in his chair.

"I love you, too, Tom." Soft words, gently spoken, and then Ellen was gone.

Tom leaned forward, and put the phone in its cradle. It rang under his hand.

"We got sperm!" Eberhardt shouted it, covering the phone's mouthpiece with the palm of his hand. DiGrazia looked up from his desk, McMillan away from his computer. Constantine felt like a fifth wheel, and there was still much she did not understand; the index cards had all been entered, there was nothing more for her to do besides answer the phones that never seemed to stop ringing, taking messages for Dominick DiGrazia, who was always on another line.

Eberhardt congratulated whomever he was speaking to, told him he'd done good work, and he was giving him further instructions when DiGrazia touched Constantine's shoulder, and she spun.

"This is the in-law's home address, and phone number. Their names are Christine and Stanley Lewan, legally changed from Lewandowski. Here's a current picture of Ellen Moran. You need to find her, and stay with her." DiGrazia flashed a humorless smile. "If anyone can win her trust, it's you." He handed her a sheet of paper he'd taken from his stacks, and a glossy picture that had been removed from the Moran's house.

"You think *she* . . . ?"

"At this point I think she might just be in danger. The second killer's still loose. Keep in mind, Schmidt called the Moran house last night. I thought he'd called to speak with Tom, but his call might have sent Ellen over the edge." He turned to McMillan. "You getting anything?"

McMillan spoke without looking up from the terminal. "I got eight names aren't on the original arrest cards."

"Only eight? We got lucky."

"Way lucky."

"Can you print them out?"

"Just a second." McMillan's voice was soft and far away, he typed at the keyboard, lost in concentration. DiGrazia knew enough to leave him alone. He steered Constantine back to his side of the boxing ring. He looked both exhausted and exhilarated.

"How are you doing for sleep?" he asked, and he reminded her of the same detective she had worked with, before she'd shot off her mouth and expressed her doubts in the car, earlier that morning.

"Deprived," Constantine said. When it didn't register with him, she added, "Look, Nick, I'm sorry for what I said in the car, I hadn't thought it out."

He waved it off. "I wouldn't have let you through the door

if I thought you believed it." Constantine decided that he could be a prick without half trying.

Eberhardt was coming up on them fast.

"You were right, Dom! We got the sperm off the bedsheets, the mattress covers, even the pillows. Our boy's prolific as hell. Klimick called it, and I quote, 'copious amounts' of our boy's spermatozoa. He wants us to find out what the boy's been eating after we catch him."

"We'll DNA-match this motherfucker, it'll nail him to the wall."

"We've got to find him first, and charge him. Link him to the murder. Masturbation's not a crime, and neither is being someone's roommate."

Constantine thought, There goes Ellen. But it didn't mean she hadn't done it, it only meant that Schmidt had a roommate who liked to jerk off.

McMillan said, "We'll find him, and to hell with that roommate nonsense. We've still got the partial print off Veronica's upper bridge." He turned in his chair, faced the three of them. They all moved closer to him now that he didn't seem to need privacy. "I ran a program matching all of our eight missing names against the list you had me pull up this morning. It was a bust."

"*Shit.*" DiGrazia barked it.

"Yeah, but remember, that was limited, we not only went way back, we snatched them out of violent criminals only. I'm running a program now with all *those* names, against anyone been inside a state loony farm, or institution for the criminally insane, for anything at all, depression, insomnia, I don't give a shit. We'll get present whereabouts, last known addresses, phone numbers if they got them. Got the eight missing one's flagged for faster attention."

"You can *do* that?" Eberhardt said.

"The list'll print out in a second, the eight names you wanted, Dominick."

"What about warrants?" Constantine asked.

"Don't need a warrant for state or federal institutions. Confidentiality laws still apply as far as doctor-patient goes, but the names and files—addresses and such—of everyone treated with public funds is public access, as is the general nature of their treatment, and its expense to the taxpayers."

Constantine, knowing the parameters of the district she worked in every day, said, "You checking the Veteran's Administration?"

McMillan said, "God*damn*it," and turned hurriedly back to the computer.

DiGrazia was looking at her approvingly as he asked McMillan, "How long will this take?"

"Gonna take another half hour at least to program a search of the goddamn VA. Then it could be two minutes, or it could be two days. Lots of people get treated in this state, more than I ever thought, at least, so I'm only going back five years on the first pass."

"The first five don't click, go back five more, then five more."

Constantine did not want to leave the room. She found reasons to stay, thought of questions to ask, of statements to make. She said, "What are the odds that our boy is one of the eight missing names?"

"Even money," McMillan said.

"What makes you think he's been on a mental ward?"

DiGrazia answered her. "Schmidt didn't grab him out of thin air. He picked our boy with a lot of care, then played him like a violin. He knew a healthy, scared seventeen-year-old woman could beat the shit out of him with one hand tied behind her back—"

Eberhardt cut him off with, "Or he wasn't crazy enough to do the butcher work himself."

DiGrazia said, "He grabbed some sick, miserable, fantasy-fueled son of a bitch, and stoked his fires, got him all warmed up inside. Drank with him, moved him into his own *house*, became his best friend, went over and over it with him every night, and kept him out of harm's way until the time was right. The guy was upstairs listening while I was talking to Schmidt last night." Constantine wondered how he knew that, but DiGrazia didn't elaborate.

Constantine did not want to ask why they were only checking Illinois institutions.

So she said, "How long do you think we have before the public finds out about this?"

"It'll be on the ten o'clock news for sure, maybe even at six," Eberhardt said. "They've been talking to the neighbors, they'll know that someone else was staying there. Or at least suspect. And that's all it takes to set them off." He shrugged. "DiGrazia sent police artists out with Identikits, don't think the media won't find out about that."

DiGrazia broke the bad news. "Parker's already smoothing the way for us right now. Whatever we want, we got, at least for tonight. Alvarez knows what we're doing, and why, and he's keeping his mouth shut for the time being, but he's advising the superintendent to request FBI involvement first thing in the morning. It's a smart move. If we don't get lucky tonight, the bosses can blame everything on them. Alvarez has got to cover himself. We need a pinch tonight."

"Tomorrow morning won't be soon enough," McMillan said. "There'll be a dozen accidental shootings before morning if we don't catch this second guy quick, and the feds won't take the rap for one of them, *we* will. Word gets out about him stalking around? *I* wouldn't want to try and sneak into my house with my shoes in my hand tonight."

Constantine hadn't thought about that.

All she'd heard in the last hour were the sounds of phones ringing, male voices shouting into them, or back and forth across the room. She looked down at the paper, at the picture in her hand. The woman was lovely, her vibrance shone brightly, even through the harsh single camera eye.

"They're not home? You're sure?" The address was way down in Hegewisch, a long drive during rush hour, at the beginning of the construction season.

"We've got the guard in our pocket, he'll call as soon as either one of them arrives. And we've got a squad in the vicinity."

"It's still a media circus, I'll bet."

"They'll be wanting to know how he *feels*," McMillan said.

"Or how long he'll wait to file the lawsuit."

"Get over to her parents' house, Janice. She's there. She was spotted driving her father's car out of the police station lot just a couple of minutes after we let the doctor go."

284

"While *we* were being de-fucking-briefed."

"It indicates an argument between them."

"Or she didn't want her father's car towed."

Constantine wanted with all her heart to stay right there in that room, wanted to be in for the end of it, right there with DiGrazia, putting the cuffs on this butcherous son of a bitch. She could smell it in the air, she knew that they were closing in on him. The feeling infected the room, she could see it in all of their eyes.

"And you guys just have to wait for a match now?"

"There're a few moves we can still make. I'm going to run down the eight names Jimmy pulled out of the computer." DiGrazia was walking her to the door. He was whispering when he said, "Alvarez has already made your position permanent, you go into SOS, in plainclothes, just as soon as this is over."

"Why didn't you tell me when you figured out about the second guy?"

"I thought you'd get it for yourself."

"And you didn't want me out of patrol if I wasn't bright enough to do that." DiGrazia did not answer her, or respond to the quiet anger in her voice.

She stopped at the door. He didn't move to unlock it, or to throw back the inside bolt. She said, "I meant what I said, Nick, I'm sorry. And I'm not saying it because you and your buddy got me into SOS. I shouldn't have—"

"It's all right. Believe me, I understand."

Something in the way he said it made her ask, "What do you mean?"

"In the first place, the SOS assignment wouldn't have happened if you hadn't worked your ass off to prove you were as good as anyone they have."

DiGrazia looked over his shoulder, as if to make certain that neither of the other men was close enough to hear him, before he said, "And the other thing, well, we both know, it's . . . cultural." Constantine saw his cheeks blush just before he spurted out, "It's the way we're trained to act toward each other."

Act toward each other? What was he saying?

Whatever it was, it was all he was *going* to say on the subject, because now he was throwing back the bolt, then unlocking the door, pulling it toward them. Janice stepped through it, but Di-Grazia stopped her.

"Janice, listen to me. Be very careful. Remember what you said last night: a woman's capable of the same behavior as a man."

"You think *she* was in on it?" Janice thought she saw where he was going with it, had to stop and put her hand on the doorway. She said, "You don't think she did *Nancy* . . ."

"Don't quote me, but I wouldn't be real surprised to find out she did Schmidt."

"To get back at—"

"Go find her, Janice. Stick to her close until we can exclude her. If she'll talk to you, great, if she won't, just turn into her shadow." He stopped and thought a second. "Scratch that. If you can't get next to her, radio in, we'll get somebody else to stake her out, you've done enough for one day."

"You'll radio me if you get a match, though, right? No matter what?"

"Hold on." DiGrazia walked hurriedly over to his desk, picked up his cell phone, and came back to Constantine, handed it to her. "If we get a match, I'll call you. You'll be in on the pinch with me and McMillan."

DiGrazia closed the door in her face.

CHAPTER
35

Constantine had to wait a while before she could pull out of the parking lot, street traffic was heavy, but the pedestrians were worse. Bicycles, walkers, rollerbladers, shoeshine scammers, and joggers clogged the sidewalk. A beggar sat on the thin metal barrier that separated the lot from the sidewalk, waving a *StreetWise* paper at everyone who passed. He didn't get a lot of takers.

What was all this business with men carrying their t-shirts while they jogged? Were they just showing off, or did the material scratch their nipples? Constantine hadn't done any running since she'd graduated from the academy.

It had been a different world back then, not just for the few women in the department, but for everyone in the country.

She thought about hitting the Chevy's siren to get the attention of the creeps who wouldn't allow her to pull out, but the bosses frowned on that, memos had been circulated. It was bad public relations in a time when everyone in the city already viewed themselves as an oppressed minority, living under a police state.

Constantine could tell today's female rookies a thing or two about oppression, but she never did, she allowed the younger women the soothing balm of self-pity when they went on about sexism in the department, in the locker room after their shifts. She didn't want to be viewed by them as some know-it-all old lady.

Constantine looked out at the young people passing, ignoring her as easily as they ignored the beggar on the divider. She took out DiGrazia's cellular, and punched in a number.

"Hello, Brandy? It's Janice Constantine." Brandy was a sixty-four-year-old widow who had been a housewife before her husband had died, at which point she had taken on the mantle of the merry widow. Brandy had never worked outside of the home. She thought that Constantine's job was dangerous and filled with excitement; Brandy greatly admired Janice Constantine.

She was also Constantine's sponsor in Alcoholics Anonymous.

Brandy's admiration never broadened into awe—Constantine had to bite her tongue and listen as Brandy gave her hell for missing this morning's scheduled carry-the-message meeting at the inpatient Alcoholism Treatment Center down at Igalls Memorial Hospital. Constantine had forgotten all about the monthly responsibility.

She at last broke in with, "I'm sorry I didn't make it there, I hope the meeting went well." Wrong thing to say. Constantine rolled her eyes as Brandy started to give her a full account of the meeting.

"Brandy? *Bran*dy? You still go to the midnight meeting at the Mustard Seed, don't you?"

Brandy told her that she certainly did, didn't Constantine remember that Brandy went to three meetings almost every day? She was appalled as she told Constantine that she hadn't made it last night, though, because the eight o'clock meeting in the church basement had run way over, and she'd been tired, but Brandy had heard all about it from people who'd been watching television throughout the night, or earlier today. The entire recovery community had been buzzing over the news that one of their own, one of their precious new people, was being sought by the police on the very first night that he'd come to them, looking for help.

"Can you find out for me what Terry said? If he told anyone where he was planning to go after the meeting?" For one of the very few times in Constantine's memory, Brandy was at a loss for words.

Constantine could almost hear her thinking, wondering if she would be breaking any moral or ethical canons, balancing that against her innate desire to gossip. She had to fight the urge to tell Brandy to make up her fucking mind, right *now!* Instead, Constantine waited. Brandy finally told her that she'd see what she could do, and, as Constantine was finally able to pull out into the street, she told Brandy she'd have to call her back, she'd give her an hour.

DiGrazia still hadn't given her the goddamn cell phone number.

Hegewisch is a Far South Side neighborhood which is divided into two sections, one of which is referred to as Arizona—which is situated east of the railroad tracks—the other section is simply referred to as Hegewisch. No one knows why this is. Its borders are Torrence Avenue and Wolf Lake to the west and east, the village of Burnham to the south, and the East Side on the north. A snaky curved road separates Hegewisch from the East Side. A large yellow sign on this road warns motorists to slow down, and gives the number of the dead who, over the years, hadn't.

There are old, shingle-sided homes in parts of Arizona, and the main drag, Baltimore Avenue, the shopping area, is in Hegewisch. There is one Catholic grade school on either side of the tracks, St. Columba to the east, St. Florian to the west. St. Columba's has the distinction of facing Szarek's Auto, the only car dealership in the neighborhood.

Hegewisch has two funeral parlors.

Both areas have plenty of taverns, at least one on every commercial block, sometimes as many as four. Residential streets generally have their tavern on the corner, where men have been stopping off for generations, on their way home from working the steel mills. It has been more than one small male Hegewisch resident's fondest wish to grow up and stop off in these places after work, have a shot and a beer, like Dad.

The steel mills are closed now, but the taverns are still open.

Constantine drove past a vacant lot in the Arizona section of Hegewisch now, looking for the Lewan's address on a block where most of the lawns were bright green, but where few houses had their address numbers displayed. Several teenaged white males were in the lot, drinking beer out of quart bottles in full daylight, holding what she hoped were cigarettes in cupped hands, as they glowered at the obvious unmarked police vehicle. Constantine glowered back. She pulled over to the curb, rolled down her window.

"This is Avenue N; where's One-two-nine-two-two?"

No answer. Constantine sighed. She rolled up the window, took the radio mike into hand, and pretended to speak into it, then put it back, opened the door of the car, and stepped out onto the cracked asphalt. She put her hands on her hips. Behind her, the small, urban jungle that was Wolf Lake Park seemed shadowy and forbidding.

"There's two squad cars on the way. You boys old enough to drink?" For once in her career, Constantine's gender worked in her favor, she understood that if she'd been male, the boys would have run off by this time. All that kept them rooted to the lot was their false sense of machismo.

One of the boys put his bottle down, though, then stepped in front of it, as if to hide it from her view.

She would have to make this quick; the longer she waited, the higher the odds were that they would fight their urges and would bolt. They would lose their nerve as time passed, thinking that two squad cars were on the way to pick them up. Constantine focused in on the boy who had made the feeble attempt to hide his bottle.

"Hey, you—" The kid pointed to himself. "—yeah, you. Answer my question and I'll call the squads off." She saw that he was very dirty, his hair was thin already, his eyes were set close to his nose. She wondered about his parentage, she felt a sudden surge of sorrow directed toward him, and fought it off.

"One-two-nine-two-two?" the kid asked. Constantine nodded. He jerked his head down the street. "There's only two or three houses got addresses on 'em." Constantine had already discovered that. He said, "Middle of the block, the one with the green and white awning. Matches the grass, it's the Lewans you want, right?"

"You're smarter than you look," Constantine said, rather than thanking him. She was doing him a small favor, the others might not razz him so much for talking with her if they thought he'd been insulted.

The young man took umbrage at her remark, though, pointed his finger at her and said, "Yeah? Well, don't be too fucking *sure* about that!"

Constantine got back into the car without response, thinking that it was punishment enough for the kid just to have to be who he was.

Constantine stepped onto the concrete front porch and rang the bell. She looked out at the desolate block. There were no houses on the other side of the street, just thickets and trees, forest that wasn't deep. She could smell Wolf Lake. She could smell, too, the stench coming from the chemical plants just across Wolf Lake in Whiting, Indiana. Constantine breathed through her mouth. She looked back at the door.

"Mrs. Lewan?" The old heavyset woman was looking at her suspiciously through the small, diamond-shaped glass of a front door that had four different locks. There was an empty dirt driveway next to the house. Wild grass and weeds grew between the identical areas where the car's tires had carved out grooves. Constantine had seen from the street that there wasn't a garage out back. She wouldn't want to drive through an alley in this neighborhood, either. She was glad to see that someone was home.

Constantine held her photo identification up to the glass. "I'm—Detective—Janice Constantine. I'm looking for your daughter, Ellen?"

She saw the old woman look hurriedly behind Constantine, as if seeking danger, an accomplice, something that could cause her harm if she dared to open the door. The old woman shook her head.

"Ellen's gone." *Gone.* Not *She's not here.* Which meant that she had *been* there.

"Took your car?" The old woman bit her lip, as if wondering how much trouble she could get into if she refused to answer the question.

"Do you have a warrant?" the old woman said, and Constantine gave her a bright smile.

"Warrant? What for? I don't want to arrest Ellen, I want to help her."

Constantine heard a male voice raised in query, saw the old woman look back over her shoulder, heard her say, "It's a detective looking for Ellen . . ." Constantine knew that if the window extended low enough, she would see the old woman dry-washing her hands as she spoke. "A *woman*." She watched the relief flood the old woman's face as she stepped aside, and her husband took over.

"Help you?"

Constantine tried again, identifying herself as she held her ID up to the glass. She heard locks thrown, and stepped back so the old man could open the screen door for her.

"Come on in, Officer," the old man said. "You ain't missed Ellen by more than ten minutes."

Constantine stepped into the house, and stopped at the sight of the small shotgun that was propped up against the wall. She looked at it, her right hand slowly creeping up her side.

"It's a four-ten, with birdshot. Goddamn kids, when they ain't trying to rob you, they're running around here like wild animals, they ride their bikes all over your lawn."

"On the lawn."

"You know how much work goes into making a lawn look like that?"

A fence would have been easier, and legal, but Constantine didn't mention this. Instead, she said, "That's a fine lawn, Mr. Lewan, you see it the second you turn the corner."

Smiling, Mr. Lewan asked her if she'd like a cup of coffee.

CHAPTER
36

"Nobody smokes anymore, and they don't want *you* to, either," Mr. Lewan said. "It's gettin' so's they don't even want to let you do it in the privacy of your own home."

Constantine nodded her head in sympathy, the two of them smoking at the kitchen table, while the Mr. Coffee machine dripped noisily behind them. Mrs. Lewan was busy setting out metal spoons, putting saucers and cups down in front of them, not missing a word that either of them spoke. Her long-simmering resentments were disclosed by the manner in which she slammed the utensils down. Constantine imagined that if pressed to do so, the woman could not count the number of times she had served her husband and his guests. How many of his lectures on smoking had she been forced to sit through, while nodding at his superior wisdom?

It's cultural . . . It's the way we're trained to act toward each other.

Constantine saw the reality of Mrs. Lewan—what Ellen Moran had learned through years of practical study, Constantine divined in the course of a careful visual analysis. Watching Mrs. Lewan perform her tasks, Constantine thought she now understood what DiGrazia had been trying to say. A not-too distant squeal of rubber interrupted her thoughts.

"Hear that? Happens all night the past ten years, the cops never do nothing about it, either. Avenue O's just one block over, U.S. Forty-one, it'll take you all the way to Florida, you want it to. I first bought this house, it was a two-lane strip of road. The only niggers you ever saw were the ones fishing Wolf Lake on weekends, and they knew better than to try and park their Cadillacs on *this* block. You could sleep out in the yard if you wanted to, in those days. For God's sake, we used to leave the doors unlocked."

Mrs. Lewan said, "Until that Speck business." She put a hand to her mouth as her husband gave her a look. Infamous Chicago murders were no doubt not a favored topic of conversation in the Lewan household. They'd rather discuss the good old days, and disclose their bigotry to strangers.

Constantine kept her expression neutral as she said, "Did Ellen say where she was going?"

"Said she was going home. Borrowed my car, because she couldn't get her own car out of the garage because of all the media . . ."

Constantine let him talk for a minute, hiding her disappointment, her anger at Mrs. Lewan, her even greater anger at the husband. Mrs. Lewan poured her coffee. Constantine thanked her, reached for the sugar. She wished that Mrs. Lewan would sit down.

"You said you came here to protect Ellen?" Mr. Lewan was cut off in midword by his wife. He stared at her, open-mouthed and shocked.

"Yes, ma'am."

"Thank heaven for that. All that business about Tom's life getting dragged up all over again, I've been terrified all day that she'd have a miscarriage."

Constantine stopped stirring her coffee.

"What did you say?"

"Christine . . ." Mr. Lewan's warning was potent, but it didn't stop his wife.

"Well, I *was*."

Constantine said, "Ellen's pregnant?"

"And don't think we ain't been worried about it." Mr. Lewan had a sudden, sly look about him. Constantine suspected before he even opened his mouth that he was about to tell her a lie. "First thing we thought about when we heard the news about the killing. We knew what happened last time, what—whoever—did to the baby. Tom's first wife's baby, I mean."

Constantine had not had a chance to read Schmidt's files. She did know that Ellen hadn't married Dr. Moran until three years after Nancy's death. The *Sun-Tribune* article had not mentioned the fetus in Nancy's purse, not in sensitive acknowledgment that their readers would be eating breakfast while they read the piece, but because they hadn't been told. But these people were Dr. Moran's in-laws; surely, through the course of the years, the topic had been discussed among them.

Constantine might have let any suspicions she had pass quickly from her mind if Mr. Lewan hadn't been such a poor liar. But, like all poor liars, Mr. Lewan now tried to quickly change the subject, afraid that he'd been caught in the first lie, compounding it with another.

"They had to dig all that up, put *our* names in the papers, too, like we had something to do with any of it. We wouldn't talk to the reporters when they called, and we ain't talked to them yet today. They had to go and dig up Todd's death and everything, couldn't even show respect for the dead. We didn't even know who Tom Moran *was* until years after the first wife—you know."

"Well, that's not true," Mrs. Lewan said, and her husband shot her another glare. Constantine stood up, looking at the woman. Her wrinkled face held the peculiar expression that the faces of children hold when they know they're being naughty and know it, but simply don't care.

"Goddamnit, Christine!" Mr. Lewan nearly shouted the words.

"We've got all those pictures . . ." Mrs. Lewan was wringing her hands now, delighting in the way she'd stood up to her husband, but no doubt pretending to be afraid so he wouldn't know she'd done it on purpose. Constantine decided that Mrs. Lewan knew her role well. And why not? She'd spent her entire life studying for the part.

It's cultural . . .

DiGrazia's word echoed in Constantine's head, and she now used that cultural divide to her advantage.

Constantine moved in very close to Mrs. Lewan, and her voice was pure steel when she said, "I need to see those pictures, ma'am." She put her hand out in a traffic-stopping motion as Mr. Lewan opened his mouth. Constantine didn't bother to look at him. "I need to see them right *now,* Mrs. Lewan."

Mrs. Lewan looked at her husband, who was now sullenly silent. Constantine watched the old woman's face as it changed expression, as simulated fear was replaced by the genuine kind. Bullies fold quickly, Constantine had seen it before. She couldn't give the woman an inch, knew that if she let up on her for even a second, the woman would turn to her husband for guidance, and that would be the end for Constantine, she'd never see the pictures. She positioned her body so that Mrs. Lewan could not see past her to her husband.

Her voice was harsh, professional, and accusing when she said, "I didn't drop in for a cup of coffee, lady, I'm investigating a murder here. Show me those pictures, Mrs. Lewan. You could get yourself in a lot of trouble if I have to go get a court order."

Mr. Lewan was still fuming silently as his wife led Constantine out of the kitchen.

There were, literally, thousands of them. Small pictures, large pictures, black and white, and in color. Thousands of tiny paint chips were missing from the bedroom walls, where Ellen had once had the pictures secured with tape.

"This was Ellen's room," Mrs. Lewan said. "She had these hung up *everywhere.*" Constantine believed her. "There used to be more, even, but Todd—our son—he used to sneak in here and steal them." There was a bitter reverberation in Mrs. Lewan's voice.

Constantine did not look up at her. She was thinking furiously, making her connections, putting things together that might not even be close to the truth. She didn't know exactly what she should say, or how she should say it, but she did know that she could still not afford to show this woman any kindness.

She also knew that if her husband came in, Constantine would threaten him with arrest if he didn't leave the room immediately. She needed to be alone with this woman, needed another five minutes to straighten out her thoughts. She wished, for just a second, that DiGrazia was here, then banished such thoughts from her mind.

It's cultural ...

Mrs. Lewan's subservience to her husband was cultural, too. Bred into her since the time that she'd been just a little girl. She would bury her resentment at him and take it out on other people. Generally, in Constantine's experience, on the kids. A woman such as this would have been taught through her mother's actions and words that her highest ambition in life was to serve the man of the family, the husband. The fucking breadwinner. Constantine knew how that would seethe within women such as Mrs. Lewan, how it would distort their life views.

As Constantine's had been distorted earlier that day, when she'd automatically assumed that DiGrazia had a hidden agenda, hadn't taken her out of patrol because she was a good, experienced copper, but rather because she was expendable, a middle-aged woman who didn't matter.

Well, fuck a whole big bunch of *that* thinking.

Constantine concentrated on the pictures again now, saw that they were mostly candid shots, some taken from a distance, some close-up. Some caught Tom Moran smiling at the lens, others caught him frowning. Mostly, they were fuzzy, out of focus, as he moved, walking, or sat talking to somebody who obviously wasn't Ellen Lewan.

A number of the pictures were of Dr. Moran and his first wife, Nancy.

Constantine could almost feel the desperation Ellen had felt as she'd snapped the pictures, as she'd longed for him, wanted him, as she'd fallen in love with the man from a distance. Did they speak? Was he even aware that she existed? How did she feel about the wife, about Nancy?

Ellen had quit the rape crisis center when they'd allowed men to work as counselors.

The tape had torn off some of the corners when it had been removed, off-white photographic paper replaced the fading images of a young and intense medical student. There were many more pictures of him frowning than there were of him smiling.

"How many pictures did she have of Nancy Moran?" Constantine looked up as she spoke, holding dozens of pictures in her hands. She let them slide back into the large cardboard box. Her look held no compassion, and it warned the old woman not to lie.

"I don't—Todd took most of them. She had a lot of them, though, at one time. I don't remember." Constantine was afraid that she was losing her, she had to be careful here.

Constantine sat on an old bed in a room that was filled with ancient tears and silent screams. She felt as if she were back in Mike Schmidt's basement. She could feel Ellen's longing, her need for approval from an adult male figure . . .

Constantine started, and the pictures fell from her fingers.

"How old was she when it started? How long did it go on? Goddamn you, lady, answer me!" Constantine rose from the bed, put her hand on Mrs. Lewan's arm. She was careful not to squeeze, she did not want to leave any marks.

She said, "You can answer me here, in your own house, or in an interrogation room down at headquarters, it makes no kind of fucking difference to me, lady. Either way, I'll get the truth out of you."

"I don't know if I should say anymore . . ."

"You knew what was happening, don't pretend you didn't!" Constantine did not raise her voice, but her words pierced the old woman like a shout, and she started.

"You like your house, Christine?" The woman was trembling. Constantine kept her mind focused on what she suspected—what she knew—had occurred in this room, and lost any sense of sympathy she might ordinarily have felt.

"You like living in this house? Want to spend the rest of your life in a cell down in Dwight? How about your old man, want to see him go to Statesville? Accessory to murder gets you as much time as if you did the act yourself, and there's no statute of limitations, no time limit for murder." Constantine shook her slightly, and the old woman began to cry.

"Talk to me, Christine, you tell me the truth right this minute!"

"That'll be enough out of you," Mr. Lewan's terrified voice came from the doorway, and Constantine turned angrily to face him. He was trembling, too. Constantine could tell from the way the barrel of the shotgun wavered back and forth as he held it close in to his shoulder.

"Stan, *don't!*" Mrs. Lewan stepped back, not doing Constantine any favors by screaming.

As calmly as she could, Constantine said, "Mr. Lewan, put that shotgun down. Do you know what'll happen to you if you shoot a cop? What'll happen to Christine?"

"Stan, I didn't say anything, I didn't tell her anything, I was afraid I'd get in trouble if I didn't show her the pictures!"

Constantine took a huge risk. "What you did to Ellen is too far in the past for it to get you in any trouble today. All I want from either of you is for you to tell me if you knew beforehand that Ellen killed Nancy Moran."

"He never touched Ellen! Don't you say he did!" Mrs. Lewan shouted it as Mr. Lewan wavered in the doorway, the shotgun now held loosely, down around his hip. It was a small-bore weapon, but they were in a tiny room. Whether it was loaded with birdshot or buckshot didn't matter, if he pulled the trigger at this range, Constantine would have a serious problem. His face now betrayed shock more than anger or fear, what Constantine had said had rocked him.

She said now, "Mr. Lewan, put down the weapon." Constantine hadn't moved an inch since she'd turned to face him. Her voice held the ring of command. She didn't know how he'd react if she reached for her own weapon. She repeated her order, and this time it had effect.

Fractionally, inch by inch, the shotgun lowered, until the barrel was pointing at the floor.

"I wouldn't shoot anyone."

"Sure you wouldn't, I understand. All right, Mr. Lewan. Now I want you to lean over and put the weapon down on the carpet there. That's right. Now step away from it, back, go on."

"Don't arrest him!" Mrs. Lewan shouted. She ran to her husband's side. "It was Todd, it was *Todd,* not Stan! Stan never hurt Ellen, Stan would never hurt her! I never even told him about it, he doesn't even know!" Mr. Lewan stepped back in fear as Constantine snatched the shotgun up off the floor. She held it by its slight wooden stock as she broke it open and discovered it to be empty. She could see the old man, a toothless tiger, waving it at the paperboy. Constantine's shoulders slumped in relief.

Should she place him under arrest? It was a judgment call. She had enough to get the old man locked away, but explaining things to the responding patrol units would waste valuable time. Constantine didn't want him for waving a gun around, and besides, she could always come back. Where were these two old people going to run off to? Constantine looked at them, her spirits sinking as she realized that even if she could make a case, no jury would convict two pathetic old people like these two.

They were out in the hallway now, and Mr. Lewan was attempting to push the old woman off him as she desperately tried to cling to him. He was shocked, devastated. He stood pushing at his wife with flabby arms.

His expression told Constantine all she needed to know. Mrs. Lewan had been right. Her husband hadn't known.

She took the empty weapon with her as she walked quickly out of the house.

CHAPTER
37

Neal's eyes were wide, as if he were witnessing a vision of Christ. Eddie thought that that just might be the case. He had been speaking for over an hour, and his mouth was very dry. He'd drunk several glasses of water, poured them into a paper cup from the watcher pitcher on his bedstand, but he couldn't make the dryness go away, and that bothered him, as it affected the earnestness of his delivery.

At some point in his recitation, Eddie had sat up. He didn't remember sitting up. He'd told Neal everything, went back all the way and started at the beginning, told him about the dogs, the cats, the birds, the fires he had set as a child.

He told Neal about them all, the men, the women. He told Neal about last night, told him about this morning. He'd told him about Schmidt.

Neal hadn't spoken a word, nor had he complained about the smacking sounds Eddie kept making as his tongue constantly got caught on the dry roof of his mouth.

Eddie felt free.

He felt his knees under his elbows, he felt very strong and powerful. His anger was gone, as was his sadness. He knew that a small smile was nearly always on his lips. He knew that

Neal was impressed, knew that the revelations he'd shared with the younger man had freed Neal from his own inner suffering.

Neal was looking at him through wide eyes, with respect, with astonishment. Eddie wanted to kiss him, and would have, if he hadn't sensed that doing so would frighten the younger man away.

"Schmidt wanted me to put the body in a *church*," Eddie whispered now. He laughed softly. "Mike said he had the entire file on me locked up in his lawyer's safe, said the guy had instructions to mail it to the cops if anything happened to Mike. He thought I was as stupid as he was, thought I didn't see how paranoid he was. The file was in his basement all the time, taped up in a box. Oh, he thought he was so sly." Eddie giggled. "Said he knew what I was the first time he saw me."

"And that's why you killed him?" Neal spoke his first words since Eddie had begun to talk. Eddie, watching them float over to him on a cloud of ignorance, wanted to bless him. The words weren't as clear in the air as they'd been. He blew at the cloud of ignorance, saw it quickly disappear. Was that a sign of his power, or was he losing his internal jubilation? Eddie fought off a momentary terror. Dr. Warren was in the building, Dr. Warren would give him some more of the pills if Eddie asked him to do so.

To Neal, he said, "Schmidt was at the prison gate when I got released. Took me in, brought me to his house. He would sit there drinking at night, telling me what he was going to let me do; he was offering me Heaven, Neal, letting me do what he wanted me to do in the privacy and safety of his own house, in the basement. The last few weeks were the happiest time of my life. He told me he'd been keeping tabs on me since he'd first arrested me years ago, had asked the department of corrections to alert him when I was scheduled to get out of Canton Correctional. He was waiting for me outside the prison gates, like a little kid waiting for Santa Claus. He'd been waiting for this day for a long, long time. I had no idea that when he called in the debt, it would be to do something I wanted to do!" Eddie collapsed in a fit of laughter. "Schmidt thought he was just making me do his dirty work for him. In the meantime, there I was, eating his food, drinking his booze, listening to the stories, loving every second of it." A far-away look of rapture came onto Eddie's face.

"When I snatched her, when she was in the basement, the last week? That was the best time. Schmidt told me I had to be careful, had to wait, but he didn't have to tell me that, I wouldn't have harmed that child for the world until I was ready." He looked over at Neal and gave him a beatific smile.

"Can you imagine how beautiful it was, how fulfilling? I'd only have to open the basement *door,* and she'd start begging. I don't remember ever being so sexually stimulated in my life. I never had time like that before, never had the luxury of having days and days to hear one of them scream, to hear them beg."

"But if Schmidt did all that for you, why did you kill him?"

"He would have *told* on me. He was very angry when I didn't put the body in the church, the way he wanted." Eddie's tone dripped with disgust. "I would never put a body in a church, anyone who knows me knows I'd never do a thing like that. I'm a *Catholic,* for God's sake."

Neal was filled with terror. He tried to hide it, but Eddie could tell. He smelled the man's fear, felt his own muscles grow stronger as they fed off Neal's fright. He had to be careful of that, had to fight it down. Feeling that happen to him had always been one of his indicators, had always made Eddie start to think strange thoughts.

"But *I* know . . ."

"I know you'd never tell on me, Neal."

"No . . ." Neal's voice was a whisper.

"Because you love me."

"Oh, man, Eddie."

The room fell silent.

"So where do we go from here?" Eddie asked. Baring his soul had made him hungry. He usually ate only for fuel, being hungry was almost fun. "Where do we eat?"

"The cafeteria." Neal did not look hungry. "It's down the hall, to the left, I'll take you there." Neal seemed lost in his thoughts, as his voice was far away, distracted, as he said, "Then some of us have individual counseling till around eight, then we're free for the rest of the night. We can go to the day room and watch a movie, or we can come back to our rooms if we want. A lot of guys come back and catch a nap so they can go to Sarge's midnight meeting."

"Sarge's midnight meeting." Eddie felt resentment try to barge in on his tranquility. Who was Sarge, to have a meeting? Sarge—and the rest of them—were nothing next to him. And now Neal knew of his greatness.

"Eddie?" Eddie looked up. His name was floating all around the room. Neal must have called it out a dozen times before he'd heard him. The words were fading into air far more rapidly than they had been.

"Hmm?"

"You want me to show you where the cafeteria is?"

"Yes, please," Eddie said, and rose shakily to his feet.

The room couldn't contain him, he felt himself absorb it. He followed Neal to the door, had to restrain himself from putting his arm around Neal's shoulders. In the few steps it took them to get to the door, Eddie noticed that Neal was walking strangely, was somehow cringing as he walked, as if he were expecting Eddie to attack him at any moment.

Eddie felt confused. He thought telling Neal his secrets would bring them closer together. He felt a flash of paranoia, felt the drugs Dr. Warren had given him *whoosh* to the rescue, felt them overcome his panic, but only barely, not like before.

It wasn't as good as it had been, Eddie could actually feel the drugs begin to drain out of his system.

Eddie was beginning to feel like Eddie again.

He was about to ask Neal what was wrong when Neal opened the door, and the Big Cop from TV walked past the room, glancing in at him briefly, without any particular curiosity.

Eddie froze, felt hysteria envelope him, felt himself begin to shake. He somehow managed to reach out and push the door closed, somehow understood that the Big Cop didn't know what Eddie looked like, because he had just kept walking.

But he was there, he was looking for him. He'd somehow found out Eddie's name, found out where Eddie was. It was just a matter of time now.

Neal was looking at him, his mouth open, saying something. Eddie couldn't hear him, couldn't see the words floating in the air anymore. He didn't feel strong, didn't feel powerful. He felt his legs go weak beneath him, and he forced himself to stumble toward the bed.

"Eddie? *Eddie!*" Neal's voice was loud, the young man right there in front of him, kneeling down now, in front of Eddie.

Neal was the only one who knew, and Dr. Warren had his suspicions, had asked him about the girl in the alley. Schmidt was dead. One of them had done it, had told the Big Cop about Eddie. Eddie did know Neal could have done it, maybe by mental telepathy. Eddie believed in such things.

And so Eddie reached out quick, nimble hands and wrapped them around Neal's throat before the young man could scream. He pressed in hard with his thumbs, sending his devastating streak of betrayal down from his heart, on into his fingers. Neal's windpipe was crushed before he could even react to the assault. Eddie, knowing this, lowered him quietly to the floor, and lay atop him, not letting go, watching Neal's eyes closely until the light of life faded out of them, and he died.

DiGrazia pressed the bell and waited, and a clicking sound alerted him that he could open the door to the clinic. The guard who'd been sitting just inside began to carefully inspect DiGrazia's identification. After several seconds, DiGrazia snatched it out of his hand.

"Dr. Moran's expecting me," he said.

The angry guard slapped his nightstick threateningly against the side of his leg as he led DiGrazia silently down a corridor through what was obviously some sort of residential hall. Rooms were on either side of the hallway, some had their doors open, others had them closed. He saw watchful, paranoid, or expectant faces through the open doors. He'd been carrying his jacket over his arm, and now he put it on in order to hide his badge and weapon.

The second to the last door before the end of the hallway suddenly opened, and DiGrazia looked in at the occupants, saw a young man standing in front of a big, slim, older guy, a man around his own age. He noticed the look of horror that passed across the older patient's face. DiGrazia felt as if he were somehow violating the man's privacy. He looked away as he walked on.

The guard unlocked one side of a large double door. He pushed it open. He pointed down the hallway. "Moran's the third door down. I'll leave this door unlocked for you, so I ain't got to come back."

DiGrazia stepped through, and the door was slammed shut behind him with far more force than was necessary.

McMillan sat playing cards with Eberhardt, waiting for the computer to sound off, which would alert him to a match. Di-Grazia had said to beep him if it did, he would be at the VA hospital for an hour or so. He would call only one of the six numbers in the room, he'd told them to keep the line clear. McMillan and Eberhardt ignored the constant ringing of the other five phones, two tired men who had been awake since late the night before, but too keyed up and excited to think about trying to get some rest. Neither man felt the urge to explain things to anyone, especially to bosses. That was DiGrazia's job.

"What do you think of Constantine?" McMillan asked, making conversation. He threw down a three of spades. Eberhardt swept it up into his hand.

"Good looking twenty years ago, maybe, but she put on a lot of miles over hard road since."

"I mean as a *cop*."

"She's a cop, all right." Eberhardt dropped the queen of hearts onto the pile. McMillan couldn't use it. He drew from the face-down deck. "I was mad after that set-to with Stefaniak and Hill. I asked her what she wanted, and I thought she was going to shoot me."

"She might well have," McMillan said. "She's a pretty tough cookie."

"Don't run across her very often, down where I work."

McMillan discarded, paused a second, waiting for Eberhardt to reach for his discard before spreading out his hand. Eberhardt looked up at him. McMillan had been holding the card, knowing it was the last one Eberhardt needed.

McMillan said, "Rum. You know, for a doctor—and a white

306

man—you're a pretty predictable guy. Maybe there's hope for us yet . . ."

Eberhardt was opening his mouth to respond when someone began pounding on the door at the same moment that the computer behind them began to beep.

CHAPTER 38

"The blood results surprised me, I have to tell you. You all right, Dr. Moran?" DiGrazia leaned forward in his chair, in a solicitous manner. Moran nodded his head. He looked pale and afraid, and now DiGrazia wondered why the man had even allowed him to come here.

DiGrazia said, "The midnight-shift guard at your subdivision couldn't remember the time you came in or left, although he did remember both occurrences." He shrugged. "You live close to the wrought-iron fence. The guard in the vehicle must have been cooping somewhere."

"He has a schedule. A route. Circles through the area at various times of the night," Moran said.

"It wouldn't be very hard to watch him pass, jump the fence, dump the blood, and get back over before he finished a circuit," said DiGrazia.

"I would have told that to the other two detectives, if they hadn't been—if they'd let me," Tom said.

"You said you were planning on coming to us, didn't you, Doctor?" The question took Moran by surprise.

"Yes. I talked to my wife about it earlier today. I wanted to see if I could help. How did you know?"

DiGrazia ignored the question, and said, "But not to solve Nancy's murder."

It was a simple statement, spoken softly. Yet Moran visibly started, as if he'd been physically attacked.

"Doctor, there're only the two of us in this room. And I'm not interrogating you. We know you didn't kill Veronica Davene, you're clear. And *I* know you didn't kill Nancy."

"How do you know that?"

"Because Mike Schmidt questioned you, and at that time, he was the single best interrogator the police department had ever seen."

"But he always thought I was guilty."

"If you had been, he'd have gotten you to confess. It was one of the things he could never deal with, what led him to become— what wrecked him. You're not a psychopath, Doctor. You feel emotion, I saw it this morning. Schmidt would have gotten it out of you, if you'd done it."

"He almost did, anyway. He almost had me believing I'd done it. If the law professors hadn't found out I was being held . . . I don't even want to think about it." DiGrazia suspected that was due more to his memory of the fear he'd felt that morning than to his twenty-year-old recollection of Mike Schmidt's interrogative techniques.

"Why, Detective DiGrazia. *Why* did he hound me?"

DiGrazia was unwilling to give him an adequate response, so he only shook his head.

Moran pointed over his shoulder, at the computer on the small desk behind him. "You know, this little thing changed the world. Fifteen, even ten years ago, I was spending every minute I could in libraries, checking out long, professional, boring books about the few real progressional murderers there were in the world. They were written by scholars. There was no such thing as a profile, there was no Behavioral Science Unit, none of the so-called true-crime books, movies, or TV had invaded our culture, hadn't yet turned everyone into analysts about such killers.

"Now I can look up police reports. Even search certain declassified police and FBI files that someone got through the Freedom of Information Act, and posted on the Internet. I've been studying them for years, Mr. DiGrazia. They've become very . . . let's just say important to me. I may know as much about them as Park Deitz or Robert Ressler."

DiGrazia sat silently and very still, willing his body not to move a single muscle. Moran's voice was soft, distant, and dreamy, intimate in the office.

"I know more about progressional killers than I do about almost anything else, I guess." He looked over at DiGrazia, expecting a response. DiGrazia was disappointed by his understanding that he'd have to personally extricate the information he'd come here to get out of the man, and he'd have to do it slowly. He'd thought for certain the doctor had been about to volunteer what he wanted.

"You could call me an expert."

"And you found what you were looking for, didn't you?" DiGrazia asked him.

Constantine threw the cellular phone down in disgust on James McMillan's desk, then stood looking anxiously over his shoulder as McMillan sat in the chair, looking at the name that was flashing in red on the color monitor. Every time the name turned red, the computer gave out with a little beep.

"There's our man," Eberhardt said. A cream-colored file folder was on the desk next to the computer; Constantine knew that pictures lay within it, color photos memorializing what had been done to Veronica Davene. She read the name off the computer.

"Richard Edward Milles."

"Got a good ring to it, don't it?" McMillan said.

"Page DiGrazia," Eberhardt said.

"I ran the goddamn cell phone dead trying to call you guys, why didn't you pick it up?"

"He told us to just answer one line. You called the wrong one."

Constantine was dialing DiGrazia's number. She had to open the file to get it off the sheet. She turned Veronica's pictures over, she'd seen enough pictures for one night. She closed the file as soon as she had the number.

"Terry told a group of people last night that he'd be checking himself into an alcohol treatment center. He asked for help getting in, but he wouldn't stick around or go in right then, wouldn't go right into a detox last night. He said he had to work."

"Can you use that thing to find out where he went?"

"Not if it's a private hospital."

Several beeps alerted her that she'd reached DiGrazia's pager, and Constantine punched in the number, added 911 behind it, so DiGrazia would know it was an emergency.

"Can you run Milles's name against any other state but Illinois?"

"Doing it." Constantine was pleased that McMillan hadn't thought of it first.

"Why aren't you with Ellen?" Eberhardt said as she hung up.

"DiGrazia was right again. Ellen left her parents' house ten minutes before I got there." Constantine couldn't help herself, she had to show off a little. "I found out who killed Nancy Moran, though."

"What?" Both men turned to her in unison.

"Ellen did it," she said.

Dr. Moran said, "Mr. DiGrazia, I'm not sure that I like this line of questioning."

"Give me a week, two weeks, I can come back and give you a name. Give me that much time with the files. I might not be able to make a case, but I'd bet that I could give you the same name you're thinking of right this minute. And you might not like it very much if I did that, would you, Doctor? You said on the phone you were going to help me. You said the same thing this afternoon, before the judge showed up. Help me, Doctor. Help me now."

"Schmidt never figured it out."

Tacit acceptance between them that Moran had the information DiGrazia was seeking.

"Schmidt turned into a drunk with tunnel vision. He never saw past you." Even with what he had learned about the man, DiGrazia felt, as he said this, as if he were betraying his ex-partner. He knew he had to give the doctor another small kernel of truth.

"Schmidt's oldest daughter was murdered by her piano

teacher. He pleaded not guilty, and at first Schmidt backed him up. He could not believe that a man he had approved in advance could be capable of killing his little girl."

"Oh, God."

"And the brass knew what it did to him, when he finally saw past his suffering and came around to accepting the truth. He was in court every single day, and he went crazy when they didn't give the man the death penalty."

"What happened to him?" Moran drew in a deep breath. "Schmidt killed him, didn't he."

DiGrazia tossed a computer printout sheet on the desk. There were nine names on the sheet; eight had been printed out by McMillan, DiGrazia had written the last name down himself. "He's the last name there, the one that's written down. He got out of Pontiac last year, served twenty-two years, the first fifteen of them in the maximum-security mental ward." DiGrazia paused, almost formally.

Then he said, "Do you recognize the name, Doctor?"

DiGrazia waited, carefully watching Moran's face. Moran pursed his lips. Moran shook his head. "No," he said, looking up at DiGrazia.

DiGrazia did his best to hide his bitter, frustrating disappointment. "Do you recognize *any* of the names?" Moran looked down again. He seemed to be carefully studying the list.

"None of them. Why would I?"

"You called the clinic late last night, and then again this morning, right before you were arrested. We've got an eight-hundred number, we've taken hundreds of calls since they showed Terry's picture on the screen. Most callers say Terry's their brother-in-law in disguise, living a secret life. A dozen calls came from inside this hospital, from a different ward. Terry's here, in the detox unit, you called and set it up for him, smoothed the way. I'd like to speak with him, the three of us together. We don't need to bring anyone else in on this, we don't even need to intrude on his therapy. I just want to talk to him."

"Terry didn't kill anyone!"

"Terry and Schmidt were a lot alike, Dr. Moran."

"I can't do this to him."

"I don't think I have to tell you how long it would take me to get a warrant."

Moran, surprisingly, smiled. It began as a slight twitch at the edges of his mouth, then stretched to cover his face. It was a smile of admiration.

"I have to hand it to you, Mr. DiGrazia. You had me going there for a minute."

"I beg your pardon?"

"You were threatening Terry to get me to talk, you think I'll—what, confess?—before I'd let you hurt Terry."

"If you're lying, you're the best at it I've ever seen, sir. That, or you should have been a lawyer."

"Do I need one, Mr. DiGrazia?"

"I already spoke to Judge Haney, I called him right after you agreed to let me come talk to you."

"Then you know he's not representing me anymore. You know I could have helped you? I could probably have led you to Schmidt."

"Schmidt blew it himself. His need for revenge, to nail you, finally got him killed."

"I can understand the feeling."

"You know who killed Nancy, don't you, Dr. Moran?"

Moran slowly nodded his head.

"I think I might," he said, as DiGrazia's beeper went off.

"Richard Edward Milles," Constantine said into the phone. She squinted at the long rap sheet that McMillan had printed out. "DOB three-eighteen, fifty-three; brown, blue; six-and-one-quarter, a hundred-and-seventy-five. Charged with: Burglary, seven times. Sexual Assault, two times. Chicago PD charged him with one count of intimidation, it doesn't say what for, but it's during the same month as the first sexual assault charges. Convictions: three, got probation for the first sex crime, and the intimidation. Did time for one of the burglaries, and four years in Canton Correctional on the sexual assault: guess who the arresting officer was on the second sexual assault? I'll give you a hint. Milles was sent up four years this month, released three weeks ago."

"Mike Schmidt," DiGrazia said into her ear.

"You got it. Now listen, Nicky, Ellen wasn't at her parents' house, but I got them to show me her old room, and get this, she had maybe two thousand pictures of Tom Moran in a box, she had them pinned to her walls, *she had an obsession with him twenty years ago, Nicky!*"

"You're saying Ellen Moran killed Nancy Moran, twenty years ago, Detective, is that what you're telling me?" Constantine didn't understand what he was doing. She heard the scream on the other end of the line, someone in the room with DiGrazia was shouting, then the phone went dead in her hand.

"Jesus Christ," Constantine said. She looked at Eberhardt. He wasn't a cop. McMillan had to man the computer, dig up everything there was on Richard Edward Milles. There were maybe two hundred cops right upstairs who would love to go with her to find DiGrazia, but they hadn't been in on it from the beginning, and that was important to Constantine.

How many cops did you need to go find a guy in the VA Hospital? Still, she hadn't liked the sound of the scream. But there was something that bothered her even more.

She'd been in such a hurry to tell DiGrazia what she'd discovered that she hadn't told him the most important thing about Richard Edward Milles.

"I'm going over to the VA hospital," Constantine said to McMillan and Eberhardt.

CHAPTER
39

Frank told the cab driver to pull over when he spotted the liquor store, and he paid the man, grabbed the cardboard suitcase filled with his clothes, and got out of the cab without giving the driver a tip. The cabbie's curses followed Frank, the man shouting in a language Frank didn't understand, but he wouldn't have paid any attention to the words even if they'd been shouted in perfect English. His money was his own, and he had more important things to do with it than to hand it over to foreigners.

Frank walked into the small store and waited impatiently in line as package customers bought their liquor, as lottery tickets were ordered. The clerk wearing the turban punched the numbers into a blue machine. The small bottles of whiskey lining the shelves behind the man beckoned to Frank, lovingly called his name, and it was all he could do to keep still. On a small table next to the man—beyond arm-reach from the counter—was an open cigar box filled with different brands of loose cigarettes. A handwritten sign announced that the cigarettes were for sale at fifty cents apiece. The clerk was burly, and he had a phone to his ear, was smiling as he spoke into it, speaking in what sounded to be the same language that the cab driver had used when he'd cursed at Frank just moments ago. The clerk called all of his customers "sir" or "ma'am."

Frank breathed through his mouth, shaking with his need. The only alcohol he'd had all day had been the beers the cop had given him, and he had fought the urge, as he'd packed his few possessions, to run down to the gas station and at least pick up a six-pack. Frank hadn't had the nerve to ask the hotel manager for a refund on the room. He'd been excited at the prospect of moving in with his brother, Tommy. Tommy would want him to quit drinking, but Frank would worry about that when he had to, he didn't have to concern himself with that now.

Tommy had told Frank that he'd loved him. That he was going to take good care of him. Love and cab rides, a new home to look forward to, all of this in one day was heady business for a man like Frank. He needed a drink to calm himself down, to get through these first few hours of adjustment. The VA hospital was only a few blocks away, he could sip his whiskey as he walked, hide whatever was left inside his suitcase, for later on.

Around him, in the store, neighborhood street people were doing their daily liquor shopping. A videocamera behind the clerk roamed the store, from left to right. A small TV was on a stand beside the camera, flickering a poor image of a baseball game that nobody seemed interested in watching. Frank was relieved when he figured out that nobody seemed to care that he was the only Caucasian in the store.

Frank moved one spot closer to the counter. The door opened, and a young man came in, took his place behind Frank. The next patron asked for QuickPicks. Frank stepped in close, tasting the alcohol already, as he looked over at the bottles. There was now only one human being standing between Frank and heaven.

"Hurry it up, Abdul," the young man behind Frank said, and the clerk dropped his smile. He glared at the young man behind Frank, but not in a way that invited violence, more in a superior, haughty manner that a politician might use when confronted with a surly constituent. The young man behind him shoved at Frank's shoulder, as if doing so would make the clerk move more quickly.

The customer in front of Frank at last stepped aside, and Frank muttered, "Bottle of Four Roses." He hadn't responded to the shove.

"Would you like a pint, or a half pint, sir?" The clerk was still looking with disapproval at the young man behind Frank.

"Pint." Frank had a ten-dollar bill in his hand, change from the twenty that his brother Tom had given him. His own cherished singles were safe in his left front pocket. Frank felt the young man shove his shoulder again, harder this time. He lowered his head in submission.

"Gimme a goddamn pack of Kool, Abdul. I ain't got all fuckin' day to be watchin' you handin' out Four Roses to winos." Frank looked up and watched the clerk take his time putting the bottle into a bag. Frank hadn't wanted a bag. He wanted his whiskey, and he wanted to get out of there.

"My name is not Abdul." Frank was viciously pushed aside just as he was accepting the bottle.

"Wait, sir! You did not pay!" The clerk turned to the young man, enraged, shouting and pointing his thumb back over his shoulder. "You are on the camera, sir, you are on the camera, sir!"

"I don't give a fuck about your television! Gimme a pack of Kool, motherfucker!"

"You wait your turn!" The clerk was livid but frightened, moving around in the small enclosure behind the counter, the phone forgotten, on the counter now, as he held a hand out to Frank. "You pay first, sir."

The young man was wearing very long shorts that did not fit him very well; they hung down from the center of his hips, and extended well past his knees. He had on a tight, white, sleeveless undershirt that exposed long, thin muscles; despite his youth, his head had been shaved close to the skull. There was a thick rope of shiny gold hanging around his neck. Frank thought the young man was, at most, in his middle teens. The young man held his arms out in a familiar gesture, a pose: arms extended wide, bent at the elbows, fingers pointing down and inward; the stance of a street thug just before he started a brawl.

Or pulled out a weapon.

The clerk must have recognized this himself, as his hand disappeared under the counter and came out with a pistol that seemed small in his thick hand, a hand that was shaking terribly as he pointed the weapon at the young man.

"You leave now, you are not welcome here!"

"I'm welcome here as long as I got money!"

Knowledge that he was on videotape was all that kept Frank in the store. He hadn't paid, and his image was on a machine. Frank had been arrested for shoplifting before, and he knew that you didn't get treated the same way for that as you did for something like vagrancy. The cops could be cruel to thieves. The scene had drawn a crowd, the window was filled with faces, people enjoying a violent diversion that had nothing to do with themselves. The store was suddenly silent, the announcer of the Cubs game the only voice to be heard, cheerfully giving everyone the batting statistics on the man who was standing in front of home plate. Frank, standing stone still, wished himself invisible.

The young man moved in close, arms out wide now, in a crucifixion pose.

"Come on, shoot me, you A-rab son of a *bitch! Shoot* an unarmed man!" A murmur grew outside, a collective intake of breath at the young man's audacity. The clerk tried to put down the weapon, but the young man wouldn't let him, had stepped into it, his chest thrust out, smiling at the clerk now as he played to his audience, a young man who had no doubt already outlived many of his friends, thinking that he himself had nothing to lose, and proving it to the world.

"You gonna kill me, or are you gonna give me my pack of squares?"

"Leave my store!"

The young man laughed wildly as he leaned down, grabbed the barrel of the weapon, and held it between his eyes.

"Come on, Ab-*dul.* You got the balls, or you smooth down there, like a GI-Joe doll?"

The young man pulled on the weapon again, and it went off in the clerk's hand. He shouted loudly in fear and surprise as the young man collapsed on the floor. The crowd outside the store gasped, and then the small window behind the clerk's head exploded as somebody threw a brick through the glass. Frank had the ten dollar bill in one hand, the bottle of Four Roses in the other. His suitcase was on the floor, next to the young man's body.

Frank stopped caring about the videotape, didn't step into the blood to retrieve his suitcase. The store was under attack now, the clerk frantically shouting into the phone. Frank turned and ran out of the store. He didn't stop until he was a block away, hearing sirens, Frank crying, sniveling, as his fingers fumbled with the cap, as he finally got it open, as he held the bottle to his mouth and drank until he found himself sucking on air.

If Sarge had been able to see Frank, he would have envied him his whiskey.

He sat on the edge of his cot, alone, his roommate at dinner, along with everyone else on the ward, Sarge with his eyes closed tight, his hands together, as if in prayer, held close to his chest in a protective gesture.

What could protect him now? Could anyone help him, could anyone save him? Sarge didn't know what to do, who he could talk to. Moran was the head guy, but he was only here part of the time, an administrator more than a working shrink, and besides, Moran wanted Sarge out of here, Dr. Warren had told Sarge that, just last night. Sarge knew that he couldn't go to Dr. Warren, either. Warren was Eddie's friend, Warren had even given Eddie his home phone number, and he'd personally called the orderlies last night, preparing them for Eddie's arrival. Warren had been coming into the hospital in the middle of the night, just to see Eddie.

Eddie had told the group last night that he'd spoken with Dr. Warren about his problems, had told them that he didn't think that Warren had believed him. Warren had to be crazy. Sarge believed him. Sarge believed the hell out of him.

Even if one-fifth of what Sarge had heard was true, Eddie was the most frightening man Sarge had ever come across. And he suspected, by the way Eddie had spoken to Neal, by the tone of Eddie's voice, by the smacking, dry-mouth sounds Eddie constantly made as he talked, that Eddie was under the influence of powerful, mind-altering drugs.

What was a man like Eddie capable of, with his inhibitions removed?

Eddie. Sarge thought of the name with contempt. The last time he had checked himself in, he'd insisted on being called Rick. Due to his trustee status on the ward, Sarge had access to the circular files. He knew the man's real name. Richard Edward Milles.

Sarge had heard Eddie and Neal leaving for dinner, so he had a little time to think. The doors to the rooms did not have locks. If Eddie somehow found out that Sarge had listened in . . .

There was a pay phone in the day room, Sarge could get to it while they were all at dinner. Call 911 and tell them what he knew. Sarge had access to TV and the papers, had heard, seen, and read about what had happened in the alley the night before. He knew what Eddie had done. Would he have to give them his name? They'd have a tape recording of his voice. Dr. Warren would find out that it was Sarge who had called, and would put Sarge out on the street.

On the street, Sarge knew, he would die.

Now he wished, not for the first time, that he'd been killed in Vietnam. As much and as often as he'd prayed for survival when he'd been over there, Sarge understood, in hindsight, that an anonymous bullet through the head would have saved him thirty years of pain and suffering. Sarge put a hand over his mouth to cover the moan that was trying to escape him, found that it did little good. He curled up on his cot, taking deep breaths, puffing out his cheeks to blow them out, trying to regain control of himself.

The more he thought about it, the more he understood that there was no one who could help him, no one he could turn to. Sarge was one of the few men on the ward who was trusted with shaving equipment, but he wasn't allowed to have it in his room, nor in his possession. He would calm himself down, and go see the orderly. Tell him he felt the need to shave. Sarge was trusted, Sarge was a known quantity.

He could use the disposable razor to slash the inside of his arm, from wrist to elbow. As soon as he calmed down. He had to make himself calm down first, so the orderly would not be suspicious.

"Eddie, you have to calm down," Dr. Warren caught himself, knowing his voice betrayed his fear, knowing too that a man such as Eddie equated fear with nourishment.

He thought of ways out, ways to save himself, as he faced a

human monster who stood before him, chest heaving, fists at his side, making accusations of betrayal in a low, tight voice, accusations that might well cost Dr. Warren his life. Warren had spent his entire career surrounded by mental illness, but this was the first time he had ever personally encountered evil.

"I'm going to walk over to my desk now, Eddie. Your medication's in the middle drawer—"

"Fuck the medication! You're not going to drug me out again, turn me into a zombie!"

"I don't know what you're talking about, Eddie." Warren knew he'd have to use the name every chance he could, try to make the man think of himself as a human being, as good old Eddie, Dr. Warren's pal. "It made you feel better when you took it earlier, didn't it?"

"You called the Big Cop on me! I saw him walking by, out in the hall!"

"Eddie, there are no cops out in the hall. You have to believe me, Eddie." Warren saw the look of confusion on Eddie's face, and ran at it with everything he had. "I gave you a mild hallucinogenic drug, Eddie. Tell me, were you seeing other things? Of course you were. But they were good things, weren't they, Eddie?"

He could see Eddie vacillating, saw the man's mouth open wide, as if remembering a particular horror. Dr. Warren did not know about Neal, he thought that Eddie was merely having doubts about his allegations toward Warren.

"There are good and bad hallucinations, Eddie. You've experienced both this afternoon. That's all it is. I would never betray you, Eddie, you have to believe that. And I can prove it."

Eddie jumped on that.

"Prove it, prove you wouldn't."

Eddie's fists were now merely hands, rapidly patting the sides of his legs. He appeared to be a petulant child, angry over an imagined slight, worried about his punishment.

Warren didn't change his expression or the tone of his voice when he said, "I would have turned you in before, wouldn't I have, Eddie? If I were going to do it, I mean? I would have turned you in when you first told me about your problems, years ago, about how you solved them. Think about it, Eddie. You didn't tell me anything new today."

"But you *knew*." The monster was hidden within him now, Eddie was the pathetic creature he had been when he'd first come into Warren's office. Warren watched him make his shaky way across the room, saw Eddie carefully sit down on the couch, saw him lower his head into his hands. "But you *knew!* You even asked me about it, you asked me about last night!"

"Let me give you some more medication, Eddie."

"I have to leave, Dr. Warren, I have to get out of here, right now." Eddie had looked up, was talking quickly, staring at Warren. Warren watched him metamorphose, saw the creature within him fighting to get out, and the view was the ugliest that Warren could recall. It could go either way, Eddie or the beast could win. Warren had to do his best not to let his revulsion show.

Eddie said, "You're going to take me out of here, Dr. Warren. You're going to give me some medication, and let me go. I'll talk to you all you want, tell you everything you want to know, but not in here. Not locked up. You have to get me out of here."

Thank God. Eddie had given him a way out.

Dr. Warren opened the middle drawer of his desk. He did not mention that Eddie had signed commitment papers, and he wanted Eddie under before he had a chance to remember that he had done so. Warren looked at the assorted bottles, Eddie's treatment plan, thought out in advance, each drug chosen with care.

"Of course, Eddie. If that's what you really want." Warren shook two pills out of each bottle, there were ten pills on his desk when he was finished. Too many? Would Eddie notice? Less might not have the desired effect. Warren had to take the chance.

He walked over to the water cooler, and re-created his earlier movements, dropped the pills into a paper cone, filled a second one with water.

"You want out, Eddie? All you ever had to do was ask. When have I ever not been a friend to you? I've always accommodated your wishes. You've never just been another patient to me, Eddie. I've always thought of you as my friend." He was almost there. "One of my closest friends."

Dr. Warren handed Eddie the cups.

"Take your medication, Eddie. We'll talk a little bit until you calm down, and then we'll get you out of here while Neal and the rest are still having din—"

Eddie leaped to his feet and slapped both cups out of Dr. Warren's hands at the mention of Neal's name.

CHAPTER
40

Constantine saw the drunken man wandering around on the sidewalk as she double-parked next to DiGrazia's unmarked squad. He looked familiar to her, and that surprised her. He wasn't ranting and raving, wasn't falling down drunk, but he'd been hitting it pretty good, that was obvious. She got out of the car and approached the hospital cautiously. She pushed back the hem of her wrinkled jacket, rested it on the other side of her weapon.

She was meaning to pass him, just walk on by, but he stepped into her way, a look of despair on his face. "All right, I give up." There was a quiver in the man's voice.

"That's all right, buddy," Constantine said, but he didn't move. "Tell you what, you really want to confess, go on down about four blocks south, then one more west. That's the Twenty-eighth District headquarters, they'll take your statement over there."

"You don't . . . ?"

"Naw, I don't." Constantine gave him a wide berth, walked past him, a piece of paper in her left hand, her right hand ready to draw her weapon, if she had no other choice. The first sound of footsteps behind her, and she'd take him down and cuff him.

He could wait facedown on the little patch of grass while she spoke with DiGrazia, told him what else McMillan's computer had said about Richard Edward Milles.

Why do these guys always come with three names?

Constantine could see the man now, in the reflection of the glass door directly in front of her, the drunk was still standing on the sidewalk, watching her.

"This the VA hospital?" he asked.

"Detox is around the other side," Constantine said, as she pressed the buzzer, peered in trying to see if anybody was in there. Crazy people had always frightened her. She'd never let that stop her from confronting them when she'd had no other choice.

"Detox." The man spat the word out. "My brother works here, you know."

"Yeah? That's good," Constantine said. She pressed the buzzer again, "Me, I got a brother in Harvard."

"Harvard?"

"Yeah, in the science lab."

The man was coming closer now. Constantine was sorry that she'd spoken.

"What's he do there?" the man asked.

"He's in a jar, he's got two heads."

Some dimwit in a rent-a-cop uniform was looking out at her now, looked quickly down at her gun, then back at her face. He made a *what-do-you-want* motion with his hands. "Goddamnit," Constantine said, and reached into her pocket for her wallet ID. She held it up to the glass. She glared at the rent-a-cop.

"You want to open this door, Ace?" Constantine shouted the words, knowing he could hear them. "Or you want to be charged with obstruction of justice."

The man pushed the door handle, then let go of it, and Constantine had to scramble to keep it from slamming in her face. She shook her head in disgust, then pinned the man with a glare.

"Where's Dr. Moran's office?" she demanded, and heard the voice close behind her say, "That's him, that's my brother."

She turned to face the man, and the door hit her on the hip. The surly rent-a-cop wasn't helping her out one bit.

"Tommy Moran, he's my little brother," the drunk said.

*   *   *

"You know as well as I do that my wife didn't have anything to do with Nancy's death!" Moran shouted the words at DiGrazia, who accepted them in much the same manner that a statue accepts rain. Moran stood up quickly, then sat back down again. "Was that some cop trick, some setup?" He was breathing heavily, staring hard at DiGrazia. DiGrazia didn't move, didn't even blink.

"Goddamnit, I've had about enough of this—" Moran rose again, and now, so did DiGrazia.

"You might want to call a lawyer, Dr. Moran, for your wife."

"She won't need a lawyer!"

DiGrazia stood over him, looked down into Moran's face. He felt no shame over the fear that was stamped all over it, took no responsibility for what he'd done to put it there.

"One of our detectives has proof that she killed Nancy." DiGrazia turned toward the door. "I'm putting out a pickup order for her."

"You can't—"

"Watch me."

DiGrazia had his hand on the doorknob when Moran shouted, "It was Todd, goddamnit! It was Todd who killed Nancy!"

Todd?

DiGrazia let go of the door, turned to face Moran. "Who the hell—" then he got it.

"Ellen's brother."

"I think so, I don't know, nobody knows." Moran walked around to his desk, flopped down in his chair. He pulled open a drawer, ignoring DiGrazia while he popped the lid on a bottle, shook two pills into his hand, tossed them into his mouth and swallowed them dry. He unlocked his bottom drawer, took out a large pile of papers, and threw them on the desk. The papers slid across the desk; most of them fell to the floor. They'd been folded, letter style, as if they hadn't been sent in a single bunch, but had been mailed individually. DiGrazia, knowing what he now did, could see Schmidt doing something like that.

"Take a look, go ahead. They were from our pal, Schmidt. There was never a return address on any of the letters, and they were postmarked from different zip codes, but he sent them."

326

DiGrazia looked down, recognized the letters immediately. Moran said, "They're police reports, copies of notes, statements. Hospital reports. He mailed me one every day, to my house."

"Your wife—"

"My wife didn't know, she worked different shifts. I'd find excuses to go home at lunch, to get there just as the mail came, or right after."

"When did they start arriving?"

"Late February, early March. Sometimes Post-its would be on them, little block-printed lettering with small, ugly allegations."

"Doctor, let me ask you a question." DiGrazia almost savored the moment. He loved getting his man. It was the challenge, the thrill of closing the trap around the suspect, outsmarting criminals, that appealed to him. It was the main reason—perhaps the only reason—that DiGrazia stayed in police work.

Now he walked over to the desk, turned the computer printout around, and circled the third name down. "This name mean anything to you?"

"Richard Edward Milles." Moran seemed puzzled at the change of topic. He shook his head. "No. But I can look it up."

"Why don't you do that?"

"Will you leave Ellen out of this?"

"I'll check Todd out from top to bottom first, I give you my word on that."

Moran looked at him, as if trying to judge the value of DiGrazia's word. "Todd killed himself fifteen years ago," Tom said. DiGrazia did not seem surprised to hear it.

There was a soft knock on the door, and Moran looked over at it with distaste, with fear. He looked at DiGrazia, who shook his head. He hadn't brought anyone with him. Moran seemed to believe him.

Moran walked over to the door, opened it, and DiGrazia looked out at a fat man in late middle age, who seemed terrified at the sight of them. He was bent over, as if from a burden.

"Dr. Moran. I have to talk to you right away."

"Not right now, Sarge," Moran said to the fat man. His voice was surprisingly calm. DiGrazia looked over at him, eyes narrowed, wondering about him. He had changed attitude and tone as quickly as any stage actor, slipped into his professional doctor's role without the slightest hesitation. DiGrazia fleetingly wondered if Schmidt had been right about him all along.

"I wouldn't bother you, Doctor, I know you're busy, but it's an emergency," the fat man said.

"What is it, Sarge?" Moran's voice was tightly controlled. DiGrazia was standing close to them, watching them interact, thinking, the piece of paper in his hand, the circled name highlighted. The man Moran called Sarge looked over at it, his mouth working, eyes wide. He watched as Sarge visibly started.

"He's *here*," Sarge spoke to DiGrazia now, rather than to Moran. The doctor answered him, but DiGrazia was already in motion.

"Who's here?"

"Milles," DiGrazia said. He had moved in close to Sarge, held the paper out in front of him. He shoved it under the man's nose. "Richard Edward Milles. Where is he?"

Sarge opened his mouth to answer, but Dr. Warren's scream cut him off before he could say a word.

Eddie cut the scream off with a hard blow to the throat, did a quick turn and followed it up with an elbow strike to the same area. He wanted time alone with this man, with his betrayer, but Warren's scream prevented that from happening. Eddie had to live with that, but not for very long. In Warren's attempts to befriend him, he'd given Eddie his home phone number and address; Eddie had been to the doctor's house years ago, had spoken to him there.

Dr. Warren, Eddie knew, had a wife, and two young children. Eddie was looking forward to visiting them.

Eddie frantically grabbed up several of the pills from the floor, popped them into his mouth as he ran to Warren's door. He was holding a paperweight from Dr. Warren's desk in his hand, one of these things with fake snow inside, with a little cabin encased in liquid, inside thick round glass. It was the best he could do. Eddie had no plan. All he knew was that he had to get past the orderlies, the guard, and somehow get out the door, into the outside world.

He threw the door open and ran out into the hall, saw that the corridor was nearly empty, that most of the residents were still in the cafeteria, or in their rooms. At the end of the corridor, Eddie saw that the door to the outside was open, the guard was standing there with his club in his belt, staring at a fat, old blonde woman who had her back turned toward the guard. She was saying something to a man standing on the sidewalk. The man she was talking to looked like a resident of the facility.

Keep talking, lady . . .

"What's goin' on . . . ?" the young black orderly was stepping around the intake-station desk as Eddie ran past, and Eddie hit him hard on the side of the head with the paperweight, managed to hold on to it as the orderly fell hard to the floor, Eddie not breaking stride as he ran for freedom. A nurse screamed behind him.

The guard and the woman both turned just as Eddie reached them. The guard was fumbling with his nightstick as Eddie shouldered him aside, the woman was reaching for a pistol. Eddie hit her with the paperweight. She fell to her knees as blood exploded out of the side of her head. Eddie let out a small breath at the sight. Something tore inside him at the thought that he didn't have time to stick around and play.

But she was bleeding . . .

And still reaching for her weapon. Where was the Big Cop? Eddie straddled her, hit her again. This time, she went down flat on her face. Eddie felt himself stiffen, astride her broad back. He dropped the paperweight and grabbed the woman's gun out of its holster.

Something was on top of him, smothering him. Eddie lashed out at it with the gun. It had to be the Big Cop, or the guard. Eddie, panicking, fumbled with the weapon, trying to find the trigger. He felt sudden dullness in the side of his head, again, then once more, and realized that someone was punching him in the head, trying to knock him out.

It couldn't be the Big Cop, the Big Cop would have just shot him. It had to be the guard.

Eddie felt the ferocious blow to his stomach, felt the wind rush out of his lungs. He threw himself off the woman, flattened himself on the ground, the weapon beneath him, Eddie finally managing to get his finger on the trigger as someone grabbed him by the hair and drew his head back, hard.

Eddie saw black stars flashing in his vision, felt the forearm tightening around his throat, heard someone shouting, then a bunch of voices were screaming. He leaned back, pointed the pistol away from himself and behind him, fired a single shot. Whoever had been choking him screamed in terror or pain, and the pressure let up. Eddie pushed away.

The Big Cop was in front of him now, at the entrance to the clinic, a large weapon in his hand, calling Eddie Richard, telling Richard to drop the gun or he'd blow his fucking head off. The useless guard was cowering on the tiny lawn. The woman was prone beside Eddie, the man he'd shot behind him. Eddie could feel the man's fingers trying to grab onto his legs.

Eddie was out of breath, still struggling to breathe, the punch in the middle of his stomach had hurt him badly. But he had enough strength left to pull a trigger if he had to. He pointed the pistol at the woman's back.

"You get away from me!"

The Big Cop was holding his weapon in both hands. A tall, slender man in a suit was just behind him, holding back the curious residents who were gathering at the door, wanting to see what was going on. The Big Cop's gun was steady, the hole in the barrel seemed to Eddie the size of a cannon.

"I'll shoot her, I swear to Christ I will!"

"Drop the gun, Richard. There's nowhere you can go, nothing you can do. It's over. The doctors can help you, they can make it go away."

Eddie had the hammer back on the woman's gun. He now slowly moved the barrel up, until it was resting at the base of the woman's skull. He heard her moan, heard cars squealing to a halt on the street behind him.

"You drop *your* gun, or I'll shoot her." Eddie was amazed at how calmly he was able to say this. His belly had stopped hurting, he was even breathing well.

The drugs. He'd taken the drugs. That was it. They'd get him through this. For all Eddie knew, this was all just another hallucination.

He was thinking this when something slammed into his hand, hard, and the pistol barrel jerked away. Eddie heard screaming, close in his ear, an animal growl, and he fired twice in terror into the ground as something heavy fell upon him.

DiGrazia saw Frank Moran rising slowly to his feet, saw the blood pouring from his chest, heard from ten feet away the obvious sounds of a sucking chest wound. He saw this without taking his eyes away from Milles, saw this without moving his aim one inch. Milles was on his ass, sitting on the small lawn, had his weapon on the back of Constantine's head. Bad call, that one; he should have shot the man when he'd been pointing it at her back. He might have missed the spine.

DiGrazia kept his face expressionless as Frank steadied himself, looking down at Milles, shaking his head repeatedly, as if he'd had enough of something, wasn't going to take anymore. There was a moment when DiGrazia's finger tightened on the trigger, when he was willing to take the chance that Milles's dying reflexive actions wouldn't cause him to squeeze the trigger and kill Constantine. It was just a momentary thing, then DiGrazia eased up on the trigger.

He was aware of the crowd gathering on the sidewalk, the crowd across the street watching, moving into the street and blocking traffic as they joined the other gawkers. He heard Moran behind him, shouting at the mental patients.

He saw Frank pull back his foot, felt his lips forming a shout, wanting the man not to do it, then Frank kicked at the weapon, almost fell as his foot connected, and then he was on top of Milles, holding him down, wrestling and punching, biting at the man, making animal noises. Milles still had the weapon in his hand as DiGrazia ran toward the two of them.

DiGrazia stomped down hard on Milles's fingers, leaned down and twisted the weapon free, as Milles screamed, as Frank Moran's teeth dug into Milles's neck. DiGrazia used Constantine's weapon, rather than his own, and slapped Milles hard behind the ear. Milles went limp, but Frank kept biting at him. DiGrazia pried him off Milles, shouting for Tom Moran to come and help him.

He'd have shot Milles through the head if the crowd hadn't been watching.

DiGrazia didn't want to, but he went by the book; he cuffed Milles before he turned to see how Constantine was doing. She was on her back now, trying to get up. There was a baseball-sized lump on the side of her head. Her left eye was swollen shut. DiGrazia heard sirens growing louder as the ambulances and squad cars raced toward the hospital. He cradled Constantine in his arms, and she looked at him vaguely through her one good eye.

"Got his ass," she said.

"We got his ass," DiGrazia replied.

"I—"

"Shh." DiGrazia smoothed back her hair, whispered for her to be quiet. Constantine's face twisted into an impatient, angry expression.

"Print matched from the partial, on the bridge. We got his ass."

"Yes, we do."

"He was *here*. You didn't let me tell you on the phone."

"He was a patient." DiGrazia heard angry cops demanding that the crowds disperse. He felt the hot glare of camera lights fall upon him.

"No, *before*. He's been here before!" Constantine was slurring her words. The pupil of her left eye was tiny. Goddamnit, where were those fucking paramedics?

She said, "Dr. Warren. He treated him four years ago. Look into it for me, Nicky. That son of a bitch. If he knew all along . . ."

"Let me at her." The voice was female and harsh, right at DiGrazia's ear. The paramedic knelt beside DiGrazia, hurried and angry. "The fucking box is still down the block. We got news vans and private vehicles blocking the area for three blocks around."

"Take care of her," DiGrazia said, rising to his feet. A different paramedic was working furiously on Frank Moran. Seeing the cuffs, they'd left Milles for last. DiGrazia saw the emergency lights of the ambulance, far away.

It took him less than two minutes to get the block cleared of traffic. Six lawsuits would eventually be filed against him for the manner in which he did it, but the "box"—the first ambulance—had Janice Constantine inside it and was rolling to the hospital before the outraged curses and screams of citizens and reporters stopped echoing in the concrete canyon that srrounded them.

CHAPTER
41

Constantine felt the pain in her head, felt the doctors manipulating her face under bright, harsh lights. She heard their voices, heard them speak to her, the doctors calling her by her first name. She hated when they did that, but she was in no position to complain. Her husband Luke was holding her hand as she waited for X-rays, and she squeezed it, hard, letting only the man she loved know how much fear she was holding inside. She knew that bones in the side of her head were at least partially crushed, suspected that part of her skull was fractured. Her face had swollen so badly that she couldn't even talk anymore. She'd seen plenty of people with lesser injuries die from hemorrhaging in the brain.

They wouldn't let her husband come into the X-ray room with her, and she reluctantly gave up his hand as the technician wheeled her inside the sterile room. "Stay awake, Janice, Janice can you hear me?" What did this dim bulb expect her to do, answer?

Constantine knew the importance of staying awake, knew, too, that she could be given nothing for the pain. The doctors would want to know if her head took to feeling any worse. She stuck her tongue into the roof of her mouth, relaxed her jaw as much as she was able. It hurt less that way.

As they wheeled her out of the X-ray room, her hand was taken again. When she looked up, it was not her husband holding her, but rather, Nicky DiGrazia. Constantine tried to nod at him, but that hurt too much, so she tried to smile. The tears that formed in DiGrazia's eyes told her how grotesque her attempt must have seemed.

DiGrazia's was the first face she saw when she awakened, lying on her back in a hospital bed, her head swallowed up by thick white bandages. After her initial fear subsided, her good eye looked around frantically, seeking someone, anyone, in the room. And there he was, sitting in a chair beside the bed.

DiGrazia wasn't holding a book or magazine in his hands. He hadn't been watching TV. He was holding the buzzer, the thing that summoned the nurse. She imagined him sitting there throughout the night, watching her chest rise and fall, making sure there were no changes in her breathing patterns, and she was glad.

DiGrazia spoke to her quickly, before Constantine could try to open her mouth.

"You've got a fractured skull, don't try to talk." DiGrazia placed the buzzer on the mattress next to her hand, as if it now embarrassed him. "There's concussion, but—thank God—no bleeding. You'll wind up with a small depression in the left side of your head. You'll be in here a few days. Luke left to get the kids off to school. They were here, too, earlier. Your older daughter, Alicia, sat outside the door all night, with the cop. She left for work a little while ago." DiGrazia smiled. "Alicia told Mary Murine from Channel Four news to go fuck herself when she tried to interview her about your condition."

Constantine held a thumb up. Pain shot through her face as she said, "Milles."

"Goddamnit! Don't try to talk, Janice—"

"*Milles!*" Constantine closed her eye as pain flashed red throughout her skull.

"All right, all right, calm down, for Christ's sake." DiGrazia shook his head. If Constantine had been able to, she would have smiled. She could use the way she looked to get her way with him—for a while, at least—and she would do that until DiGrazia figured it out and stopped giving in. It would be fun while it lasted.

"Milles didn't get as lucky as you did; steel's harder than glass. I gave him a pretty good shot with your pistol, they had to open up his skull to relieve the pressure. He's in a coma, upstairs, under police guard." DiGrazia smiled ruefully. "You're not gonna believe this, but the doctors balked about cuffing him to the bed. He's on the fourth floor, in Intensive Care. We convinced them that they didn't want him waking up and running loose in here."

Constantine closed her eye, then opened it quickly. She did not like the vivid image that had formed on it closed. So she looked at the white walls, at the TV hanging from a platform, behind DiGrazia. She felt the bandage over her other eye, wondered if she'd lost its use. She felt lucky to be alive.

"Frank Moran saved you. I had a bead on Milles, but he had your weapon pointed at the back of your head, I couldn't shoot him. Milles had already shot Frank in the chest, but Frank got to his feet, kicked the gun, and wrestled with our boy until I could disable him."

There were a thousand questions she wanted to ask him, but she couldn't do that now. She didn't even want to write them out, she didn't have the energy.

"Frank made it, he was in surgery most of the night, over at Mercy, but he's alive. Enforced detox. Like you with the cigarettes." Constantine wished he hadn't said that. She felt the urge to light up. "No-smoking facility, Janice," DiGrazia said.

"Moran."

"Janice, you have to stop trying to—" DiGrazia held up his hand before Constantine could repeat herself. "All right, goddamnit, just stop it!" He compressed his lips, glared at her, took a deep breath. Janice's heart lifted at the sight.

"That's the only thing you figured wrong. Ellen didn't kill Nancy, we think her brother Todd did. He had cancer, and everyone thought he'd killed himself to escape the pain. There was incest—Tom Moran disclosed it to us—just as you guessed at the parents' house. Maybe he was feeling guilty about it at the end—about what he'd been doing—and tried—in a very disturbed way—to give his sister the one thing she wanted more than anything else in the world. Nobody knows.

"We've decided that Ellen doesn't have to find out about her husband's suspicions. He claims he finally figured it out in March, when *another* killer committed suicide in Portland. After finding out he had pancreatic cancer, he went straight from the hospital to his in-laws' house, shot them both, then himself when the cops were closing in on him. Who knows? Nancy wasn't our case. But it sounds good to me."

Which was good enough for Constantine.

"They're threatening to file a lawsuit against you, by the way, the Lewans, I mean. Imagine that? A hero cop, found a serial killer single-handedly . . ." DiGrazia smiled as Constantine raised her eyebrow.

"Eberhardt, Jimmy McMillan, and I, we had a little discussion last night, while the medics were working on your head. Your suggestion about the VA hospital was what rang the gong for us, Janice. We asked Parker to tell them at the press conference that it was you who solved it, working under his personal authority. As soon as you can, you'll have to tell me how you picked up on the incest angle; I can't figure out how you did it. What? Why are you waving at me? No—don't try to talk!"

Janice lowered her middle finger. She closed her eyes for a moment, and when she opened them again, DiGrazia seemed sheepish.

"You were right about Warren, too. We found Milles's file in his office. Milles had taken it out of one of the cardboard boxes in Schmidt's basement. Warren almost died, would have, if Dr. Moran hadn't performed an emergency tracheotomy. He had to use a pen; ever try to find a sharp object on a mental ward? Warren's lawyer tried to deny his client knew what Milles was doing, but we got his ass on a search of the den at his house— you're gonna love this: Warren was writing a *book!*"

Again, Constantine looked away. She wondered how long he'd known. Three years, at least, she'd bet. DiGrazia's voice came to her through her self-imposed darkness.

"We've got dozens of tapes, CD-ROMS—are you sure you want me to tell you about this now?"

Constantine waved a weak hand for him to continue.

"Milles would get the urge every few months, jump into a beater, and travel around the country, waiting for an inner impulse to tell him when to stop. He never used the same method twice, Janice, and he was very careful who he picked. He says on one of the tapes that he killed a young guy because he wouldn't give him a handout on the street. Followed him until he passed an alley, shoved him in, and stabbed him once through the heart. We've got copies of him confessing to thirty killings."

"Roni?" Constantine's speech was slurred. She hoped it was from medication. She reached up and rubbed lightly at the thick patch of bandage over her eye.

"No outright confession on tape about that one, but we've got allusions to it, plus two terrified guys at the hospital who've given complete statements—for whatever they're worth. Roni's the only murder we've charged him with. We'll have him nailed down, with the partial print, the DNA. FBI took over the investigation, by the way, so the government lawyers'll be the ones who'll have to find ways around the confidentiality laws, unless we get lucky and he dies upstairs. Even if he lives, we've got his ass cold. But I'd hate to see Warren walk."

Not as much as Constantine. She wondered how Dr. Warren felt about that possibility.

When she looked back at DiGrazia, he had his hands folded between his legs, his eyebrows raised, his eyes wide, looking around the room. They lighted on Constantine, and he hurriedly looked away. Constantine frowned, until DiGrazia began to hum—then she got it.

He was joking around. Dominick fucking DiGrazia—the enigmatic, complicated, multilayered sphinx—was joking around! Maybe he wasn't such a miserable human being when there wasn't a serial killer running loose in his city.

Constantine stared at him until he stopped humming, and he was smiling when he responded to her open-handed, rolling motion.

"Bad news first: SOS is out. The good news is, Parker nixed it, because he wants you for himself." DiGrazia rubbed his stomach now, not a good sign for what he was about to say.

He seemed inordinately self-conscious as he said, "You want to partner up with me? They've been on me for three years, since Schmidt retired and I went on my own."

Constantine looked at him, understanding that he was no longer fooling around.

She would have to tell him that she wasn't going to sit still for any of his teacher-student bullshit, that if they were going to be partners, she would have to be one in more than name only. And she'd have to talk to him about his attitude. And she wasn't going out on any more coffee runs, either, ever.

But she could do all that at another time. At the moment, Constantine just held out her hand, and he leaned over and took it, shook it carefully, sealing the deal. Surprising her yet again, DiGrazia seemed relieved.

He cleared his throat before he said, "There's one more thing, Janice, something you should know, if we're going to work together."

Constantine thought, "Here it comes," as she remembered Rosen's warning, what Tina had said about DiGrazia. She cautioned herself to not respond when he told her, to act as if it didn't matter. She wondered if she could twist her face into an expression to show that she was offended by his even thinking it was important enough to discuss with her.

There was a light tap on the door, and a very attractive woman stuck her head inside, looked around, then walked in and let the door shut behind her.

A doctor, no doubt. Thank God. Constantine needed something for her pain. Where was her white coat? Constantine lay in shock as the woman walked up to DiGrazia, smiling, but without a lot of humor. She kissed his offered cheek.

"My breath gotta be like a dragon's," DiGrazia said, as he rose and slipped his arm around the woman's waist.

"Parker said you'd probably be here. You need to get some sleep, Nicky." Constantine hadn't thought about that, he'd guarded her all night without having slept in—what?—two days.

"Bonita, I'd like you to meet Janice Constantine, my new partner. Janice, this is my wife, Bonita. Don't bother getting up."

It's the culture . . .

Bonita just touched Constantine's hand, as if afraid that it had been bruised in the fight.

"He doesn't have to tell me who *you* are, your face was all over the television last night, and on the front pages of both papers this morning. They're calling you a hero." Bonita looked up into her husband's eyes, and tightened the arm around his waist.

"Come on, you. You're coming home with me right now, or they'll have to find a bed for you here."

"You gonna knock me out?"

"Kick your ass right here, my man, you don't come and get some sleep."

DiGrazia looked over at Constantine, his smile fading, looking at her with a critical eye. "You going to be all right?"

She gave him a thumbs up, then dropped it, waved her hand again. DiGrazia looked at her, shaking his head. She waved her hand faster. DiGrazia shrugged.

"Wha war u gna tl me!" Her head, Jesus, did it hurt her head to talk.

"Janice, don't try to talk!"

Bonita said, "I think she wants to know what you said, was there something you were going to tell her?"

Constantine began a vigorous nod, but the pain stopped her.

"Oh, yeah, you should know something, Janice."

DiGrazia paused, stiffened up, and looked up at Constantine gravely. She waited.

"I'm not real easy to get along with."

"No shit," Constantine said.

Bonita said, "She said—"

"I know what she said," DiGrazia replied, as he opened a hand and held it out toward Janice in a farewell gesture, palm open wide.

"Take good care, partner," Dominick DiGrazia said, as Bonita led him reluctantly toward the door.

Hours later, after visiting time was over, and Luke and the kids had left, Constantine, afraid, was lightly dozing, in the twilight world between consciousness and sleep, when DiGrazia slipped back into the room. She heard him tiptoe around, felt the nurse's buzzer gently taken off her second pillow. She heard him sit down, taking his time. He thought she was asleep, and she let him keep on thinking that. Constantine wondered if DiGrazia's eagle eyes had caught sight of the single tear that dropped from her good eye, down onto the sheet. She hoped that if they did, he would believe it to be just a natural secretion, due to the concussion.

She heard him settle himself in for the night, and she no longer felt afraid.